The
Weeping Woman

ALSO BY ZOÉ VALDÉS

Yocandra in the Paradise of Nada

I Gave You All I Had

Dear First Love

The Weeping Woman

A Novel

ZOÉ VALDÉS

TRANSLATED FROM THE SPANISH
BY DAVID FRYE

Arcade Publishing • New York

3-16

First English-language Edition

This is a work of fiction. Names, places, characters, and incidents are either the products of the author's imagination or are used fictitiously.

Arcade Publishing books may be purchased in bulk at special discounts for sales promotion, corporate gifts, fund-raising, or educational purposes. Special editions can also be created to specifications. For details, contact the Special Sales Department, Arcade Publishing, 307 West 36th Street, 11th Floor, New York, NY 10018 or arcade@skyhorsepublishing.com.

Arcade Publishing® is a registered trademark of Skyhorse Publishing, Inc.®, a Delaware corporation.

Visit our website at www.arcadepub.com.

10 9 8 7 6 5 4 3 2 1

Library of Congress Cataloging-in-Publication Data

Names: Valdés, Zoé, 1959–
Title: The weeping woman : a novel / Zoe Valdes ; translated by David Frye.
Other titles: Mujer que llora. English
Description: New York : Arcade Publishing, 2016. | Originally published as La mujer que llora (Barcelona : Planeta, 2013).
Identifiers: LCCN 2015043905 (print) | LCCN 2015047897 (ebook) | ISBN 9781628725810 (hardback) | ISBN 9781628726299 (Ebook)
Subjects: LCSH: Maar, Dora—
Fiction. | Picasso, Pablo, 1881–1973—Fiction. | Psychological fiction. | BISAC: FICTION / Contemporary Women. | FICTION / Psychological. | FICTION / Biographical. | GSAFD: Biographical fiction. | Historical fiction.
Classification: LCC PQ7390.V342 M8513 2016 (print) | LCC PQ7390.V342 (ebook) | DDC 863/.64—dc23
LC record available at http://lccn.loc.gov/2015043905

Cover design by Georgia Morrissey
Cover photo: Shutterstock

Printed in the United States of America

To Dora Maar, James Lord, and Ramón Unzueta, in memoriam
To Bernard Minoret and Ana D'Atri
To Marcela Rossiter

I walk alone across a vast landscape.
The weather is fine. Not sunny though.
The minutes do not pass.
For the longest time, no friends, no people
walking by.
I walk alone. I talk, alone.

Je n'ai pas été la "maitresse" de Picasso; il fut mon
"maître."
I was not Picasso's "mistress"; he was my "master."

—DORA MAAR

Dora wanted to go down in history without a need
for words.

—JAMES LORD

PART I

HOT THOUGHTS

Bernard. Paris, 2007

I stood on the balcony, looking at the flow of traffic. I let my gaze drift down to the bench on Boulevard Bourdon where a young couple sat kissing, probably the same bench where Bouvard and Pécuchet had sat and talked under 92-degree heat in Gustave Flaubert's novel. It's so pleasant, so enchanting, so delightful to watch young lovers kiss in Paris: deep kisses, all tongue. Robert Doisneau took the greatest photos of Parisian kisses ever.

I stepped away from the window and crossed the living room. A woman's life is an unending litany; when the litany ceases, desire comes to a halt and the season of hot thoughts begins. That's the time when your body cools and fever takes savage hold of your psyche. Not that life has ended, only paused before turning around, lurching noisily back to a start, and heading toward the second childhood that drowsily awaits us with death.

The rain had cleared up two hours earlier, and when the sun emerged I breathed a deep lungful of the welcome air of spring, wafting through the large window that cinematically framed our courtyard garden.

Bernard was expecting me at his house on Rue de Beaune in Saint-Germain-des-Prés. I wore a thin new dress, perhaps too thin. As the saying goes, *En avril, ne te découvre pas d'un fil,* "In April, don't take off a single thread," meaning, don't be too hasty about putting away your coat in April, the chill can be treacherous, liable to return without warning, so you run a real risk of catching a cold. But I didn't feel like wearing an overcoat, a raincoat, not even a jacket. How I missed summer! And in my childish longing I decided to dress as if it were summer already and we were enjoying the dry, soporific heat of Paris in July.

Spring, spring at last, after a long and brutal winter! The banks of snow piled high on sidewalks were in the past, slush-covered streets a memory. Yet I nonetheless covered up with a thin black lambskin raincoat, just in case.

I didn't want to keep Bernard waiting too long; this would be the second time I met him.

We'd first met in December, before Christmas, introduced in a darkened movie theater several minutes after the film had already started. We could only exchange a few pleasantries in the flickering dark; we didn't want to bother the fellow sitting near us. It was the premiere of a film by one of Bernard's friends, starring that actress I liked so much. . . . I'm having a brain freeze, can't remember the title of the film. Oh, of course, now the actress's name is coming back to me, Nathalie Baye. The film was really good, the first feature by a new producer who'd worked as a screenwriter before. Bernard himself was—and is—a scriptwriter for major French producers, and he rubs shoulders with the cream of Parisian society; as they say here, he "knows everyone in Paris." He had been friends with Marie-Laure de Noailles, Leonor Fini, Dora Maar. . . . Bernard is a writer, the coauthor of *Les Salons*. He's a good writer, though that's not how he's ever wanted to view himself. I knew he was good friends with James Lord, and when some Cuban friends of mine spoke briefly but intensely about him, I asked them to introduce us. He's been successful as a scriptwriter and is still an elegant gentleman, classy, poised, but with a touch of shyness that speaks well of him yet makes it hard for him to communicate with others.

That same night, after the premiere, we ate at a restaurant "for artists and writers," his words, where he presented me to the grandson of a Parisian grande dame, one of those blue-bloods, the kind with a high-class first name, a string of fancy surnames, and piles of money to match, all neatly tucked away in Swiss banks, I'd guess. She also had plenty of antique jewels, fur coats, minks, paintings by prestigious painters, and her photo in the society pages of *Paris Match* every week, guaranteed. A real patroness of intellectuals and troubled avant-garde artists. In other words, nothing that impressed me; I've always had to work hard to put beans on the table. But I still acted fascinated by the topic of the grande dame and made clichéd compliments about her fortune so as not to dishearten her young grandson, who was grateful I pretended to care about his grandmother. The kid had the most beautiful blue eyes I'd ever seen, a watery Caribbean blue.

That night, when Bernard and I really talked for the first time and sized each other up through our words (so French of us), he kept asking me what I liked most about France and the French. I don't remember my exact words, some nonsense I'm sure, something like, "the love of art, the sophisticated eroticism, the sensuality, the giddy passion one feels from being in Paris." Whereas he concluded, "What I value most is the conversation. We French know how to talk with each other."

"True," I agreed. "There was a time when Cubans also knew how to have good conversations. Nowadays, you only get strident soliloquys, jarring rants, all unbearably boring."

"My poor dear"—he pronounced the phrase, *ma pauvre dame*, with well-aimed, ostentatious pity—"all that will be over some day, I assure you."

"Anyway, people are losing the gift of conversation here in Paris, too. There are still a few circles of intellectuals, no doubt, where people know how to converse, but in other venues one's conversation partners tend to be rather crude." I made my retort with French-style prissiness, that is, by openly discounting the exquisite (because Gallic) yet clichéd virtue of being a good conversationalist. The French are experts at treating your talents as worthless, which was exactly the number I pulled on him at that curiously uncomfortable moment, staring at him point-blank as if to throw him off balance.

I've learned from the French how to use their own statements against them, paying them back in their own coin, and in the same tone.

Bernard pretended not to hear, another subtle French-style retort. "We should be more open, I like gregarious people. Cubans are gregarious."

"A bit too much, *un peu beaucoup trop*," I noted.

Bernard burst into a guffaw that he stifled by covering his mouth with a napkin. "All that will change, the consequences of the 'illness,'" he traced air quotes, "will soon pass, you'll see, it won't be long."

I wanted to believe it, but I preferred to change the subject.

"Monsieur Minoret," I called him by his last name.

"Please, call me Bernard."

"Bernard. I wanted to meet you because I would like to write a novel about someone you knew very well, a long time ago."

"Let's talk as friends, then," he said, lifting the cup of Dom Pérignon champagne, a pure delight of golden bubbles, to his lips.

"A great literary moment," I complimented the champagne, and this amused him.

"Let's order dinner first. Do you like oysters?"

"Of course. I love them. The first time I tried oysters, caviar, and champagne was before I went into definitive exile from Cuba. No, not in Havana, not at all; it was on the first time I was here in Paris, I tried them at the Jules Verne restaurant, you know, on the second floor of the Eiffel Tower. Someone else paid, of course; at the time I couldn't afford fish and chips, let alone oysters. When I first savored that quivering delicacy still moving in its shell, I said to myself: 'Come on, what am I doing eating mealy old chickpeas in Cuba?' I was just twenty-three."

"I'm sorry, chicken and peas?"

Feeling rushed by the waiter standing ready to take our *commande*, I waved to Bernard not to worry about the misunderstanding; my use of the Cuban word for garbanzos had confused him. He gave the waiter our order. "We'll start with a fine Claret, number six."

In the meantime, I scrutinized his face. Bernard had reached a venerable age some time back, yet his face was still as smooth as a baby's skin. Small, lively eyes the color of honey, rosy lips, clear cheeks pampered with creams and cosmetics. He pouted his lips in a very Parisian sneer, and when he said, *"Oui, oui,"* the syllables stretched out into a sigh. He was tall, trim, and had no nasal twang in his voice.

As we dined, I dropped the name of the woman I was interested in. "Dora Maar, the great artist. I'd like to know more about that woman. I mean to write about her, though I know she loathed the idea of writers delving into her life; she didn't trust them. She said more than once she didn't want anything written about her, since it would be 'only be tabloid trash.' And she added that 'writers are backstabbers, because they write about what they know.' So true, because that means writers should be more imaginative. I've read a lot, seen her paintings, the exhibit about her at the Picasso museum and, of course, the novel about her life, or rather, about her life with Picasso, terrific. Along with other books that portray her as a difficult woman."

"Ah, Dora, Dora, little Dora." He smiled gently. "Have you read James Lord's book?"

"*Dora and Picasso*, of course. It was in his book I found out you knew her and had been friends with her. It has a photo that shows you all glowing with youth under the Italian sun—Dora, James Lord, and you. Dora not quite as youthful as you, Monsieur Minoret, of course. It's a pretty overexposed photo, out in the sun—luminous, radiant."

"I thought we were talking as friends? No need to call me Monsieur."

"Of course, sorry. I wanted to know more about that trip to Venice. If I understand correctly, it was only five days, just the three of you—"

He interrupted, sharply. "We'll meet again to talk about Dora on some other occasion. Just the two of us. Actually, it was an eight-day trip, counting the return journey."

I realized he preferred to be discrete about his feelings, or simply to keep them hidden when others were present, in this case the young man with the indigo eyes.

"I'm going on a trip soon, but I'll be back in March," I told him.

"Then let's make a date right now for April 2." Again he raised his glass of Dom Pérignon to his lips without breaking his glance, keeping his eyes fixed on mine.

"Perfect, perfect." I took out my day-planner and made an entry. "I won't forget—it's my daughter's birthday."

"You're afraid you'll forget the date?" He half-frowned as he watched me jot it down in the planner.

"No, no, it's just a thing I have. I have this obsession with constantly writing everything down," I responded, flustered.

Three and a half months later I was in a taxi on my way to Bernard's house. We'd agreed to have lunch at a restaurant around the corner.

I pressed the doorbell, which jingled like a buzzer instead of tolling the classic doorbell chime. I rang again. A hearty voice from upstairs asked who was there. I announced my name, somewhat shyly, and the door opened. I took the ancient elevator up. My mind was a jumble of thoughts, all disconnected; I remembered a song by a Cuban folk singer that made me laugh, about a girl, a cat, and a padlocked gate; from there my memories skipped to the night I went to a restaurant with my husband and a woman I still thought was my friend.

She and I had been introduced by one of those resentful gays who treat people so shabbily they give homosexuality a bad name.

He wanted to become a writer come what may, but his lack of culture was frightful. Renata, that was the woman he introduced me to, immediately made herself the center of attention and set about concocting plans for my husband—work plans, of course—and suddenly everything he and I had built up together was worthless in her eyes. According to her, she had all the answers; she'd step in and, let there be no doubt, she'd personally fix my husband's career, clear up "those minor details" that stood in the way of his film career, and all that. With her help, he'd make tons of money, she confidently asserted. "If you don't have money," she said, "you can't make films," which may be glaringly obvious, but her saying so didn't simply bother me, it wounded me deeply. From then on, everything was money and more money and projects, to be filmed her way. In a word, nothing interesting, another pile of garbage in this stupid, hypocritical world, a total waste of time.

Of course I felt guilty for wanting, as usual, to build a friendship where there was no chance of one. It's an incurable bad habit of mine.

The woman had just turned fifty-nine and didn't look it; besides still being quite beautiful, she'd taken good care of herself, but "it's still fifty-nine years, and she's having trouble dealing with the intimate fears her age entails," I told myself.

Wasting no time, the guy she thought was her best friend—that is, her worst enemy—told me about her fears, how she was starting to see the passing years as a slippery slope leading inexorably down to the end, old age.

Renata is a woman who lives for money, married to a man who makes unbelievable, unspeakable mountains of cash, yet she always does her own thing, buying stuff everywhere, splurging, like every woman who doesn't know what to do with her husband's money. She constantly boasts how rich she is, looking down on all other women, married or divorced, with or without a profession, just because we've put work above gold-digging.

In that conversation, on the night of the disastrous dinner, she admitted she'd tried out every religion in the world, past and present, before settling on the very fashionable Islam. Her husband is an Arab sheikh. Well, her problem.

Suddenly, out of the blue, she asked me if I was attracted to women—because she wasn't, "not at all." Was it because I was eyeing her too intensely? Actually, I was studying her makeup: very expensive, smartly applied to a face like chiseled marble.

Yet despite her husband's wealth, Renata worked; at least, she told us she worked, or I seemed to gather as much, or she used to work, though not so much or so often anymore; that is, she was still working, but not that much, only "sporadically," seasonally; meanwhile, her "best friend" was making sure everybody knew that Renata's husband, the Saudi sheikh, was loaded with dough, or rather with gold and oil, so filthy rich it was disgusting, freeing Renata from having to lift a finger. Despite her friend's gossip, Renata swore she was working, or at least she made a show of it. When she talked about her work, her tongue stumbled, repeating phrases unsteadily. I couldn't say for sure exactly what kind of work she did; she insisted that she was one of the few women who made millions in interior design. She'd become a millionaire working exclusively as a decorator. Which her best friend corroborates. From the amount of gossip he spreads about her, he's her worst enemy, but she still hasn't figured it out; give her time.

"Men are so terribly stupid, they bore the hell out of me," I blurted out without thinking. She admitted that she hated women. And before you know it, she's sniveling about her bad luck. I can't stand people who've barely known hardship but carry on about ridiculous trifles. Back up, that's too harsh, depends on how each person defines suffering. Now I'm the one complaining about women like her, petulant fools whining about every little thing, completely lacking in dignity.

It's quite true what Doris Lessing wrote somewhere, about how men came into the world after women, how they're inferior to us, and how some of us women act like such idiots we even envy men their good fortune and try to imitate them.

The elevator stopped at the floor where I was going. Even as I stepped out, I also thought about trifles such as forgetting to take out the garbage, forgetting to hem my daughter's dress. Yes, that tends to happen to me, I mix up my more-or-less good ideas with everyday trivialities. "Nothing to feel guilty about," I thought defensively.

Worse still are the women who make such a big deal of their gender that they start off using their vaginas as their ID cards and end up treating them as their bank accounts.

A man of about forty opened the green door for me; he had a very youthful appearance, but his face told another story, that he was forty or more years old and had been through a lot, yet he was still tall, dark, and handsome, with a nice body from working out. He didn't introduce himself, didn't give his name. Nor did he offer his hand affably, but instead comported himself as if stripped of emotion, and though it all happened very quickly he had time to make a show of curt officiousness. "A servant," I immediately guessed.

All he politely asked of me was to sit in the living room, where he said I should wait for Monsieur Minoret (as he called Bernard). He was, without question, a fine-looking butler, attractive, discreet, and polite.

I nodded and slipped into the living room, one of my high heels catching on the worn carpet that filled the entire room from wall to wall, as antiquated as the elevator or older. The sofa was also green, the same hue as the door. The walls, illuminated by carnation-shaped lamps, shimmered in gold tones tinged with Venetian orange.

I studied the furnishings: refined, elegant, clean, each item a sign of its owner's loyalty to a memory, an era, a person; a Picasso drawing, a portrait of Bernard. Another pointillist drawing, a profile of a young man whose gaze went off the paper and beyond the frame, toward a gloomy room aglow in Pompeiian green. Bernard now suddenly emerged from that very room and strode confidently to my side. Haughty, refined; in a few long strides there he was at my side, or at the side of his portrait hanging next to me, and he pointed to the framed, yellowing Bristol board.

"This is my favorite drawing, a portrait Dora Maar did of me," he remarked with pride. "She gave it to me in exchange for lace and linens—shawls, sheets, pillowcases, curtains, a whole pile of bedding; she loved that sort of sophistication, white linens. But enough of that, let's cut to the chase. I didn't actually know Dora all that well, perhaps not very deeply, but I did have a certain friendship with her, brief but close, thanks to Lord. My real friend was Leonor Fini, among the highly intelligent, beautiful, and quite extraordinary women of that period. But the little I knew about Dora made an impression on me. Without a doubt, she was one of the most brilliant women I have ever met."

I reminded Bernard that I was only interested in those five days in Venice ("Eight days, counting the return trip," he reiterated), during which they must have talked about all sorts of personal, and very intimate, things. Was Dora really in love with James Lord? Was he with her? How did Bernard feel around the two of them?

"I felt quite at ease with her. Dora was charming with me. Nothing odd passed between us, except perhaps an intense spirit of rapport. The truth is, it was a trip on which nothing in particular happened. We just wanted to walk around, James and I, relive the city, visit the museums, the churches. Dora was going there for the first time. She had this dream of visiting Venice, and we made it come true. James wanted to give her the adventure she'd been itching for all her life. Well, 'itching' is a manner of speaking. At that time we used to travel by car, by train, and nothing ever tired us out, because we were full of aspirations, blooming with good health and life's vigor. Doris arrived in Venice after James and me.

We put up at the Hotel Europa and waited for her there. James and I had already ended a relationship that went beyond friendship; that is to say, our sex life had become less important to us, it barely existed. James was getting to know me in a different way, he was crazy about my compulsions, he catered to my smallest whims and desires. I was becoming reacquainted with Dora, and I loved seeing her act like a little girl, rushing to get to the canals, but instead of a walk along a canal, as many as there were, we'd wash up in a museum and pay homage to a sculpture or prostrate ourselves before a fantastic painting, the way people once venerated the Virgin in a shrine. We had an intensely good time on that trip, and culturally we grew even more. What I mean is, James and I grew more cultured, since Dora herself was already a woman with a great deal of culture. We were cultured, too, but being younger, less so."

I asked Bernard, while sipping at the tap water I'd been served in fine Baccarat crystal, if Dora was a talkative sort, if she wore her feelings on her sleeve.

"No, not so much. She needed to be loved, that's for sure. She was a middle-aged woman, mature, yet she behaved like a fifteen-year-old girl, like these shy young women who are also rebellious and brash and always demand to be the center of attention. I gave her a lot of attention and enjoyed talking with her about the little everyday things; we didn't necessarily have any heavy, substantial conversations, nothing like that. Just simple topics. Or else she'd tell us the story of her life with Picasso, over and over again."

"And James Lord?"

"James was a gentleman, a *chevalier servant*, a platonic lover. James is an extremely busy man, you should meet him; I'll do what I can to introduce you two. . . . Should we head for the restaurant? I'm a bit worried, you see, it may be packed, it's nearly lunchtime already. In Paris, kitchens close early."

He stuck his arms through the sleeves of a beige raincoat.

"Aren't you a little underdressed?" he asked, narrowing his eyes, which gave him a feline look.

I shook my head no, kept quiet, and took a last, panoramic look around.

Suddenly, Bernard spun round and ran to the room that I fancied Pompeiian, where he rummaged around in a drawer. I couldn't see him from where I stood, but I heard his hands riffling through papers.

"I found what I wanted to give you! I almost forgot. The pages from my diary on that trip; I'll make you a copy."

I heard the screak of the copier continuously spitting out pages.

"They don't say much, nothing terribly important, just a few notes I jotted down, and I don't even remember when I wrote them, or why."

I stuck the copies in my purse after giving them a once-over.

"I'll read them when I get home, if you don't mind."

He said he didn't, not at all, and also shook his head a vigorous no to tell me he didn't mind one bit, then he wrapped a scarf around his neck, and we hurried off to the restaurant.

The Art Nouveau restaurant awning was also green, and the thick velvet curtain over the doorway was emerald, green as can be.

"Everything's green as can be today," I muttered.

"I like green, I have a lot of green in my life; it's my favorite color," Bernard said with infectious enthusiasm.

I began to ransack my brain for my own favorite color in case Bernard asked me, but he didn't. Red, blue, yellow, ochre? Gold? I'd painted in gold a lot during a period in my life when I spent hours before canvases that ended up glowing in gold and copper. My paintings weren't exactly sublime, quite the opposite, but I won't die regretting that I never tried, that's for sure.

No, he never even wondered what my favorite color was. He started reading the menu, though he already knew it by heart.

They sat us at a narrow little table by the door, and we ordered *confit de canard*, champagne, water, an apple tart with fresh cream, and coffee to finish off.

"This might come as a letdown, but I don't have many stories about her to tell, only personal impressions, notes scattered in my memory like brush strokes, and also, of course, I'm proud to own several of her works," he whispered.

"Photographs or paintings?" I was much more interested in her photography, because, to tell the truth, I didn't know all that much about her work as a painter.

"Paintings. Though she wasn't a great painter. And of course, I have the drawings she did of me, and one very subtle landscape, in oils."

"She was the greatest photographer of her time. She got into painting to humor Picasso. Everyone knows that she was the first to do a graphic study of a painter's work in progress, and the painter was Picasso, and the painting was none other than his masterpiece, *Guernica*," I recited.

"She wasn't a bad painter, either," Bernard quickly corrected himself. "That was her cross, she dug her own grave when she photographed *Guernica*. Picasso never forgave her."

"I know. Someone even wrote that she was the one who suggested he should replace the sun in *Guernica* with a light bulb, and to top it off, she slammed him with, 'You don't know how to paint suns' or 'Your suns never come out right.' On the other hand, when it comes to politics, let's be honest. . . . Picasso had done nothing, or nearly nothing, either for or against his fellow Spaniards during their Civil War. Dora couldn't stand that. She demanded, pleaded that he show them support, told him history would judge him if he didn't. Is it true that Picasso had dealings with the Nazis, that he received them in his studio and sold them paintings? You know, some books have it that Hitler considered Picasso an enemy, but the Nazis dropped by to keep tabs on him, and, who knows. Paul Éluard said—"

Bernard burst out laughing. It was a small dining area, and people turned to look at us. I lowered my gaze and stared at my hands folded on the table. Sometimes I observe my hands as if they're not mine, detached from me.

"What sort of books are you reading? Please, don't get in so far over your head. Nobody goes around accusing Picasso, nobody speaks badly about him, back off, don't touch. Picasso would never have done anything like that. Picasso, my dear, is a god. The Nazis banned his works, removed them from galleries, but he did feel forced to receive the Germans every time they dropped by. He wasn't the only one, as you can imagine. Éluard could say whatever nonsense he wanted, yes, he could, and indeed he did."

I bit my lower lip, embarrassed by my slipup; I sensed the snake was about to bite.

At a small table in front of us, a woman sat smoking, alone. She had finished her lunch and was flicking the ashes onto the leftovers on the plate. She had fleshy lips, a straight nose, a slightly protruding forehead. Her eyes were yellow, oddly puffy, the strangest greenish-yellow color.

"Behind you, Monsieur Minoret, there's a woman with yellow eyes," I whispered.

"Ah, yellow eyes! Like Jacques Dutronc, the singer and actor, the one who played Vincent Van Gogh on the screen. His eyes are the color of golden honey," Bernard said without turning around. "Should we be on first names? Oh, I think we already went through this." Again he turned his inquiring eyes on me.

I said, without looking away from the woman with the rounded head that reminded me of Dora Maar's, that I preferred keeping things more formal. I could never talk to him as if we were old friends, it felt too uncomfortable.

He agreed with a shrug, acting cross.

"Tell me the truth. Why are you so interested in Dora Maar?" he asked while he rummaged through his sport coat pockets for something.

"Because she was a great artist, because she was an enigmatic woman, because she fell head-over-heels in love with Picasso and suffered in silence after their breakup. Apparently, she stopped having sex at thirty-eight. With all the friends she once had, she ended up completely alone. But after everything I've read about the people in her circle, I also became very interested in you. In your connection with Picasso, of course, and in you as a society person and a writer, and in Lord as the platonic lover. Isn't it true that you all wanted to get at Picasso through her? I met Dora briefly, in passing." I didn't want to say any more.

He blinked at that last statement, but he saw how I was trembling and didn't pursue it, latching onto what most interested him. "Dora gave up her sex life at thirty-six. But it was her choice. As for the rest of us trying to be friends with Picasso—what else would you expect? I mean, Picasso. Though I was already friends with him through other people."

"She was already Dora Maar; when she and Picasso met, she was already a great artist, well-established and acclaimed by the Surrealists."

"Of course, of course, but hardly anyone noticed that detail."

"Detail? Sharing her life with Picasso was a detail? He wouldn't have painted *Guernica* without her."

"There are a lot of things Picasso wouldn't have done without her. But he was Picasso."

The woman in front of me looked at her watch, pulled a cell phone from her purse, dialed a number. She tried again and this time, it seemed from the way her face relaxed, the person on the other end had finally bothered to pick up. She talked with her free hand cupped over her mouth, while lowering her head to avoid the glances of the other diners. Soon enough, she put the phone away, lit another cigarette, lowered her eyes slightly, half-closing them. Now her eyes had a damp sheen and were speckled with tones of gray. She was weeping.

"Almost everything written about Picasso has it that Dora wept rivers, that she grimaced, screamed, and contorted her face until she looked horrible."

"I never saw her weep, except in Picasso's portraits." Bernard sat entranced with the delicate play of light and shadow on the sidewalk, on the other side of the window that separated us from the street. "No, Dora wasn't a crybaby, far from it. Not every book talks about her in such vain speculations, or falsehoods in my opinion, which not only attempt to drag her down, but also insult those of us who witnessed those years," he declared.

I was tempted to tell him a bit more about myself, about my life in Cuba and my more recent life here in exile. I was about to assure him that I didn't cry anymore, that my tears had dried. But sometimes I felt an anger burning deep down inside me, though by a great effort of spiritual concentration I could calm down. My blind rage would disappear as quickly as it had come. And, above all, I wanted to tell him, I felt very alone, profoundly vulnerable, with no one to help me. I didn't say any of this, I kept quiet, as I tend to do more and more these days, keeping quiet and burying it all inside me. Then I write, which relieves me, and it seems I can forget everything that made me so furious. I've turned all my tears into written words. Everything I might have wept, I've poured out onto paper. I've set down everything I could have wept in writing. I opened my mouth, closed it, thinking better of telling him.

"You were about to say something?" He spoke to me in the informal tone that I felt unable to use with him.

"No, Monsieur Minoret, nothing important. It's just that, well, you see, from where I'm sitting, there's that woman in front of me, alone. She's started crying, and now her eyes have turned gray."

"Eyes that change colors like the weather. Dora had the most beautiful eyes, nothing escaped them. She saw what no one else could see. Don't worry about that weeping woman. She isn't a

portrait by Picasso. And only portraits by Picasso deserve the attention of people like ourselves."

"She could have been one of his models, she's so beautiful,"
I stuttered. "I'm not interested in Dora Maar because she was
Picasso's lover. I care about her apart from Picasso, because I was
drawn to her life, and her art, and most of all to her work as a
photographer. I've been a fan of hers since I saw her photograph,
Père Ubu, with its deep meaning and immense Surrealist power.
An enigmatic little animal with a hairless snout and outlandish
claws. Though I also greatly admire the photos she took before she
ended her affair with Georges Bataille: the exotic photos of Assia;
Leonor Fini—another great Surrealist, from Argentina, just like
Dora (that's why they had so much in common); the portraits she
printed of Picasso himself. I fell in love with her work and the story
of her later life. And then I was immediately intrigued by those
five or eight days in Venice—eight, counting the return journey,
of course. Such a strange trip, nobody knows the details except
you two. At the time, as you know better than anyone, she was
utterly devoted to James Lord, from romantic rather than maternal
impulses, I'd guess, while he was more devoted to Picasso than
to Dora, and perhaps more than to you as well. Who were you
devoted to, emotionally?"

"Both of them, I was devoted to both. Or rather, I was devoted to
belonging to the twentieth century. To becoming an icon. By then,
on that trip, Dora had mellowed, she was easier to be around."

"After that trip, Dora decided to break off all ties, she shut herself in her house on Rue de Savoie and rarely left except to go to
Mass. She met with James Lord a few more times, shunned unin-
vited company," I rasped. "You know, women who shut themselves
off almost move me to tears."

"This isn't news to you if you've read a great deal about her, but
I'll remind you, Dora always said: 'After Picasso, God.'" He ordered
another coffee, black and strong.

"I know, I know, it makes sense. Surrealism set her free, and on the other hand, her love for Picasso turned her into a fugitive and at the same time imprisoned her in her own life story, a victim of her blind passion, silenced by her own frenzy."

We got up to leave.

There, a short distance away, the woman was quietly dabbing her tears with a lace handkerchief embroidered with the initials E M. She didn't even notice us leaving, saying goodbye to the owner of the restaurant, or, immediately afterwards, nodding in her direction. She never stopped staring straight ahead, on purpose, to avoid making eye contact with us, focusing on nothing, or perhaps on forgiveness, on the sadness of forgetting.

Out on the street, Bernard stopped me, gently grasping my elbow.

"Dora wasn't such a creature of passion, don't think that. Dora was an artist of great intelligence. Love overwhelmed her, made a fool of her. . . . She didn't weep on the outside, she wept on the inside, let all her tears flow inward, flooding her soul."

Bernard walked, tall and slim, taking quick, youthful steps, just ahead of me. I followed, studying his movements, trying to commit every detail about his appearance to my memory.

"Let's go up to my house, I want to show you Dora's painting, her famous rugged landscape."

The painting was hanging on one of the walls of the kitchen. I couldn't tell if it was a landscape or a fanciful Surrealist abstraction. The colors—greenish hues, blues, browns, blacks—formed a disgusting splotch in my mind, like a five-dimensional construction, difficult to grasp. It was a gloomy, dark painting, and I found its gloom at once repellent and intoxicating. The light entering through the window toned down the sadness that dominated the scene, in that bachelor's kitchen.

"Why did you say you were interested in me? You told me already, didn't you," Bernard said.

"Because you could have written Dora's story, but didn't," I answered, quickly, reverting to the formal tone; I still resisted his familiar attitude.

"Well, yes, I always wanted to be a writer, but I don't think I am one."

"No? After all you've written, you're not a writer? Your screenplays, at least."

"Not a great writer. I never wrote a great work, that's what I mean. I'm talking about my habitual lack of focus, bah, it isn't worth the trouble, I don't know. . . . Not that I'm all *that* unfocused or uncommitted to my own ideas. Those are just excuses for my habitual laziness." Bernard crossed the hallway and glided toward the living room.

The discreet servant offered me coffee or some liquor, perhaps a cognac, I don't remember exactly what sort of drink it was, but I do recall how I replied to his politeness. "No, thank you," I murmured; "I've got to rush home to send that article to the newspaper," I was thinking. "I've got to rush home and finish my womanly chores," I joked aloud. Bernard smiled, getting my satiric meaning, as he indicated with an ironic glance.

"Women aren't what they used to be, that is all too obvious."

"Well, now tell me about the men."

"We men are still the same, nothing about us has changed, there are no surprises. We're just that, nothing but men."

Why are there no surprises? Because all men are focused on courting power. Women are a secondary target of seduction for them now. Above all, first off, they need, or desperately want, to seduce power. There's no need to wonder why. The answer is simple: women have also begun to covet it. And to capture it.

Dora. Venice, 1958

She arrived in Venice on a May Day. She hadn't even settled into her hotel when she jotted in her diary, "Arrived May 1, International Workers' Day." It was ten past noon. Almost everyone was apparently asleep, because the city was shrouded in an odd, dense silence. But no, not asleep: resting, perhaps hiding from her; she guessed they were trying to avoid her. She smiled to herself. Why did everything have to revolve around her? At least, that was the way she always thought. She smiled to herself whenever she started to feel she mattered to someone else. She wet her lips with the tip of her tongue. It was a gesture she'd had for years, a private habit that reminded her of why Maya Walter-Widmaier, Picasso's first daughter, had called her "Lady Slobber."

She opened the window in her room. The sun bathed her cheeks. She closed her eyes. "Every honest story takes place through an open window and with eyes closed," she told herself. In November she would turn fifty-one, she suddenly recalled, and a hot flash shot up her neck.

Her face was brimming with peacefulness, as shown by the sunlight, her clear skin, her gently closed, pressed lips; her nostrils flared as they did when she first entered the basement where Georges Bataille, the philosopher and writer of magnificent erotic novels, received her and invited her to sit on the edge of his bed, surrounded by porn magazines. The way she sat on the edge of the mattress in this first encounter with Bataille inspired him to create the character of Xénie, immortalized in his erotic novel *Blue of Noon*.

She liked the smell of the narrow street, which let off an unsettling odor of dank walls, honeysuckles and irises, burnt jasmine. She opened her eyes wide. She would have loved to paint that mossy crevice. "No, no, forget it," she told herself. Probably, if no later vision obscured and surpassed the scene before her now, when she got back to Paris she would put a new canvas on the easel and paint that cleft with its fine, shiny green covering. She gloried in the idea of returning to her artistic work. "Art." Such a stiff word, so harsh. Her desire to take photographs or paint quickly evaporated.

"Art, after all, can only embellish the truth. It is not the truth in itself."

She half-closed the wooden blinds of the windows, letting a shimmering cone of light play onto the carpet. She longed for the darkness of her apartment, she missed the sound of Parisian silence. Here in the city of canals, she heard the muffled roar of the sea in slow motion, sounding as if the water would rise high as her throat and drown her. She pronounced the forbidden name once more: "Picasso." Her voice still had its birdlike lilt, as Bernard and James confirmed. Her voice was still lovely, like Xénie's.

"C et B." That's what James and Dora called Picasso. *Cher et Beau,* "our Beloved and Beautiful," was always jealous of Georges Bataille, her first love, the lover who initiated her.

She never called Bataille by his first name nor Picasso either. Never "Pablo," always "Picasso." "Men who have made their surnames famous no longer need a first name," she once said in a flash of wit.

James and Bernard welcomed her to Venice. James was cloyingly sweet, Bernard seductively charming. All this unsought attention was beginning to repulse her; being mixed up in dramas that had nothing to do with her was terribly boring. But at the same time, she didn't want to be without company, alone, no, it wasn't time for that, not yet.

Fourteen years and fourteen days earlier she had been admitted to the Sainte-Anne Hospital, escorted (not exactly accompanied) by Paul Éluard, Picasso, and Jacques Lacan, the eminent psychiatrist and psychoanalyst. Lacan signed Dora in under a fake name that still brings a small ironic smile to her face: Lucienne Tecta, "Covered Light." Or in Spanish, Luz Escondida. Did he mean that she could use that name? She, who up to that moment had been permanently overexposed as Picasso's lover, in the eyes of everyone, of every camera?

Fourteen years and fourteen days and a torrent of electroshocks administered by Lacan himself later, Dora Maar still sensed that last vestige of desire, or of jealousy. She had not changed all that much since then, since Lucienne Tecta, the woman who had been committed by the only man she loved and two of her best friends to the Sainte-Anne Psychiatric Hospital. She distrusted Lacan at first, until he slowly began to win her over. Not so Éluard. In Paul she saw a brother. Then, Picasso. . . . Pablo Picasso was bigger than God. How could she not give him all her faith? She gave him her life. And he'd used her life to do the only thing he knew how: he bled her and painted her with her own blood. She offered up her mind to him. The weeping woman. Weeping, weeping, weeping. . . . In a litany. The word "weeping" echoed against the fretwork Moorish ceiling embossed in red and gold.

After that experience, she thought she'd renounced desire. But not completely, for just now a slight reminiscence of pleasure had pulsed through her and given her goose bumps from head to toe.

She studied the objects around her: commonplace, public furnishings, pretentious copies of antiquities. She took the pictures down from the wall and hid them under the bed. A painting by Picasso would look very nice there—the canvas in which she— she rubbed her eyes aggressively, feeling drowsy—in which she was depicted as an animal forged of steel, as if her fingers moved rhythmically like sharpened scissor blades, slicing her blouse. The portrait in which she was weeping, weeping, weeping incessantly. In every painting she is weeping, wailing for all eternity.

"I do not love you, I feel no attraction to you." She relived those words in the painter's mouth, lips taut and dry, the words the surly Spaniard pronounced with his eyes glued to a canvas. Gleeful to humiliate her.

She had not been able to erase those words, uttered with such bored brutality, from her mind. Had he said it wearily? Or the opposite, with feverish intensity, like everything that came from Picasso? No matter; so much time had passed. Or perhaps not even enough time. Not too much, not sufficient. "Perhaps I haven't gotten over it as much as I had thought," she wavered, anguished.

She remembered one of the most painful scenes in her life. Picasso was sitting in Le Catalan, the restaurant on Rue Saint-André des Arts, with the Hungarian-born photographer Brassaï and Gilberte Brassaï, with the poet Paul Éluard, and with Éluard's lover, Nusch, such a delicate woman she seemed she might shatter into a thousand pieces, shimmering with beauty, with fragile yet indelible loveliness, like that of a trapeze artist whose every death-defying move on the high wire leaves a lasting impression.

She counted more people, nine altogether, and she spotted the seat they had saved for her. Picasso was smiling, recounting unusually wicked stories, talking very loud, chewing on a chunk of baguette, ordering a chateaubriand steak. He was the center; no one thought of him as anything less than a god. He was the most important thing in this world and in every possible world.

She had recognized him from a distance. She entered the restaurant slowly. She would have liked to smile, to be friendly with the others, in short, to act naturally, but she couldn't swing it. She knew she looked too serious, that she was about to cry, she knew Picasso wouldn't appreciate the tense look on her face, her tedious appearance, bordering on insufferable.

Time snaps back to the present, as in a Surrealist story.

But now she's in the past, the past in which she went by the name of Lucienne Tecta, in which she was locked in a dark room, bound in restraints, her teeth clinched. Her brain bursting with light and frothy spittle. The man she once loved jamming his thumb into her pituitary. She felt so tired then, she stopped eating, lost weight. Her backside was riddled with needle marks from the injections, her arms scratched and covered in bruises. They had to trim her nails to the quick to keep her from mangling her arms in her fits of self-revulsion. Then she started tearing out clumps of her hair, chewing it up and swallowing it down. She vomited hair balls, like a cat.

And if she'd had a key, a shard of glass, a sharp point of any cutting object, she would have plunged it into her neck, into her jugular vein.

But back to the table at Le Catalan. She sensed that something had broken, irreparably. She was already sick of guessing how good a time he had of it when she was wasn't around, she couldn't stand seeing him so friendly around others, much less put up with his acting gruff and regretful around her. Picasso was a different person, enraptured with his flirtatiousness, when she wasn't there: he was likeable, almost gentle. Finally, Dora reached the table, sat down, after discreetly saying hello; he—God—looked at her for a second and kept on talking, gesturing wildly, angrily demanding his chateaubriand. Out of the blue, he poked her forearm with the tip of his knife, as if to tell her, "Hey you, pay attention!"

She still doesn't know why, but all of a sudden Dora came out with the whole thing about how she couldn't stand him anymore, wouldn't stay with him one minute longer, she was leaving, she never wanted to see him again. She stomped out in a fury. She suspected he might follow her, but not far, a couple of yards at most, the bare minimum. She was wrong: he ran after her, much farther than she had imagined. He grabbed her by the shoulders, laying his minotaur hooves on her.

It surprised him that those green eyes, Dora's eyes that changed like the weather, were now dry and furious, that she stared directly at him with a dignity, a sharpness, that he found discomfiting, that she was struggling feebly to free herself from the rough hands pinning down her arms, that she was fighting back, though without making a fuss about it, in cold and calculating way.

"Weep, Dora, weep!" He shook her violently.

A single tear shined like a diamond in the corner of her eye.

He studied the track of that tear, as if it were a trickle of paint running down the canvas of one of his paintings: astonishing, amazing! An erection bulged under the fly of his pants, dribbling from the tip. He ejaculated at the same time that the teardrop fell from her chin to the breast of her blouse.

At last she managed to escape his powerful porcupine quills. He caught her again, she began to wail, more and more quietly, suffocating in her own moans.

She remembered nothing more. Actually, she did not want to remember one more iota of that pitiful sequence of absurdities that filled her with such shame.

Picasso cried for help, as if she were the one who had dug in her nails, not the other way around.

Sure enough, Lacan and Éluard showed up to help their friend Picasso. Not to help her, no. She was an obstacle to clear out of the way, for the time being, so that the Great Genius would feel free. Free from her! At least, that was the idea that Dora formed about what they doing to her, how they were forcing her to suffer. How could she have been so naïve? How could she have gotten depressed to the point of seeming crazy, even to the point of actually making herself ill?

In that moment *The Weeping Woman* was born, an inexhaustible theme in Picasso's work. Dora Maar, the artist, the beloved partner, the lover, had only just succumbed.

Outside it was raining, as it so often does in Venice, with a sublime impertinence that only seems believable in novels. All the water falling at once, soaking even your bones, and the puddles turning to muddled mirrors, splattered and worn.

In a window up above the street, a woman of water closed the shutters.

With the same gesture, years ago she had closed the shutters of a hospital room. The darkness had healed her, she who had been radiant, a creature who loved light and sought it out, who relished lying under the sun in gardens to photograph the clouds, was now coming back from darkness to life, slowly, regaining her sanity, through the emanations of shadows.

Nothing around her, under this rainstorm, jibed with the imaginary shadows that had once kept her so penned in but that now extended a hand to her in truce.

Dora closed the window, but the playful cones of light still peeked in through the blinds. Then she lowered the wooden slats with her fingertips, quietly.

"I'd become too high-strung," she whispered. Her hands trembled slightly.

She studied the bare walls in the semi-darkness.

She worried about the Picasso paintings she had left hanging on the walls of her house in Paris; she felt a desperate urge to return, to sit down again on the shiny leather of her ratty armchair, facing them, impatient to gaze at them and take care of them, if only by staring blankly into them, losing herself in each masterful brushstroke.

She would descend the staircase silently, without a suitcase, leaving behind everything she had brought with her and escaping unencumbered by those heavy, useless objects, making do with just her purse, catching the water taxi and making her way back to Paris. Good God, how could she have left those paintings alone with no one to look after them? She had been through hard times but had always refused to sell Picasso's important works, not a single one of his masterly paintings. She had, however, sold some of his drawings at prices that today would seem ludicrous, and later she might even sell the famous painting *Bodegón*, then still hanging in her living room. Yes, perhaps she would decide to sell it sometime, but it would have to be to a friend or acquaintance, someone she really trusted.

On the other hand, one day she would die and there'd be no one to take care of the works that Picasso had dedicated to her. It was her entire fortune. Nothing, she had nothing else, only her Picassos, and that was enough! What a burden! Why did she suffer economic hardship yet resist selling off any of her valuable paintings by him? A friend asked her one day, in the vulgar way typical of those who think friendship allows them to use any tone of voice they want, why she didn't solve her problems by selling her ex-lover's paintings. From that moment, Dora never wanted to see that fellow again, ever. Nobody could be her friend who didn't understand that she cherished her life itself less than she did those lavish canvases: her paintings, the paintings Picasso had dedicated to her.

Alone, she became increasingly isolated, meeting fewer people; when it came down to it, this solitude was all her fault, her responsibility. People, seemingly so busy, began to forget her, or didn't forget her, but life always outstrips memory. Dora then held demented conversations with their portraits, the ones of her old friends that Picasso had painted, and in a ritornello or perhaps an eternal soliloquy, she would also converse with the portraits he had done of her.

Hesitating, she dropped her small suitcase, placed the shopping basket she used as a purse in the middle of the floor, opened the door, and stood a few moments with her hand on the doorknob, her mind a blank.

She came back in. She would only be away for five days, she asked for only five days, eight or nine at most, plus the return trip; she thought maybe they could stay at Balthus's castle on the way back. Perhaps eight or nine days, tops. No one in Paris would notice her sudden getaway, except for the building caretaker, always sticking her nose in what was none of her business. It would do her good to get away, as long as it was for art's sake, for the memory of art, for art's impact on that city created by the icons of water: Venice.

She still loved James and felt curious about Bernard, longed to get to know him better. Five or eight days of conversation with them would be healthy for her, would transform her memories of her vacation with James in Ménerbes, at the house Picasso had given her; these new experiences would displace the old ones. She would take the trip to Venice as an escape, a getaway, a sort of evasion therapy. Would James still feel the same about her? Could it be true that he was still interested in marrying her? She was getting carried away here. James Lord had never proposed to her; yes, he had hinted at it, but that was quite another thing, a hint was very different from an proposal made on the fly, ephemerally inserted in the middle of some banal conversation. In any case, she would never consent to marry anyone. She had given herself to him, to Him alone, like so, capitalized, to Picasso, to God. Her God.

She went back to the middle of the room, unpacked, hung her clothes in the wardrobe, undid the bed, lay down on the mattress, and looked at the ceiling for a long time; after a while, she closed her eyes.

Opening, closing the eyelids, the present, the past. With an imperceptible movement of her lids she could shift from now to memories, and this was her life, this was what it all came down to: rambling and remembering. The routes her rambles took her on grew shorter and shorter in contrast to the inexhaustible trajectory of her memory. Now it was all just walking on an imaginary high wire; down below her were the arched windows of Rue d'Astorg, twisted, glinting like liquid, as in her Surrealist photos.

She lay there half napping, dreaming that a little girl with blond curls stood laughing beside her, but at the same time she began to hear a wail coming from the front door. She slipped lightly down a hallway toward the door. It was open, and a shadow was slipping through, toward the staircase. She was walking around naked, her thighs as white as milk, her breasts swaying, her hair loose. She closed the door heavily. She went back to bed; the little girl was gone. She opened a bottle of pills and swallowed a fistful; her mouth went dry.

"Dora, Dora . . ."

Someone knocking on the door.

"Coming." A cramp clenched her toes. She sat up in bed with difficulty.

At last, she dashed to the bathroom, decorated in flamingo-pink tiles and flagstones, and vomited. She washed up. On the mirror some previous guest had written in lipstick, in English: "Just I love you. I killed you."

So it was, that was life, just love another person, sing the other's praises, and then murder that person. She had been wrong, had confused love with eroticism in the period when she'd met Georges Bataille and become his lover, and he'd initiated her as a lover who fell headlong into passion; then it was time for the next type of love, artistic love, her love of Surrealism; then came true love, the great love, her love of Pablo Picasso, and to top it off, her love of Communism. After all these excesses, what else could she expect but disillusion.

Love was nothing but mere love, without its trappings, and at the end, death. Life should be no more than that, loving others without expecting anything on their part. Not even expecting them to love you. Her life now was loving God.

She left her room refreshed, her hands scented with a flowery cream and her neck with a subtle cologne. James and Bernard were waiting for her in the lobby. They wore sporty clothes, light colors, both looked radiant. They were young, and therein lay the secret of their peculiar glow.

Dora, on the other hand, was already on a one-way journey, was beginning to age just when she was feeling her youngest. She regretted having worn the dress with the tiny flowers against navy blue and the round collar, thinking it made her look too provincial. She smiled and continued skipping down the stairs; they let her take the lead.

She came out onto the narrow street, and a fresh breeze from the canal caressed her face. She sensed that her friends, behind her, were gazing at her with a certain amount of pity.

"Dora, where do you want us to go?"

"Wherever you two want, or wherever our old homesick feet lead us."

"Let's roam around. If you don't get lost in Venice, you can't really know the city," Bernard remarked.

"Let's get lost, then," Dora murmured.

"Later on we can have dinner at that small restaurant on the canal, the one where they make the delicious shrimp with the red Venetian sauce," James suggested.

The other two agreed.

Without a word, they walked about the narrow streets, which were strangely empty for that time of year.

"I'd like to try out Caffè Florian."

"You see, Bernard," James protested, "we'll never be able to surprise her. We had planned to take you there tomorrow for breakfast, Dora, but we thought it better to give you the biggest surprise possible by taking you there blindfolded."

Dora gave him an amused yet domineering look. "Never dare put a blindfold on me. Never, ever." Throughout their years of friendship, sometimes she spoke to him casually, and sometimes, as now, her tone with him was emphatically formal. "I shall never be a woman whose gaze is hidden, never allow my gaze to be blindfolded."

Bernard lagged behind, James waited for him, Dora continued ahead of them.

"I know, Bernard, I also get frightened by the hasty answers she bursts out with lately, but I think it's her age, she's getting old," whispered James, who loved making her out to be a bit older than she was.

Dora paced quickly along the narrow street. Suddenly, she stopped in front of a shop window, which the owner had filled with a display of all sorts of telescopes, ancient, modern, various sizes. Her father's face took hold of her memories and transformed them into startling visions.

My father, Joseph Markovitch, was born in Siskak, Croatia. He was a certified architect in Vienna and Zagreb. He arrived in France in 1896 and four years later was named commissioner of the Austro-Hungarian pavilion at the Universal Exposition in Paris. There he met my mother, Louise Julie Voisin, a small country girl born in Cognac on February 28, 1877. Henriette Theodora Markovitch was born on November 22, 1907, on Rue d'Assas.

That's what she had jotted down when she tried writing her memoirs. She later dropped the project, finding it presumptuous and a waste of time. The same year she was born, Picasso painted *Les Demoiselles d'Avignon*.

When she was three, the little girl traveled with her parents to Buenos Aires; she only remembered the unnerving sensation of the Earth rolling beneath her feet and of being thrust back into a womb, an iron womb this time. Her father made his fortune building monuments. "Who doesn't remember," she wondered, "that remarkable seven-story edifice on the corner of Alem and Cangallo?" Her father would climb, with her in his arms, up to the observatory in the gilded oval cupola and let her gaze at the sky with the strange optical devices he had installed at the pinnacle.

"Dora, *observe* the stars, Dora, *observe*, how beautiful." Her father had started shortening her name to Dora.

Then the telescope would aim low and, seen through the lens, the smallest details in the harbor would look enormous: the ships coming and going as they left for Europe or returned, the yellowish waves tinged with florescent orange in the Río de la Plata.

To the age of thirteen, she lived in Argentina with her parents; then they returned to Paris. During those thirteen years she did what all young girls do: study, play, get to know life through the experiences of the adults closest to her, make up stories, dream of what she would be when she grew up, who she would fall in love with, what fate had in store for her. The adults closest to her were her parents. As an only daughter, she was pampered by Joseph and Julie, who did their best to clothe her properly, teach her good manners, and give her a good education. They could afford it, they had the economic resources, and they also worked very hard to offer her a full, untroubled life.

Every evening at dusk she would climb up to the observatory, with or without her father. She had become an expert with the optical instruments, focusing them, turning from one to the next to measure distances, using them to observe the stars. She had given each star its own name; she wished now that she could recall them all, but she couldn't. She could only hear the distant voice of her father, Joseph. "Dora, don't close your eyes to the immensity of the universe, *observe, observe,* Dora." He repeated this so often that she ended up thinking the observatory was actually called an "observadora."

A man behind the window—the owner of the Venetian shop— motioned for her to come inside. She finally awoke from her reverie. James and Bernard were walking slowly, quite a ways beyond.

She realized she was annoying them with her delay and ought to catch up.

She passed by a hat shop. Her mother also made fancy hats in Buenos Aires, but instead these hats brought back memories of Picasso. The hats and the fluttering birds pinned to the ornaments Dora wore in her unkempt hair, or sometimes in her well-combed hair, depending on the circumstances, while tears stained the fronts of her blouses, in the paintings in which he immortalized her.

Her friends waited for her impatiently. "So tell us, Dora. Do you like Venice, or not?"

She nodded.

"We knew you'd love this city," James added.

She said nothing to encourage him. James waited for her to respond, and when she didn't he reproached her. "I get it, I get it, you knew it all before I ever found out."

"I didn't say anything, I kept quiet, because I didn't want to disappoint you by saying something prissy or foolish," she said as she smoothed her raven black hair, in which a few gray hairs were just beginning to show up on either side of the part.

They continued on their rambling course, stopping every now and then on a small bridge to watch the gondolas, some carrying pairs of lovers, others crammed with families with children.

Dora stopped in front of a vendor of shoes for gondoliers made from felt, velvet, and stitched leather, in every color, radiant colors. She looked through them, handled them, kept on walking. Bernard approached her, smiling. "Would you like a gondolier's shoe like one of those? What size do you wear?"

"No, Bernard, I don't need any."

She never needed anything, but, like all women, presents delighted her; she adored surprises. If she'd said yes to Bernard, if she had admitted that she'd liked the shoes, it wouldn't have counted as a present when he gave them to her, just an empty gesture occasioned by a whim, not a true gift.

"I only wanted to see how they were made, how they were sewn," she answered, nonplussed.

"But Dora, please, I want to give you a pair as a gift," Bernard insisted.

"No, no, Bernard, I already said no. Thank you, but don't insist."

She was annoyed by the obvious efforts Bernard was making to regale her in order to create a more comfortable, trusting space for himself between her and James. At least, that was how she interpreted the young man's persistent attempts to bring his friendliness to her attention.

Her head, her mind, open and free, soared once more.

There was a time when things might have played out differently. There was a time when perhaps she was better-natured; no doubt she was sweet, generous, caring, even funny. But she was aware that she had become embittered years ago; she often noticed that her rudeness repelled others. She couldn't afford the luxury of recalling in detail how she used to be, so it would take effort for her to compare her past and present behavior.

Not long ago, when Picasso was still the center of her life, she wasted no time in self-reflection; she had even forgotten that the way others treated her depended on how the painter treated her, had even blotted out what her relationships with friends—some of them short-lived and superficial—had been like, all the ins and outs and intrigues of friendship. Before, she only saw things through Picasso's eyes, was totally devoted to him, to his talent, to his demands. And Picasso, due to his extreme possessiveness, succeeded in isolating her from everyone, demanding that she work only and exclusively with him, hand in hand, face to face, joined at the hip.

Even when she was with other people, she felt psychically bound to him, though she was not physically by his side. Even when she was listening to other people, even when the subject at hand had nothing to do with either of them, her only point of reference was him, no one and nothing else. And no concern enticed her away or distracted her from her focus, her central core: Picasso.

When he started getting aggressive, he was hotheaded though not verbally abusive, bad-tempered to the point of losing self-control; she also began changing, pouring into him like wet clay poured into a mold, and acquiring her lover's personality traits. Then he changed again, in turn, and at times took on Dora's style. She couldn't understand how he had managed to steal her personality and take over all her attributes, her good, kind, just qualities. She, on the other hand, had inherited the worst in his character, his tediousness, his bad moods, and a fleeting sense of sweetness and insincerity.

"What are you thinking about?" Bernard interrupted.

"Oh, nothing. The Grand Canal is beautiful at nightfall." She lowered her eyes.

They were facing the Grand Canal, also surprisingly empty, which still seemed strange on such a beautiful spring day.

"Dora will never admit she's thinking about anything," James joked. "But she always looks like she's got something on her mind and that she'll suddenly barrage us with questions."

"Why are there so few people? I see hardly any tourists. I thought Venice would be overrun with them." Dora looked back at the canal, directly away from James.

In perfect Italian, Bernard asked a gondolier what was going on, and he told them, "Today is Workers' Day, May 1, *e questo.* . . ." The young man's lengthy explanation went on until his gondola disappeared around a corner.

"*Grazie mille! A rivederci!*" Bernard called out.

"I'm exhausted. Let's grab a seat in a café." Dora's face was pale, beads of sweat dotting her forehead and upper lip.

They ended up, inevitably enough, in the sumptuous Caffè Florian. They stayed there a long time. Fascinated, Dora took in every nook and cranny of the legendary place, which she described as being "straight out of a novel" and which reminded her of Balthus's paintings, though she couldn't say why. She had two hot chocolates with cream and a dessert that looked a tower of meringue. They remained there, engrossed in the ambience of the café, until it started to fill up with foreign visitors like them, though some were repeat visitors, as well as also true regulars, the real locals. Then they began to feel removed, out of place, out of touch with the history and rituals of the city, so they decided to go for another walk. After wandering for a while, they took a table at a charming little café next door to the hotel.

Settled in a corner in the small café, they watched other newcomers. Dora sat with her back against the wall, next to the front window, where she could study the few passersby, her face bathed in sunlight. They ordered *café crème*. Bernard and James started planning an itinerary to go museum hopping and satisfy Dora's urgent desire to get to know the works of Bellini, Titian, Carpaccio, Tintoretto, the mosaics of Piazza San Marco and Torcello. Dora leaned her head against the back of the chair, closed her eyes, and fell into passing trance.

Through a fog, she made out the image of her mother. Dora was lying down, asleep in her bed, in Paris, and her mother planted herself in the doorway. Standing at the threshold, her face was hard, and she was naked. She must have been sixty, but there were no wrinkles on her body, her pubis was shaved. Dora went to ask her something, but she lost the thread of her dream, shifted in her café seat. Yet she fell asleep again. The second time, she dreamed that her mother and grandmother had died and that she had removed them from the grave. In the casket, they both looked putrid, their flesh greenish, covered in sores, and yet they half-raised their eyelids. They whispered to her, calling for Dorita, their poor little Dora, "Come here, my little girl." "Good girl," her grandmother murmured.

"Sorry, I must have dozed off, I'm so tired." Dora rubbed her eyelids with a white handkerchief she pulled from her pocketbook. A veritable relic of a purse, completely out of fashion, a gift from Picasso.

"Don't worry, it was only five minutes," James commented.

"It seemed like hours, centuries." She looked at her watch, with its delicate silver hands. "Whenever you want, we can take off again."

"If you're ready, let's go now, right?" Bernard folded his newspaper, and he and James got up to leave.

Dora took a sip of water and hung her purse on her shoulder. No avoiding it, she'd have to see Venice now. Until a few days ago she only had to imagine it, now she had to face it with all her senses awake to the adventure of confronting Venice head on.

James. Paris, 2006

I picked up the receiver and dialed the number, feeling nervous. I don't like to disappoint anyone who's set aside time to see me, I'm punctual to a fault, but I had no choice, I couldn't help it, I could arrive late or not go at all.

"*Bonjour*, Bernard," I stuttered. "I can't go with you to visit James Lord today."

He greeted me politely, but he was annoyed by my unexpected announcement.

"Well, that's quite a disappointment." He dropped the friendly tone, no doubt because I'd put him in a foul mood. "You arranged to meet James Lord with me. He's a difficult and busy man; besides, tomorrow he's going skiing and the day after he's leaving for the United States. You won't get a chance to see him for months, if then. It won't be easy to get another chance to meet him."

"Bernard, I apologize, my daughter has a fever."

He thought I was making it up. When I saw how offended he was, I changed my mind.

"Don't worry, I'll catch a taxi right now and be at your place in twenty minutes."

"Fine, I'll expect you, but I'm warning you that we'll be half an hour late as it is. James won't appreciate your being late; he's quite the stickler for time."

I left my daughter with our au pair, an Italian nanny. She still had a fever, but it was going down.

It wasn't easy to find a taxi driver who would agree to take me as far as the Bastille Market, closed due to a protest march. I called Bernard just as he was leaving his apartment. He descended the stairs uneasily while I waited for him in the cab; when he left the building, I got out of the cab to greet him with the usual kiss on each cheek, then invited him to ride with me.

"You didn't need to pick me up in a car, we're just a few steps away; we'll walk," he grumbled, refusing to get into the cab.

I paid the driver. We strode to a building that was relatively nearby. I could tell that Bernard was rattled; he also kept up his cool tone, expressing his obvious displeasure.

"I'm warning you, James Lord has not been in a good mood lately," he remarked as he rang the doorbell. "And, to top it off, we show up late."

The door opened, the door latch pulled by a cord running down from the upper floor. We climbed up an exceedingly steep set of red, worm-eaten wooden steps. In one of the hallways we were greeted by distinguished portraits of our host painted by Picasso, readily recognizable images that had been reproduced in any number of art catalogues.

"These are the originals. It's crazy to keep them here, I'm surprised no one's stolen them yet!" Bernard finally gave a little smile as his friend opened the door of the apartment.

James Lord wore a brown jacket, and pants a shade lighter than tan. He looked haughty, attractive, very attentive to his studied gestures, aware of his own elegance, and quite similar to Bernard in style. A style that evoked a whole era. With poorly concealed arrogance, he shook my hand, displaying a studied curtness while avoiding my gaze. His face was serious and, I think, even a little tense; he was clearly annoyed with me for arriving late.

I apologized profusely, but he made sure that I realized he had lost forty-five minutes of his life waiting for some stranger who was—putting it bluntly—about to stick her nose into his private dealings with Dora Maar.

James Lord, the anxious target of my anxious hopes, sprawled back on one of the side couches.

I waited until he'd finished making himself comfortable, though he did so by sitting up very straight, and then I sat on an impeccably white sofa. On the wall behind me hung a portrait of our host by Giacometti. After this visit, I watched a number of documentaries and clips on television, YouTube, the Internet, that show James Lord talking about his relationships with Picasso and Dora Maar, and he always appears sitting on the same white couch where I had comfortably parked my behind. Him and behind him, his portrait, protecting him, glorifying him. Sitting down so casually, without asking first, without waiting for permission, in what was clearly and undeniably his usual seat, was a heedless error, one I wouldn't have committed had I known better. Bernard remained on his feet, nervously pacing from wall to wall, pretending to scrutinize the various paintings, which I am sure he had looked at more than once and already knew by heart.

I explained why I was there. I was interested in the trip to Venice, of only eight days, that the three of them had taken together. I wanted to tell the story, "Preferably in a novel," I stammered. He didn't bat an eyelid, nor did he look straight at me, staring off into space, at some vague point in front of him.

"What was Dora like?" I inquired.

He gave me no specifics.

"Dora was a great artist. It's all in my book," was his entire answer.

I pulled his book *Picasso and Dora* out of my handbag and handed it to him.

"Would you please sign it for me?"

He took no notice of the passages I had underlined. He scrawled a few lines. Now, with the passing of time, I realize that he showed more kindness in his inscription than in the way he behaved, or tried to appear, when I was there with him on that afternoon:

> *Pour Zoé, avec ma pensée cordiale, en attendant de voir moi-même vu par vous!*
>
> JAMES LORD
>
> *Paris, le 3 janvier 2007*

> To Zoé, with my kindest regards, looking forward to seeing me seen by you!
>
> JAMES LORD
>
> Paris, January 3, 2007

A bit later, Bernard came up with an excuse to leave, saying he had to meet someone and was in a hurry. He said this in a way calculated to emphasize his fake hesitation. I suspect he actually felt uncomfortable being around Lord and me.

Before he left, Bernard made a point of praising me, adding some very flattering opinions of his own, repeating the kind remarks others had made about me and playing up all the most positive parts. Then he was off like a shot, out the door and gone for the rest of the afternoon.

James and I remained alone. He kept quiet, still staring fixedly at the empty spot in front of him, while I didn't dare ask another question, afraid to break the spell that had settled on us. Yes, there was a bit of magic, perhaps the enchantment of my flimsy excuses. And so we sat in silence for some twenty minutes.

"There was already one lady who came around to investigate us," he said with a gentle sigh.

"I've read her book, too." This was the biography by the Argentine journalist and writer Alicia Dujovne Ortiz, *Dora Maar, prisonnière du regard*, published by Grasset. "It's an excellent biography.

I've read it carefully and I'll gladly use it as a reference. Reading that book was what put me on the trail of the Venice trip."

That last sentence was barely audible. He shrugged.

Finally, I dared to ask, "James, did you love Dora?"

Another silence fell on us, even deeper than the first. All my attention was concentrated on the face of the man sitting at an oblique angle to my left. His eyes, reddened, grew moist; he began weeping discreetly.

"Dora was the most beautiful thing that ever happened to me. I loved her dearly," he finally answered.

I don't know why, but I doubted what he was saying. His tears seemed theatrical, and I felt annoyed by his excessively dramatic weeping. In his book I read his self-portrait, his view of himself, and he had not exactly made himself out to be a loving angel; instead, he rather betrayed himself by giving a straightforward description. The relationship of Dora Maar and James Lord was overshadowed by Picasso. They were united in their enormous adoration of the artist, hers being greater than his, of course. It is no accident that Lord titled his book *Picasso and Dora*.

"How did you get my book? It's out of print, you know."

"I found one copy left, published by Séguier. I bought it at the exhibition at the Picasso Museum about both of them, Dora and Picasso."

"Please, do you think I'm going to forget who published the book? You're telling me things I already know," James regained his authoritative tone.

Once more silence returned, so thick we could have cut it with hedge-trimmers.

After a while he started speaking to me in English. I interrupted him. "Excuse me, Señor Lord." I purposely called him both and "Lord" and *señor*, which means "lord" in Spanish. "I understand English well enough but can't express myself fluently in it. I'd rather we continued speaking French."

He spoke French with a strong American accent, much stronger than my accent, and I figured it was worse when he was upset. Just then that's what happened: he mangled and butchered the language.

"Dora was a great woman, a tremendous artist. Why are you so interested in telling the story of that five-day trip, plus three days on the road, that we did with her, that she did with us, with Bernard and me, in Venice? Yes, it was really eight days, if we count the trip back and the night we spent at the painter Balthus's house."

I recognized that he hadn't mentioned his relationship with Bernard and that he had emphasized that bit about "the painter Balthus," as if I didn't know who Balthus was.

"I know who Balthus is. And again, I'm interested in the trip, in that special moment, because it was the last time she fulfilled an illusion. I've always been drawn to those turning points in lives of artists, of Surrealists and pure souls like her. Dora was, without a doubt, a key ingredient in the precious alchemy of Surrealism."

I wasn't telling him the truth.

The truth was that I felt as empty as she had, scraping the bottom of my barrel of illusions, that I didn't even have any illusions of God left, much less of freedom. Or that my god was poetry, and poetry barely consoled me. And that I was also very far from believing that either Dora or I had been pure.

"Do you feel sad?" he asked disconsolately, and without waiting for my reply he went on, "I do too, very sad."

"I was born sad. And this exile has lasted too long. I get the impression that few people understand us. Besides, a few imbeciles have tried to crush me; I feel alone, so alone."

"We're all alone. Let time do its work." He paused. "You'll get used to it. Dora did. Forgive me for mixing up *tu* and *vous* when I talk with you. Time heals all wounds."

I shrugged, though I won't deny that I felt uncomfortable whenever he addressed me informally, as *tu*, since it forced me to treat him in kind, but I wasn't going to try and stop him.

"Is that the only possible solution: let time do its work?" I searched his face. "Time passes, and then along comes death, and suddenly it's all over for us."

"The only solution is to go with time's flow, accept isolation, let forgetfulness bear it away. The rest is merely last illusions, lost illusions. . . . Death is natural, it's part of life." He smiled at the allusion he'd made to Honoré de Balzac's famous novel, one of the longest in *La Comédie humaine*, without directly citing it.

When he noticed that I made no comment and had no intention of making one, he felt obliged to ask me, "Have you read Balzac?"

"Yes, of course I've read *Lost Illusions*. Having lived under a totalitarian regime doesn't necessarily mean you're ignorant; the regime imposes ignorance, of course, but on the other hand, you can superimpose yourself and get an education under the table. My education is vast but chaotic. That's the downside: under a totalitarian system you can't be educated in a natural, organic way."

"Well, if you've read *Lost Illusions*, you'll know what I mean. That's life: a long, lonely journey, and a sky heaped with sorrow-laden clouds all around."

A short time went by in silence.

"Please excuse me. I leave early tomorrow, very early, to go skiing in Switzerland, and I need to pack my things. It's seven o'clock now. We should call it an evening."

I had arrived at 5:45. He stood up from the couch, walked over, and lifted my chin in his hand.

"You may wonder why an eighty-year-old dares to go skiing and put himself at such an irresponsible risk. Oh, I like the look you're giving me," he said, pausing. "You have such honest eyes, beautiful, sweet, and at the same time there's a feline spark behind your pupils, a tigress's eyes."

I smiled. "No, Señor Lord, I wasn't wondering anything of the sort about you. Exercise is good for older people."

I made this trite remark as I gently freed myself from his hand and put on my overcoat.

"My body needs the exercise: skiing, hurling myself down that icy, white mountain. Plunging right into it, losing myself in the cottony depths of the snow. I also long to breathe mountain air. Yes, you're right, well, that's what I am: an older person."

I realized that we had nothing left to say to each other, but that he was trying to be polite, well-mannered, to the end. James Lord had already written everything he was going to say in his book, and I could tell he was reluctant to stir the memories of his years with Dora.

I ran my eyes once more across the paintings, the white-washed walls, the white-upholstered furniture, the bone or ivory carpeting. Everything in that apartment elicited a nauseating sensation of immaculate perfection.

The strict orderliness, the whiteness, the fastidious, bleach-scented cleanliness made me slightly queasy; still, I held my breath for a few seconds, overcome more by feelings than by fumes, then quickly recovered.

James Lord shook my hand; I searched his eyes as he clasped my hand in his. His eyes seemed melancholy. We smiled and said goodbye. I never saw him again.

I came home feeling I'd just gotten back from a trip in a time machine, but a trip to the future. My daughter was over her fever; I sent the nanny home. My husband had left for work. I got into bed with my daughter, both of us worn out.

In the wee hours of the night I was awakened by my vibrating cell phone. I answered the call as soon as I was out of my daughter's room.

"Hi, this is Yendi. I just got to Paris. It's my first time here! Can you believe it? I hope you remember me! I'm a huge fan of yours! I'm Renán's wife."

I wasn't at all thrilled about getting a call so late at night, especially not from this Yendi, who I knew fleetingly from Cuba. I also knew Renán, but at least he was an amazing musician, composer, jazz pianist, and he'd been the boyfriend of a dear friend of mine on the island.

"Thanks for calling, Yendi." I went for polite. "How's Renán? Listen, it's so late here, you must realize it's nearly morning. Call back tomorrow. Please."

"Renán? Great, he's great, but we're kind of separated. . . . Yes, yes, I understand, it's late. I'll call tomorrow and tell you the whole story."

I took a shower. Her call intrigued me; I couldn't imagine what in the world that woman was doing here, in Paris. And why had she called us in the middle of the night? What on earth for?

I staggered back, perfumed and clumsily disrobed, into bed. My husband arrived a bit later. He left his bags with the camera and tripod in the living room, washed up and got into bed beside me, and gave me a back rub. "His hands work wonders," I thought.

"How'd your day go?" he whispered.

"Fine, but I didn't get much from talking to James Lord. I don't think he found me interesting at all, or at least not very much. So he didn't open up, and I didn't get any useful information. But still, I got the experience of being with him, he signed his book for me, and I took a good look at him close up. He's still an attractive man."

"An eighty-year-old man, attractive?" He stopped rubbing my back.

"Yes, because he's refined, persuasive, charming, and all that gives him the air of a great lord. Sure, he's a bit pretentious, that's to be expected. He's also very American, though he pretends not to be. That's the way Americans who have hangups about being Americans act."

"Anything else?"

"Keep rubbing my back, come on, please."

He strummed a steady beat on my shoulder blades with his fingertips.

"Anything else?" he insisted.

"No, nothing else. Oh, I forgot, Yendi called a little while back, Renán's wife. She came to Paris alone, without him."

"Yendi alone, without Renán, in Paris?"

"I thought it was strange, too. She called maybe two hours ago, late, real late. She said she'd give us a call tomorrow."

"Did you ask her what she's doing here or why she called?"

"No, that's all she told me, and I didn't know how to react, you know? She caught me by surprise. I didn't know how to deal with it."

"Doesn't matter, we'll find out tomorrow what her deal is."

We hugged each other for a while, until I started breathing deeply and he did too. He turned over. So did I.

I woke up around eight in the morning. My husband had taken our daughter to school. I had a headache, so I took an extra-strength Ibuprofen, and at that moment the phone rang.

"*Bonjour.* I couldn't hit the trail as early as I wanted, but I'm about to leave. I got a ticket for a more reasonable departure time. Bernard gave me your number since you forgot to give it to me." It was James Lord.

"Oh, Señor Lord, forgive me, it was an unpardonable oversight." I was trying to be as polite and formal as possible. "How fortunate that Bernard Minoret corrected my mistake."

"The only thing I wanted to tell you is that you should never forget I loved Dora, perhaps even more than I loved Picasso. But I did love Picasso very much, and I will always love him. Sometimes I would fall asleep in front of a blank canvas, and when I awoke Picasso would be there, already painting. Then I spent whole days watching the work unfold, watching him work, in a state of total devotion. We only left to get a bite to eat, then got back to the canvas. He got back to the canvas, that is. On returning, I'd curl up like a puppy on a few cushions to admire the artist at work, I'd drift off again and dream that all the figures were stepping out of the canvas and talking to me, flirting with me. And we'd seduce each other. . . ."

"Don't worry, Mr. Lord. I won't do anything inappropriate. I tend to write only about what inspires the truth in me, even if it's a lie. Literature, you know, is a lie that tells the truth."

"Nicely put, I'll quote that one." He cleared his throat. "Is your daughter feeling better?"

"Much better, she's back in school today. Thank you for asking, Señor Lord." I didn't tell him that the phrase he'd found so nicely wasn't mine but by the Mexican writer Juan Rulfo.

We said goodbye with some affection. Again I wished him a wonderful winter holiday and hung up the phone.

My cell was vibrating again. It was Yendi with her nasally, squawking voice. She said she'd be by in fifteen minutes. All I could do was agree; she'd taken me by surprise again and once more I acted like an idiot.

I dressed in a hurry; I only had time to drink a cup of coffee and change purses. In the elevator I felt dizzy, never a good sign, and a twinge of pain ran up my back, like a chill deep inside me, and lasted longer than it should have. I was trembling when I go to the front door.

Yendi was already mashing the doorbell. I noticed the disappointment in her face. "Oh, you came down. I thought I might go up and see your place."

"I'd rather take you out for coffee, I've got some guys painting upstairs, and it's not really a good time for visitors," I lied badly.

We went to a café on Rue Francs Bourgeois, in Le Marais. On our way there, Yendi told me she was in Paris because she'd won a grant. I asked her which one and she couldn't remember, or didn't want to tell me. Then she said she was writing a novel about Anaïs Nin and it was coming along nicely. She showed me a folder full of paper, but when she opened it there was nothing written there, just a lot of blank pages and a birth certificate, which Yendi said was evidence that Anaïs Nin had been born in Cuba. Yet as I remembered, Anaïs Nin had often said, whenever anyone asked her, that she was born in Paris. You can read it in her books and even see her saying it in an interview posted on YouTube.

"I owe this novel to you. I admire you so much! You won't remember this, but a long time ago you told me about the *Diaries* of Anaïs Nin. You even loaned me a copy!"

I didn't remember, but it was true that I'd read those books tons of times and had recommended them right and left, and I've also written and published about them.

I wasn't aware that Yendi was now a writer; she used to be an actress, mediocre at best, and had produced a documentary, equally mediocre, about some woman painter she had imitated without success, and she'd shown me a thin book of her poetry, worthless, though I was forced to write a review of it out of politeness since she insisted so vehemently. And now she was telling me she was writing novels, with one on the way and another in the planning stage. I had my doubts, knowing how manipulative she could be and how serial exaggerators like her are so often motivated by envy.

I'd heard all about her back in Havana. Several people, including one of her former boyfriends, had warned me of her neuroses and her constant fits of exaggeration. Nevertheless, I sucked it up and pretended to pay attention to everything she said, even though I was nearly bored to death and couldn't hide the fact.

After enduring an endless stream of nonsense, I announced that I had to go, that some coworkers were expecting me to deal with an issue at work that was hanging over me.

"Wait, you haven't told me if you're still writing." She grasped at my coat with her little claws, like a shipwrecked sailor grasping at a plank, in a phony gesture that reeked of desperation.

"I'm still at it, same as always, until my brains dry up." I got up and paid, but she also got up, even though half her beer remained and she hadn't finished her croque-monsieur.

"I'll go with you," she said, acting as if I were the one who wanted her company.

I was starting to get nervous. "You can walk with me for just a few blocks. My meeting is for employees only: you can't be there."

"Don't worry, I have to meet somebody, too. A very famous person, a Cuban musician who lives here, everybody knows him. He's giving a concert at the Olympia, a huge deal! I'll only be in France a couple of days, then I'm off to Barcelona to meet an old lover, the painter—"

"I don't want to know his name. Your husband is a friend of ours. I don't want you to tell me your stories about lovers, or about anything." I was blunt; she started to sob.

"Did you know my mother died? She was crazy, totally nuts. Renán doesn't understand me, he's so into himself, such a control freak, he doesn't even give me any money. . . . Fabio is different." She finally got out the name of the painter I hadn't wanted to hear. "He's kind, gentle, generous. . . . I feel so alone, things in Cuba aren't going well for me at all, it's so messed up. Luckily, I have the Colombian author who supports me—"

"We're all alone," I crudely interrupted, thinking of James Lord. "My mother also passed away, and exile hasn't been easy; it's been a long, hard struggle. People who stayed in Cuba complain, but those of us who left also have it hard, and nobody understands us or cares about us. More and more people keep leaving, but fewer and fewer understand us. Everyone's leaving, everyone's leaving. . . . But those who've been coming over lately aren't like earlier exiles, they arrive ready to fight tooth and nail, with a mindset formed under the dictatorship. Everyone's leaving, everyone's leaving," I repeated naïvely.

Without my realizing it, we had ended up in front of Victor Hugo's house in the Place des Vosges. I invited her to see the museum, and though she didn't seem very enthusiastic, she agreed, not wanting to look like an idiot.

"Everyone's leaving," I went on in a kind of litany. "Everyone's leaving."

She looked at me suddenly with a glint in her eye, which gleamed slyly, or lethally, or bent on malice, like the eye of a rat. But she didn't say a word, and turned back to gaze at what was straight ahead.

"What a tiny bed!" she remarked as she looked at Victor Hugo's bed.

"In those days people were smaller."

"I could fit in that bed—I'm just a little thing, a slip of a girl!"

I nodded. It didn't escape me that she had said nothing about my mother's passing away in exile. It made no difference to her; she didn't even show a little sympathy.

We walked back through the museum, seeing it in reverse, and left the building. It was very cold and gray and starting to snow.

"Did you know I'm a French citizen now?" she said with a start.

"No. You turned French in Cuba? How did you swing that? I mean, did they give you French nationalization papers while you were living in Havana?"

"Of course, thanks to Renán. His mother is French, and I'm married to him, so, well, they gave it to me. The guy who's the French ambassador is one of ours, and he pulled some strings for me." She winked.

"What do you mean, 'He's one of ours'?" I asked.

"Oh, nothing, nothing, just that he loves everything about us, he's nuts about all things Cuban," she squawked.

That was the last straw. My family—my husband, my daughter, and I—had spent years waiting for a residence permit; then we applied for naturalization and even in spite of the huge number of fees we paid, the government agencies turned us down. I had to wait for my Spanish citizenship papers before they'd give me

French residency. Once I was a European citizen, I could choose the nationality of the country where I wished to reside and then, only after all that time, did we reapply for French nationalization. It took five years before they gave it to us.

"You're lucky. Few people get in so quickly." I took a breath, trying to keep calm.

"I knew how things were done, that's all. Right? It's a matter of pulling strings. I've known which strings to pull," she announced, shamelessly.

I nodded, having no doubts that, for sure, she had left no string unpulled.

She fished a fancy cell phone out of her overcoat pocket and dialed the famous musician who—according to her—had a concert booked at the Olympia. They agreed to meet at a trendy club. Just as soon as she finished her call we said goodbye, and that was it, or so I hope. I've never seen her again, and I don't think I ever will see her again for the rest of my life; obviously, in the future I'll avoid any possible encounter with that repulsive creature. Encounters like this cut a few years off your lifespan.

Yet now I mentally had to dip into that encounter, and it's loathsome that every time I think about James Lord I'll have to remember her, because this all took place in less than twenty-four hours. That is, I met him, and that same night—the wee hours of the overnight, that is—Yendi called. The next day I couldn't avoid encountering her, and when I finally managed to get rid of that repulsive individual I felt terrible, because I realized that meeting her had dulled my impressions of James Lord. Somehow, that woman showed up and threw everything off. She filled my day with gloom. People like her cast a pall over the brightest places they pass through. And now I remember that Yendi had also been there during that attempted demonstration in Cuba, the one I had participated in with Lefty Sotera, Lena, and Apple Pie. Though when the shitstorm started, she went over to the oppressors' side.

That evening, still upset, I wondered if I had told her too much, and convinced myself that I hadn't, since I'd done my best to talk as little as possible. In the end things hadn't gone as I'd hoped, I later discovered, because when someone comes to steal from you, they'll take anything you leave in reach, no matter how insignificant. In this case it was a simple phrase I'd said without thinking, a heartbroken comment I made that she turned into the title of a fairly insipid and unoriginal novel, *Everyone's Leaving*. "Everyone's leaving" was also a line in a song I wrote for Mónica Molina, which became the theme song for the film *La Bostella* by Édouard Baer.

Hours later, I wanted to go back to thinking about my meeting with James Lord; I tried my hardest to focus on how he looked, but instead of my memories of him, all I kept seeing was Yendi, and her greedy mug, and the falsity she constantly flaunts, which brings out the worst of her defects: envy, seasoned with a dash of the evil eye. I might add that she has the stupidest smile I've ever seen. A rodent angel, with mousy little teeth, flapping her bat wings in every direction. A dark, insensitive, destructive creature.

Dora. 1939 and 1958

The three of them had entered a palazzo facing the Grand Canal. It was a fabulous place: red velvet curtains draped heavily down the huge picture windows, golden pompom ropes gathering them to either side, and sunlight peered in to frolic with its refractions in the fancy Murano glasswork. Not only were the decorations, lamps, and dishes made from this fine, delicate, marvelous blown glass, but some of the furniture—armoires, chests of drawers—were made with exquisitely beveled mirrors in a stunning, baroque style. Extraordinary.

The light refracted everywhere, creating even more magnificent spaces, making the rooms look twice their size. Dora stood transfixed before this opulence, but soon her good taste led her to see that there was nothing elegant about it, that it was all a sort of conjurer's bric-a-brac trick, a gilded cage concocted to fool the weak of spirit. Still, it was attention-grabbing. That was the perfect term for it: attention-grabbing. Though she did like the ceiling lamps, the Chinese silk tapestries, and the ancient drawings on the fragile, delicate cloth lamp shades.

Bernard attempted to make himself comfortable on a chaise longue upholstered in fuchsia, but he was so tall his body looked ridiculous on it, like a tiger balancing on a ping-pong ball. The upholstery on the rest of the furniture ranged from leopard skin to shades of violet, purple, gold, black, and red.

"Our friend's apartment is all so eclectic. In Paris, however, he lives much more modestly."

"Paris is Paris. Venice is different, Venice is lush exuberance. From what I've seen, here you almost have to display a style that connotes wealth." Dora knew she wasn't making a valid point; she just wanted to respond to Bernard. "How did you and James come to know this Venetian gentleman?"

"He's an art dealer and an antiquarian we met years ago at one of Marie-Laure de Noailles's get-togethers. Odd you've never crossed paths with him."

"Maybe I've seen him before and simply didn't notice him." Dora was looking out at the Grand Canal, sitting on the window ledge; the pearly mist rising from the water belonged in a supernatural Flemish landscape painting. "Here comes James," she announced, and her face lit up. She felt more at ease with her friend there.

She watched James approach the palazzo and draw the key from his pants pocket. He was returning from the market loaded down with Italian cheeses, wines, and prosciutto. Dora went to open the orange-tinted glass door of the foyer for him. He hurried through to the kitchen and put the groceries away.

"Why don't we stay here instead of going back to the hotel?" Bernard asked from his outlandish, uncomfortable settee.

"The owner has some friends coming in this evening, and they're staying here!" James shouted from the kitchen. "We can share the place with them, but not for very long."

Dora wanted to help out. She prepared a tray of cheese and pro-sciutto; they opened the bottle of Chianti and toasted to friendship and to art. Bernard switched to a more comfortable seat and turned down the wine; he preferred champagne, his Dom Pérignon, to which he was vexatiously addicted in spite of the cost.

"Cold-bloodedly and obscenely expensive," he stressed, self-conscious about his problematic addiction.

James thumbed through an art catalogue while Dora, once more seated on the window ledge, gazed out at canal's the magnificent width and the slowly undulating water in it.

"This reminds me of the day I arrived in Buenos Aires with my parents. My mother was holding my hand so tightly, her nails were digging into my palm. Louise Julie Voisin, my poor mother, was terrified. She knew that in Argentina any French woman was assumed to be the worst. 'French woman' was synonymous with 'prostitute.' At a very young age I felt, or was made to feel, like a whore."

Bernard looked at Dora. All the light of the setting sun enveloped her, and she too looked like a crystal glass, a vestal trapped between mirrors reflecting multiple spaces, her image repeated in each of them. A shattered crystal, as in the first painting Picasso gave her, his first disjointed portrait of her, painted on April 1, 1939.

Her head was depicted as a garden made up of miniscule blues and lilac patches. Picasso titled it *Tête de femme* (Head of a Woman). The lower part of the image is in profile, with the chin, mouth, and nose sharp-edged; the rest of the face is like a separate patch of forest in which part of the nose protrudes and disappears behind the trompe l'oeil, creating an illusion of shimmering depth; the forehead and cheeks appear to be exaggerated by the light of a miner's lantern. The startled eyes peer into the unfathomable abyss of the implausible. Back then, Dora had seemed very sweet and submissive, while now her features had hardened, so that even with her image shattered into a mirage of a thousand quicksilvered pieces, she emanated a harmony that purified and cleansed the air around them.

Bernard kept watching her with intense, disturbing curiosity. He enjoyed talking with this austere woman, and he had just discovered a fascination with Dora in himself that prompted him to sporadic fits of tenderness. He searched deep down for an explanation: why was he so attracted to her? Because being around this woman, who had been not merely Picasso's muse but his sexual and intellectual partner, gave him a very special sense of peace, immersed him in a state of sublime art reverie, as if looking at her, talking to her, was the same as standing before a painting by the master, leaving him enchanted and subdued by its kaleidoscopic splendor. A living work of art, inevitably spoiled, marred by the disturbing essence of our unavoidably vulgar human nature.

"What are you thinking about, Dora?" Bernard teased. "I know you're not going to tell me, because you never think about anything."

"Memories, I only remember useless things."

The grayish, rainy day seemed ready to flow into the river, down the giant storm drain formed by the gaping hole of the horizon. Mist cloaked the fantasy world. It was much cooler than forecast, and the coming winter seemed likely to be much harsher than had been expected. She was running to Picasso's studio with a baguette under her arm. Suddenly, a woman stepped in front of her and stopped her short.

"Miss, were you aware that this painter sells paintings to just anyone? And not only his own paintings, he also sells whatever other artists have given him for safekeeping. He's sold off paintings by Wifredo Lam, drawings by Max Jacob—poor Max Jacob, after Max put him up in his house! Did you know what he said when he found out that his supposedly best friend, Max Jacob, was in a Nazi camp? He said Max would save himself, he'd fly the coop, because 'Max is an angel.' That stuck-up Spaniard has got to be an imbecile!"

She watched the woman and listened, distressed. A fine drizzle blurred her vision. The woman who had bumped into her, seeming to jump out from nowhere, had a swollen, toad-like face, and though you could tell she had once been beautiful, she might be about seventy now. Bulging yellow eyes flittering in their sockets; smile full of nicotine-stained teeth; chubby, restless hands. She was monstrously fat, dressed in a tight, bottle-green tailored suit, the front of her blouse stained with garbanzo purée. Dora was in a rush. "I'm sorry, madam, I can't stay, the bread is getting wet."

She was sure the woman was wrong, that Picasso had never sold any of Wifredo Lam's works. Lam was too wary to leave his paintings in unsafe hands, especially if he'd signed them, since he never signed a painting until he had already sold it to a future owner who wouldn't double-cross him, someone with plenty money whom he could keep track of as a collector.

Dora felt her bladder was about to burst, she got chills, she was dying to get home and use the bathroom. Picasso must be hungry, as he always was. Hungry as an ox.

Her shoes were full of water, the soles were worn through, but her lover didn't want her to buy new ones. Why, what did she need them for? She started shivering, couldn't stop her lips from trembling or her teeth from chattering. But just thinking about the man she loved more than anyone in the world and how he was waiting for her at home, she hummed softly. He hadn't wanted her to wear her best coat either, the chinchilla. With that fancy fur on, she looked too formal, beautiful, and elegant. Ugly shoes, ugly shoes, she had to wear ugly shoes! Forget about expensive coats, no luxuries!

She climbed the steps two at a time, running upstairs with difficulty, squeezing her thighs together not to piss herself; she opened the door out of breath. Jaume Sabartés was peeking out from behind a screen; she couldn't see him but could make out his hunched silhouette.

She opened the second door and entered the painter's studio. A very young soldier was snoozing on the cushions; he looked healthy and very handsome; she had enough time to notice he was half-naked and very provocative in his careless pose, as if offering himself up from the beyond, shameless in his dreams. Picasso was painting, a cigarette butt clenched in his teeth.

"Who's that?"

"Nobody, an American soldier," he answered dryly, curtly.

Dora looked at the cushions; the man was gone.

"He disappeared." Dora dried her temples with a paint-splattered rag. She was dripping wet.

"Yes, I know, that's what always happens. He appears, he disappears, sometimes I think he isn't real and that I've made him up, that he's a hallucination, a mere figment of my imagination."

Dora was convinced it was true, that the young soldier existed only in Picasso's imaginary world, and now in hers, for she blindly believed everything the Master asserted, especially when he was huffing and puffing feverishly before a canvas.

She heated some turnip soup, fried some chicken breasts, daubed the bread with oil. "Come and eat, it's cold and you've been working a long time."

"But who asked you for food? I don't want to eat. It isn't time for me to eat! Stop interrupting me, get out of my way!" He slapped his brushes and snorted, his face throbbing with anger.

Dora's reply was to look distressed.

"Oh, so now it's weeping time. The weeping woman! And here come the tears again. When I tell you to. . . . You're going to drive me crazy, you're pushing me to the edge with your tears! You and your tango tears. . . ."

He got dressed, bundled up, and went outside, slamming the door behind him.

Dora wavered in momentary shame but then ran after her lover. He was walking too fast and disappeared among the pedestrians. A bit later she caught sight of him entering a nearby café. She held back, straggling on purpose, then walked past the establishment and spied him through the steamed-up window. That was a period when everyone spied on everybody.

Inside, the Master was having a roaring good time with some buddies, regulars of the café, while the owner served him a pot-au-feu, a boiling soup featuring a huge bone whose marrow flavored the oregano-scented broth, a few vegetables, bread, and that's it. The painter devoured the dish with a ferocious appetite.

When he got back he was in a better mood, and the soldier was still there, seemingly asleep. The Great Genius, moved to pity, lauded the soldier's beauty. "A dream, a genuine dream!"

In her distress, Dora had bitten her lips bloody.

After a bit, tired of waiting for the painter to notice that she was there, she got up from the armchair, violently grabbed her coat, and fled headlong, running in terror down the stairs. She never wanted to hear his name again, ever. She was still young, why not find someone else? Why not fall in love with some other man? Why not drop the artist and go off with someone who'd love and admire her the way she really deserved, as the genius that she also was? Because she loved the Great Genius and wasn't able to love anyone else, couldn't leave him, was ready to sacrifice everything for him, including herself. She wanted to throw herself in the Seine, kill herself, die tragically, she longed to disappear; yes, that's what she'd do, she'd disappear, she'd punish Picasso. But maybe he wouldn't see her suicide as a punishment but as liberation. She blew her nose into a sketch she had doodled on a napkin and wept disconsolately.

She continued walking along the bank of the Seine; the booksellers watched her progress with some foreboding, jittery. It's true that she was stumbling like a madwoman at a suffocating and unstoppable pace, acting terrified and looking depressingly like an angry woman, an abandoned woman, a wounded beast. Madness produces dread in others.

How could she free herself from the trauma of Picasso? Did he love her as much as she loved him, she ceaselessly wondered? No, he didn't love her: the Great Genius couldn't love anyone but himself. Then she changed her tune: she could put up with him, she kept telling herself, yes, yes, she could endure his egotism to any degree. With no complaints, and then she'd be the perfect lover, the guardian angel, the servant who only appeared when he called, at the precise moments when the Master had a concrete need of her presence. No, Dora couldn't behave like a servant to the man she loved. That wasn't love, no, not at all, not her concept of love. How could a woman as intelligent as she was behave in such an unbearably submissive way?

"Picasso is such a bastard," she thought, and immediately regretted the thought, begging for forgiveness in an anguished prayer while kneeling before a statue of the Virgin in a corner niche on the wall bordering the Seine. Why before the Virgin? She was a committed atheist, an unbeliever. Well, because the Virgin was different, somehow, the Virgin was a woman, she'd understand what Dora was going through better than anyone else could. Then she burst out laughing, her hand bleeding from being dragged, scraped, against the river wall. Was she going crazy? Not at all, not at all; quite the contrary, excessive sanity was her worst defect. It was merely that she was suffering, feeling very high-strung, too high-strung and sad, she was shivering with cold. She saw the clotted blood on her hand, she licked the wound, and her saliva allayed the sting.

She entered a café, pulled up a chair, ordered a hot chocolate, and drank it in small sips. The liquid warmed her stomach, and she feel better, fortified. She watched the people walking by through the frosted window; a couple kissing under a street lamp with nerve-racking passion, utterly absorbed in their desire, deeply immersed in pleasure. Did he love her as much as she obviously loved him, judging by the expression of surrender in her lips? Men always love less. It depends on the woman. There are all sorts of women! Women savage at love, women clumsy at submitting! Women so sharp, so sneaky, that they always figure out how to get the men to love them so they'll profit from their loving!

"I'd love to go on a trip," Dora murmured.

The waiter, who hadn't quite heard, asked if she had ordered something.

"No, sorry, just talking to myself, please don't think I'm crazy. . . . I'm not crazy or sick.

The waiter went on to the next table and took care of some Swedes sitting there. They were two couples, and the city had made a good impression on them. Dora listened absently as they showered praise on Paris in perfect French. They raved about this first trip of theirs to a gentleman who had just happened in, talking at first from table to table, until the man got up and joined them at their table to assure himself that everything was going well for them and that his new Swedish friends were having a grand time. Dora noticed that the old man emphasized the word "Swedish" so the owner would realize they were foreigners.

"*Tout baigne, mes amis les suédois?*" The old man's face grew blurry through Dora's tears.

Dora asked the waiter for the check, paid, and went back out.

The street was empty; it was starting to snow. From far away, another woman was walking toward her, on the other side of the street. She was very pretty, young, sassy, thin, just the type to catch the Spaniard's eye. Had she gone to visit Picasso? Could she be one of Picasso's lovers, coming back from making love with him? No, no, he wasn't cheating on her yet, Dora comforted herself, not yet.

Yes, it was a young woman, not exactly pretty, but by her shape she was the type of woman the artist might find attractive. Blond, sublime green eyes, shock of straight and slightly flaxen hair, a soft complexion. She wasn't vulgar, and she knew how to walk—that is, she walked with a sway in her hips, as if she were dancing, undulating with the rhythmic disdain of a languid mermaid (that was the sort of cultured catcall men gave women in the tropics, the Great Genius had told her). Walking forward, it became evident that there was something scatterbrained about her sashay, with a dash of concealed, understated passion. "Face of a phony," Dora thought; however, the other woman clacked her heels against the sidewalk with firm steps. Dora crossed to the sidewalk where the woman was walking.

They barely touched as they passed. The woman had given Dora a sidelong glance; Dora felt she had smiled at her impudently, even cynically. She backtracked and tugged on the woman's arm. "You're coming from Picasso's studio, right? Tell me, you meddling nobody."

"Hey, what's with you, are you crazy? Let go of me, leave me alone!" She fended off the artist's claws as best she could.

"Picasso, the name Picasso means something to you, right? Have you slept with him? What a bitch!" Dora's eyes were blood-shot, she couldn't control her jealousy, all her rage came foaming out at the corners of her mouth.

"Who, what? Please, let go of me. I don't know what you're talking about!"

Dora—dissociated from herself, disconnected from her true being, possessed by complexes and rancor yet merely the lover of the painter, who was already married to that plump blonde Marie-Thérèse Walter and who, on top of it all, was the father of a young girl and a good-for-nothing son whom the blonde insisted on treating as her own—went on stamping her feet and hurling insults. . . . Exhausted, weeping, at last she let go of the woman; but doubt was a thorn in her side, for deep down she was sure that the girl was shamelessly lying to her.

"She must have gone to see Picasso, she must have slept with him, he must have begged her to let him paint her. . . ." And he'd done his part in all of it, especially painting her, except that the face on the painting would never be that of this baby-faced whore, but hers, her own face, the face of the weeping woman. Weeping, weep-ing, weeping, echoing ceaselessly, unbearably, in an endless and vul-gar litany. Her temples pounded in throbbing, shooting pain.

The other woman went away cursing Dora, turning around to look from time to time. She was carrying a notebook under her arm;

it fell to the ground and she scurried to pick it up, then tucked it safely inside her large, time-worn leather purse.

Did this episode, which recently ran through her mind while she contemplated the chalk-white landscape of the Grand Canal, really happen like that, or was her memory beginning to play tricks on her? Were these constantly crumbling fragments of memories, or this series of memory lapses, a product of what she herself had seen of life, or were they just her attempts to string together stories others had told her after she was committed to the Sainte-Anne Hospital?

Bernard again asked her to share her thoughts.

She refused, giving him the slippery and scarcely believable answer, "I swear, I'm not thinking about anything."

Now she only wanted to recall the moment she first met Kiki de Montparnasse at La Rotonde. Kiki was singing for American soldiers and passing the hat. Dora thought she was a great artist, though others scorned her. Kiki had modeled for Foujita, Modigliani, Derain, Soutine, and also for Picasso.

Kiki de Montparnasse was undeniably a beautiful woman, but heavyset, though very happily so. In fact, at that time, being fat was fashionable. She just wanted to caress those chubby cheeks and stare captivated at her lines, to pet her like you'd pet a stray puppy, not a wanton woman; she wasn't voluptuous, no, not by any means. Her body was like an overstuffed cushion, inviting you to sink on in. Her hairstyle was laughable, even ridiculous, with straight hair and short bangs that came out limp from the shower, and her eyes were unusually small and totally impish.

Dora admired Kiki from the first photograph she saw of her, the one shot by Man Ray, *Le Violon d'Ingres*, where you can appreciate Kiki's narrow waist, her fabulous backside, her wide hips, her exuberant ass. A terrific ass, a voluminous monstrosity, ready-made for the camera.

Dora saw herself in that photograph; if she didn't watch her diet, before long her own rump would look like the model's. So she wanted to meet Kiki, she looked her up and found her. They met in the summer of 1924 at a bar in Montparnasse. Afterwards, following the trail of that beautifully photographed backside and its owner, Dora luckily met the photographer, Man Ray. He was not pleasant at all the first time she approached him, in fact quite the contrary: rude and evasive. Until she told him her full name and he wanted to identify himself as a Jew, just like her. If her name was originally Markovitch, his was Radnitzky. Dora insisted that her last name was not Jewish in origin at all; her continual need to clarify this led to innumerable misunderstandings later on.

Man Ray listened, rather dully, to Dora's tales of her life as an emerging (and in his opinion, unskilled) artist, so he paid little attention to her career as a Surrealist photographer, at least not at that moment; he was more attentive to her form and her oval face, leading him to be immediately captivated by her impatient (his words) and devastating beauty.

Bernard came over and placed his hand affectionately on her back; she didn't pull back, and yet he perceived a gentle rejection, telling him that his gesture was unwelcome.

James had just prepared a wonderful breakfast for them with loving care. He invited them to the table. Dora had a ravenous appetite and had no qualms admitting it, with a cheerful smile, she always had an appetite that she ought to conceal, and besides, she gained weight too easily; she smiled again, this time with a touch of shame. The lukewarm sun climbed with agonizing slowness through a hazy sky.

She gained weight too fast, her hips, already round enough, were starting to look terrible, misshapen, grotesque, and this made her feel handicapped, unattractive. She knew she no longer enjoyed the youthfulness of Kiki de Montparnasse.

Now so much time has passed that today she's practically an old woman, so she can eat whatever she feels like, can stuff herself with food, sweets, anything she wants. She ought to be more worried about diabetes than outward beauty. But precisely now, when she no longer has to please anyone, she's lost her sense of taste, her discriminating palate. Before, everything she tasted was delightful, deliciously succulent. Even back during the trip to Venice, every mouthful tasted bitter and insipid, and nevertheless she needed to eat, to chew, to fill her belly, feel some warmth in her guts. Her guts would grow lukewarm, but just then her feet would get stiff with cold. She didn't know why, for many years, her feet tended to get cold and upset her digestion.

James squatted in front of her and massaged her feet with his large, robust hands. Using his fist, he pressed the soles of her foot, from heels to toes. Her heels hurt her terribly, as if needles were constantly piercing them. "It's the weight," she told herself, "too much weight."

And to think, she'd been a slender child, although, true enough, she had a very heavy, serious character; but as for weight, she was light as a feather, ethereal, had no appetite. Yet there was never a smile, never a toothy grin on her lips, and no one could swear to ever seeing her jump for joy. That's not to say she was a depressive teenager, certainly not. She remembered herself instead as always stern but happy, though her hard, tough features alarmed people. Her chin hinted at this aspect of her personality: the deep-rooted toughness of the uprooted. Nevertheless, she pretended she was managing to float among the others, with the lightness her Argentine childhood imparted to her, very much despite her abundant, shiny, jet-black hair, her clear, sharp eyes, and her robust arms and legs.

As a teenager she was so light she could dance the tango, pretty much behind her mother's back; she would dance cheek-to-cheek with a shadow, her back like a tigress's, her legs coiled around the abyss.

Naturally, she danced the "respectable tango," as the decent families called it back then, but in the end it was still a tango. "The sisters' tango," they also called it, and the most feverish and sensual moves took place in that sisterhood. The more refined a tango seemed, the more obscene; the obscenity was unleashed in the dancers' fevered imaginations. I'm speaking of ballroom tango, not the slum tango of the outer districts.

Dora danced and danced, swept away by the rhythm of her ripening desire, turning, circling, losing herself in a whirlpool of kisses though they were nothing but dreams, shimmying and swaying so sweetly and smoothly she couldn't stop even when her mother insisted, flying off and away through an open window.

"Every good story is written through an open window," she thought with eyes closed, "every honest story." Then she remembered the iron-barred window at the Sainte-Anne Hospital, in the Psychiatric Unit, and her desires to transform into a ringed-neck dove, and how she succeeded in doing so, in her own mind, when it was unhinged.

And with that same lightness, at the threshold of adolescence she reached Paris. As soon as she set foot on the sidewalks of Saint-Germaine-des-Prés she lost this misty gift, even as she began, on the other hand, to melt herself down and pour herself into a mold, or to rid herself of all the worries inherited from an imploding family. Then her body became transparent, fugitive, stunning in its flight. Her body became a sort of perpetual wanderer.

She walked all over Paris with the voices purring to her inside her head, a genuine chorus, a whole crowd addressing her from within her head, familiarly. She used to leave the Lycée Molière and get lost, wandering with her friends for hours all up and down Avenue Foch. She loved going her own way, roaming around with no set goal, getting lost in Paris like anybody else, mercurial and ordinary; and thanks to this very ordinariness, which adolescence gave her and old age would take away, she could feel supremely natural and free.

Like every intelligent girl, Dora aspired to learn more and more, to know everything. What she desired and treasured most of all was knowledge.

She started going to get-togethers, what they called "surprise parties," and there she met Louis Chavance, another great artist in a city full of artists, famous playwright, film editor, actor; she considered him her first lover, with whom she frequented the Café de Flore and whom she ambiguously accompanied everywhere. There she also met the writer Georges Bataille, another great and unforgettable lover, and in this period Picasso stepped up, unsurprisingly, or better said, not shockingly. Because Dora intuitively knew that he was the one she had always been unconsciously waiting for.

At that time Dora wore a pageboy haircut, and so her profile lost even more of her former imbalance. Her excess of spirit began to weigh down her arms, her legs, her cheeks. Dora wanted to be on her own and she moved to a place she would immortalize in her photographs: 29 Rue d'Astorg, with her mother.

It was probably then, after she moved, that she began to lose interest in superficialities; only the most profound things astonished her, and she adopted an unprejudiced attitude; pumping others for information, she got rid of consistency and seriousness, though she became noticeably more mysterious, because she never revealed any secrets. However, others suspected that she was storing up the flame of desire—the double flame that Octavio Paz wrote about, the flame of desire and the flame of love—and that only a demonic force could capture her and set her afire forevermore. Her yearning for knowledge turned into a ceaseless pursuit of desire and love. In the meantime, an artist was born.

Max Jacob saw her as an Etruscan lady and heaped flattery on her. Max was certainly an angel, but he couldn't escape the

Nazi camp; his singed wings weren't up to it. He died there, like everyone else, like his dearest sister, of pneumonia and typhus, crushed by life. Dora could never forgive herself, though none of it was her fault. Maybe they could have done something, but they didn't. . . . This has always been her most painful memory, her torment.

On April 5, 1942, Max described half-jokingly to Jean Cocteau the time a member of the Gestapo had visited him, and how he'd interrogated him in his room. "He was a round-shouldered man (an Edmond Jaloux type), accompanied by a soldier:

'Police!'"

Jacob answered the door, pretending to be delighted, pronouncing the word emphatically, "*Enchanté!*" And, inviting him to move closer to the warmth of the fireplace, he commented on how cold it had been that year.

"What sort of things do you write?"

"What a pity I don't have my books here. . . . Though I do have a booklet with a few of my verses. May I give it to you? Would like me to sign it? Please tell me your name, thank you! How shall I sign it? 'In friendship'? Why not! I'll write, 'To commemorate. . . .'"

And on the part of the Gestapo, the interrogation continued on its dry, impetuous path.

In a letter dated July 18, Max Jacob wrote to another friend, Conrad Moricand:

The Paris security detachment ordered Saint-Benoît-sur-Loire to personally see to it that I was wearing the yellow star. Two daring gendarmes arrived and were able to confirm that I had been corrected.

Dora's martyrdom, her torment, was her friend's unstoppable descent into the inferno. Without a doubt, this was the most painful of her regrets.

"Why did you quit photography, Dora? Was it to take up painting?" Bernard asked.

It was not a question she really wanted to deal with; she preferred to avoid it, to send him off on another tangent. "Dear Bernard, I started out with painting. My father was an architect, and I wanted to follow in his footsteps by using my artistic talents. I can't explain why, maybe it was just a childish whim, that's probably what it was for me. The fact is, I went to the School for the Arts because I wanted to learn how to draw. I studied at André Lhote's famous studio, the one everybody enrolled in, especially the Argentines, who are always up on the latest trends in art."

Dora's mind began to fly, unstoppably.

"Montparnasse supplanted Montmartre in the hearts of painters. Going to Rue d'Odessa, the tiny street where Lhote had his atelier, opened up a huge range of possibilities for me. Not that Lhote was easy to get along with; he had a shortcoming that we all accepted because it was outweighed by his immense wisdom: he was extremely demanding of his students, intolerably severe and acrimonious, and with him you either learned or you died of shame. His was the best atelier in Paris. So I devoted myself to painting, and I learned from him how to mix colors, to make sensible palettes, to structure a composition in spatial terms. He introduced me to the intricacies of perspective, so that later I could break it, smash it to pieces, crush it."

"I've never been clear whether Lhote was an artist," James interrupted.

"Lhote never managed to become the great artist he believed himself to be, but for me he was a great expert. He was uniquely unflappable, tenacious, and sharp. One of my most cherished prizes came from his classes: my friendship with Henri Cartier-Bresson, who gave me a taste for photography. Though that was a later chapter, as you know. I've always admitted that I owe the whole beginning of my career to Lhote, his *Treatise on Landscape*

Painting, his studio, and his views about Cubism. Nevertheless, his methods weren't suited to someone like me who depends too much on passion." She scrutinized James with a sidelong gaze, a gesture Bernard did not fail to notice.

James sat back and listened to Dora unperturbed, or feigning deep calm, absorbed by her words, even though he knew this story by heart.

"I was more interested in angles and geometry; that was Cartier-Bresson's fault. I say 'fault' because he instilled me with the shortcoming of looking at things from several points of view at once, a shortcoming I thank him for teaching me, because he infected me with the divine virus of focusing on what is hidden and of breaking things down into triangles. I learned abstraction through a photogenic appreciation of reality. Though I have to admit that Lhote also loved the 'aerial perspective,' as he called it, the fluid rhythms of rhomboids, and the dense power of line. These are all concepts that he pioneered, and they are all still in use. There was one phrase of his, however, that has resonated with me, that has been reinforced in so many ways, like glittering splinters of a broken mirror reflected in liquid: the one where he explored the tremendous value of negative space. Your head, for example, is a negative space."

"So why don't you paint me?" Bernard was enraptured by Dora's knowledge. "Though you've painted me before, but I'd love you to paint the physical changes that have been taking place in me over the years."

"I'll paint you again, Bernard, you have a very interesting head and a flawless nose. Everything I like about faces is in yours. I'll do it again, count on it."

James cleared his throat, somewhat dubious about the words of praise Dora directed at his friend.

"Don't act jealous, James, I've painted you many times; but besides, Picasso painted you. You don't need anyone else to immortalize you. I painted you sitting on the bench, our bench, under the fig tree in Ménerbes; that was an unforgettable, unrepeatable afternoon."

The word "unrepeatable" sounded like slapping a permanent seal on a top secret document. Blushing, James went to put a record on the old phonograph. Fréhel's voice invaded the room.

"Actually, I have to admit it was Marcel Zahar, the art critic, who urged me to enter the École de Photographie de la Ville de Paris," Dora went on. "Cartier-Bresson has never wanted to express his thoughts, or even talk at all, about our friendship. I don't know why he doesn't mention us; perhaps he's afraid Picasso will start to ignore him. Well, I was also coming from far away; it's only logical and natural that the so-called "one-minute" photographers who swarmed all over Buenos Aires made a huge impression on my memories. For me, finding the man hiding behind that wooden box on a tripod, with a black cloth over his head, summed up the whole mystery of staring contemplatively at the famous imaginary 'birdie' that the stranger always asked me to watch. Was the birdie inside the box, or on top of the one-minute photographer's head, or in some inaccessible spot where I couldn't quite see its always-invoked, never-seen profile? Cartier-Bresson must never have understood where I was coming from, or coming back from. . . ."

"And your other teachers?" He searched her limpid eyes.

"You didn't let me finish, Bernard. I was going to say that even though I had a great teacher, which I've never tried to hide, I rarely mention him; he is one of my secret treasures: Emmanuel Sougez. It was unquestionably Sougez who gave me individual lessons in photography and convinced me that photography was my art. He introduced me to Pierre Kefer. Or was it Louis Chavance? Just mentioning that guy's name annoys me; he's always thought he 'discovered' me. Typically rude playwright. Anyway, I met Pierre Kefer—he was quite a character. I set up my first studio with him at his house in Neuilly."

"I suppose he could help you out."

"Of course. Pierre was rich, from a prominent family, a society man, and he lived in a lovely mansion. He went all out to get me to go in with him, and he succeeded. He eradicated all the arrogance and bad temper I had back then. But I don't know, perhaps I owe the impetus, the *élan vital*, to the journal *L'Art vivant*. In their October 1934 issue, Jacques Guenne described my early work with a wealth of detail, and he did such a stunning job that I wrapped myself in his elegant praise like a warm, protective blanket of affection and recognition. Later, I began to see things more clearly and I did a lot of fashion photography."

"See, Bernard? With Dora nothing is ever the last word."

"It's true, James. The only last word in my life was Picasso."

Fréhel's voice on the phonograph sounded more nasal than ever.

James now realized why Picasso always said she was like a man: not only because her crude reactions intimidated him, but also because he couldn't put his finger on what she meant by her lapidary phrases. A phrase Picasso constantly repeated. "For me, Dora is a man." When he was asked to create a statue of Guillaume Apollinaire, he gave them an old image of Dora that he'd cast in bronze. Dora was a man for him, perhaps because of the lack of definition that had always characterized her, or because of her absolutely unyielding frankness in the face of any situation; and no matter how unstable she might appear to be, she inevitably came straight at you, like a well-aimed punch to the gut, always with a nettlesome remark that left you speechless. Her remark burned, sent flying like a flaming arrow without a lot of thought.

"I've lived in many places and with the best people I could find. . . . I was also the assistant of the Polish photographer, Harry Ossip Meerson."

Bernard was bowled over. "No. Really? The famous American photographer?"

"He became a naturalized American later, but he was always Polish," Dora explained.

"He's taken lots of photos of Marlene Dietrich," Bernard noted.

"She was his ticket to success. Her face was like a landscape. That's how Josef von Sternberg described it, the Austrian-American film director who made films such as *The Blue Angel* and *Morocco*. The architect of Marlene's stardom."

James drew the curtains closed. A bloodstained cloud reddened every color in the room.

Suddenly, Dora's eyes began flittering restlessly in their sockets, as if trying to leap in time to unlikely recesses of her memory. To those shards of memory left behind in the cells of the psychiatric hospital, where she beat her head with hands bruised black and blue, where she gnawed with her teeth and aching gums at doors made of stone.

Bernard and James. Me. Paris, 2009

His hands trembled at times — especially his right hand — from early Parkinson's, very slightly, scarcely noticeable. I looked up and met his fluttering eyes the color of honey, or rather of gold. He kept silent a long time, and I didn't dare upset the invisible barrier that stood between us. Bernard's eyelid was also trembling persistently.

Bernard had been expecting me for too long. I had disappeared for the meantime to write another novel, but though he suspected otherwise, I hadn't given up on the idea of using literature to understand why Dora Maar had felt forced to withdraw from all her friends, choosing never to see them again, after that trip to Venice.

I don't know if I'll be able to clarify anything, I'm not convinced literature is up to the task. Perhaps I'll only manage to make an even more tangled mess of the facts and cast an even darker shadow over the evidence.

Bernard was sitting in front of me in the Café de Flore, half-shutting his eyelids, like a tabby cat. I wouldn't have known how to answer if he'd asked me why I had disappeared for so long. More than three years had passed since I had even phoned him.

An unfathomable silence washed between his eyes and mine.

He didn't ask at all about my seclusion. He had aged a little, nothing very visible. However, you could barely tell his age from his trembling fingers; his skin had lost none of its youthful freshness.

Finally, he spoke. "What about her attracted you? Or rather, how did you find out she existed? Did you hear about her in Havana or in Paris?" He extracted a moist towelette from its envelope and cleaned his hands, finger by finger. He waited for me to reply while he examined the edges of his nails minutely; he was a fanatic for scrupulous cleanliness.

The *grisaille*, that dull, enervating monotony of gray, was settling on the streets of Paris; suddenly a ray of sunlight broke through the clouds. At that moment I began my story.

"It was in Havana, in the early nineties, when I got my hands on a book of photography that I had been aching to have for a long time. I hadn't been able to acquire it by honest means, so I traded a few pounds of powdered milk to get it from a friend who had stolen it from the library of a Dutch diplomat. One of the perks of totalitarian life: swapping stuff. I had already read about Dora Maar but I hadn't seen any of her photographs."

The shadow of one of my friends, Lena, fell in skewed proportions across the wall. Sunlight, tinged by the ivory or bone-white curtains, flooded the terrace in an orangey glow. Lena looked magnificent; her smiling blue eyes filled the room with cheer. She was naked.

I was leafing through the book of photographs that a friend had sent me from Paris. And I opened it precisely to the page where Assia, Dora's beautiful model, was posing for that photo in which her body flows softly across the wall, shockingly beautiful, gigantic, her nipple like the prow of a boat.

"We're going to be late," Lena prodded me while she got dressed. "Apple Pie won't forgive us."

"Have you seen Dora Maar's photographs?" I asked Lena, excited.

"Never heard of her." Lena put on a slip under her skirt.

"I'm not surprised, it isn't your fault. In this country we live in the most shameful ignorance."

"You haven't told me who she is." She lit a cigarette, took a puff, set it back in the ashtray, wiped the sweat from her brow with a graceful linen handkerchief. "What a shitstorm! I don't think it's a great idea for us to go out walking on the Malecón on a blazing hot day like this. Or having to wrap ourselves in the flag. And to top it off, we'll be there with who the fuck knows. . . . We gotta be crazy! The last thing we'll know out there is who's who."

"What do you mean, 'who's who'?" I was still engrossed by the images in the book.

Lena shrugged and picked the cigarette back up from the ashtray, took a deep drag, pointed at the book. "So tell me already, who's this Dora you're so fascinated about?"

"A Surrealist photographer, a painter too. Picasso's lover."

"Picasso? What a stud! Picasso's lover, you say?" Lena kept asking, as if she were deaf.

"Yes, and Georges Bataille's. Picasso painted his fill of her, and his filth of her, too."

"I don't get it, I prefer the kind of filth you get your fill of the other way, lying down." Lena stubbed out the cigarette, went to the kitchen, grabbed a tangerine and began to peel it. I don't think she was very interested in the topic of Dora Maar and Picasso, though she pretended otherwise.

"It's a good thing you had one tangerine left, because I'm about-to-faint starving. Speaking of photography and these people you find so fascinating—Picasso, Dora—are you bringing the camera?"

I nodded. We finished getting our stuff together and went outside. The atmosphere was tense, or so it seemed to us. Lena kept sucking on the tangerine peels and spitting them onto the asphalt.

"You nervous?" Her eyes fell on mine. Sea-blue eyes, liquid eyes, watery dreamlike eyes.

"No," I replied, uncertain. "I don't want to think about what we're going to do."

We walked a long stretch in silence along the Malecón, heading toward Havana Bay.

Around Calle Salud we met up with Apple Pie. She was with Lefty Sotera, bus driver and part-time baseball player.

"Wass'up?" Lefty greeted us, visibly nervous.

Apple Pie kissed our cheeks, and we kissed hers. Normally, we talked in a natural way to avoid suspicion, but now we didn't even dare whisper a few words. A while later other people joined up, and before long there were about thirty of us there. Among them I recognized Yendi, younger than us, slippery, the one who had tried to get into my house by way of her painter boyfriend. Thirty people—or more, or maybe less.

"Plenty have showed up, anyway, and, as always, more blacks than whites," I said to myself. Given the fear of repression that exists in that country, getting an opposition rally of thirty together was quite a feat.

We had agreed that Lefty Sotera would be in charge of operations, but the poor guy had suddenly blown a fuse and was moving in slow motion, as if he'd gone loopy and didn't know what to do.

Apple Pie pulled out a thermos and started pouring shots of coffee into cardboard cone cups for everyone. She was a young woman with very rosy skin, honey-colored eyes, a small mouth, short, and restless by nature, nervous for no reason, though at this moment we all had reason to be nervous. She adjusted her bra after she finished pouring the coffee; she was busty, and her bra seemed two sizes too small. The sun was starting to burn her delicate skin. She complained that she was thirsty, and she had been so focused on making sure there'd be coffee, she'd made a large pot before she left and had forgotten to bring water.

"We're all thirsty," Lefty Sotera pointed out. "Good job of forgetting, Apple Pie. OK, everybody, listen up, on my order we're going to unfurl our banners and march together toward the American embassy. I doubt they'll let us get that far. Most likely they'll intercept us on the way, but we'll try. Ready?"

There were murmurs of assent. The sea was calm, shimmering in its Caribbean blue. There wasn't a cloud in the sky.

"Do you think the police will detain us?" an older man asked.

"Yes, *purete*." ("*Purete* means 'grandfather' in Havana slang," I explained to Bernard.) "Of course they'll arrest us, and let me tell you, if you want to leave you still have time to run away. More than likely they're going to beat us up. We have to be ready to get a good stomping, to get arrested, to get taken down to Villamarista or one of those detention centers; and, by the way, we should also be ready to pretend we're crazy and we all forgot our names."

"Don't worry, I can take it," the old man boasted. "My grandfather fought in the war for independence."

At Lefty Sotera's signal we pulled out our banners and marched forward, linked arm in arm. We waved our placards in the air and shouted out, demanding freedom for political prisoners. Freedom! Freedom! Freedom!

The first police appeared right away, and then two truckloads of "spontaneous crowds": members of the Rapid Response Brigades. Yendi slipped away, moving farther and farther from us until she surreptitiously joined the crowd of repressors.

We hadn't marched even fifty yards.

"Someone tipped them off before we got here, that's got to be it, maybe someone who's taking part in the protest right now," Lena whispered.

"It was her," Apple Pie pointed at Yendi.

We didn't stop. For a few short minutes, we, the police, and the "spontaneous crowds" watched each other like tigers on the prowl.

One of the police approached us, and the march ended.

"You can't do this," he ordered.

These words had hardly left his lips when the "spontaneous crowd" jumped out of the trucks armed with clubs, brass knuckles, and pipe wrenches and ran at us. We started running away at top speed, scattering like a bucket of marbles.

They began hurling huge rocks, some of which hit us. I saw them beating people all around me, and I got beaten as well. Yendi vanished into a military jeep.

I managed to slip loose from one of the paramilitaries, who had grabbed me by the back of my blouse; I ran and ran until I was about to faint. I ducked into the courtyard of some apartment building. A curtain opened and a hand pulled me inside. The woman hid me under a bed. My pursuers entered the courtyard, but they didn't dare to search the building.

Apple Pie, Lena, and I regrouped two hours later in the basement of my house. Apple Pie had gotten a good drubbing on her back. Lena had a bloody lip and nose. My lower back was throbbing, and my shoulder was dislocated. Lena set it right with a tug; I saw stars and a flash of pain.

Lefty Sotera joined us in the apartment about three hours after we arrived. He was missing patches of hair, they had knocked one of his teeth loose, and there was a swollen black welt on his lip, topped with a dot of clotted blood. His clothes were in tatters, and his knees had huge abrasions that left bloody halos on his torn pants.

"They grabbed me around Calle San Lázaro and laid into me good with their sticks and clubs, bashed me all they wanted. Luckily, a bus full of people stopped at the same spot where they were working me over, some of the passengers got off and defended me, just imagine, people who know me from my bus route, so I managed to escape. The police never showed up, and in the middle of the brawl one of the attackers turned his back for a second and I took off running, I ducked inside a building I know by heart, like the palm of my hand. I went up to the rooftop and from there I started jumping roof to roof. Now you can call me the Wild Cat, the Malaysian Tiger." He laughed. "They couldn't lay a hand on me!"

We listened with rapt attention, lost in a haze, to his description of this episode. I went to the medicine cabinet to get what little we had: iodine, Mercurochrome, gauze, cotton; at least it was something. Luckily, one of my neighbors, who worked at a hospital, kept me supplied with some of what she pilfered. We treated each other's wounds as best as we could.

I was afraid my friends would go outside, I asked them to stay and keep me company. And so we kept anything terrible from happening to them.

Night fell.

I boiled some potatoes and fried some eggs: dinner.

Another neighbor loaned me a few spoonfuls of his coffee ration. We had hot coffee with sugar: heaven!

"Next time we can't make the mistake of inviting so many people we don't know," Apple Pie commented.

Lefty Sotera flew into a rage. "Then we shouldn't call it a 'protest against the dictatorship'! Then it'll be like a harmless little stroll in the park! You've got to be fucking joking!"

"I agree with her," Lena said. "Don't you see, we can't even count on the foreign press to protect us?"

"Did you invite the foreign press?" I asked while I lit a joint. "We can't afford the luxury of letting assholes like Yendi be in on it."

"Of course we invited the Yankee press agencies, but they didn't bother to show up. Journalists live in fear of being expelled from Cuba. That Yendi's an informer; who invited her?" Lefty Sotera pricked his lip with a red-hot needle, dark blood oozed from the nick. I passed the doobie to Lena and helped my friend out, washing his wound with water from a small pitcher. "Who the fuck invited her?"

We looked at each other shrugging, nobody knew. It hadn't been any of us.

"What a piece-of-shit country," Lena sighed.

"What a piece-of-shit world, you mean!" I couldn't contain my anger.

"You call this a country? A pigsty of an island is what it is, but it's what we have to deal with." Apple Pie wept in frustration.

Lefty Sotera noticed the photography book lying on top of a pile of books in a corner of the living room. Sitting down on the cold tiles of the floor, he leafed through the pages.

"Look." He pointed to the photo of Assia by Dora Maar. "Looks like you, Lena."

Lena clicked her tongue. "Maybe I look like her shadow," she joked.

"Yeah, if we keep on eating sweet potato bread we'll all end up fat," Apple Pie yawned.

"Sweet potato isn't fattening, it's better than flour, especially for maintaining a healthy scalp," I said.

We went to sleep; the women slept in the bed. Lefty Sotera slept on a cot, uncomfortably enough. Around midnight he moved to the bed, with us. He was on fire.

We made love and wept in each other's arms. We were still young, we were full of desires, and we had a feeling we'd never be free.

Bernard lifted the glass of Demoiselle champagne to his lips (Dom Pérignon wasn't on the menu at the café that day) and swirled the cold liquid in his mouth, savoring it.

"You've gone to bed with girls? So you've gone to bed with girls." His eyes gleamed malevolently.

I chose to remain silent; I had no reason to answer.

"Your silence is tantalizing." He smiled maliciously but immediately changed the topic: "I'll continue my story, if you're still interested. The second afternoon, we were sitting on the steps of a palazzo, tired from hoofing it around Venice. That morning we had visited the Basilica of Santa Maria, and from there we'd gone on foot to Peggy Guggenheim's residence—she was opening her house to the public as a museum. James wanted Peggy and Dora to meet, but it didn't work out well, they didn't hit it off.

"Dora was absolutely astonished by the Henry Moore statue that still stands by the entrance. We couldn't take photos of ourselves that time, we'd forgotten the camera, but it was a shame to lose that image of Dora studying the sculpture, rubbing the bronze with her hand as if trying to make it even smoother.

"Then, that same afternoon, sitting at the bottom of those steps, we got her to start talking about her work as a photographer. She had never talked about it so openly before. James and I were stunned, really stupefied; we were all ears. I don't remember what James did to get her talking like that about her flings with Assia. Photographic flings, lesbian fascination; she may have felt the same with the Surrealist painter Leonor Fini, whom she photographed half-undressed, holding a cat between her legs; and she certainly did with Nusch Éluard. Dora had been a daring, free-spirited girl. Our Dora, without realizing it, had been a forerunner, a driving force behind so many artistic and sexual trends. I was very good friends with Leonor Fini, who organized some very entertaining, lavishly theatrical Surrealist gatherings in Corsica."

"Do you know if Dora knew Remedios Varo, the Spanish Surrealist?"

"She must have, but she never talked to me about her. The thing is, before the Venice trip I wasn't very close to Dora, not really even as friends, even though I knew a lot about her and enjoyed seeing her now and then. I didn't have much to do with Remedios Varo either. With Dora, just those five days in Venice, where each minute felt like centuries to us, and the three days back to Paris by car. I don't mean we found her boring to be around, not in the least. Quite the contrary, for me each minute with her was timeless, never-ending. I don't know if she had the same experience, but for me, with my sense of time, it meant a lot, it certainly did. I can remember her in such vivid detail that even now I see her image superimposed over yours, as if she were really here."

He rested his head in his hands, his eyes fixed on a private moment from the past.

"We returned from Venice by car. It rained a lot. Dora and James argued the whole time. I did the driving, and every time the

85

car broke down it was up to me to fix it. She would get out and hold a huge umbrella over me as I worked. We got soaked on that trip, it rained so much. And that was how I began to love her. And I think she also loved me. We began to love each other at the very end. When I first came to know her, Dora impressed me as an egotistical woman. I had only seen her a few times, but I knew all about the strangeness of her relationship with James, who I always told to be careful, since his ambiguous signals might get her to make a fool of herself if she clung to a false illusion. Dora was ambivalent, and she could be very stingy, proud, bad-tempered, domineering. Intrigue fascinated her. . . . And yet she was the most charming, seductive person I ever knew; I found her enchanting. An exceptional woman who didn't have the slightest idea how exceptional she was, and who wore herself out as a result, trying to become what she already was. More importantly, she was an artist with a uniquely generous soul."

PART II

I'VE SET DOWN ALL MY TEARS IN WRITING

Dora and me. Venice, 1958–Paris, 2009

Dora haunted my dreams. In the misty gloom of night her hands wrung each other and wrung mine. Hands with long thin fingers that she constantly rubbed, one hand against the other, gently; she also inspected them closely, tracing the arteries that showed through her translucent skin and following them as they ran into tiny veins that led to happier memories.

Georges Bataille described her as a woman incapable of love. Xénie-Dora, in response, wrote him an angry letter, insulting and reproaching him for understanding nothing about the years when her suffering turned her into a peerless, unique artist who loved others experimentally through art and the prism of her sadness. Bataille did not understood young Dora's artistic love-play.

In fact, Bataille felt abandoned. His spiteful description of Dora was merely an expression of his bitterness, the reproach of a predatory seducer who had let his biggest prey get away, the woman he thought he had turned into an expert in sadism and masochism and a submissive object of lesbian love. But Dora would not be dominated.

Years later, just when she began to feel that Picasso was rejecting her, Bataille wrote to her again, this time appreciating her real worth. Now he was the one who felt like a damp shadow, a vanishing presence. Sadness fit him like a glove; sick and frail, he hoped his former muse's friendship would make him feel better. And it did. She went straight to him, the writer who thought eroticism was earthy and childish, yet who hadn't been able to decode the playful messages his lover had been sending him with her body and her art back then.

To stick to the real story, however, Dora hadn't actually abandoned him, as he used to complain behind her back to their mutual friends. Contrary to what he told everyone, he had dumped her for the writer Colette. So Dora left, more heavyhearted than heartbroken, pretending she was the one dropping him so as not to come off looking worse. The breakup left no scars, at least not visible ones. Dora was young, she recovered quickly, especially since he wasn't the god she was aspiring to worship.

The Blue of Noon, the novel where Georges Bataille introduced the character of Xénie inspired by Dora, who shared the leading role with Simone Weil and Colette, who ultimately betrayed her, was published in 1957. The next year Dora decided to go into seclusion decisively, serenely, and apparently without regrets.

Neither James nor Bernard knew if Dora had read Bataille's novel. No copy of it was ever found among the piles of books in her library after her death to prove that she had read it. Perhaps she did so in secret. Keeping the secret even from herself, in a state of absolute emotional rapture and denial. Or she preferred to remain unaware, ignorant of the Dora she had been for Bataille and who now appeared in a novel, defined as a proud young woman whose spirit was spiced with unwonted perversity.

Her hands, back to studying them in close detail. Her hands bled while she, on her knees, anxiously awaited her punishment, the physical torture, the pinches, the blows.

Intelligent women, contrary to what one might think, are fond of cruelty.

Bataille tended to take a few liberties too many, though for Dora surely the hardest part was finding herself reflected in a character described as bisexual, rather banal, and even superficial, by someone she respected as a fine observer and literary luminary.

"I was the crowned queen," Dora sighed.

Indeed, in 1935 and 1936 she must have been a queen of Surrealism; her photos were easily as good as those of the acknowledged masters.

Thanks to Pierre Kefer she was able to move her studio from 29 Rue d'Astorg next door to 29B, renting it from Daniel-Henry Kahnweiler, Picasso's art dealer. She liked the neighborhood for its elegance as well as the fact that Picasso himself lived in a distinguished apartment not far from there, and also had his studio nearby at 23 Rue La Boétie.

The apartment at 29 Rue d'Astorg not only became Dora's home; she also made it into one of the most famous and impeccable Surrealist images, pouring into it all her pain as a smothered daughter suffocated by her mother's overprotective and crushing presence.

This photo, titled 29, *rue d'Astorg*, makes you feel queasy as soon as you look at it. An arcade as seen through a funhouse mirror; at the far end, a tiny door letting in a bit of light. And in the foreground, the grotesque body of an adolescent girl whose misshapen head resembles a pond turtle's. She wears disheveled clothes and her arms, legs, and feet are elephantine, absurdly chubby. Sitting at a bench, the girl tugs at her dress; her feet, shod in school shoes, dangle bashfully. The bench looks ready to tip over, unbalanced by the stunted girl's own shadow; she is taking off, rising from the ground, giving the bench a vibrant impulse to levitate. The girl's long neck looks like a finger, but it can also look like an arm or a penis; the shape is undeniably phallic. It is a fascinating image, not only for its Surrealist content, but for the intimate perspective it affords, fraught with the heavy load of dreams and torments that hounded and pervaded the artist. In this photo, Dora produced a work of art inspired by adolescent desire, her initiation into erotic adventure, her maiden voyage into brutal sensuality; we witness an unstable trio, a dubious concoction, culminating here in a hellish nightmare.

Leaning against a window in the Bridge of Sighs, Dora now looks at her hands in the foreground; below them, in the distance, gondolas transport tourists through the gray Venetian waterways. Hers are the hands of a middle-aged woman, the hands of a woman who has no man's body to caress. Hers were the first artist's hands to love and pay homage to Picasso, the first to glide with mysterious force toward him, to find him, just as he found art: "I do not seek, I find." She still had the scar from that wound, from the time she slipped while plunging a knife between her fingers into the wooden tabletop and cut herself.

But she had not come to Picasso on her own. Intuitively, she had been following the clues that fate and people had left along the trail that led to him. It was a woman's voice that first set her on Picasso's trail: the beguiling voice of Musidora.

Like André Breton, who said he had reinvented the feminine ideal through the exotic singer, Dora was enchanted by Musidora. Musidora was described as "a modern-day fairy, adorably given to wickedness," with a seductively childish voice. Breton turned her into a divine and divinating figure, a martyr for all desires, a perverse everchild.

In Musidora, Dora saw an infinitely powerful audacity. Though she found something more: a message for herself, given that she took photographs with her eyes clear of recurrent vices, and she also focused on her subjects using the unconscious. (All this would later appear in Alicia Dujovne Ortiz's biography of Dora.) And her unconscious led Dora from Musidora to Picasso. Before that, however, her most loyal friend (or at least she was his), Paul Éluard, entered like a ray of light contoured by broken shadow, his face turned devoutly toward freedom, his wide, round forehead a prow searching forward. This photo no doubt inspired Picasso when he later painted portraits of the poet. Éluard illuminated the trail to Picasso; Musidora blazed it, step by step.

A history that swings both ways

The poet Éluard was responsible for something just as horrendous as Picasso's treatment of Max Jacob. When Picasso was asked to do something to free Jacob from the transit camp for Auschwitz-bound prisoners, Picasso responded with a remark too trivial and evasive to count as poetic, at a time when even poetry was more often harmful than helpful. Jean Cocteau could have saved Jacob, but the letter he wrote that might have secured his release arrived too late.

Éluard, for his part, saved many people with his poem "Liberty," and today its lines still inspire hundreds of thousands of political prisoners around the world. That was Éluard the poet. Éluard the Communist, on the other hand, informed on a friend and got him killed. He was expelled from the Surrealist movement, but he came back; same with the Communist Party; half-expelled, half-rehabilitated, but always coming back the same way he left: by constraint. It was a time when people didn't know, or barely knew, that Communism was blameworthy.

Despite the known horrors and regrets occasioned by Éluard's fickleness, Dora loved him like an older brother and a usually affectionate mentor; she admired him as the great Surrealist poet, because she understood him better than anyone.

The painter De Chirico, however, thought Éluard was a mystical cretin, and he thought the same of Picasso. But the stupidity supposedly reflected in Éluard's face was exactly what had tenderly and sublimely seduced Dora.

To top it off, "Gala the Druggie," as the Russian muse was known when she was married to Éluard, left her first husband for the mustachioed Salvador Dalí, never to return. The poet could never get over her desertion, which has its own place in the annals of Surrealism. Call it a desertion for the history books. Éluard did not immediately recover, turning his abandonment into an interminable, depressing whine, which his friends listened to pityingly, especially Dora. Éluard felt belittled, excluded from the life of the only woman who acted as his muse and who revealed herself to be her own work of art. Gala Dalí took off, even though she could have stayed with Éluard collecting lovers with his knowledge and consent. But perhaps Gala needed to belong to one man alone, and not to any man but to a mad, ardent, fertile, and entertaining genius. Everything she perceived of Éluard's love, Gala's exaggeratedly dramatic style of passion, gradually became unbearable to him. So much so, that when she shared him with Max Ernst, Éluard kept repeating—as an excuse, pretending all this meant jack to him—that he preferred his woman's lover to his woman herself. That was Éluard. And that was what Dora loved about Éluard: his complaisant fragility, his evasive attitude to being scorned by the woman he loved, his broadminded championing of every point of view when they argued about people's sexuality, and so many other sides of his complex personality, his ability to stage all these blind spots, with their sex organs fully exposed, as if genitals talked among themselves, had brains of their own, minds that could hold forth on diverse subjects, like a film by Alain Robbe-Grillet, the writer and filmmaker known for his theory of the *Nouveau Roman*.

Musidora led Dora to Breton, Breton to Éluard; by another route, as we shouldn't neglect the influence of Georges Bataille in her life or in their life together, Éluard led her to Nusch, her great friend, her double. And they led her to a certain Pablo Picasso.

Nusch was Dora's best friend and confidante. Her real name was María Benz. Her father was a circus performer; she also did some acting, playing very minor roles at the Grand Guignol. There Éluard discovered her. She looked like a sickly child, pale, tubercular, prominent bones, so fragile anyone would think she was about to come apart at the seams like an old rag doll. Yet her pearly-white complexion, blond hair, and those same bones jutting out at every angle could all be captured by the camera in a way that made her look like a monumental Nordic beauty playing the role of a lifetime: acting out her own death in every portrait.

The "swinger," as Breton contemptuously called Éluard because of his continual mixed-up relationships, got married a week before Breton, on August 14, 1934, to Nusch, that young woman whose delicately balanced swan's neck couldn't have been a greater temptation to depravity. Dora remembers in minute detail Nusch's bridal dress, the naughty wink Nusch gave Dora, the complicity that instantly sprang up between the two of them. In those days there were still pleasure-loving girls in the world who couldn't wait to get married, join nuptially as man and wife, with the idea that desire and love could abide forever.

After that first festive meeting and with their deepening friendship, Dora began to photograph Nusch incessantly, following a mysterious need to capture and immortalize Nusch for herself alone, with some degree of jealousy, almost of morbid egotism.

The "swinger," however, couldn't help, years later, going back to his old ways, with Dora and Nusch, with other women, with any woman who crossed his path.

Greek games

Dora was standing still, balanced on a rickety chair, photographing Picasso's studio from above, capturing a bird's-eye view, a technique that had become a sort of obsessive tic with her. Éluard and Nusch dropped by, or "slipped in on the sly," as they put it. Nusch, ravishingly beautiful, posed seductively for the lens. Dora pressed the shutter, hoping to capture Nusch just so, enveloped in a pale white halo.

Éluard made a conspiratorial gesture that Nusch understood implicitly. She began to disrobe, and once nude, she set herself before the painter. When Picasso, who hadn't stopped painting, saw the young woman offering herself to him, he didn't wait, he stripped off what little clothing he was wearing, charged Nusch like a bull, and tossed her on the cot.

Dora never understood why Éluard forced Nusch to go to bed with Picasso in front of her. But these were things, she supposed at the time, that Surrealist women had to accept for the sake of their friendship, of her friend's poetry, of the Surrealist movement itself, as free as she herself had been in her Bataille period. In any case, Dora never forgot Nusch's melancholy look, her compulsive motions, her moans, more like those of a wounded animal in terror than in heat. Dora felt terribly ashamed of Picasso, snorting like bull, covered in sweat, on top of her best friend's body. But this feeling vanished instantly when Nusch's face transformed, looking as if she had fainted dead away, until at last Dora realized she was smiling with pleasure, rolling her eyes.

Éluard smoothed his hair, and his bulging forehead seemed about to burst with fury, with sensual pleasure, with everything he needed to be able to write a poem worthy of Paul Éluard.

Dora always wanted to be like Nusch, so much so that she ended up falling in love with her. In love with her theatrical lovemaking and her histrionic sexual surrender.

Being stout, Dora silently envied the actress's childlike looks, her sickly body that was for the first time being nourished by the poet and his poetry, her fine hands, the nails she photographed sunk into her feverish cheeks. Her enigmatic face, veiled by a finely drawn spider's web.

Dora's best models were Nusch and Picasso; when she photographed them she felt she was surrendering to them forever, in the same state of sublimation she attained in orgasm.

Dora, looking out over the magnificent landscape for the soul that is Venice, admits to herself that she had been deeply in love with Nusch, that she wished she had been the one who made love to Nusch, not Picasso, though Éluard never would have been understood; or maybe he would have but it never occurred to him to suggest she make love to his wife. Besides, they were all—all or most of the Surrealist men—trying to interest Picasso in their wives. Picasso, after all, was Picasso, and recreational sex and voyeurism were growing in importance. An indescribable frenzy was overwhelming them. The sexual object was becoming even more desirable and delectable.

Dora kissed her on the lips, after shooting the photo in which Nusch's eyes glistened moistly like two drops of liquid indigo. Nusch didn't push her away, didn't say anything. She just shifted positions smoothly and very gradually. Afterwards Dora began to dream she was making love with Nusch's shadow, with her double, enveloped in a florescent halo. Or with a spider with Nusch's head.

Another time, while shooting the Vicomtesse de Noailles, the moneyed patron of the Surrealists, Dora realized she could fall in love with women more readily than with men. But then she corrected herself: she wasn't interested in men, she was only interested in one man; she had loved Picasso, while she might have loved many women. First, Nusch. Second, certainly, Leonor Fini, her painter friend. Third might have been Marie-Laure de Noailles.

Marie-Laure had an additional allure: she seemed to have no bones, her flesh wrapped around the wind, the breeze, and her body unfathomably gentle, impossible to describe and even harder to capture in a photograph. She was pure air. Marie-Laure's body was a Surrealist assemblage of skin, held aloft by a desire to clothe nothingness, veil the void, and costume the abyss.

She was married to the Vicomte de Noailles, an ideal lover, for he understood and accepted everything, couldn't have been more tolerant. Not that he had much choice; she was already a blue-blood, a direct descendant of the Marquis de Sade. Her great-grandmother on her mother's side, the Countess of Chevigné, inspired Marcel Proust to create the character of the Duchesse de Guermantes. Marie-Laure had been lucky enough to have a father of renowned ancestry, a Jewish banker, Bischoffsheim, not an easy last name but one that opened all sorts of doors, cousin to the Baron Hirsch who founded the Jewish colonies in Argentina.

Her whole history fascinated Dora, and, like so many other artists, she aspired to be added to the list of the Vicomtesse's inner circle. And, while Picasso, Balthus, Dalí, Giacometti, and Óscar Domínguez (a painter and the patroness's vulgar lover) painted the aristocratic lady with bones of smoke, Dora photographed her.

The rich woman who produced many of Luis Buñuel's films remained close to Dora, faithful to the end.

And she had already foreseen this, long ago, while she watched the shimmering gondolas. She knew that Marie-Laure would never leave her side, ever, because Marie-Laure's greatest treasure was her great generosity and dependable loyalty, though her loyalty would later be debatable, since if James Lord had allowed her she would have taken him to bed during the week that Lord spent at her fabulous summertime mansion.

Dora was walking in silence now along the Grand Canal. She began to recall how many times she had abandoned Marie-Laure. Just as Picasso had abandoned her, she had left Yves Tanguy, the painter and sculptor, another of her lovers. "Maybe it's all a punishment," she droned under her breath in a litany, "maybe it's the worst of all punishments." No act will go unpunished.

Before Picasso, she was the one who left the men. Much like Bataille, Tanguy had begun to smother her, and she could no longer bear his stifling presence or even manage to look him in the eye, avoiding his gaze, ashamed he might discover she no longer loved him. Tanguy suffered, but men get over breakups quicker than women. A woman dies every time she is deserted. Every time a man is abandoned, he is reborn. And her relationship with Tanguy hadn't lasted, not like the ten years she lived with Picasso. "*Petit Yves qui vous aime*" was the sweet inscription he wrote her in a book: "Little Yves, who loves you."

And then came Picasso. All love, all betrayal.

She had given the ten best years of her life to Pablo Picasso, and it was as if she had thrown them into the sea, as if they had sunk to the bottom of the ocean. After him, she no longer knew how to live. The rest could only be compared to a form of survival that, paradoxically, came from the vital impulse bequeathed by those ten years.

She went back to the hotel. James was waiting for her at the front entrance, wearing a white linen shirt and lightweight beige pants. He was utterly good-looking, very handsome, and she now tried to believe she might begin to love again.

Étourdissement. Dora, Éluard, Picasso. And me. Paris, 2010

Étourdissement is not an easy word to translate from French. From the verb *étourdir*, "to stun," it retains a connotation of pending tragedy without being over-the-top. Yet I can think of no more apt word to get across the feeling that overwhelmed me as never before. I hadn't slept for days. So many years of reading Paul Éluard's poem "Liberté" in public, because I thought he'd been expelled from the French Communist Party and had never rejoined; so many years of being flat wrong, of living a lie, a lie repeated so often it had almost become the truth, as happens under totalitarianism.

I learned of this error, to my own horror, from the writer and essayist Jeannine Verdès-Leroux. And though I will always love Éluard's poem and continue to quote it, because it is a great poem quite in spite of who wrote it, and it will remain a literary symbol of freedom, it won't be the same, I won't read it as I used to. When I mentioned this to Jeannine, her response was dreadfully definitive. "In any case, he didn't give a damn about his poem!" she said in an anguished but authoritative voice.

I have the same feelings toward Pablo Picasso. We know from a number of sources that he did not cover himself with glory, at least not as much as we had been told, during the eight months before the Germans invaded France, nor did he comport himself well with his women. But his art, much of it, still captivates me. Quite in spite of who made it. Nowadays, to be sure, I don't look at Picasso as I used to, just as I can never read Éluard's poem in the same way.

Paul Éluard arrived at Surrealism even before Surrealism itself did, before Dadaism did, because he was a Surrealist before World War I, and he was close to André Breton, first as a friend, then as a poet. Both were briefly active in the Communist Party in 1925; later they distanced themselves from the party, fed up with and fearful of what they were already beginning to learn about it: the horror. Éluard was actually expelled, though he later rejoined. André Breton never again set foot in the party, being influenced by the thought of Leon Trotsky.

In 1935, Breton and Éluard traveled to Prague, where they had the good fortune of meeting a number of famous writers, poets, and critics. They became friends with the historian and literary theorist Záviš Kalandra, born in 1902, beloved by all. This experience was incredible for them both. They returned to France in raptures about the way they'd been able to take the pulse of genuine poetic and political movements that were on the rise even inside a nascent dissidence.

In 1942 Éluard went back to the French Communist Party and stuck with it till his death, a move that forced him to write incredibly hideous and even totally Stalinist poems such as his "Ode to Stalin" (1950). He had not, however, entirely forgotten that experience in Prague, and it ate away at him not to accept it for what it really was: an awakening to the truth.

I also wrote poems with communist overtones, though none quite so horrendous; I was sixteen years old and very confused. I'm not sorry, I'm ashamed of my stupid naivety, of how gullible I was to believe everything they told me.

In 1950, Záviš Kalandra—the friend Éluard and Breton had met in Prague—was arrested, accused of spying and conspiracy, and savagely tortured. He was forced to read a mea culpa in front of a tribunal and had to agree to everything the regime ordered him to do, for as we know, at every trial in the USSR and in the "popular democracies," the accused was obliged to testify to whatever the

Communist Party demanded. Thus destroyed, Kalandra was never again the same.

André Breton issued a major appeal with the aim of demanding Kalandra's release; all the important writers, from Paul Claudel to Marcel Camus, from François Mauriac to Jean-Paul Sartre, signed his petition. Not so Éluard.

In the June 14, 1950, issue of *Combat*, Breton published an open letter to Éluard: "How, in your heart of hearts, can you bear so grave a debasement of Man in the person of one who has proven to be your friend?" Éluard responded: "I have too much work to do with the innocent people who proclaim their innocence to deal with the guilty who proclaim their guilt." You can find this quote in the June 19–25, 1950, issue of *Action*. Záviš Kalandra was executed. He was forty-eight.

Max Jacob, Picasso's friend, was arrested by the Germans and imprisoned in the Drancy internment camp for deportees. There he died there on March 5, 1944, some say from pneumonia, others say typhus, or both. First he had to live through the torture of seeing his younger sister, Myrté-Léa, dragged to the same camp and later deported.

Jacob wrote to his friends, trying to get them to do something for his dearest sister. Sacha Guitry responded that, if worse came to worst, he could help Jacob but not his relatives. A short time later, on the February 24, 1944, Jacob was arrested. He could have escaped through his back door, but he sat on his bed and waited. From the train, from his dark cell, he wrote to Jean Cocteau and Picasso with a plea for help. Cocteau scrambled to respond, but in spite of his letter and the petition (which, by the way, was never confirmed to have been signed by the poet's other friends), the letter with the release order that he had obtained from the German ambassador, Otto Abetz, arrived too late.

I've said it before: when Picasso was asked to help free Jacob, which he should have been able to do given his relationships and his friends' relationships, he answered with a pitiful excuse. The scene took place in Le Catalan. "It isn't worth doing anything. Max Jacob is an angel; he'll be able to fly the coop." A very Picasso statement. You can even imagine the poet, winged like the dove of peace, flying across a sky painted by the Spaniard. According to others, rather than an angel, Picasso actually called Max Jacob a *lutin*, a *duende*, a sprite.

Max Jacob died at Drancy, the antechamber of extermination, the limbo on the way to Auschwitz, very ill and perhaps still hopeful. My mind replays this incident in slow motion and cannot erase the letter he wrote to Cocteau:

Dear Jean:

I write to you from a train, thanks to the kindness of the gendarmes who surround us.

We'll soon be in Drancy. That is all I can say.

Sacha [Guitry] said, when told about my sister, "If it had been him, I could have done something!"

Well, it is me.

A hug,

MAX

He also wrote to André Salmon from the train, urging him to ask Picasso, one of his oldest friends, to do everything possible. And one last message before he was locked in the icy cell for those waiting to be deported: "May Salmon, Picasso, Moricand do something for me."

As he was dying, the great poet Max Jacob saw trees passing by overhead; he shouted, he yelled, and shortly he began to fall quiet. The pain in his lungs made him cry out convulsively that someone was plunging a dagger into his chest; in the end, he grew calm. "I am with God—and you have the face of an angel." Those were his last words.

I once loved and admired Picasso; today I can only view his work coldly, with artistic admiration, of course, but nothing else. I'm done with tenderness. I cannot conceive of art apart from love. But this deep love has left me. Perhaps, with time, I will be able to warm up to his work again.

The great Polish Nobel laureate Czesław Miłosz, who served as a diplomat after the war, requested political asylum in 1950. He also became a professor in the United States and returned to Cracow in the last years of his life, dying there in 2004. The last sentence of his *Letter to Picasso*, published in the June 1956 issue of *Preuves*, pages 5 and 7, in case anyone wants to check, reminds the painter: "If the support you lent to the terror mattered, your indignation would also have mattered. It is therefore just to point a finger at your thoughtlessness, lest it be forgotten by your future biographers."

His biographers have been very careful not to bear it in mind.

Few are unaware that Pablo Picasso had to be begged and kept people waiting when time came to help his fellow Spaniards in the struggle against fascism, which is not to say that he had anything to do with fascism himself. He, like many others, kept quiet, or rather circumspect, for a long time. Until the day three German police entered his studio and insulted him, calling him "a degenerate, a Communist, and a Jew." It would be unjust, therefore, to not mention that it was Dora Maar who managed to convince him that he had to do something through his art. Another fact too often whitewashed in those daunting historical tomes that shower Picasso with praise and flattery while reducing Dora to the role of the unhinged lover.

I can imagine Dora, in her big-shouldered leather coat and those clunky shoes with the hollow wooden heels, begging Picasso to make some small gesture, even a simple statement of solidarity. Finally he did so, and that's what counts. But Max Jacob wasn't saved, and Picasso could have done it, with his enormous influence. He waited around and did nothing. His waiting made all the difference.

However, the Great Genius didn't waste much time on great events that would have made him more famous than he already was, being too caught up instead in his orgies and in his engravings, which so obsessed him. In any case, there will always be a good pretext to excuse him; after all, it's Pablo Picasso. And in the end, nothing better to erase memories of dark doings than sex and the pristine impact of art. Art and the death's head that Picasso idolized.

I'm tossing and turning, can't get to sleep. Paul Éluard, a traitor. Paul Éluard, the author of the poem "Liberty." The poem that for years—through all the long years of my exile—I've been reciting to everyone who needs to understand what liberty is: life and desire. Art and life.

This is history, too: disillusionment the hard way, censored rage.

What else must Picasso's secretary, Jaume Sabartés, have seen? He must have seen much more than this; what else? I ask this relentlessly. But he had to keep quiet; he chose to keep quiet. The poet, the secretary, had to remain loyal to the Great Genius, the man-monument, the historic artist. I capitalize "Genius," and rightly so, I think, for of course that's what he was; but doubt creeps in when I write "man," a word encompassing the simple grandeur of human beings who are honest and fight for truth.

Dora, however, didn't begin to doubt Picasso's "manhood" until the day he stopped gazing attentively at her body, and she noticed he was starting to forget the delicious curves and hollows of her nakedness. Picasso stopped noticing her, stopped desiring her, while becoming enraptured with her mind. Or perhaps that was all she had left, her irksome and insufferable intellect.

Meanwhile, her body grew more and more rigid. Like a cracked terracotta statue. She walked beside him, and he turned away from her, or she sensed that he was turning away from her. It wasn't like the man had suddenly stopped being masculine and virile. No, the man had ceased to desire her and to desire himself. The man wasn't interested in the war either, or in the suffering of others unless it was art; he dreamed of peace and painted it daily. The man stopped being a man and became the great, historical artist, the Great Genius, the renowned property of the public. "My party is my painting," he smugly proclaimed.

His kisses weren't the same, he began to possess her even more brusquely, savagely. The little man became a minotaur, snorting, puffing, on top of her body. He scratched at her armpits until blood flowed in thin rivulets. He scratched at her breasts. With his nails he scrawled on Bristol board, "Dora Maar's blood." And the stain bled into the paper. He gleefully painted with her blood.

Dora tried to force herself to cry, but she couldn't. Dora squeezed out her tears, but they refused to run down her cheeks. Dora acted out a grimace of pain, but her shame undercut her efforts. Then Picasso shook her violently by her black-and-blue shoulders: "Weep, Dora, weep, Dora!"

The woman, at that instant, recalled her father's words, "Observe, observe, Dora!" in the distant observatory of her childhood, off in Buenos Aires.

Her splendid body, eggless as the body of Lautrémont's female shark, had ceased to inspire the Master; but her tears, her suffering, fired his excitement and roused him to paroxysms. She sighed, relieved. This wasn't the end. No, not yet. As long as she shed tears, he would not abandon her.

She could understand that her real power consisted in the fact that, up until this moment, of all his women, she had been the most often painted, the most often portrayed. But, instantly erased by her own evanescent, treacherously silent tears. "Stolent." Silent, stolen tears.

James and me. Paris, 2010

I hadn't seen James Lord for quite some time. I hadn't called Bernard again either. The novel was on hold, time was passing; time flies, their lives fly, my life flies.

I was afraid I might not see them again, and I foresaw precisely that happening: my never seeing them again. Then the phone rang. I spoke for a while with the writer Guillermo Cabrera Infante's widow, Miriam Gómez, who lives in London. I hung up thinking about a thousand things at once. I took a bath, got out a black dress and put it on, and left for the Ars Atelier gallery on Rue Quincampoix.

That night there was a private preview there of an exhibition by the Cuban Surrealist Jorge Camacho, who was paying homage to another Surrealist painter, the Chilean Roberto Matta. The exhibition was called "Le Grand Transparent." It was magnificent. Camacho's fine-grained drawings did honor to the title, exemplifying a grand transparency of line, a clarity of time in the alchemy of verses and words drawn from the depths of dreams.

When the gallery closed, a group of us decided to go eat at a Lebanese restaurant recommended by my friend Tania, who collects art.

Halfway through dinner, I learned that James Lord had died. I couldn't believe it. Impossible. Another Cuban painter, Ramón Leandro, passed the news along to me, and he assured me it was true. I didn't want to accept it. It couldn't be.

I went home and sat down to write, and to really think about them. About James, about Bernard, about Dora. . . . Until I was seized by nervous, hysterical, absurd sobbing. I decided to take a shower and let out all my tears under the hot water.

I wept, heartbroken, conjuring up Dora, James, and Bernard; thinking about the trip to Venice that she had so desired and that Bernard and James had made a present of to her to make her wish come true.

I barely slept, dawn caught me sitting on the sofa, my legs drawn up against my stomach, staring blankly at the dawn-red ceiling. I waited until a reasonable hour, then phoned James's house. No one answered. I didn't dare call Bernard. To this day I haven't tried again.

James Lord had died. "He's dead," I recited dully, achingly.

I began to reread his book, *Picasso and Dora*, at first in French, then I downloaded it in Spanish.

I read and read the French text nonstop, my face wet with tears. Now that James is gone, there's a new dimension to his writing, it has acquired the weightiness of a last word spoken by someone who will never speak again, the treasured echo of a voice I'll never hear again, though he never spoke much and was a rather quiet sort, or maybe I should say "reserved," not quite the same thing as "quiet." He's dead, and we won't be able to meet anymore at his apartment, and I won't be able to hear his asides on Dora, Picasso, Surrealism, and Cubism, or let him watch me tenderheartedly, or listen to his cloying, coy praise for the color of my eyes.

I won't have James to ask about Dora anymore, won't be able to find out whether that trip was the total nightmare he made it out to be in his book or whether, as Bernard declared in our first meeting, "Nothing at all happened, she just felt more comfortable around me than around James. She and I just became reacquainted, and we got on fabulously, and we shared stories and jokes. We had fun the whole time, while James got left behind. But that's not strange, she wanted to give him a good thump on the head, teach him a lesson, and I was a good means for her to do that. Dora was pretty malicious, not that it was easy to spot that side of her. Really, we laughed a lot. She came back to Paris with us in the same car. She got carsick. The car broke down a few times, and while James was doing everything he could to fix it, with no luck, we'd get down from the vehicle and split our sides laughing, reminiscing about people we hung out with, like Picasso and Marie-Laure de Noailles. Dora had the most beautiful voice I've ever heard, as I've told you before, and of all the Surrealist women I knew, she was the most intelligent."

I never asked Bernard what he thought about Picasso as a friend, as an ordinary man without the protective cover of being the great artist. He wasn't forthcoming with details, either, but he always insisted that Dora was a difficult woman. Too cerebral, excessively intelligent. Her intelligence had displaced her libido. Too coldly rational, too aware of her body's terrifying temperature. An extremely dangerous temperature for a man who sweated from hot spells in the middle of winter. Dora harassed him with her breath, but he needed her harassment, just as he needed to have kids scampering around him, the imaginary kids who played in the courtyard of his house on Grands Augustins, who wandered about all day long in his head. Three wars and Dora had aged him. Unforgivable.

"Why didn't she have children with Picasso?" I wonder. "After she broke off with Picasso, why didn't she establish a stable relationship with James Lord?" And I answer my own questions. "Her child was Picasso, because he was her everything, her double, he was her womb, her sexuality, her birth; he was her desire, her pleasure, and her acute suffering. He was her only child, and he was the death of her."

"My children, good or bad, have their own lives and never deceive or bring shame on their father. And you have a lot under your control, my love," Picasso reminded her in the home of his friend and collector Douglas Cooper.

At which she angrily shot back, "Yes, a whole orphanage."

She could be tough with him, but she refused to be friends with anyone who expressed doubts about Picasso and wasn't up to her standards.

James loved Picasso as much as she did, though not with the same level of devotion. James loved her in that she was an extension of Picasso's genius. She had sensed this from the first day she met James in Picasso's studio and, later, when the cigarette lighter incident took place.

Dora never entirely liked James, but she loved him, because she knew he loved Picasso through her. And there couldn't be any relationship between her and any other person that didn't go through Picasso.

Today I confirmed it on the Internet: James Lord is dead. He will never read this book. It took me so long, so *affreusement* long to finish it. *Affreusement* was a favorite word of that man who enlisted as an American soldier during World War II without a second's hesitation, solely because he wanted to meet Pablo Picasso so desperately, so vehemently. *Affreusement*. "Horriblemente" in Spanish; in English, "frightfully." I prefer the French. My language is abandoning me, and I begin to find myself possessed by the language in which I sought refuge, in this city that had given me a second life.

When I asked him if he had loved Picasso, he replied, with the submissiveness of a frustrated artist and lover, that he had loved him *affreusement*.

"I was his sleeping soldier." A metaphor to sweeten the deception of pretending to sleep so that Picasso would gaze on him.

"And did you love Dora?"

"I loved Dora more than anyone in the world." His eyes teared up. "With Picasso I was audacious and in awe. With Dora, I was just thankful and surprised."

In his book *Picasso and Dora*, Lord did not leave out the story of the kiss Picasso gave him, a rare thing to see between two men in the United States but fairly common in Europe. James felt that this kiss signified much than a show or a declaration of friendship.

"Was Picasso your lover?"

"Not at all. I was Picasso's lover. Platonic, of course, and per- haps just a bit more, as can only happen within the mirages pro- duced by art."

"And Dora? Did you isolate her from the rest of the world, or was it Picasso who monopolized her and swallowed her up?"

"I didn't isolate Dora, and Picasso didn't monopolize her. Dora was a broken woman; I suspect she'd always been so. When I met her, she hadn't yet withdrawn completely from society. She did that bit by bit, gradually. Her definitive break took place long after we returned from our trip to Venice. We talked every day by telephone, we met almost daily; of course we talked about painting and Picasso, which became our mutual obsessions, but especially hers. The separation broke her, she couldn't console herself, she harbored too much bitterness and resentment. Dora wanted to be a famous painter, since Picasso was the one who steered her from photogra- phy toward painting. She was sure she would be recognized, sooner or later, as an accomplished artist, but she never was. Maybe some day! Some of her paintings weren't bad at all, though I preferred her drawings and watercolors. Curiously, she never wanted to show me any of her photos."

"Notice that you just said 'I preferred'—why does a woman, a woman artist, always have to be judged, evaluated, and pigeonholed by the men who supposedly love her? Did you love her as an artist? How could you love her as a woman, then? Aren't you gay?"

James Lord rubbed his hands slowly, deliberately, his eyes fixed straight ahead on the wall, avoiding my gaze.

"In a certain sense I loved her as a man loves a woman. It was a great, loving friendship she and I had. I loved her without feeling a desire to possess her physically because, to be frank, I have never felt attracted to women. Dora knew that, but she may have also felt it would be different with her. I am a gay man who loved Dora Maar, if that's how you want to look at it. There was one moment when I did feel physical desire for her: on the island of Porquerolles, on the beach. She was emerging from the sea, like a water goddess; she looked great in the sea, and she knew it. But my sexual and intellectual infatuation soon passed. I have loved a few women because I wanted to be like them."

This time I was the one rubbing my hands against my coat. I'd gotten cold and felt nervous. I persisted, "I read in an interview you did some time back that you had erotic dreams about Picasso."

"Yes, I did, I still do, I still caress Picasso in my dreams, and he penetrates me, like a bull. . . . The bull, for me, is Picasso's desire." He stopped, blushing. "Which, honestly, is what the famous painting of the bull possessing Dora Maar conjures up. I didn't just love Picasso, I was obsessed with him. Even when I was awake I dreamed these erotic images, and I can still imagine his hand squeezing my penis. . . . Sorry, forgive me. I once saw him in his underpants, in his studio, he didn't make the slightest advance toward me, but if he had I would have responded more than blissfully, euphorically, would have surrendered completely."

James Lord forced a melancholy smile.

Now, in the deep of night, cloaked in this shadowy silence, I recall the hazy light floating in the air that afternoon, and his hands still rubbing each other, his long legs crossed, his shiny English loafers, the slight tremor in his right foot. Straight torso leaning back into the impeccably white sofa, full head of handsome white hair, misty eyes, and a reflection of *Ubu Roi* by Alfred Jarry in those eyes. *Père Ubu*, the Surrealist animal in Dora Maar's photo, bearing the whole weight of hyperreality.

"Did you know that Picasso loved to say, 'I'm a lesbian'?"

"Of course I knew, I often heard him say it!"

It was one of his pithy expressions. We both burst out laughing.

"He also used the line, 'Painting is just my way of keeping a diary,'" I added.

A hush fell. Dense.

NOTES FROM MY RED VELVET JOURNAL:
Dora. Venice, 1958 / Bernard. Paris, 2008 / Me. Paris and Venice, 2008

Dora

I leave the hotel and decide I'm going to take a gondola ride. While the gondolier shimmers through the water with his large oar, and long before he turns a corner intoning, "Oweeeeee!" in his young, virile voice, I sense for the first time in years that I'm recovering the placidity of pleasure, I feel pleasure again settling in my body, I rediscover my legs and remember how the writer, filmmaker, and artist Jean Cocteau, dressed as a character from one of his works, affecting nobility with princely gestures and flittering a fistful of courtesies, decked out like a mysterious duke, prodigious in praises, used to compliment my legs. Also the actor Jean-Louis Barrault, inevitably half-undressed, approached me to bestow the most unexpected flattery and even sassy, fiery comments in praise of my sensuality, adding that my gaze seemed to have been carved by the day's sea mist.

"You have a lovely mouth," Barrault whispered, and I trembled within, though I showed myself strong as a castle wall on the outside, muscles all tensed, as if I were a marble statue, my neck a column of Murano glass, my face angled back, my expression evasive and aquiline.

"Yes, quite a beautiful mouth, lost in thought, reflective," Jean Cocteau agreed, while finishing a detailed sketch of my face on paper and in spoken words.

I sense that the old woman inside me is claiming more and more space, and yet I was always old, the younger I was the older I felt, or guessed myself to be.

I know that I didn't appeal to either of them, Cocteau or Barrault; I've never appealed to men with the blazing desire they demand. Picasso loved me for my intelligence, but he didn't approve of my body. He made a pastime of calling me fat, saying, "Better watch out, Dora, you've put on weight," then snatching the spoon right out of my hands not to let me overeat. He didn't like skinny women, either, though; he couldn't stand a woman whose bones jutted into his skin.

I yearned to be as beautiful as Leonor Fini, seductive and vibrant; not so much a painter, anyone would agree, as a *cocotte*, a Victorian courtesan, a Pigalle Quarter whore from the times of Toulouse-Lautrec, with torn stockings around her ankles, a cat nestling between her thighs, shapely, strong legs that looked carved from tourmaline. Leonor kept after me, insisting that I photograph her. She never found out I was dying to do so, but what I most wanted was not to seem unwelcome. Leonor Fini was more Argentine than any of us have been for ages, and much more Surrealist than Remedios Varo or me, more translucent, given her lucidity. A woman of anthracite, sometimes of diamond or fire; an opaline, pearlescent woman.

When Picasso abandoned me, Leonor Fini was always there *à portée de main*, at my fingertips, to console me, but I didn't want her consolation or any other woman's. I only wanted to be around men, and I accepted them as a string of punishments.

This was how I took Georges Hugnet, the poet. He was impressed by my Surrealist photos, the ones Picasso loathed, at least that's what he said, though deep down he didn't really feel any disdain for them. Hugnet was moved by seeing my photos, so he published my *29, rue d'Astorg* in a collection of postcards. Every inch a man, good, patient, intelligent, a faithful man. His friendship did me more good than bad, though all my friendships with men, without exception, harmed me. However, like the good creature of contradictions that I am, I find men easier to put up with as friends than women. Women I can only love, like a man.

Georges Hugnet died before his death, faded away in life, young at heart though old in years. We shut ourselves in for hours at my apartment on Rue de Savoie; his wife never understood our relationship, but she didn't give a damn what might happen so long as he was happy, and I think she likes me because she recognizes that I did make him happy, I distracted her husband and kept the worst from happening, kept him from getting bored with life, and she owes me that debt of gratitude. I photographed him, painted him. But I never managed to capture how very beautiful and deep he was. I have never been satisfied with my photographs of men, or with my paintings of them. What good is personal satisfaction when you've lived with an undisputed genius? Everything I might do will look small and ugly next to his extraordinary art.

Who cares if I was Georges Hugnet's lover? Nothing of him belonged to me, unlike every particle in Picasso's body. Nor did any part of me infiltrate Hugnet's soul. A young soul, virtuous and sincere to the end.

It is no secret that my whole life changed the day Picasso discovered Man Ray's photograph of me, the one in which I wear a feathered headdress and a soft gaze. Everything changed then, the day my independence was fated to be wiped out and I was to be nullified as an artist. I don't know how Man Ray could capture that gaze, I never gazed sweetly at anyone. Picasso should have reproached me for it. Picasso, who hated the sad women who looked at him with the eyes of slaughtered sheep. Picasso loved me through that photo. No, excuse me, Picasso loved that photo first, not me. The thing that existed for him, the object of his admiration, was the photo. And then he wanted to love the woman Man Ray had photographed. For Picasso love always was always filtered through art, through his artistic eye. Rather than a weeping woman, instead of that fanciful nothingness that is the artistic whole, for him I was a Man Ray photograph, an image of a woman with a falsely sweet gaze, sensual, wearing feathers on her head, with full lips, and the perfect hands, the tiny hands of a porcelain doll.

A primitive woman floated in that photograph, which superficially pretended to be an image of me, though it wasn't me, it wasn't the static, rigid woman I am now; it was still the water-woman, a torrent of watery clay. That image was the chance product of observation and contemplation: Man Ray asked for a particular pose — or rather, he suggested one, since he never imposed anything — and so I was captured forever as the object that would seduce the Great Genius.

Picasso fell in love with the Amazon, the savage woman, the gruff, stubborn woman who skittered to hide behind feathers while putting on a sugary-sweet, blurry face. My hands turned into trophies by the strength of Picasso's prodigious imagination. Tiny hands that didn't square with my uncouth-looking face, a face to tone down and put on display in the glass exhibit case that the god of painters needed to equip himself with a feminine ideal and quench his thirst, though it be with a single drop from the water-woman, the woman who would become his perpetual watering hole.

I always preferred the other photo Man Ray took, the gentle one that shows my face plain, without all that photographic manipulation: my pupils float in the teary lakes of my eyes, my mouth looks slightly open, loopy, my nose is as delicate, my nostrils more closed than in the earlier picture, eyebrows are thin, everything is a line in this face I used to have, wrapped between my arms draped in black cloth, my small ear barely to be seen, like a skittish little bird. Here, in this simple photo, I am a genuinely liquid, crystalline woman; here I'm already the woman Picasso stole for his paintings, all tears, all lines, all reverie, all gut feeling.

Picasso and I met in the middle of one of my most famous weeping sessions. In a film. After that photo by Man Ray, when we both aspired to find ourselves in the world we sensed in premonitions, a world conceptualized only by Surrealism. The only thing left was for us to meet in a novel or in a film.

And the latter happened: he was in the audience, watching, and I was up on screen. Not as an actress, not at all. But as the set photographer. Our chance meeting was on the set of Jean Renoir's *The Crime of Monsieur Lange*. When I photographed Sylvia weeping as she watched the train's departure, I was forever frozen there, recast as that image. I photographed everything my doleful dreams sensed about Sylvia. I shot her weeping disconsolately. Picasso saw her weeping in the movie hall; he must have been deeply moved to see a woman weeping so copiously, without trying to hide her tears, exposing her weeping as if she were spreading her legs, naked, whimpering shamelessly, immodestly, healthily, with unwonted wildness. Sylvia crushed a handkerchief into her lips, chewed the corners of its tear-stained cloth. The handkerchief opened up like a white rose between her pearly teeth. From the other end of the movie hall, hidden in darkness, I watched the same scene, delighting in my work, and my vulva went wet as I thought of the beautiful photograph I had gotten of Sylvia Bataille.

I don't remember if I said hello to Picasso before I settled into my seat. Later on he said that I did, that we nodded to each other from a distance, and that afterwards he made out who I was in the dark by my shape, by the impetuosity of my body, and he especially recalled tracing my silhouette in his mind. It was just as he described and painted me later: in his eyes I was silently weeping. So even when he was a stranger I was already weeping in his mind, in the deepest and most incorruptible part of his artist's soul, wailing for the man who intuited I would love him till I died, and the man I was wailing for was none other than himself, though not even I knew who it would be at the time, and yet there he was, living and breathing just a few steps from me. And he was already sure that he would be the one I'd go crazy for. There I was, a woman in the movie hall, weeping like a Mary Magdalene, waiting on the Master, the Great Genius, who would pluck the petals from the white rose between my teeth and form me once again into a great and famous portrait though I was nothing but a woman, desired and then forgotten. Without knowing it, I yearned to have his ferocious will conquer mine, I hoped that the immensity of his talent would snuff out my own, I was overwhelmed by the power flowing from this man whom I invented and desired, who had not yet defined the vast and restless outer reaches of his shadowy power.

I won't deny what no one can have failed to notice, that the focus of my work, the core of my life, has been the twisted image of tragedy, which hasn't unfolded in all of its splendor because I was never brave enough, nor on the other hand meticulously methodical enough, to balance the solidity of art and the adventure of love. Two opposing forces, which together, locked in a wild struggle, destroy the spontaneity and freedom of fragile beings and so create the true tragedy, which is that hostilities persist forever.

The day I met Picasso—he could tell the story better than I could—he even told it to Françoise Gilot, who later told and wrote the story in turn to everyone, right and left. That day, I was still gullible; not exactly naïve, but too trusting. I should digress and let you know that I suffered and was terribly jealous of her. However, to be fair, I must admit she could give Picasso what he longed for, what he most missed: youth and children. More rebelliousness and personal egotism. Without her rebelliousness, without her egotism, if she hadn't ousted him from her life as she did, Picasso would have gotten bored and turned her into another pushover, a patsy who killed herself in the same pitiful way all the other women did. Picasso never stopped making his women jealous of his art, but with Françoise Gilot he suffered exactly what he'd made some of us go through: aloofness, indifference, disdain, humiliation. She offered him a supple, almost adolescent love that later morphed into a motherly, vestal love, greatly strengthening his love for her, because it came from a mother, the person to whom nothing can be denied. The person who gives life itself continuity, eternity by bloodline. And that's something that only comes with children. No work of art will do it. Of all his women, Françoise proved the most skilled.

In October 1935, I was a fresh, daring, beautiful young woman. I knew it, and I knew I could use my beauty to arouse strange emotions in men, charming them with more than just my body, for my intelligence and brightness shined through even if I sheathed myself in a heavy black cloth dress, even with my shiny black hair combed straight back, even in clunky high-heels. Men would stare at me, and their stares would pass right through my clothes, undressing me. They realized they found me irresistible at first glance, and after a second look they'd start to find something deeply unsettling about me, something that wouldn't let them forget me. I became the drug that every man needs to reaffirm his virility, but their virility numbed their souls.

I walked into the café Les Deux Magots and immediately noticed a pair of large round eyes gaping at my body. I didn't know who was staring at me nor did I care to know. All I cared was how hard he was staring and how I reacted by bringing out my bestial side. I tried to appear all sweetness and light, even making my face friendly, I traipsed around the café as if dancing to a luscious melody, a waltz, a tango, a minuet. The large round eyes followed my every move.

I don't know who he is, he doesn't know who I am. Paul Éluard answers when the stranger quietly asks a question, or so I guess. Paul Éluard whispers to him that I am Dora Maar, a sturdy soul, a Surrealist soul, an indomitable woman who beat Georges Bataille at his own game and tossed him aside (when in reality he was the one who left me for Colette).

And yet I walked into the Les Deux Magots meaning to yield to the man of my life if by any chance I met him, if fate threw us together, intending to throw myself at his feet. I longed for this meeting to take place, because I had been living obdurately and exclusively for the moment when I would no longer have a doubt that this was man I'd been imagining since adolescence.

The large round eyes then climbed up and up my body, nibbled my ears. They paused at my eyes. I resisted their magnetic gaze without batting a lash. They dropped slightly down and to one side from my right ear to fix on my lips, as if the stranger were shooting thousands of tiny needles into my skin.

I wore a pair of black gloves embroidered with pink rosettes; I took the glove off of my right hand, and then the round black eyes took hold of my waist and forced me to sit.

I opened my purse, pulled out the knife with the sharpened point. I placed my left hand, still gloved, on the table and carved its outline into the wooden table with the point of the knife. The large round eyes capered about the table's edge. Eyes closed, I tried to plunge the knife into the wood between my fingers, leaving success up to chance. I barely felt any pain, almost nothing. When I opened my eyes, the outer edge of my hand was bleeding and my tortured fingers throbbed.

The stranger's large, odd eyes drilled into the drops of blood. The glove steeped in rich red fluid. The large round eyes now sat astride my spirit. In front of me sat the stranger, who was no stranger at all. It was none other than Pablo Picasso, demanding my blood-soaked glove. He wasn't the sort of man, much less the sort of painter, who would needed to have an object to be able to recall it. Picasso had a memory for objects like no one else, because even before things existed he had already divined them. No object escaped his visual ability or his memory. He always kept my glove in the case where he stored his treasured fetishes. The valuable thing about my glove was the blood, obviously. I found that out later when I saw him dipping his brush in the cotton pads saturated with my menstrual flow.

Just as I later found out that the valuable thing about me wasn't the wrapping, which is me, but my heart, that pulsing mass crudely congealed into an unexplored mound, a virgin landscape.

I thought he would ask for my hand, and he took my glove. That little, bald man with the face of a mad monkey, abnormally wide eyes, acerbic tongue, pants hiked up too high for my taste, skinny arms compared to his rather broad torso, grim, but with enormous power in his black eyes, with great manly power in the way he grabbed the glove and stuffed it into his pocket, determined to keep that object at all cost, he left without saying one word. At least, all I remember are those dark eyes, like two bright red, dripping nails from Christ's crucifix.

Some time afterwards, that man, the owner of those bulging, excruciating eyes would be laughing with me as we embraced for the first time in bed. I was twenty-four springtimes old, and he was, on the outside, a shriveled old man of fifty-four battered winters.

Even so, I already felt I was intellectually older than he was. And he continued to be a child playing his favorite game: loving you until he tore you to bits. The child who would never give it up. The child who would torture you with his other favorite game, the one between brushes and a blank canvas.

Bernard, nearly tepid

Bernard took one of her hands in his. They were sitting at a table in front of a small café near the gallery where some of Balthus's paintings were on exhibit.

Dora allowed him to seize her hand, barely noticing; since her solitary gondola ride, her mind had taken refuge in the past, her past with Picasso, and she couldn't stop thinking in an irksome litany how much she would have loved to have made this trip with him.

It was in the past, precisely, that she and Picasso had traveled to Italy; he had invited her, just so, springing it suddenly on her, the way he always gave surprises: "Let's go to Florence and see all those masterpieces." But once in Genoa, crabby and visibly fed up, he started badmouthing Botticelli, Rafael, Michelangelo, and the rest, shouting that he wouldn't give a penny for any of that hideous rubbish, that he wouldn't trade the lot of them for his one Cézanne. And then they had to clear out because his fury tormented him and ruined their visit by driving her mad.

"Your hand is so small," Bernard said.

She withdrew it. It wasn't the first time he had noticed how small her hands were.

Bernard felt a desire to describe those fingers, the nails like delicate scales about to detach. No, Dora hadn't been as beautiful as her friend Leonor Fini, but he had no doubts about her obvious mystique, all concentrated in her eyes, in her lips, in her hands, but above all in her voice. He would have loved to be a great writer so he could rapturously describe the tone of Dora's voice. Clouds resounding in the throat of a sparrow; incisive and torrential, watery as air laden with fat raindrops in a downpour. Then he asked her a semi-foolish question, as if to get her to loosen up and speak candidly.

"Dora, what do you expect from James?"

Leaden silence.

It wasn't exactly a question she could easily answer.

"Didn't you know he and I were a couple? Of course you must know we're just very close friends now."

She turned away, fixing her half-closed eyes on a pigeon that was pecking at a pebble and continually cleaning its beak.

"Do you love him?"

She turned, now, to look at him straight on.

"Yes, to be honest. At one time I thought we might live together," she murmured.

"You thought? You don't think so anymore? Would you like him to marry you?" Bernard hesitated before asking such a daring question point-blank.

She shrugged. She was like a frightened child; he'd never seen her like this. Never before had he dared to emotionally corner the woman who so humbled him as an artist.

"I'm not sure James would want to." Bernard wanted to hurt her, plunge the knife into the wound.

She put a quick stop to it.

"Please, Bernard, leave it. What possible interest is this of yours? Do you want to hear my confession?"

"I'd like to write, become a great writer, I'd love it if you could be the main character in my greatest work, that's all," he stammered.

"Oh, please, no, I was only someone's model, the clay that Pablo Picasso molded. Isn't that enough? For me it is. I'm nobody now. Whatever I managed to become during my relationship with Picasso, I'm not that now, it's all gone and forgotten, I'm worthless.

Find another model you can use, I don't know, some queen perhaps. Queen Margot might be good for a thick novel with hundreds
of pages; or a king, make up a king with palaces and courtesans. Or
go for Pablo Picasso himself." She loved to savor her tormentor's
name. "Pablo Picasso." She also enjoyed switching suddenly and
speaking to her friends in a formal, distant tone. "Please, Bernard.
You have no right."

The silk ribbon around her hair came undone; the breeze tus-
sled her untied locks. She modestly hurried to retie them into an
austere bun.

"All James and I have in common is our friendship with Picasso,
he must have explained that to you. We both feel an intense love for
his work. We're linked by our memories of that era; nothing more.
I love James, perhaps I got my hopes up, but now I know that we
could never have anything real between us. The fact that someone
is here with us confirms that fact."

She was referring to Bernard's presence.

She adjusted the round collar of her dress.

Bernard took a sip of the Campari with lemon. He was a young,
good-looking man, more stubborn than passionate; he knew his
greatest strength was fighting a one-on-one contest on the field of
ambiguous seduction; well, after his deep love of literature, he told
himself. He should reverse the order of those two if he wants to
succeed as a writer, he thought.

A long silence held. Finally, she asked when James was planning to show up, she was getting hungry and she wasn't ready to
wait for him much longer.

"I figure he won't be long. I went out book shopping, you know,
and as you can imagine he set off to do what he's fondest of: buying
trinkets and baubles."

She pulled a pocket mirror from her purse, examined herself
on the sly, wet her lips with the tip of her tongue, and hurriedly
put it back. A few gray hairs were beginning to show along her

temples, forcing her to reject her own faded image as a woman with no way out.

Bernard took out his notepad and started jotting down phrases. Dora, impatient, ordered another vodka and orange juice. The waiter leaned over and whispered in her ear, "You are a very beautiful *signora*."

Dora knew that compliments formed part of the customary ritual of gallantry among Venetian waiters.

She observed a woman sitting down at the next table over who was also retouching her makeup, using the same gestures she had a moment before; now she was looking at herself in a compact.

Finally, in the distance, the silhouette of James Lord appeared.

Bernard was still engrossed in his notebook. Dora didn't make the slightest movement to acknowledge the presence of the newcomer.

"Here I am. I guess I'm late enough to get you angry, you'll be ragging on me for a whole year." James was carrying a few packages, and he tossed off the joke in an ironic tone.

Bernard looked up; the setting sun hit him right in the eyes.

"Yes, you're late, and you do it on purpose, typical for a spoiled and callous character like yours," she complained.

James had brought presents for his friends; they each smiled appreciatively. For him, a long, blue Murano crystal pen. For her, a graceful little velvet hat with feathers, and a pair of black gloves embroidered with small red flowers. The flowers looked like drops of clotted blood embossed on the slippery, stretchy fabric.

In her purse, Dora still carried the knife with which she had pierced her flesh on the doomed or blessed day she met Picasso. But now she preferred to keep that implement where it was, buried amid the banality of objects hastily tossed to the bottom of her sorry old excuse of a purse, a gift from her once and only love.

Shadows, arabesques

I spent the whole livelong day looking for a spot in a café where I could sit and write comfortably without anyone talking to me or bugging me with their endless noisy conversations. Venetians love to gab.

At last I found one overlooking the canal, fairly modest, with a few little tables on the sidewalk in front. From there I could watch the gondolas as they turned and passed directly in front.

In one gondola I spotted a dark, smooth-complexioned woman in a black dress with purple flowers, fitted tight around the waist, the sort of dress that had been in style after the war, with a broad skirt and belted waist. She stepped off the gondola and sat at the table next to mine. She ordered a vodka and orange juice.

To observe her more easily, I thought I'd pretend to be fixing my makeup, so I pulled out my compact and studied her closely in the little round mirror, powdering my face and touching up my lipstick over and over. She looked like no ordinary woman; there was something haughty and regal, extraordinary and arrogant about her. Perhaps it was her manner of carrying herself, the way she sat so straight, with a certain rigidity that elongated her back like a leopard's, like the backs of the women in Ingres's harem painting. She was waiting for someone, no doubt. Just as I was, with the air of expectation typical of a woman who is beginning to age.

I, well past thirty at the time, was waiting for the man I had chosen to go with me on this trip to Venice. My husband. Finally, he appeared with our young daughter in tow. She was pouting, thirsty, hungry, and sleepy.

"We can't stay, look how crabby Attys is."

"Give her to me."

I sat her in my lap, where, leaning against my breast, she fell asleep instantly.

"Did you get to see the Balthus exhibition?"

I nodded.

"I'm worn out from all the walking I did, especially with the little one on my shoulders. I met Roberto in Caffè Florian, The place was packed.

He meant the Cuban painter Roberto García York.

"Did you manage to write anything?"

I shook my head.

"What's up? How come you're not talking?"

"Nothing, nothing's up, I just don't feel like talking."

For quite some time our conversations had become more or less the same: short, concise. Yet I loved him, and he, though he never told me so, loved me too. This triangle was our life: him, our daughter, me. Indestructible; no one could break it.

Why did we love each other almost without having to talk? There was nothing we needed to say. Just by looking at each other we guessed the other's thoughts.

From the start of our relationship I knew he was an artist of unique gifts, that he was capable, at any moment, of coming up with a solution to anything that confronted him, that his creative potential was uncanny.

We understood each other because of his filmmaking, a cinema of protest that sang of life and liberty. We went into exile together, and we brought with us our greatest treasure, our finest work: the little one, our daughter.

Nothing was easy in exile. He started making documentaries about painters. The act of making films brought us closer together, his work, not mine (my writing came between us); getting to know the painters, researching their work, painting their stories with a camera, made us a single being. It was a venture that became our world and sealed our love. Yet while I was always involved in his work, he was never very interested in mine. He never read what I wrote. He was afraid of reading me.

I liked it better that way. At the time I thought (and I still think now) that one day I'll die, before he does, and then he can calmly read what I have written for the little one and for him.

The woman sitting at the table next to ours must have been in her fifties, perhaps younger; she uncrossed her legs, put her elbows on the rough wood of the table, gazed intently up and down the street, displeased. No doubt at all, she was waiting for someone who was running late. My husband focused on her.

Opposite the woman a faded man was talking, but she didn't see him, she was waiting for another man.

"She looks like an old girlfriend of mine."

Yes, my husband is an expert in talking to me about his former girlfriends when we're on a trip that was supposed to be romantic, when we ought to be forgetting about all of our exes and focusing on us. But now he was insisting on pointing out the remarkable resemblance this woman had to his former girlfriend, who had evidently been an important part of his life.

He pulled the camera from his backpack and snapped a photo of the little one and me. The woman was in the background.

"She must have been a lot older than you, because that woman's sure over the hill, I mean, practically ready for an old-age home," I interrupted sarcastically.

"No way, not at all. Are you blind? Put on your glasses, come on."

"Now all of a sudden I'm the old lady who's going blind," I thought. I refused to put on my glasses. The little one whimpered and woke with a start, asking for food.

"I'm hungry, mommy, hungry!"

We ordered a pizza. I cut a slice into little pieces and fed them to her. She chewed and swallowed noisily; the woman made an unpleasant face when the little one gurgled her water.

Finally, by and by, a tall, good-looking man appeared carrying bags of gifts. The woman looked inside the bags and smiled, accepting the man's offering.

The little one finished chewing and slurping her pizza, we paid and left. We jumped into a gondola that left us off in front of our house; we were staying in a lavish apartment that we'd rented from a Parisian antiquarian, right on the Grand Canal.

We put the little one to bed in the room next to ours. I played with her for a while until she crashed.

I undressed in our room, in front of the mirror on which someone had scrawled with lipstick, in bad English, "Just I love you. I killed you."

My husband stood behind me, his erection jutting between my thighs. I turned and offered him my lips. While he kissed me passionately, I was thinking about Dora Maar, about the passionate kisses she must have exchanged with Picasso. About how hard love is between two artists. About how easy it is for a woman to seduce a man—physically, rather than intellectually.

And about the fact that, when you finally do seduce him intellectually, it is possible that desire, once satisfied, is extinguished.

Dora through the kaleidoscope

She couldn't understand how she had gotten it into her head to take a trip to Venice. It wasn't about needing a change of scenery, getting to know the city she would have once loved revisiting with Picasso, nor did she really care at this point to understand what was really going on between herself and James, since she'd guessed long ago that all they had in common was Picasso's art and genius; they didn't even share their love for him. She loved the man and the creator, the God. James adored Picasso's work, lusted after it; the painter himself was now secondary for him.

She walked slowly through Piazza San Marco, among the crowd. "Éluard, Éluard," she murmured. She closed her eyes. "*Dégoût.*" She suddenly heard the word, or thought she heard it. "Loathing." The word that had been found written on a piece of paper next to the corpse of René Crevel, the young gay poet who had asked Éluard to attempt a reconciliation with André Breton in order to raise Breton's awareness and iron out differences between Surrealists and Communists, and whom Éluard ignored. And so began the pain of broken relationships, the great antagonism between them, the politically committed artists, first with art, then with everything else, once mistrust and discord had been sown and were spreading among the Communists.

The Communists were suspicious of the Surrealists, accusing them of being traitors, Trotskyites. Dora signed petitions and letters on both sides, running from one to the other to talk about how politics was destroying everything, but she never lost any of her faith in art nor, unfortunately, in the political ideology to which she clung for dear life.

Dora, the great artist and the Surrealist muse, stooped so low as to become a first-rate ideological extremist with a strong totalitarian streak. It's true that in that strained era you didn't have any other choice, but she could also have fallen much lower and flirted with Fascism, in addition to accepting Communism as the only path, with the naïveté typical of those who feel guilty about finding hope only in the liberating act of creation.

It saddened Dora to see the direction Georges Bataille was heading. He smoked more than ever, he ate little and poorly. Éluard refused to sign Bataille's letter arguing that Hitler's brutality was better than "the slobbering excitation of diplomats and politicians!" Éluard also broke with Breton, blaming him for everything that was happening around them. He avoided any reconciliation with the father of Surrealism and traveled to Barcelona to participate in an homage to Picasso. She sensed that something ugly was going to occur, and the foreboding pained her more than her suffering for what was going on every day.

Nevertheless she sought a refuge, a sort of empty loft of the imagination where she could harbor a bit of peace. This refuge consisted of her trust in her friends, and theirs in her. She couldn't blame Éluard for becoming inseparable friends with Nusch. With Nusch and with Picasso. A time even came when Picasso couldn't live without them, especially not without Nusch.

While Picasso was carving a monumental sculpture of his wife Marie-Thérèse Walter, Nusch and Éluard were staying with him at his place in Boisgeloup, keeping him entertained by reading poems and talking to him about painting, though talk about painting was what least interested him. They were reinventing the world through art. A world they knew they were losing, a world on the verge of catastrophe, but one they stubbornly kept trying to save minute by minute. Every brushstroke by Picasso proved it. Bull's head. Death's head.

Nusch and Éluard invited Dora to visit the Master in his chateau. Dora photographed the imposing front door, snapped pictures
of every nook and cranny, of Rue du Chêne d'Huy, of the critic
Roland Penrose overwhelmed with emotion and gesturing hysteri-
cally in front of the door to the house of the Genius of the Century.

When she crossed the threshold, she smelled the jasmine in
bloom and a kind of strange summertime aroma imbuing the whole
house and bathing her skin in warmth.

Pablo Picasso was waiting in the anteroom with his son Paulo,
the child he'd had with the Russian ballerina Olga Khokhlova: his
first wife, his first offspring.

Dora felt she shouldn't be there, that the sooner she fled from
that place the less risk she would be exposing herself to. Nevertheless she went ahead, drawn by the savage look in those eyes, by that
sarcastic smile; spellbound, she kept taking photos, more and more
pictures of the house, of everything inside it, and especially of its
owner. Captivated, she followed those large black eyes, which she
had already run into on an occasion that had a very special place
in her memory. Seen through his eyes, she became transparent,
uneasy, nervous, despondent, caught up in the rhythm of a dance
she couldn't shake; she was upset at her dependence on this space,
adopting the squalid pose as willing partner and at the same time
forced lover, like the pose of a wounded beast that seeks a hiding
spot or that is about to be hit by a hunter's flaming arrow or poisoned dart.

Picasso never stopped gazing at her, fascinated by her visual
perception as a photographer, by her movements, like those of a
trapped gazelle. She was—it had to be said—quite different from
every other woman he had known. He and she had many things in
common, and they shared a commitment to beauty and a dizzying
creativity centering on the unusual.

Right away he longed to make her his muse. Her black hair
was like the southern breeze, her body lavished him with familiar

movements, instantly recognizable to his sense of smell, of touch, undulating as if in a carefully choreographed underwater dance: every time she got behind the camera she thrust her hips forward, opening her pelvis; when she stepped away from the camera, her body went back to her strict pose as a prudent, intelligent woman, even slightly pedantic and vain.

Hearing her speak his native tongue, Spanish, he could foresee her panting erotically, picturing his heavy hands on her backside, squeezing it, pinching it red. He quickly conceived how she might become a second mother to him, giving birth to him while consuming him in the sexual act.

Picasso knew and was enormously proud of the fact that she had been the literary model for Georges Bataille, one of Bataille's "deviant lovers," as he later sarcastically described her. However, the Dora and Bataille affair had endured and would endure forever, including in the timeless form of a literary work. No, theirs had not just mere sexual encounters. Dora had conquered the philosopher. As the Spaniard planned to conquer her. He did it, of course, he certainly did: he conquered her, subdued her, so that he could paint her, illuminate her in his paintings and extinguish her light in real life. She succeeded, it's true, in seducing him with her ideas rather than with her thoughts. Because her profound and fervent thinking ended up exhausting him.

Picasso was always well aware that Dora's beauty derived from her effectiveness at enticing people with her ideas first, and only then with her ability to control every attribute of her body and make it the focus of desire. Once she was on the altar, whether it was up on a pedestal where she would set the rules and rebuff every proposition, or on the contrary, later on, down below in the garbage where she would accept the most unimaginable abasements, Dora always was the one who held the power. Her power had to be destroyed.

Dora—he saw this right away—would not be the mother, like Marie-Thérèse, mother to Maya, Picasso's second daughter, nor like the tyrannical Olga. Dora was, at last, the artist; but she was also the matron who remembered him from his halcyon days in the bordellos of Barcelona's Barrio Chino. At first glance she looked like an exotic girl from the south, a mestizo beauty with a fun hint of flippancy, sweet, luscious, eloquent. Mysterious, cultured, and dangerously intuitive. Why not destroy her by weighing her down with all the obnoxiousness he was capable of?

He felt an urgent need to penetrate her world and puzzle it out. Like the time he wanted to puzzle out the soul of that simple gypsy with whom he lived shut up in a cave for a while, the one who later appeared in his paintings as a figure radiating innocence, fiery eroticism, tender wisdom. . . . Picasso realized that one of the characteristics he found most attractive about Dora was the idea that he could relive with her the passionate moments of his intense bucolic fling with a country kid. She was very manly. A real he-man, that woman. Her masculinity bolstered his desire.

There would be time in the future to tell Dora about his fleeting youthful homosexual affair. About how he had yearned to experience everything about sex, how he'd wanted to try everything that piqued the appetite of his desire. But for now she could wait to learn these secrets, he'd confess them to her later on. Dora was this new woman, the one before his eyes right now, and also that boy, that model, who seemed to have escaped from one of his future paintings. The two, joined as one, were perfection itself, Socrates's androgynous being, rolling toward the light.

If Picasso was such an open-minded man, why was she now so strongly opposed to James's homosexuality and his relationship with Bernard? To tell the truth, she didn't mind seeing them together; what bothered her was having to share James on that trip to Venice, the only trip she would ever take with him. Her last trip. Though Bernard showered her with flattery and did everything he could to reassure her that he wouldn't come between her and her friend,

Dora couldn't avoid feeling jealous about the traces of the love relationship the two men had shared.

Nor could she bear imagining them making love, and yet she couldn't help constantly envisioning their naked bodies entwined in the act of love.

That's why she was out so early now, walking around the plaza over and over again, making its oval circuit, trying to push away the image of the young pair, each sucking the other's sex, an image that frequently disturbed her dreams.

Then her mind turned again to the suicide of René Crevel, the young gay poet everyone made fun of, the one who'd been marginalized by most for being homosexual, for being "wimpy," as his most envious rivals put it. And, she told herself, that fascinating and creative era had gone to ruin when they gave in to the Nazis, and again when they ended the savagery and blotted out the horror of Fascism but then, instead of wanting to be free, latched onto the Communist terror. When they traded one brute for another. Did they have any other choice? Yes, the choice of freedom, but once they'd won it, like most young people, they didn't know what to do with it.

Or they did, but they swapped it for debauchery, for an unbridled sexuality that only got them riled with each other and amused the enemy once again. They did not know how to juggle freedom and desire. They couldn't turn sex into poetry. They sullied everything with politics and polemics.

Picasso had probably been more daring than she, because he was able to take sex in a different and more savage way, in a much more vigorous, childish, emotional, abiding way, mingling it with his pleasure at his own courage in toning down his manliness, in sodomizing her, and in becoming a totally sexual being.

Picasso, moreover, awakened amazingly possessive impulses in everyone who met him. We can be so deeply affected by somebody else's courage and talent that we'll instantly succumb to our desperate, agonizing desire to possess him, to appropriate his whole being.

Such was the case of Pere Mañach. Dora was amused by the gripping old stories of ardent pursuits that were attributed to this gay gallery owner. He had offered Picasso lots of money for his work, but in consequence he wouldn't let him alone for a minute. It got so bad Picasso had to pretend he was going to bed with his friend Manuel Hugué and let Mañach catch him there, a thrilling sight for Mañach but rather unexpected for Manuel, in order to get him off his back.

"Dora, hey!" James Lord was waving to her from the door of Saint Mark's Basilica.

She smiled, happy she could witness the spectacle of the young James Lord calling to her from the atrium of the church. He was so close; she wanted to run to him, hug him, tell him everything she had remembered during this long early morning walk. But she held back. No, she shouldn't break the spell woven by the respect she had so painstakingly established between herself and the eternally aspiring writer and artist, whom she had first met while he slept at Picasso's feet as the artist put the finishing touches on one of his finest works: a contemplation of bold and fleeting youth.

Dora was only too aware that James would write about her one day, and she didn't want to mar her image of exquisite and austere good looks, which allowed her to put Surrealism behind her and remake herself as the existential shadow behind the faces in those Man Ray photographs, which no longer had anything to do with her. Because you could say that those faces had been shot precisely so that Picasso would discover her, love her, and paint her. And now none of those stories existed; the multiple versions of her face invented by Man Ray had evaporated. Nothing existed, except in the intimacy of memory. Thinking it over, not even in the sinister promiscuity of recollections. Nothing existed but the paintings in which Picasso had immortalized her.

James was waving tactfully, a tender smile on his lips, just as he had in that little shop in the Parisian neighborhood they shared, the day he met her for the second time in his life.

The shop was barely lit. She turned around with a package she had just bought and tried out a tedious cliché, "So we meet again."

And he replied with the even more trite, "What a surprise."

The absurdity of the cliché did sound less rough and inexpressive than their spontaneous indifference, which spoke volumes.

Impression of the inner life of Dora, 1958. The Bridge of Sighs

But to stop remembering I'd have to kill myself.

Around eleven at night, after dinner, I told James and Bernard I was going for a walk. They wanted to come with me, but I begged them, reluctantly, to let me be alone for a while; besides, I wanted them to get some time together, too, take a walk by themselves, exchange a few words in keeping with their intimate friendship, and enjoy a city they would undoubtedly return to someday, though they would never forget a single detail about Venice from that trip, precisely because they had taken it with me.

I walked toward the Bridge of Sighs, quite near where we were staying. The water flowed dark and oily from the miasma that filled the lagoon. "I'll never share a kiss with the one I love under this bridge, nor make a wish, as the legend suggests," I told myself sadly.

A while later I decided it would be best if I threw myself into the canal and ended it once and for all, but then I thought about my two young friends. It was a selfish decision; they didn't deserve to suffer such an act of melodramatic foolishness. Even the act of dying calls for elegance and, above all, good manners and self-restraint. But could I really want to end my life?

"What would those two do with my body if they found it intact?" I wondered, and almost burst out laughing.

Then they sure wouldn't ever forget our grisly sojourn in Venice.

I was condemned to the doleful reverberation of memories, to continue living under their constant drip, drip, drip, coming more and more often, more stridently, more gut-wrenchingly. Most of my acquaintances expected I would commit suicide after Picasso left. Even Picasso suspected I would. I didn't, and I never will. For the simple, ironic purpose of proving them wrong and not giving the painter the satisfaction. They'd all think I was a miserable wretch if I did. But he's the height of misery, not me. Because he never loved anyone. He didn't know how to love.

When he left me, he transferred the quantum of cruelty he used to invest in crushing me to his work, which was already cruel enough in itself.

All of a sudden, a shadow caught my eye. The dark form glided, or so it seemed to me, from the entrance to an alley, along the edge of the canal, and up to the stone balustrade where I was standing. It spread its arms, which transformed into two immense white wings. It was an angel, or a sprite, I thought. When it stepped into the light, I realized it was a man wearing a tuxedo with a pair of immense blue wings fixed to the back and a mask covered with white sequins.

"Who are you? What do you want with me?" I asked, pointedly.

"I'm going as Marlene Dietrich. It's Carnival, didn't you know?"

"Well, you don't look much like Marlene Dietrich. And you're lying, it isn't Carnival," I added, teasingly.

"Of course I do, I look just like her, at least the tux. It's the same one she wore in the film *The Moroccans*. I had to take off so much weight to fit into it. But no matter, doesn't make any difference. All that matters is keeping up appearances. . . ." The man ran away from me along the waterfront, and in the distance I saw him duck through the door of a palazzo flecked with flamingo-pink paint.

I can't conjure up the image of an angel without thinking back to Max Jacob and the heyday of Le Bateau-Lavoir in Montmartre, at 13 Rue Ravignan, where so many artists lived and painted, where poor Fernande Olivier became Picasso's model and his lover. Yet nowadays most of the people who go on pilgrimages to that narrow, eloquent space think of it as nothing but Picasso's shrine and studio.

It's true that Picasso lived and worked there, but he did so as one among many artists who were joining forces, all with the common objective of creating and changing the direction of art. It was there, though, that Picasso also took off on a seemingly frivolous tack in his painting: his Rose Period. For a man as rough and coarse as Picasso seemed to be, the Rose Period was when a brashly feminine world burst into his art. Perhaps it came from the woman who showed up and turned him into a severe Iberian male, Fernande Olivier, who truly initiated him in the role of the untamable macho, mounting women like a bull, snorting and foaming, in extended amorous group attacks, in orgies, where her beauty stood out among the vulgar attractions of the other young women.

Max Jacob was an angel, a *duende*, a sprite; Picasso was right to call him that, suddenly so poetic that the words sounded suspiciously evasive on his lips. Max loved the Spaniard and the Spaniard loved Max, without any doubt, but in the long term Picasso could be faithful only in his relationships with form and color, perhaps more clear-cut than his friendships in the muddied waters of love, which blinded him. Max Jacob brought him to Le Bateau-Lavoir when he could no longer keep him in his garret.

Picasso was afraid of that angel's love. Picasso was simply afraid of the sprite and didn't even take the future consequences of his fear into account. For even if Max Jacob was an angel, which he metaphorically was, he was above all a mortal creature, however immortal he was as a poet, the greatest poet, Lorca's *duende*, the very spirit of art. And there was no reason for Max to have been sent into that horror, into that threshold of hell at Drancy, final stop: Auschwitz, when he could have been rescued if his old friend had been quick and decisive instead of solemn and metaphorical; Drancy, a place from which he couldn't fly, where he died tortured and ailing, his wings incinerated.

One evening we spoke about Max Jacob. Picasso rarely did so with me, he avoided mentioning the unhappiness and suffering that

Max represented in his life, a subject on which I think he was more forthcoming with the underhanded Sabartés. And on this occasion he avoided talking about the moment when the German police took Max away, preferring to glorify the old times when he and Max met Guillaume Apollinaire and they eked out an abject living, smoking opium and misspending their youth, which was their greatest treasure then.

Jaime Sabartés was a fairly subdued man, as I've said before and want to emphasize. Sabartés only came to life when he was flattering the Master and when the Master deigned to give him his infrequent thanks. His faithful Sabartés.

What did I learn from how others reacted to the acclaimed Master? Picasso was also a great master for me, even though artistically I was a Surrealist from the start; I learned from him the true mystery of painting: that it is music, that it is literature. I learned, and I truly appreciate all the people who scorned me, because they inspired me to aim higher and higher. Though on the other hand, when they continually abused me they thought they were honoring Picasso. One of them was Sabartés.

I quit photography because the Great Genius wanted it that way, because Picasso hinted imperiously that I should, as if he were giving an order: my way or nothing, my way or the abyss. And so he suggested the idea to me because, according to him, he wanted to make me a great artist. Photography or painting. Photography or Picasso. Personally, I don't know but that I was already a great artist. Yes, perhaps I was, most likely I was. At least, others thought so, the others thought I had been great before I got together with him. And one of those who thought so was Max Jacob. However, what I really wanted to achieve was exactly and precisely along the lines of what Picasso also wanted me to achieve, what he dreamed of for me.

He almost surely left me because I didn't meet his expectations. I didn't produce the creative impression, the atmosphere of perseverance from being near him, that he expected of me.

My world fell apart the first time I wept in front of Picasso over something less than poetic; that was when I ceased to be the lover, the mother, the companion, and was reduced to the weeping woman. "Reduced" is just a way of putting it; actually he exalted me by imagining me as invariably tearful, endlessly weepy.

From then on, my presence always suggested a chain of events to him related to weeping, nothing about me interested him but my tears and my blood, not even my naked body. He soon began to lose interest altogether in my body, stopped nibbling greedily on my sharp breasts as he loved to do when we first met, turned away from the jet-black mound of my pelvis, except when my menstrual blood flowed.

Picasso yearned to see me cry again and again, again and again, endlessly; tears and blood, my cheeks and the bull writhing in the sand, death throes and blood clots. Picasso spat words like daggers, like darts, trying to hurt me, only to paint me unharmed, recreating the shock of the event on canvas. My tears became diamonds, and I gladly gave them afterwards to all the women he courted. My tears soon sold at higher prices than the most sought-after jewels in the famous salons of Paris and in art circles all over the world.

People are always ready to pay for prurience. Everything that humanity has ever sold, disguised as art, has been sheer, sick prurience. This is why I ran away from all that greed, which I neither wish nor am able to call "art." This is the real reason for my isolation, my abstinence, my bitterness, my one-way journey to worshiping the god of the unmentionable, a genuine god. After Picasso, only God. And me? No, I no longer exist.

Long-awaited conversations, and a dream about the painter Jorge Camacho

About a year and a half ago I visited the painters Jorge and Margarita Camacho. I told them I was writing about Dora Maar and Picasso. We shared a lot of laughs over anecdotes that Jorge recounted about Picasso and Wifredo Lam. I was convinced Picasso had fallen in love with the half-Chinese, half-black Cuban painter, devilishly brilliant as an artist and complicated as a human being. Camacho roared with laughter, but he was doubtful. I think it was one of the best conversations I ever had with Camacho, the Surrealist painter, one of the first Surrealists and one of the last. "Surrealism still goes on, though, it will never end," Margarita reminded me. Camacho knew that the alchemy of art derives from laughter, and he knew how to laugh, being a fine alchemist throughout his life, and now in death as well.

Several months after that mirth-filled visit, Camacho fell ill. I visited him two or three more times. Then he got so sick he couldn't even bear to let friends visit. He didn't want us to see the state he was in. Margarita took care of him to the end, and she respected his wish to let no one see him in his weakened condition.

Camacho died. The death of a friend in this mournful exile adds still more terror to the delirium tremens that has seized hold of me.

I took three pills and fell asleep. When what I really wanted was to fall dead, but I lacked the courage.

Dora Maar, naked, handed me a bar of soap.

My mother, naked, held out an apricot for me in her chapped and trembling hand.

Jorge Camacho, hiding behind some trees at Los Pajares, peered out, smiled, walked away toward a salt dune, far off, blurry.

I woke up two days later, needing to drink water, lots of water. My throat was parched and my eyes were glued shut from a conjunctivitis I had contracted in my sleep.

I went to the kitchen; on the way there I bumped into the ghost of the writer Emilia Bernal, muttering one of her poems. For an instant my fingers caught hers, she squeezed my hand tight.

We looked into each other's eyes, smiling in amazement.

Early the next morning I phoned Miriam Gómez in London, who told me she was still working on the *Complete Works* of her husband, Guillermo Cabrera Infante, and that she'd just read the Romanian translation of his novel *The Fickle Nymph*.

"You know Romanian?" I asked her.

"No, but it's very easy to read." A typically brilliant riposte from Miriam Gómez.

I hung up with Miriam and then got a call from Juan Abreu, phoning me from Barcelona to ask me to send him my photo, saying he wanted to do my portrait. "I'm too old and ugly for that," I told him. But he insisted.

I had a terrible case of insomnia. I didn't feel like doing anything. I went back to the books about Dora Maar.

For years I've watched American movies late at night. "It's better than paying for a shrink," Miriam Gómez assured me. No doubt about it. Old Japanese films, too.

At midday, invariably, I was taken by the idea that I ought to kill myself, but five minutes later I'd be filled with a squeamish love for life. "Besides, only frothing mad writers kill themselves," I would tell myself, losing heart. Or brave writers. Am I a coward?

I picked up yet another book about Communism and totalitarian states, and forget it, the same old stuff. That sharp pain, piercing my whole head, refusing to withdraw its talons from my brain, sinking into my nerves.

Mamá appeared again; she was angry, visibly upset, because I hadn't visited her grave in the Père Lachaise cemetery, because I hadn't brought her flowers on that special day, her birthday. "You didn't even bring me a tangerine," she complained; much less did I bathe her with rum the way she likes to be bathed, that is, I didn't sprinkle rum across the marble tombstone I had placed over her grave. Pink marble that cost about as much as a condo in Miami. But Mami always wanted a high-class tombstone. I would have preferred the condo, like anyone else, but that wasn't what God had in store for me. God, or whoever.

That's how things go with my dead mother. And my life with Dora Maar. Nocturnal, rough, eventful.

My life with friends and with spirits.

Yesterday I had lunch with Laure de Graumont, at her house, only steps from 29 Rue d'Astorg.

You know what 29 Rue d'Astorg is now? Offices. At night, shadows and ghosts. Vaulted rooms, filled with bundles of soulless reports and wandering forlorn spirits.

I took three more pills, it's become a habit, taking pills on the sly, it's the only way I can get through the day and sleep through the night. I chew them up and spit them out. I don't swallow them, just the saliva juice and that chalky residue that sticks like sediment to the roof of your mouth.

I redid my library, but just the sight of it made me cry. It'll all end so soon, it'll all die with me. It's a complex method of encouraging yourself.

"Shall we go to the lakeshore soon?" the spirit of Emilia Bernal asked me early the other morning.

"No, Emilia, we'll go back to the island."

"The island? God forbid!" She almost vomited and got such a dizzy spell she just about toppled over on me.

"Yeah, you're right, God forbid!" I answered resignedly, while holding her up and fanning her with one of Dulce María Loynaz's fans.

She recovered and, hiding behind a curtain, lit a lantern, and after a while I heard her broken voice recite or read a poem she had written more than half a century ago:

> Oh, I'll make you a boat of my dreams,
> light as a bundle of wicker sticks.
> My love will make you a lullaby song
> to the soft-strumming beat of the waves
> when the night, kissed by breezes from land,
> gently cradles the boat to the shore.

"I'm an exile," she murmured, "like it or not. Just like you."

Free will and Surrealist dreams, April 2011

Los Pajares. Margarita and Jorge Camacho's country home. Jorge is dressed in white, wearing a linen suit, impeccably white, just as he'd been when he introduced the Andalusian singer María Faraco, who sang boleros at a flamenco club in Almonte.

Yet I knew that Jorge was no longer with us. All that was left of him was his open hand waving us goodbye in a strange photocopied photograph that Margarita had shown to me. Jorge had only recently died.

Ricardo and I asked for some water. We had just gotten in after a long drive from Paris to Los Pajares, and we were tired and thirsty. Jorge told us of the marvelous oranges that Los Pajares produced. Suddenly, he invited us to go out, or go in, depending on how you view the angles in that dreamlike architectural limbo, through a doorway aglow with radiant light.

Jorge Camacho moved off and was slowly lost to sight, disappearing in the intense luminosity from that entrance, or exit.

I followed him, with my eyes at first, then ran after him. Ricardo stayed to talk with Margarita, who was squeezing juicy oranges in the kitchen.

Then, before my eyes, one of the most beautiful landscapes I've ever seen appeared: a grove full of splendid orange trees, the ground entirely covered with succulent, fleshy, fragrant oranges in hues ranging from golden red to bright yellow. Jorge was signaling me to follow him while he kept moving forward, slowly, through the grove. The sky was a sumptuous, brilliant blue; the sun looked like a grapefruit cut in half.

After a while, Jorge sat on the ground with his legs crossed, Zen-style; he peeled one of the oranges with his thick, twisted fingers, deformed by his brushes and dried out from turpentine, and started to suck on it as he delivered an Aristotelian discourse for me, linked it to fragments of Aristophanes's *Lysistrata*, and finished off with a description of the gorgeous face in Leonardo da Vinci's *Lady with an Ermine*.

I was sleeping next to a horse, my arms around his lustrous, thick neck, my sweat-drenched face sunken into the animal's mane. His name was Jade. We were lying down in the middle of a field; I was wearing riding pants and boots, a white long-sleeved blouse, and a long brown leather jacket. It was biting cold, the rising sun could barely warm the air, dew still dripped from the green grass. Jade sighed deeply, whinnied, and all at once leapt to his feet.

It took me a while to catch up. The two of us, the horse and I, are at the bank of a river.

It was a dream in the past tense that shifted suddenly to the present.

Jade drinks thirstily, stops, looks up at me, and I'd almost say he's happy to see me.

He's all I have in this world: this horse with his chestnut mane and coat. And this sense of absolute belonging, my human sense of ownership, makes me feel that he and I should soon undertake a long journey together.

Jade grazes on the lawn and scans the horizon from time to time.

I strip off my clothes and dive into the crystalline water. It's icy cold. When I get out, I run back and forth to air dry myself. I'm freezing. I dress hurriedly. My breakfast is a few almonds and apples I pick up off the ground.

Jade trots up to me, by my side, right next to my body, and sways his hips to show that he wants me to ride him. I jump on, bareback. The horse begins the journey, slowly at first, then at a stately gallop.

His measured and elegant stride turns into a frenetic race through a vast, unending forest.

At last we come to a village. This village transforms into a series of narrow streets. On one of these streets stands a low building with a balcony. My mother's balcony. There's Mamá, young, so lovely, in her freshly-ironed white blouse and the black skirt she used to wear to work at the Estrella Oriental restaurant. She wears her hair cut short, and there's no makeup on her face.

"Sweetie, you're back at last. But with a horse? What are you doing with a horse?"

"He's mine, Mamá. I thought he was all I had left, I thought I'd lost you, but I see you're here, waiting for me. C'mon, throw me down the key!" That's what I always shouted up to her when I got back in the wee hours after a long night of youthful partying.

"People think mothers will always be waiting for them, but sometimes it doesn't work like that. . . ." She grabs and tosses me a rusty key.

I turn it in the lock. I push the creaking door open. I run up the stairs two at a time. My best friend opens the door for me. Mama is already lying down. I give her a kiss. She is cold. The room is filled with an unbearable smell, the stench of embalming fluids.

I step out to the balcony. Jade hasn't moved from where I left him, under the flowering vines; someone has hitched a ramshackle wooden cart to him.

I go back inside; Ena helps me pick up Mamá. We carry her downstairs. I place her in the cart. Ena clambers up next to her.

I make a signal, a thin whistle escapes my lips, and Jade understands it's time to start moving.

And once more his slow, dry hoofbeats echo in the dusty lane; then we're trotting at a faster pace, and after a while the trotting turns into an unbridled gallop.

Night falls, leaden, starless. I don't know how I've survived so many nights without seeing the stars in the firmament.

Jade slows his pace; we're climbing a rocky crag. My whole body feels heavy, I'm so tired I'm nodding off. A booming crash awakes me: the cart has slipped from the tether and is hurtling off the cliff. Jade turns round and runs down the precipice in the direction the cart has fallen.

There, in the middle of that valley, I lie down next to Mamá, so warm now. I'm the one who's shivering, frozen, at this moment.

My closest friend has now become a little girl lost in the woods, clinging to a stuffed rabbit.

Jade's black eye spreads into a murky tide that floods the valley.

The painter dips his finger into the thick, dark puddle, draws the silhouette of a horse ridden by an orphan girl.

The rider's face is bathed in tears.

The man washed his hands under the water streaming from the sink, scrubbed them well, shook them dry in the air, and set about meticulously reorganizing his brushes. Before turning to face us, he stood fascinated by a new figure that had appeared where the paint was peeling away from the wall. He shaped it with a thumbnail, stripping off a bit more paint; now it looked like an insect, a small spider.

He was wearing a white cotton T-shirt, wide knee-length shorts, and white espadrilles; it was summer in Paris. In the adjoining bedroom, from which you could see into the room where he was painting, Paul Éluard, the "Milk Princess" (as he called his model), and Dora were waiting. Éluard observed, smiling, seated on a chair, his lascivious grin stretching his face into a gaunt mask.

The painter walked around the room several times, opening and closing a window, and turned to face the bed. It seemed like Nusch's naked body was floating among the sheets; he loved Nusch's face, but her body not so much. He preferred Dora's body, its precise curves, sculpted by shamelessness. A crude terracotta figurine. Nusch was all bones, a bag of bones; when he embraced her and jumped on her, he felt like he was going to break her, that she'd be encased in the embroidered linens like a fossil in a rock. He also found it hard to paint her body; he didn't know which angle of her bony humanity to begin with, yet her face, so precise with those sharpened angles and hollows, evoked perfection. He moved toward her. Nusch half-closed her eyes, but he presumed that, deep down, she was looking at Paul and Éluard was looking at her.

He easily whipped his sex out from his broad pants; he had long detested taking off his clothes, but he had no other choice but to do it and he hoped all this would be over with quickly. He, who had once so reveled in the languid ceremony of stripping off clothes and who used to take advantage of his frequent nakedness without a trace of shame, now could only manage to take out his penis and begin to masturbate hastily. Éluard made a gesture, gave a command, and Nusch obediently sat on the bed with her legs doubled under her. A second gesture from Paul, and then she opened her legs, displaying the delicate, rosy depth between her thighs.

The painter took Dora by the hand and started to undress her, her black dress slipped from her body and fell to the floor, she stepped forth, slowly and precisely, from the circle of dress where it lay puddled, first one foot, then the other. She wore no underwear. Only thin stockings held up by lace garters.

Dora naked, essential and exuberant, swelling in the painter's eyes, her breasts firm, her nipples thick and engorged, her belly timidly bulging, her thighs white and fleshy, her knees prominent, her legs straight and sculpted, her crossed ankles fitting inside the painter's huge fist, her feet small, as well as her hands, which could be crammed halfway inside the man's mouth. He pushed her gently toward Nusch.

She kissed the other woman's lips; they tasted like honey, like strawberries; the painter interrupted the kiss by caressing the breasts of the Milk Princess. Dora contemplated this fevered caress with a glazed expression. Picasso glanced at Paul, who quickly looked away. Now he was starting to touch his privates through his pants.

Dora lay down next to Nusch, and they joined their bodies together. They rubbed their mounds and breasts together. Picasso pulled Dora aside, kissed Nusch on the lips, only to then thrust his powerful, thick penis into her; the woman let out soft moans of pleasure and, from time to time, turned her head and let her vacant gaze rest on Paul: the focus of her attention was him, her paramount attraction was Paul. Nothing was more important than her universe, and for her the universe was named Paul Éluard.

Dora remained off to the side. Picasso cared only about Nusch; Paul wouldn't care for her, either, he never took an active role. Her friend Nusch's heart beat only for Éluard. Picasso pulled out from Nusch's sex and went after Dora's breasts.

She felt the painter's acrid breath on her neck, pinched his nipples, he slapped her breasts, she raised her hands to protect them, her eyes filling with tears, yet she did not flinch from his gaze. Picasso's face was turning into a black, hairy snout, the Minotaur's snout, his hands transforming into bristling, hairy hooves. His erect purple penis then thrust again and again into her violet-red vulva, more and more, accelerating in tempo, faster and faster. The Minotaur bellowed. Dora panted and wordlessly drank in the copious tears coursing down her cheeks. Nusch masturbated while watching them. Paul had moved his chair to the edge of the bed, but, vacillating, could not make up his mind to join in.

The Minotaur assaulted that beautiful, smooth undulating body with tremendous, seismic force. Dora started to emit odd, almost bovine sounds from deep in her throat, without taking her eyes off the man. The Minotaur panted more and more thickly, as if he were running lost in the woods, while also yelling obscenities in Spanish. Dora began to smile, though still whimpering; her bouncing breasts compulsively aroused the man. Dora stretched out her hand, placed it on Nusch's clitoris, starting to massage the sweet spot with frenzy. Nusch writhed her bony body between the sheets, moaning less and less timidly with pleasure.

Picasso held himself more tightly to Dora, sliding his hands under her body and grabbing her backside, which she never ceased to sway. At last the man let loose a deafening yell, and his colossal chest shivered in strange convulsions; he released a long, abundant ejaculation inside Dora. He stayed on top of her a while, then removed himself. His lover kept her serious stare fixed on him, the trace of a smile gone from her face. They kissed on the lips, and he fell to his side like a heavy bundle.

Dora and Nusch continued kissing each other, caressing each other's breasts, locking their thighs together; at last, they both reached orgasm with gentle and no less perfidious delight.

Paul stopped masturbating; a large, wet stain appeared on the front of his trousers inside a slimy halo.

Both women got up and went off to bathe each other. Together, they got into the old copper tub. Paul lay down beside Picasso.

The painter felt uncomfortable having the poet there, but he didn't move. Soon enough, both were sleeping soundly.

Outside night was falling; the heat wave had withered the rose bushes, and the geraniums were drooping in the pots that hung from the balcony.

Picasso passed his hand over his sweaty brow, gritted his jaw, uttered a few words, grumbled and cursed—sometimes in Spanish, sometimes in Catalan—though he seemed deep asleep.

Meanwhile, Nusch and Dora were drying their bodies, getting dressed, combing their hair, and deciding which restaurant to go to for dinner later.

Dora was sad, though she couldn't put her finger on the reasons why. Or perhaps she could sense those reasons but preferred not to discuss them with her friend. Éluard loved Nusch, which did not prevent him from sharing his wife with Picasso. Picasso liked his friends' wives and had no qualms about going to bed with them. In the same way, Marcelle, whom he called Eva, the wife of the painter Marcoussis, had slept and lived with him for a period. He had also made Alice Princet, Derain's wife, his lover. Eva Govel died from tuberculosis.

Was Picasso faithful to Dora? She couldn't even opt for doubt. No, he wasn't, and he never would be.

But for his part, Picasso wouldn't have stood for the slightest infidelity, not even a thought of it, nothing sexual involving any man, though perhaps with women it would be all right; well, as long as he was present and, of course, a major part of the threesome, the orgy.

A maritime face. Venice, 1958

"You have the most beautiful eyes I have ever seen."

The young fellow, in an impeccable white suit, Panama hat, and two-toned shoes, sat down next to her in the garden of that other great patron of the arts in the era of Marie-Laure de Noailles, Peggy Guggenheim. The man's only purpose was to whisper this little nothing into her ear. She smiled affably. He murmured the compliment again, and again her smile curved, even more affable. The stranger realized that this obliging gesture was the most he would ever get from his efforts at flirtation, so he stood up, walked over to the Henry Moore sculpture, turned around, observed the woman through the hole in the middle of the bronze, then walked away disappointed.

Dora also took off walking.

She looked around for the two men with her, who had gotten lost somewhere inside the Guggenheim house; she wished they'd seen how, in spite of her age, she could still attract and win the hearts of fine-looking young men, even one as comfortably well-off as her fleeting and intrusive beau, to judge by his fine clothes and polite manners. Nevertheless, whenever a man flirted with her she couldn't help thinking of Picasso.

Had she really won Picasso's heart? Yes, the first few years, despite his involvements with all those stunning women, until she got it into her mind to photograph the great artistic, social, and political event that was *Guernica*. Without saying so, Picasso would never forgive the photographic report she did on this work, no matter how much he owed her for her advice and her experience as a Surrealist photographer and painter. The first piece of photo-journalism ever published on a work of art was Dora's report on his masterpiece, but as far as he was concerned, that petty detail, bah! what did he care! It only hurt him, since her report exposed his hes-itations, the mistakes that, in his own view, he kept committing; in the opinions of others they only made his work more valuable, but in his eyes they made him feel ridiculous, mired in his own doubts. Even though figuring out which way to go next was his true motive for always searching, always discovering, always finding new things.

Then again, could she have won James Lord's heart? She couldn't be sure; nothing proved that this was a genuine love conquest. James was possessed by a homoerotic fascination with Picasso, and it was abundantly clear that his obsession consumed him. She had decided, only a short while ago, to take charge of the young American's education and refinement, thinking she ought to initiate him into a demanding Parisian art education, nothing like whatever he'd learned in a backward little town like Engle-wood, New Jersey, James's hometown. And in a certain way this would turn her into his accidental dominatrix, because on top of everything else she was considered merely his platonic mistress, given the situation of the relationship into which she had begun to invest so much.

And much later, adding to the mix, there was Bernard. In Ber-nard's case, enchantment was undeniably slow in coming, but when it did begin to appear, it was respectable and stable. In a very short time their tastes and feelings were entirely in sync, but she could only be interested in Bernard as a friend or, rather, as a passing acquaintance. A deep friendship could turn into a bigger commit-ment than a love affair, even more possessive and uncomfortable; and she'd already adopted the wise old Argentine proverb, "A lone-some ox can lick itself just fine," which is to say, you're better off on your own than saddled with boring company.

Dora got up and walked around the garden. None other than Bernard joined her. He walked with her in silence, as curious and talkative as he always was; he seemed distressed. The afternoon turned gray, and an agreeable breeze kicked up off the water. Dora's eyes also turned leaden.

"Where've you left James?"

"He's off taking notes about a Juan Gris painting," Bernard lied. In fact, James had stayed behind chatting with some young high-society Venetian women he'd just met, whom he'd already invited to come to Paris, an exchange Bernard had witnessed and found absolutely ridiculous.

"Oh, Juan Gris. Picasso couldn't stand him, did everything he could to destroy him." Dora observed with rapt attention some birds winging across the sky. "Like a bird of prey. Yes, he could be an eagle, a vulture, could sink his talons, peck away till blood flowed. . . . He treated Braque badly, called him Madame Braque, constantly made fun of him, still boasts that 'Braque was the woman who loved me most.' And Braque got back at him by saying that 'Picasso used to be a great artist, but now he's just a genius.' Deep down they adored each other."

Bernard burst out laughing. "Why do you always talk about him, about them all, as if it happened in some distant past?"

Dora looked at Bernard, surprised. "Perhaps because I've already moved on to the future."

Another heartfelt laugh from Bernard startled the little birds in a nearby grove into flight.

"Do you know when Picasso met Max Jacob? The year was 1901, it was his first exhibition in Ambroise Vollard's gallery. Picasso always thought of himself as a poet, and it was Jacob who introduced him to French poetry. The next year, in spite of the poverty that poets are supposed to put up with on their own, Picasso moved into the maid's room at his apartment on Rue Voltaire. Max Jacob even gave him his own bed. Picasso painted by night and slept by day. Max did the opposite. He stayed there for two years. Until Max acquired the Montmartre atelier at 13 Rue Ravignan for that bunch of painters who went around like beggars. André Salmon and Max Jacob were the ones who named it Le Bateau-Lavoir."

"Max truly loved him. Loved Picasso," Bernard remarked.

"Of course he did, he moved into a fleabag flat at number 7 Rue Ravignan, in the back of a courtyard, just to be near Picasso. Max lived an incredibly miserable life there, and that was also where the face of God appeared to him, on one of the walls of that flat. Years later, in 1915, the Jewish poet converted to Roman Catholicism and asked Picasso to be his godfather at his baptism. After Max Jacob's death, a few of his friends and I arranged a religious service for him at the church of Saint-Roch. Picasso stayed outside, didn't want to come in. He's never wanted to have any contact with death."

"What's *Guernica*, then?"

"Everything, except death."

"War?" Bernard asked, perplexed.

"War, life. But never death."

Suddenly, Dora thought she heard Picasso's laughter, that whinnying horse laugh he would let loose in the most unexpected places. There was a time when the artist drank a lot of wine and Anís del Mono; he also smoked hashish around the clock and split his sides laughing at any fool thing, in thunderous guffaws, until his bull neck swelled up and his heartburn made him weep, but in acute pain, and his breath smelled like vomit.

One time he vomited blood, picked up a paintbrush, and without skipping a beat started painting on canvas, using his own blood and the chunks puked up from his stomach to draw a face of Christ that melded with the image of Max Jacob.

"Did you know that Max saw Christ's face in a stain on the wall? Or are you tired of listening to me?"

"I'd heard something," Bernard mumbled.

"It happened on June 7, 1909, right when he decided to convert from Judaism to Catholicism. Picasso immediately agreed to be the godfather. Communists always end up clinging to God, and Picasso couldn't do otherwise."

Bernard made a show of being interested to hear more of the story she told so resolutely; he walked close by her side, entranced by her voice. Dora was carrying a silk handkerchief in one hand, and when she gestured it fluttered between her face and Bernard's shoulder.

"I also began to love God, just like Max, and I began to have faith through astrology. Yes, I've followed the same path Max Jacob took. There's nothing closer to one of Picasso's paintings than an astrological chart; faith, belief, science, poetry. . . ."

Bernard saw James in the distance, next to a tree, talking with some fairly good-looking guy. The young man handed him a scrap of paper on which he'd written something.

"What does it feel like to be known forever as Picasso's mistress?" Bernard asked, mouth quivering, staring all the while at the spot where his friend was exchanging all too friendly glances with this young stranger.

"As I've said before, I wasn't Picasso's *maîtresse*; he was my *maître*." Her wordplay was wonderful: in French, *maîtresse* means both "mistress" or "lover" and "dominant woman," while *maître* means "teacher" or "dominant man." *Domador de fiera furiosa en una feria*. Terrible tiger tamer under the big top. Now she was the one who laughed at the Spanish tongue-twister that had just popped into her head.

Bernard's tall, ungainly figure came to a halt. He lowered his gaze and fixed his eyes on hers. He realized he was looking at the most enigmatic of faces: a maritime face. The face of a middle-aged woman who'd been through rough seas, a face where the only trace left by those passing storms were the tracks of tears cried in solitude, tiny rivulets sprung from eyes whose lashes always seemed moist, shining. A woman alone, immaculate, painted and erased by the same artist who had created her like a major work of art.

"Was there no way to escape him?" Bernard asked.

Dora became aware that something was bothering Bernard. Finally, she saw what it was: James was going off with a very attractive, vigorous stranger.

"No, Bernard, no one escapes Picasso, ever. No one can resist him. No one dares attack him, either. His legend, his 'black magic,' will always protect him." She took him by the arm, as if pulling him aside to let him in on a secret. "Don't torture yourself, take some friendly advice, it's never worth torturing yourself."

She slipped the handkerchief around her neck and took hold of Bernard's arm.

From the distance, James noticed the pair of them; he said goodbye to the young man and walked toward his friends.

It started to drizzle; they rushed through narrow streets, the windstorm made a mess of her hair, and the blasts of rain lashed their bodies. In less than ten minutes it became a torrential downpour. They ran for shelter into the church of San Gregorio.

Bernard straggled a bit behind while James and Dora explored inside the sanctuary; he pulled out a small notebook and wrote:

Dora Maar is a great, underappreciated woman. No man has been able to love her as she deserves. James may know more about her than she does herself, because he's an expert appraiser of high-value artworks, and Dora is one, but he won't be able to stay with her to the end, either. He isn't prepared for such an undertaking. She's alone, and alone she'll remain. Picasso has turned her into an incurable recluse. I wouldn't be surprised if she turns out badly in the end, a madwoman or a saint, locked up in a madhouse or a nunnery. That is, if the nuns dared to take her in. Perhaps she won't ever be. . . . No, she isn't the sort to take her own life.

It began to drizzle, thunder boomed off rooftops and domes, and the wind whistled as it slipped through the fissures of the stained-glass windows.

Dora knelt before the altar; she seemed to be praying.

Nothing, no one. Venice, 1958

I'd like to think that what poisoned us was politics, the bad company that comes with politics and relying on ideology; the idée fixe of becoming "ideologues." Maybe, too, we were very immature, victims of our desire to be seen in public as, not so much lovers, rather as accomplices, despite all the complications of Picasso's life, and later on, much later on, to yearn for the possibility of fleeing in terror.

Picasso couldn't take any sort of criticism. I was always criticizing him, and that put him in a very bad mood. Other than the High Priestess, the writer Gertrude Stein, no one was allowed to criticize him. She, the *mamma* of every artist and writer in vogue during that "crazy time," was the best situated to put each of them in his proper place: she would send this one down the drain or place that one on a well-deserved pedestal, depending on how each one rated. She handled Ernest Hemingway with ease, however she deemed fit, and she joked and made sweet talk with Picasso or told him off based on her frame of mind. I can say, without fear being mistaken, that Stein was utterly unpredictable. She could allow herself the luxury of sneering at his genius—the genius of the Great Genius!—and of calling him a bad poet in front of everyone, of humiliating him from A to Z when Picasso took to writing. More than to writing; he took to cobbling verses that sprang from his pain and his disappointment in love, especially after he was free from the extreme duress that Olga Khokhlova, his first wife and the mother of Paulo, his first-born son, put him through and had time to write.

"You haven't suffered enough," Gertrude Stein asserted, "or the verses you've written aren't good enough for us to believe you've really suffered from love. You can't paint like Picasso and write like any old Pablo," the incomparable high priestess of the whip-like Word told him point blank. "The Russian ballerina isn't worthy of your inspiration, or you aren't worthy of the suffering she's caused you, or else not even she has made you suffer enough to chasten you as a husband and glorify you as a poet."

Gertrude Stein didn't beat around the bush.

Indeed, Olga gave Picasso nothing, not even a grief worthy of his majestic art, nor did her body inspire a single brush stroke worth his trouble; as a model, she was plenty conventional, as he often commented in annoyance.

As conventional as a classical ballerina can be who doesn't believe in her abilities and whose only aspiration as an artist is not to break the mold. What Picasso asked of us as women was to give up being conventional, to push ourselves and go beyond our limits, to leave off being women and to become paintings, immortal works of art, Surrealist girls. We had to dance barefoot for him on sharp rocks, while savagely wounding our feet. We made his hangman's job easy.

"Olga is a nobody. She set about turning into a nobody; little by little she faded away. I'm terrified of people like her, of the nobodies who could invade the planet, nobody it, undermine it," he murmured, passed out in my arms, one afternoon in the Luxembourg Garden when he was of a mind to reveal gloomy aspects of his relationships with women to me. The only one he didn't talk about was Marie-Thérèse Walter, the Vestal Mother.

Logging a windstorm in his logbook

The rain suddenly stopped. Bernard left off writing in his notebook and, feeling overwhelmed, set out to look for James. Both of them ended up waiting for me at the entrance to the church under the lintel of its solid, ancient doorway. I would have stayed there forever if I could; it had been years since I experienced the peace I felt there.

We set off walking together again. I was beginning to get a taste for walking by Bernard's side, in between the two of them. A salty mist rose from the waterfront; the mix of rainwater and canal water emitted a bogus odor, like bruised blueberries, and my senses dissolved into the damp blur of dusk.

Later, James and Bernard opted to go back to the hotel with the excuse that they needed to plan their time. In fact, I suspected they were dying to be alone, to kiss ravenously, to make love and lavish each other with affection. I'd seen it in their eyes, in the looks they gave each other, looks that left me out.

But let's imagine it were true, that they really needed to plan their time and log their hours in a logbook, in the small blue date-book Bernard carried with him: what sense does that make?

It's not my style. I've long had all the time in the world at my disposal, I don't succumb easily to the boredom of daily life, I'm not interested in cramming my life into neat compartments or pigeon-holing my existence on graph paper with the sole aim of propelling myself into an absurd headlong cosmic rush to the end.

In any case, if there's anything that truly slips through our fingers, it's life, the time we spend living, which is why we should at least pretend that our obsession for planning and organizing torments us as little as is possible. No matter how much we insist on filling our lives with content, we'll find ourselves equally emptied of content in that last dreadful or liberating moment of death.

I walked the waterfront, the waves in the Venetian canal bringing to mind that stroll along the beach in the south of France my first time there with Picasso.

We had talked in Spanish, he with an irrepressible Andalusian accent that he cranked up whenever he wanted, and I making do with my grouchy Argentine accent. Sometimes I'd throw in a few Castilian pronunciations, which would get on Picasso's nerves because he'd think I was making fun of him.

In the course of that stroll I became vaguely aware of the existence of Marie-Thérèse and little Maya, a tedious and disagreeable child, too mature for her age, who became more spiritual over the years. We all knew about Olga and his first child. I say I became "vaguely aware" because, instead of telling me straight and laying his cards on the table, he hemmed and hawed. Besides, to be honest, the less I knew about his entanglements the better. I wanted to stay out of the whole mess.

I didn't want to know anything about either of them, much less get into anyone else's business, even less untangle the tightly woven love tales of this man who loved prancing about, acting like a sultan, so proud of his harem of passionate and well-loved females. My attention was entirely focused on him, his brilliance, his art, and his way of expressing his love, so unromantic yet profoundly idyllic and passionate beside the course exterior that characterized him. I was his sultana, the noble overseer of his harem. At least that's what he led me to believe for a while.

There were few times when I was as conscious of what I was looking for as on that beach stroll in the south of France, as aware as I was then of what I had found in Picasso's persona: this man shredded my idea of what it meant to submit blindly, totally, exclusively to another person; he changed me in every sense, made me into someone else. I threw myself obediently at his feet. And I imagined that this was the notion that everyone else, the people I admired and tried to emulate, all the Surrealists (myself included), had of grand artistic love.

Though I wanted Picasso to mold me when it came to love, in the field of ideas I valued my independence too highly.

After a few months of living together off and on, politics came between us, as was then the fashion in the Surrealist camp. I was one of the women who started him on it, I admit; perhaps I let myself get carried away by my desire to be accepted as a serious, intelligent woman, firm in my convictions and thoughtful. What I didn't know was that Picasso loathed politics and, deep down, women who thought for themselves. It was my own fault, I repeat, I was the one who dragged him onto the battlefield of ideologies. Before I entered his life, he had only flirted foppishly with the Communists, but he flatly rejected all commitments to any ideology.

Others before me have said that he refused to sign any document that would get him mixed up in political decisions. Sometimes he would be filled with rage against politically committed demands to paint this or that absurdity in favor of "the cause." "The cause, what cause?" he would mutter angrily, brush clenched between his teeth. His cause was art, his battle was painting, he grumbled. Make up his mind about politics? It was beyond him.

I can't help laughing when I recall that image of Picasso imitating Hitler, mocking him, with a black paintbrush for a mustache. It happened at the beach during our first vacation, at the very time the Spanish Civil War was breaking out. We weren't the only ones who relied on humor to deal with the uncertainty that was crowding in on us, the horror we could hardly imagine we'd soon be living through. A few months later we learned of the assassination of a poet and playwright whose name back then already meant so much to Picasso and to me: Federico García Lorca.

We began to fear the worst: nothingness. Treacherous, blank nothingness. We feared that an army of nameless soldiers, nobodies, nobodies, nobodies, would spread throughout the world, marching violently through a society that would be conquered by boredom, arrogance, terror: the Empire of Nothingness. Dying of disquiet in a world lulled into quiescence.

But Picasso could split himself in half like no one else, and he publically affirmed, "Communism represents an ideal that I believe in. I think Communism aspires to achieve that ideal."

However, whatever he expressed in words or painting, it carried little weight with the fanatical ideologues. They commissioned a portrait of Stalin from him, and he painted it, inspired by a youthful image from back when the Soviet leader was nobody, or virtually no one. They kicked up a huge fuss. The Soviet embassy deemed the portrait unacceptable. Armageddon came down on him: the Communist ultraconservatives trained their spotlight on him. Picasso just kept his mouth shut, the coward. Deep down, he was nothing but a coward. The only coward who's ever had so much written about him.

How did we survive all that in occupied Paris? Like most people: by devoting ourselves discretely to art, hiding out like rats, sheltering under the power of the Great Genius, who everyone tried to court, absolutely everyone, including the enemy, though in their own way. It's true. The enemy respected Picasso. Even today nobody can explain it. Just as we still can't explain why the enemy respected so many artists and intellectuals. Maybe because they needed to enjoy themselves, and they could only find their fun in the fashionable circles of Paris.

Bernard's brown notebook

James irritates me all the time. I can't make him understand Dora. To top it off, sometimes he mistreats her, his behavior is cynical at best and not very nice. It's not his fault, I know. Dora is a dejected woman, yet conceited, and she talks too much sometimes and other times, well, she sinks into silence. But he shouldn't act so rude toward her. I know full well that Picasso treated her worse, I don't deny it, but he was the Master, the God, the Great Genius. What are we? Nothing, nobody. Maybe I'm exaggerating, but that sulfurous nothingness keeps gaining ground and corroding everything it touches.

No, it's not fair. We aren't perfect. Neither is Dora. James and I, even less. And we don't claim to be perfect friends.

Today, while we were sharing a strawberry ice cream, Dora told me about the time they moved near each other, Picasso to 7 Quai des Grands Augustins and Dora to 6 Rue de Savoie. Her face lit up with sadness as she described the places where she thought she was going to be happy. It's strange that a woman like Dora would aspire to be simply happy with a man like Picasso, and when I mentioned it to her, she said she could be happy, occasionally, and not in a conventional way. It all depends on what you expect happiness to be. Over their ten years, she experienced perhaps twenty happy moments. She didn't believe in the banal ideal of happiness, "being happy is too empty," she insisted, adding a play on the words *banalité* and *vanité*. Banality, vanity. She stumbled, she stuttered. It was an evasive reply and an unbecoming attitude, in my view, of course, after I'd given her my sincere support. "Picasso was quite brave," she says. Then she calls him just the opposite. She's insane!

Plenty has been written about the circumstances that led Picasso to abandon his apartment on Rue La Boétie, though already it had long since been left uninhabited and uncleaned, almost in ruins, because of the painter's instability and his refusal to keep living in a place where, according to him, he'd been so put down and misunderstood by Olga. That apartment reminded him of the excesses and socialite frivolities he was forced into by his Russian wife, according to what Dora told me. And yet the truth is that Picasso had also enjoyed those excesses, though it's also the case that luxury and fatuity quickly bored him.

After the honeymoon phase of that marriage, he began to yearn for a place where he could live as what he really was: an artist! He tried to go back to his old bohemian times, the days of painter and poet friends, the nights of endless debates about art and painting.

Dora found the two addresses just about perfect for her lover's new mood. During that period Picasso had broken with Jaume Sabartés; he was fed up (according to him) with his secretary's scandalmongering, his nonstop blabbering about how Picasso mistreated women, about how he was stingy, about how he'd been awful, had cruelly mistreated the people who worshiped him. "The Master," as Sabartés slavishly called him, ended up banishing him from his life for quite a long time, and Dora took advantage of this situation to seize control.

A series of coincidences at 7 Quai des Grands Augustins not only inflated Picasso's ego but filled him with morbid elation and overweening pride. That was where the playwright and actor Jean-Louis Barrault, who later costarred with Arletty in Marcel Carné's 1945 film *Children of Paradise*, found a space to rehearse his plays; it was also where the famous group Contre-Attaque debated Surrealism's usefulness to the revolution, among other political ideas. And on the corner across the street, Louis XIII had been crowned king of France in 1610, at the age of nine, after his father, Henry IV, was assassinated by a Catholic fanatic.

At those Contre-Attaque meetings, in that very apartment, Remedios Varo, Benjamin Péret, and Dora Maar got together with Georges Bataille. That was where they met the Cuban writer and ethnologist Lydia Cabrera, who didn't appreciate the irresponsibility, or frivolity, of her openly Communist colleagues at all. Nor did Remedios Varo much care for mixing Surrealism with politics, much less for talk of ideology, even though she was anti-Fascist and anti-Franco and had been persecuted and arrested for it in France. Nor did Lydia Cabrera want anything to do with Fascism, much less Communism.

But the best omen of all, according to Picasso, was that the building had served Honoré de Balzac as the inspiration for writing his short story "The Unknown Masterpiece" in 1831. Curiously, this story had many points in common with what was going on in the artistic climate of the time when Picasso moved there. The tale anticipated a true revolution in art—not in society, as had been expected. It was believed that art would cause social uprisings through its incendiary political messages, which would incite the masses to take power (Socialist Realism, straight from the Soviet Union). Picasso despised any messages in art; then again, the greatest revolutionary in art was unquestionably Picasso himself.

The short story could already be considered visionary at the time, especially because in one of the apartments in the building that appears in the tale there lived none other than the one who profoundly changed the nature of art around the world, and who took one of Balzac's recurring motifs and made it his own: that the mission of art should not be to copy nature but to express it or interpret it.

Later on, Picasso illustrated Balzac's literary gem with a series of etchings. This was the kind of sidelong experience (as the Cuban writer and essayist José Lezama Lima might say) that sets a genius afire and that multiplies not the force of his ego, as I've previously expressed but rather his creative impulse, his mysteriously all-consuming force, whose purpose is exclusively to create.

I jot down the thoughts and reminiscences of Dora Maar in this brown notebook because they will be useful someday, perhaps to me, for writing about her, or for writing about this trip, this short but intense trip on which I've learned to listen to her and interpret her drastic mood swings.

I don't know, I'm not very clear with respect to these notes. I couldn't even aspire to a prestigious future; no one would bet on my becoming a famous writer. In my blue notebook I write about James and me, and sometimes about all three.

I've tried to puzzle out carefully: which of us will have benefited most from this trip? For Dora, neither James nor I mean much more than dust in the wind, we haven't contributed anything essential to her that might help her age with any distinction due to our presence here, and we've left no impression on her, nothing enduring that's come from our minds. The only one who could transform her was Picasso. We have no choice but to face this devastating reality.

James already knew her, and her ups and downs too. It's possible that, having spent so much time with her, he's now begun to lose interest. Nor will this trip with Dora add any astonishingly profound or exceptional meaning to his life. At this point I suspect he gets more bored by her than by anyone else. His feigned expression of interest is all too blatant, as is the bored look he puts on whenever he hears another of her anecdotes about the past, where her obsession has a name: Pablo Picasso. Nevertheless, he puts up with her, because James wouldn't want to forsake his having been someone important in Dora's life, in both their lives, Picasso's, Dora's.

No doubt about it, I'm the one who comes out ahead on this trip: I've gotten to know her a little better, I've been able to hold her in my arms. I had imagined a rigid, stern, arrogant woman, and I must admit I was wrong, I was unfair. Some people are born to have every unfairness in the world contribute to people's perception of them.

Now I'm crazy about her, I'll never forget her. How could I, when she's seen something in me that nobody else ever has: my aspiration to become a serious man of letters? And she understood it.

James. A gondola ride from the heart of forgetfulness

The canal boat was waiting for him just where the gondolier had agreed to pick him up. He'd wanted to go for a stroll on his own and return by gondola to where he'd agreed to meet his friends, a restaurant near Teatro la Fenice—La Madonna, a refined place, exquisite, recommended by his Parisian friends.

Today he'd rather not have had to see Dora; he was rather tired of her company. He was suddenly beginning to regret having invited Picasso's lover to come on their trip with them.

Though he considered her his one and only true friend, he couldn't stand her when she set to harping on her relationship, immortalized in paintings, with Picasso's imposing figure (not really with Picasso himself); and he hated it when she started detailing once again, right in front of Bernard, every torment the painter had put her through. He found her behavior presumptuous and tactless, the way she used the most plaintive and pitiful aspects of her relationship with the Great Genius to seduce Bernard. He'd have liked to forget her, erase her from his life.

He ruthlessly detested it when she set about describing, for example, how much work it had been for her to photograph *Guernica*. It was a story he already knew by heart, one he'd already told to Bernard himself. But his friend wanted to make a show of being extremely interested in her revelations (this lowered James's opinion of Bernard), and then all of Venice's beauty vanished from Bernard's mind so he could bend his full attention to the storyteller and her miserable Picasso anecdotes.

The gondolier broke in upon his thoughts to ask if he already knew the city, in which case he could push on in a hurry, or if he wished instead to explore the canals at a leisurely pace while the boatman explained the history of the various palazzos.

"As you prefer. I'm in no hurry."

"This is the palazzo where the famous author from the Republic of Venice, Giacomo Casanova, lived; his book, *History of My Life*, was a grandiloquent piece of literature," the gondolier recited in proud and pompous tones. With a dismissive wave of his hand James called for a change of subject, as he was already familiar with the story.

James, somewhat put off by the gondolier's prattle, let himself be swept away by the deeply touristic chatter; it kept his thoughts from flowing freely, but he couldn't deny the musical charm of the Venetian accent.

So they disappeared into the strangely peaceful calm of the city's watery byways. As the gondolier announced the palazzos to him one by one and pointed out, now more concisely at the passenger's request, who had famously lived in which and who still lived where, James couldn't help thinking back to scenes from the studio on Grands Augustins.

Picasso inevitably loved talking about the "Phoney War"—*la drôle de guerre*, as Parisians called it—and about bullfights as if they were works of art. Only with the bombing of Guernica on April 26, 1937, did he come to perceive the enormity of war's true horrors. From then on he was conscious of the suffering and tragedy of the massacre.

Guernica was born not solely from his notorious "aesthetic narcissism," as some of his other works had been, according to what Alicia Dujovne Ortiz tells us and what Picasso himself planned to recount in a book someday, but from the genuine, searing pain he perceived in letters from his mother, which told of a Spain sunk deep in death, and from Dora's continual insistence that he must get involved, as a Spaniard, as a believer in the Republic, in the tragedy his country was struggling through.

Though he balked at the politically committed, twenty-four-hour activist Dora, it was her determination that forced him, in an act of resigned obedience, to take his proper stance as artist and as a defender of liberty.

The print *Dream and Lie of Franco*, completed long before, did not sufficiently represent for him the personal, intimate rage he felt over the thousands who had been cruelly murdered, and the hundreds left wounded and dying. "Wars end," James remembered Picasso pointing out to him once, "but hostilities persist forever."

James wished he could have been at Picasso's side when he made the decision to paint *Guernica*. He felt a healthy envy of Dora over this. But a man befogged by the artist's overpowering charm could never have seen and understood the immense effort such a colossal undertaking entailed, much less have motivated him to carry through with it. Fear paralyzes men, but motivates women.

Picasso invested a lot of physical and spiritual energy in that work. Dora did not only observe him, however; she also guided him. James told himself he wouldn't have known how to do that. It would have been extraordinary to witness those moments when the Great Genius, *Cher et Beau*, spread out the huge sheets of paper on which he drew the rough sketches that would become portions of the grand canvas. *Guernica* was more than a painting; it was a torturous birth. James wouldn't have been up to serving as its midwife.

Picasso had never allowed anyone to photograph him in the midst of such hard work before. However, he authorized Dora to proceed. He knew he wasn't giving the assignment to just anyone, knew that she was, first of all, a great Surrealist artist and, secondly, the woman he loved. This is evident in the series of extraordinary photos Dora took of *Guernica*, especially in the one where Picasso, standing on a ladder, let himself be snapped by the lens of the artist who made *Silence*, one of the best works in Surrealism, where arches keenly, neatly cleave three bodies and a shadowy and seemingly superfluous half-light reinforces a mood of undulating chaos. At center, the rumpled body of a girl, her hands crossed above her pelvis; the head of a dead woman juts over the bottom edge of the photo; and at back, a body crawls toward a holy vertigo of hollow arcades.

James could bet that Dora had secretly infused Picasso's *Guernica* with the mystery of her *Silence*. But what he most envied was the female face, so like Dora's, near the gutted horse dying in agony, tongue sticking out, and the bull that represents reflection, contemplation, and perplexity. Dora was witness, accomplice, and protagonist. *Guernica* owes much to her presence. A presence that later would get on Picasso's nerves, because he would realize that her photo series revealed, highlighted, the countless doubts and uncertainties that assailed him as he faced those eleven and a half by twenty-five and a half feet of canvas. And also because his most recognizable painting would forever enshrine the image of the weeping woman. That weeping woman is watched by another woman, kneeling and clutching a dead child, so similar to the third woman seen crawling on all fours in Dora's earlier photo, in a masterful *Guernica* sequence.

James would have loved to have appeared in the great work, to have been immortalized as his friend had. But her grandeur was not for him, and he lacked her passion for inhabiting those expanses of white, black, and gray.

Dora is everywhere in *Guernica*. Her vibrant presence is explicit not only as the photographer who once captured Sylvia Bataille, weeping in the filming of *The Crime of Monsieur Lange*, where the two of them had coincided before they met. In *Guernica*, she is reflected in every woman's face; she is all of them, even the horse, and she is there in every inch of the painting, haunted by hungry ghosts, weeping uncontrollably.

For James, *Guernica* was the most important art work of the twentieth century.

A painting never meant for Dora, not even in Picasso's wildest lies and promises. Not for her, not for anyone. Not even when he promised Marie-Thérèse that the canvas he was painting was for her and her child, that it would be dedicated to Maya and her mother.

Maya's mother, the Vestal Mother, however, didn't understand the importance of that promise, wasn't aware of the significance of the painting, which had cost Dora such efforts to bring into existence.

"You can't paint suns. Your suns turn out awful." Dora humiliated Picasso when she studied the sun in *Guernica*, easy to do in the series of photos she'd taken.

The sun was transformed into an eye, and inside the eye, a light bulb. She'd given him the idea. That was her first step toward perdition. It was unforgiveable for someone who was supposed to keep her mouth shut, a silent observer in the background, to rob him, if only for a few seconds, of his role as the great creator. That was all it took for him never to forgive her. A genius would rather give away a work of art than have to thank someone forever for giving him an idea.

James knew how much his friend Dora had suffered when Picasso broke with her, but he recognized that what he considered an artist's smug gesture on her part had killed off a wonderful relationship, which ended up benefiting James himself.

"Poor fool!" he blurted. "She dug her own grave. Her pretentions and quarreling drove him away. She should have been satisfied with what she'd been given, should have been the woman who inspired, not the one who interrupted the divine trances of the Great Genius. Dora estranged us both, herself and me, from Picasso. Estranged me, because, how could I keep loving Picasso if he no longer loved her, but only the terrifying idealization he had invented of her?"

Nothing as indelible as the illusion of silence in mirrors.
Venice, 2008

We were having breakfast when it occurred to me to bring up my project of writing a novel about three women Surrealists: first, Dora Maar; second, Remedios Varo. . . .

"And the third?" asked Roberto García York.

"A Cuban woman who actually was a Surrealist without knowing it. *El Monte* is a great piece of Surrealist writing. I'm talking about Lydia Cabrera."

He nodded as he lifted a bite of ham impaled on a silver fork to his mouth.

"You haven't considered Leonora Carrington? Or Leonor Fini? Both are tremendous, wonderful, unique, and highly creative in several fields of art. Leonor Fini in the theater—"

"Yes, of course, but what I find interesting about these three women isn't just that they were part of the Surrealist movement, and that they contributed to it, and that their paintings were Surrealist even after they renounced it, or that they weren't even aware they were Surrealists. What I hope to do is to recount small moments in their lives—brief but intense, profound, incidents."

Roberto García York sat in thought, as if he had his doubts. After a short while he acknowledged that, of all the women mentioned, he preferred Leonora Carrington and Remedios Varo; he had known them both, and also Leonor Fini. His own work, he added, was strongly influenced by those artists. But he couldn't see any special mystery about Dora Maar. I understand his position: Picasso had ultimately overshadowed the brilliance of her work.

"Even her photos, her drawings, her paintings aren't considered part of the essential Surrealist canon, which is a real injustice," Janine said as she handed a glass of orange juice to the painter.

"No, no, come off it. Dora Maar is very well known."

"As Picasso's lover," Roberto interjected. Janine's hand trembled slightly when she heard the painter's qualification. "Only those in the know are aware of her enormous legacy, not in quantity but in quality. But her fame really is based on Man Ray's famous photographs of her, and the portraits by Picasso, which by the way started commanding very good prices—and very quickly. Destiny is an amazing thing. And to think that she made sure his work would be taken such good care of. God knows where all those tremendous *Dora Maar*s that Picasso painted have ended up. To be totally honest, she wasn't a great painter, but she was the greatest Surrealist photographer. And that really would be worth showing the world."

A bit away from us, by the window, my little girl started humming a children's song while scribbling on the floor with some paper and colored pencils Roberto had given her. My husband, Ricardo, was paying attention to our conversation. Janine, always on her toes, was looking out only for the painter's demands and needs. She had been his model; now she was merely his partner. And though she took care of him, she also imposed a lot of her own tastes on him, which for the most part he disliked and found tiresome. She didn't take part in the conversation even though we'd been speaking French so she wouldn't feel left out, since she didn't speak a word of Spanish despite having lived with our friend for forty years.

"I've always been surprised by the power of domination that male artists exert over women, and how the women accept it in the most abject state of submission. Even when they try to set their own rules as homemakers, it's a false assertiveness, yet another act of astonishing deference and obedience. Wouldn't it be easier for them to refuse to give in, and to dump them?" I said to Ricardo after breakfast was done, while we were walking up around Hotel Danieli.

"What's most terrific isn't being the 'Great Genius,' as they called Picasso. What's extraordinarily sublime is loving the Great Genius, apart from understanding him, and having the naïve certainty that the meaning of life revolves around him," Ricardo pontificated.

"You say that because you're a man."

"No, that has nothing to do with it. Not because I'm a man." He paused half a beat. "Because I'm a genius."

We burst out laughing. Our girl started asking us why we were laughing like crazy.

"Mamá, what are you laughing about with Papá so crazy?" The question, structured just as she said it, was filled with the sublime, special, nearly Surrealist grace that only children have.

We strolled along the narrow streets adjoining the Grand Canal. Ricardo stayed playing with the little one in Piazza San Marco, and I looked for a quiet place where I could write in my notebook. I picked one of the many cozy cafes that lie just beyond the square.

I would write by hand, then type it all up on the computer. I ordered a Campari with lemon and started writing. The waiter came over with the tray and the iced Campari sweating up the glass, I looked up, and then I noticed a woman who strongly resembled Dora, wearing the same navy blue dress with tiny flowers and high, rounded collar that Dora has on in some photos. I took a sip and pretended to be admiring the scenery. I kept my eyes on her, following her through my Campari glass.

I couldn't imagine Dora just waiting, not with her restless attitude. Much less imagine her at the mercy of those who always took advantage of her, something she would notice with her keen intelligence: the man she loved would have to choose between his wife and his little girl, and his much younger lover. Dora remained right at the center, inconvenient, bothersome to others, especially to the one who was trying to juggle the tumultuous lives of all those love-struck women, as if he were some mere circus performer.

Guernica in the face of catastrophe

JOURNALIST: You really love the word "love," Pablo Picasso. . . .

PABLO PICASSO: I even told a girl who interviewed me for some newspaper the other day, "You know, for me there's only love."

J: You love people a lot?

PP: I really do. If I didn't have people, I'd rather be a door knob, or a flower pot, anything. . . .

J: Do you also love television? Not so much . . .

PP: Oh, I do have one, I do. I started watching it one day because they were showing Princess Margaret's wedding. Somebody loaned me a TV and I watched the princess's procession, and I kept on going after that.

J: You know what would be great? Just leave you alone in front of the cameras, totally free, you'd be able to do great stuff for the viewers, you'd make up all sorts of things. . . .

PP: Yes, most likely. Sometimes I find wonderful things on television, lovely things, things I love, things I find interesting, but other times it's just appalling. I can say that, can't I? Because it's just the two of us here alone. Oh, no, that's not true, everybody can hear me!

J: If you had to choose which period, which painting, which canvas would live on after you, which would you choose?

PP: I don't know, that's a hard question. Everything was done with the intentions we had in the moment, in the period, in the state we were all in, myself included. It's so hard to say. When it was Guernica's moment, I made *Guernica*. That was a terrible catastrophe, and the beginning of so many other catastrophes we've suffered through, wasn't it? But that's how it is. It's personal. At bottom, these are memoirs one writes for oneself. . . .

ON SCREEN: "I paint the way others write their biographies. My canvases, finished or not, are pages from my diary."

—Excerpt from Picasso's only interview on
French television; transcript from the archives
of the National Audiovisual Institute (INA).

Marie-Thérèse showed up unexpectedly. The secretary, Jaume Sabartés, was rubbing his hands in amusement, watching; he eyed the situation from behind the door with the air of a bullfighter about to win the ears and the tail in a single fight. He sided completely with Maya's mother, whom he considered the "Good One." The other woman was the "Bad One," the enemy, the upstart. The other woman was Dora Maar.

"I have a daughter with this man. It's my right to be here with him. You may go. You're nothing but *the other woman*." The Vestal Mother lay down the law.

"I have a lot more reasons to stay than you do." Dora was haughty and gruff. "I don't have any children with him, and I don't see any difference between having them and not having them."

She could have said she did have one, that the monumental painting looming before her eyes was the offspring of them both. But she thought it inappropriate.

Picasso was unfazed, anyone would say unaffected, by the scene of jealousy playing out before his eyes, but he turned his back and kept on painting as if it had nothing to do with him.

Neither of them had seen the other before, they hadn't even crossed paths accidentally. Both women thought the same thing, that the rival was more beautiful than her. But Dora had the advantage of having loitered many times around the house in Tremblay where Picasso had installed his wife and daughter, knowing that the painter was inside that building, surrounded by his family. Those were nights when she wasn't ashamed to weep pathetically in front of a taxi driver, under lashing rain or falling snow, unable to focus through the windows on the faces smiling at the man she loved more than anyone in the world.

"Which of us should leave?" Marie-Thérèse put Picasso between a rock and a *Guernica*.

"It's a difficult situation. I like each of you for different reasons. Marie-Thérèse, because she's sweet and kind, and she does everything I ask. Dora, because she's intelligent. I have no interest in making a decision. I'd rather leave things as they are. You two work it out." Picasso continued slinging paint on the canvas, smiling quietly, smugly, unable to look at either of them, pretending neither of them deserved his precious time or the selfless attention he devoted only to his painting.

Dora felt completely drained, as if her body were nothing but a formless mass of jelly, and her veins were opening of their own accord and her blood burbling out and puddling at her feet.

Marie-Thérèse struck the first blow, a punch to the jaw, then Dora grabbed her by the blond hair, so meticulously coiffed in *Belle Époque* curls. They both rolled across the floor, slapping and punching.

Picasso was dealing out brushstrokes right and left, faking indifference toward what was going on behind him, though inside he was seething in a Machiavellian frenzy. Sabartés noticed he was more elated than ever.

His women were on the floor, fighting, scratching, yanking out hair by the roots, pinching and biting each other's breasts, kicking their backsides! Wasn't it magnificent? It would have been better if they'd ended up in bed making love to him, he thought, more and more triumphant as he watched his wife and his lover getting beaten up for the cause, for him, the trophy, the talisman, the lustful object of their wrath. But he'd have to be satisfied with a brawl instead of romance.

Neither of them would ever again resemble the models that the Great Genius had immortalized in his paintings, so low had they sunk. Dora had lost all her elegance, he had sucked her dry of the last ounce of mystery, and nothing remained of the intelligence that had captivated her Master in those Man Ray photos and had enslaved him to her blinding beauty.

From the corner of his eye Picasso watched her screaming obscenities, her mouth gaping wide, her eyes red and bulging, her hair disheveled, her dress torn. This image satisfied him more than the first photographs Man Ray took, because at last he was discovering the broken woman, her tattered soul, her mouth twisted into a grimace and eyes frozen in weeping, rage inflaming her swollen flesh. This grand spectacle finished her off as an enigma. Wounded, Dora ceased to be the intelligent woman and became the tormented lover. Everything he'd loved about her, her masculine side, lost its power in this torrent of tears and moans. The gravitas vanished from her face, replaced by a melancholy frown. What emerged was the soiled, rotten, diluted, insipid woman of water.

"I liked her as much as if she'd been a man," Picasso put it on one occasion, "and, well, that day when she and Marie-Thérèse decided to fight over me, she looked like such a woman to me, I stopped loving her."

Once her masculine armor of wisdom (claimed as the exclusive property of men) was shattered, the fragility of the wounded, dying lover appeared. The hysterical tears were followed by mockery. Picasso reveled, he delighted, in ripping her to ribbons.

"I stopped loving her when she appeared to me as a regular woman, fighting with another woman, over me. . . . And the thing is, I'd seen that so many times. . . . It offered me nothing new. For the first time, Dora didn't surprise me," the Great Genius lamented.

I set my glass on the table. The woman who looked like Dora turned her gaze on me and held it there until I lowered my eyes to stare at my notebook. When I looked up again, she was gone. The sun was setting golden over Venice.

It seems the sunsets in this city are inevitably golden. I was sure some artist would be smearing a canvas, trying to capture the sobriety and elegance of the setting sun in ochre, pearl, and rose.

"Every adventure has to do with. . . ."—with leaving someplace, with running away. Where had I read that phrase? In James Lord's book?

Every adventure means losing ourselves to a new place, a place we've never thought about before, a place we've never even noticed in our dreams.

The austere aloofness of James. Venice, 1958

I should be nicer to her. At least I could try pretending better. After all, we treated her to this trip, we're the ones who invited her. At first, Bernard didn't seem as excited about it as me, but now it turns out he's gone crazy about Dora, and he never stops pointing out that I shouldn't be so prickly.

Picasso never loved her, and he treated her worse than a cow. Everyone knows that neither he nor anyone, anyone at all, loved her, certainly not him. I can't be sure that no other man loved her, not even the ones I didn't know who were trying to woo her with the idea of getting me away from her. None of them would have given her the love she gave Picasso. Not even Georges Bataille. Maybe Yves Tanguy did. So why should I love her, then? She's nothing but a woman. Or worse, she's too much more than a woman. Terrifying.

But I contradict myself, I can't help it, I love her because I could latch onto Picasso only through her, and I can't find a good explanation for that. Maybe I have to give the same explanation the painter came up with for himself: I love her because she's a real man. Her soul is male, entirely male, though wrapped in a woman's body, fragile and somewhat coarse only in appearance. I love her because she's as much of a man as Picasso. She's like him. She is him.

There's no doubt. She's an angel sculpted from mud with her wings sawed off. Or a sprite. Like Max Jacob.

Picasso painted her weeping so many times because he thought that after cutting off her wings she'd be left wracked with pain for the rest of her life. But she resisted. Does anybody know why? I do. Because she's a warrior. Invincible. She'll never be defeated.

And as far as I can remember, I've only seen her sniffle a couple of times, and almost never weep. . . . I should try to recall. . . . No, never. I've never seen her weeping.

She bites her lip when she feels scorned, humiliated, but she doesn't weep. Her eyelids fall heavily, as if she'll never open them again, but she doesn't weep.

She isn't a weeping woman. She's a broken woman. Shattered, yes, undone. At the point of evanescence, as if she were going to vanish, suddenly about to fade away, shatter into a thousand shards. A woman dry as glass.

When I watch her ordering a plate of garlic shrimp in a restaurant, I'm tempted to wrap my arms around her and kiss her on the cheeks. I can't help feeling tender or compassionate, the life she lives grieves me. Compassion is what I feel, that's the word. Her life goes on with nothing to look forward to but one day after another with nothing gained. Or maybe there is something. Perhaps she still longs for, still dreams of, the return of her tormentor, or of anyone who might take his place.

When we eat dinner, she avoids looking me in the eyes, and she always addresses her remarks to Bernard; she watches him with a smile, self-effacingly. Bernard raises his glass in a dainty toast, first to her, then to me, but I've noticed he too avoids looking at me. He locks his eyes on hers, savors every sip, and doesn't look away for a second. I calmly drink my red wine, or pretend I care about nothing, especially not the scoldings I get for how I savor my wine, which Bernard finds vulgar. It bothers Bernard when I toast with wine, a habit he considers low class, too American. He and Dora prefer Italian champagne. More power to them! I exclaim, not without some irony, and light up cigarette number who knows which. Yes, I also smoke like a chimney.

Last night I ordered several glasses of Chianti, let my drinking get out of hand. I'll never get used to drinking like a Cossack, it just took a few cups for my head to get as puffed up as a hot-air balloon and me to go around saying awful things. I got very sarcastic and wheedling and demanded that Dora explain to me how she made love with Picasso. How did he do it? How did he penetrate her? Vaginally or anally? Or both?

I can imagine it so easily, I whispered into her ear. He penetrated you with a good deal of physical cruelty. He was a delightful sadist, a brute, a genuine bastard. I can't deny it was those same qualities that made him so powerfully fascinating to me.

Last night I behaved badly, very badly, I was a fool, I admit, especially with her, but also with Bernard, who couldn't understand why I insisted on showing my worst side. I don't understand what was going through my head either. I was very drunk, and that's why I can't accept that I did it on purpose. I've been worn out for days, it's true, tired of it all, and it's because I can sense we've already experienced everything important we were going to experience. We're already almost dead.

I'm here so we won't die, won't rot all alone, and that's why I've invited her to take this trip to Venice. I mean for her to get to know the city, to enjoy herself as much as possible before she goes back to Paris, before she shuts herself up again, this time forever, with Picasso's paintings, with her idol's things, with her God's stuff, and suffers, in the end, unavoidably, the torments of remorse. I don't know what to do with Dora, I don't know. . . .

Maybe if I buy her some presents, I could make her a little happier, or if I ask her to the theater. She's so aggressively intense to be around. How could I get rid of her? I don't want to!

No, Dora will never be happy again, for one simple reason: she never was. She was never able to be. It never mattered to her.

For the last two nights I've been plagued with these damned erotic dreams about Picasso. I tell her about it over breakfast, she rolls her eyes and replies, majestically, even delightfully, "I dreamed about him each and every night for over ten years. There were moments when I was terrified to go to bed. There were nights when I would have rather died than go to sleep."

Why should I want to be cheerful? Venice, 1958

James was vulgar last night. Maybe I provoked him and didn't real-ize what I'd done. I can understand him, I haven't been friendly to him these last few days.

Why will I always have to find excuses for men?

No, this time I won't. James acted like a real ass, he was insuf-ferable, and I'm not going to forgive him so easily. It's not worth thinking about for one more second. Once more, his attitude sowed doubt in me about what kind of sexual relationship I really had with Picasso.

At the beginning of our relationship, despite the sour taste of his kisses, Picasso made me feel like a real woman. Some time later, he fell into his harsh, beastly routine.

When one lover becomes petty and insolent, that's the worst thing that can happen to sex between two artists, two perfectionists. Most of the time I felt nothing special toward him, and he got plea-sure only by hurting me.

The first symptom I noticed was when I started dropping things, my hands couldn't even hold a glass. I was always shaking inside, or else my body would tense up until it went into spasms.

And had I really gone crazy that day when Jacques Lacan and Picasso decided to commit me to the Sainte-Anne Hospital and subject me to those electroshocks? Lacan was the one who pre-scribed the treatment and signed the admittance order, it's true, but Picasso didn't do anything to stop him. And Paul Éluard was there too, backing them both up. I'm aware that Lacan thinks I had two choices, the confession box or the straitjacket. But that only proves that he doesn't know anything about me, that he doesn't know me. There was a time when I gave in to men's savage desires, to their aspirations regarding me, though they never took me into account. "Never again," I promised myself.

My room, much like a jail cell, was painted black and had no windows. The darkness swallowed up every bit of space. Or was it the other way around, all white? Was it dark or too bright? How many days was I locked up, how many years? My forehead and temples are sunk in that black hole of memory, sucked in by blinding light.

I stopped talking, eating, dreaming. I stopped loving. And living.

They insisted I switch my name. It was something we all had to do in our circle of Surrealists, friends for so many years. Our mutual trust was a comfort, but . . . I wasn't me anymore. Nor were they them. Picasso forced us to play at switching our identities, and sexes. We obeyed him because he was the Great Genius, *Cher et Beau*, Beloved and Beautiful, the Master, God. When one of them had to turn into me, that person, using my name, couldn't be anyone else, nobody but Picasso. Which meant going to bed with him, possessing me possessing himself.

The men, bare-chested, took off their briefs. The women, also with their breasts to the breeze, spread their legs and started laughing. Couples swapped, intertwining in a daring, surreally erotic swarm. Picasso tried to get me not to join. He was saving me for himself. Yet he could go to bed with all the other women, and they with all the men. They all made love with and penetrated each other. I photographed the moans of pleasure, the pointed breasts, the open lips, the magnificent pubes, the penises dripping sperm, and the mouths waiting for the heavenly manna of pleasure to wash over them.

I was supposed to be content with watching, just with observing. "Observe, observe, Dora!" the Great Genius murmured. I only had the right to observe those bodies in the sunlight, or sometimes streaked by stars. I was supposed to photograph and obey, as Picasso had trained me, while he enjoyed them all, women and men alike. If it had been a bullring, for the first time in history the bull would have worn out the picadors, the bull handlers, the audience, and even the matador, and left them all for dead. My lover didn't feel the slightest bit of tenderness or compassion, only cruelty and greed. He seemed insatiable, forgetting that I was observing every detail through the camera lens. He overlooked my presence there, watching him make love with our friends. Or maybe not, maybe he did it on purpose, to drive me even crazier. No, he wasn't forgetting at all; more like, my being there was what turned him into that ravenous beast, devouring pubes, stuffing holes, sucking nipples, clitorises, and anuses, and also letting the others do the same to him. More like, he was running riot in a whirlwind of reminiscences that excluded me because I'd never been part of them, kaleidoscopic memories of his old sexual life with Fernande, with Eva, with Olga, with Marie-Thérèse, with so many others.

Man Ray took part, only as a spectator, in the evasive and malevolent sport of photography, by my side, hardly even brushing up against me. Now, when it was his turn to carry the name "Roland Ray," he was supposed to grab Ady Fideline, the ballerina from Martinique, and make love with her nonstop, like a teenager rutting shamelessly for the first time. He handed me his camera and I was supposed to serve as the official recorder of his pleasure, so I unabashedly photographed his panting face. After a while he was spewing foam from his mouth, slobbering, and his eyes were pumped up, yellow as egg yolks.

Yes, I really felt I was going crazy during those sessions, I suffered too much from Picasso's loveless indifference, his passion for others, but it got even worse when I was subjected to his detachment, the disdain of his lust, when he started making excuses for excluding me from his filthy sexual appetite.

Nusch came up to me and tried to take away my camera so I could join in with them and add my appetites to the orgy, but Picasso interposed himself between us. And I, sincerely and regretfully, had by then lost my drive. Nusch liked it when Picasso cornered her, it was a kind of trick to get away from her consumptive husband, diligent Paul Éluard, who now would often dribble spit and breathe noisily as he decoupled from the others.

Picasso set Nusch next to Valentine Penrose, on the floor, kissing each in turn, but then it was Alice Paalen who got in between them and isolated Valentine, taking over her milky, languid, body. Valentine was a breathtakingly sensual and desirable woman. . . .

The men, like genuine children, started a pillow fight. Tired of all the futile madness, I made as if to join them, though only so they'd start caressing each other again, but Picasso made a gesture like he was going to slap me, and that stopped me cold. A newcomer filmed it all. At last Man Ray put down his camera and, annoyed, asked Picasso why he treated me like I was his daughter and not like what I was, his woman.

"She has no right to appear in these films, much less to sleep with anyone. She isn't my daughter, but it comes to the same thing, she's my lover, and I'm tired of explaining it. She's only permitted to watch."

My eyes, watery, jumped from body to body, lusting to join in the freedom that linked them. But this jubilant dance was off limits to me.

I clenched my jaw, furious, wanting to scream and show how angry I felt, but at the same time I was afraid to lose Picasso. He would have tossed me out if he'd so much as suspected I was being eaten away by jealousy and was dying to unleash my senses. And this greed was impervious to everything but jealousy; that's just how it was. It was unutterably horrible; it gnawed at my insides and froze my soul. I was about to burst with anger, to tell him off, let him know it had been weeks since we made love and when we did it, he didn't worry about whether I felt the least bit satisfied.

"You don't have to feel anything, I'm the one who should." Those were his very words, the one time I complained about his lack of interest in whether I got any pleasure.

"But Picasso, I'm a woman," I tried to explain.

"No, you aren't a woman. You're a Queen with a capital Q, and queens don't need the nonsense of pleasure, or anything at all. You, just keep me satisfied and stay the way you are, unscathed, persevering, on your throne as Queen. You should behave like Paul Éluard—he lets me do it with Nusch and he also acts the fool when Man Ray enjoys her. . . . You're a Queen, you're my Queen, and that's that, case closed. Shush!"

I didn't know what to say, I felt I could sense a very different, very egotistical love in his voice, a frustration, as if I really were his Queen and my station were high above the rest, up in a sort of observatory, from which I might contemplate the alien bedazzlements of Eros, hear the moans of naked bodies clamoring for mine, and with absolute dispassion withdraw from them and surrender to onanism in my celestial realm.

I should have exploded a thousand times from rage. Maybe if I had, I wouldn't have gone crazy. But I didn't. Picasso demanded that I remain impassive, that I show nobility of spirit, and that if I felt jealousy wrenching my guts (he never referred to the heart, he considered it vulgar), then I should start photographing, filming, offering up my voraciousness in a more solemn, artistic, magnificent, detached, and everlasting way, as when a Queen on her throne draws a line with her scepter to mark the boundary between herself and her subjects.

The warmth of those bodies ceased to captivate me, I photographed them feeling utterly aloof; besides, I found it doubly uncomfortable because I had to keep my clothes on. Not that I wanted to undress, either. My body was too stout, it annoyed me, and it put Picasso at a disadvantage; he'd already called it to my attention: "You're fat, and I do not by any means want them to see you like this." While those skinny men showed off their equally malnourished wives, following the fashion of the moment, he and I both had flamboyantly robust physiques. Women were fascinated by Picasso's body, but he knew I was beginning to sour among the men who'd abandoned the plump woman fashion of the Twenties and were coming under the sway of the addictive vision of sickly, frail women with underfed, childlike airs who were now in demand among some Surrealists. A new style imposed by the food shortages and scarcity of clothing brought about by the Great War. Picasso preferred for my body to remain hidden under a cloak of mystery. In that way, his friends could only imagine me masked behind an enigmatic exuberance touching on the unknown, as in a painting of Gala by Salvador Dalí.

I could undress and join the others only when we got together as couples, specifically only when we were with Nusch and Éluard.

Éluard sensed the awkwardness of my situation; he perceived that I was bitter, could feel my distress, but couldn't do much for me. He couldn't stand up to his friend, Picasso, so he confined himself to writing me a poem, appropriate and puerile, that wouldn't rock the friendship he kept up with the painter. Nusch pressed it into my hands one afternoon, a slip of rice paper, rolled up and scented with drops of Guerlain cologne. I kept it in an old secretary desk for years, later it traveled with me at the bottom of my purse until, from fear that the envelope and slip of paper would disintegrate, I added it to a folder of old documents and returned it to the desk:

> Figure of strength, scalding, savage,
> black hair where gold flows southward.
> Intractable unbounded.
> Useless.
> Such health erects a prison.

In Mougins, in the early years of my life with Picasso, I posed constantly for them on the beach.

Paul Éluard suggested I should let my hair grow and comb it with the ends out. I looked a little like Gala, which I hated, but I paid attention and let it grow. Then Picasso, ecstatic, started painting me like crazy. I had to put up with long hours in front of his easel, and when something didn't turn out the way he wanted, he'd insult me.

"You aren't a beautiful woman. Though you think you are, there's nothing beautiful about you. The proof is that I can't paint you right when you look normal. If you're weeping I can, because when you do that you look funny, and that amuses me, cheers me up, and my hand becomes free. But you're not a woman who tends to inspire anyone to reproduce beauty, because I can't get anything worthy of the sublime out of you. Nothing about you is sublime, just unusual; as a woman, your features look odd. Besides, there's no harmony! You pad out the whole canvas. And that frightful, puffed-up hair!"

Éluard kept writing, quietly, suborned by his own silence and embarrassed by the complaints his friend was aiming at me.

That's why all the portraits Picasso did of me at that time show me weeping. I was the weeping woman in his paintings, but I rarely wept in real life. My melancholy wasn't an actual fact, and reality didn't matter much him. He would reveal my face in oils on a canvas and proudly exclaim to his visitors, "Look at how she weeps for me!"

I had nothing extraordinary about me, but I really was filled with fury. Unusually furious, that I was. I sense I was going to turn hateful or go crazy. Furious, angry, pained, tormented; my lips were dry from vomiting so often and biting them in anger. But Picasso was unable to decode my anger, much as I wanted him to so I could at last forgive him. Picasso couldn't understand why I was frowning when he played at being the photographer, snapping a photo of Jacqueline Lamba next to me and comparing the two of us. I knew she was going to come out better than me, because I didn't feel beautiful, but he was sure to point it out to me.

"Aren't you embarrassed? You're not like her, you're nothing to look at."

I no longer knew who I was, I'd lost all perspective about myself. I appealed to the mirror, and the surface reflected a squat, dark figure full of unintelligible meanings, of codes and ciphers I could scarcely crack, much less mull over. Because of him, his insistence on the invisible nature of the body, I became a cryptic woman. Good energy no longer flowed from my body. I didn't give enduring, positive vibrations. Everything that came from me merely trickled out and soon evaporated, leaving no trace of my essence. He wanted to blast my yearnings, crush my aspirations. I accepted it because I longed for it. I allowed it more as a whim than out of love. I'd fallen in love with Picasso on a whim, as a Surrealist experiment: I yearned to find the man, the god, who could make me a goddess.

And he did it.

With all the difficulties it entailed, I was his goddess. He used me until he imagined there was nothing left of me that he could exploit and subdue, until he had finished hundreds of portraits and had decreed that, with all those paintings, I was less a person than a figure belonging to him and so, from then on, I should be very highly valued.

PART III

AN EXTRACT FROM
ALL THESE SILENCES

Bernard sheltering in my secret. Spring 2011

The friend whom Bernard and I had in common let me know this morning that the poor fellow was bedbound now, spending most of his time on the computer he kept propped on his legs, surfing for porn. Bernard had asked our friend if he had any news about me and whether I was still planning to write about the trip to Venice he and James took with Dora Maar.

"You should call him," Ramón Leandro observed.

"I don't dare," I murmured into the phone.

It wasn't that I didn't dare, it was that so much time had passed, and perhaps the product wasn't going to be what he'd expected of me, I clarified. Besides, he was finally acting his age, that is, you could really tell that he'd gotten old. He wouldn't be happy at all for me to come around visiting him after he had changed so much, much less for me to bother him with a novel that didn't reflect the true story of what happened, because that's what it was going to be, a novel, not a mere chronicle.

"I'll wait a bit longer," I assured him, "but we don't have much time left, either." Dora had been right: we writers are a bunch of boastful traitors.

The doorbell rang; I shuffled into the foyer. It was the mail. From the bundle of letters I fished out an invitation from the Maison de l'Amérique Latine. It was about a book presentation for Alicia Dujovne Ortiz's latest, a biography of St. Teresa of Ávila.

For years I'd been living with Alicia Dujovne Ortiz's biography of Dora Maar, imagining its Argentine author, dreaming of meeting her, and here a chance to do so falls into my lap. I looked for the date on the announcement; scheduled for June 20. I couldn't possibly go, as I would be in Arras then. Maybe I could send her a letter via the Maison. A letter? What an idea! To tell her what? Simple enough: that I was writing about Dora Maar, that I was concentrating on the five, or rather eight, days she spent in Venice, about which no one could ever discover anything, and about which Alicia Dujovne Ortiz herself must still be wondering, given that after this trip Dora Maar decided to shut herself off from the world for good. And that she, and the questions she raised about that brief sojourn, and Dora Maar's behavior from that time until her death, her seclusion after the trip, were what had inspired me to recreate those five day (or eight, counting the journey back) that she spent with James and Bernard under the spell of Venice's charms.

I realized I had never seen Alicia Dujovne Ortiz's face in the press, hadn't even bothered looking her up on the Internet. I went to do so. I turned on my computer. Typing rapidly, I searched through the photos in Google—it's so easy to look up people's records today. There she was. Her face spoke to me somehow, it was possible we'd met; yes, I must have run into her at some event. But no, it's some other feeling. I got the impression I'd been with her on some very special occasion, that I'd been her friend and that, in some far distant spot, we had arranged to hold a conversation about our heroine. I paced back and forth, scribbled some notes, and finally forgot all about it.

A bit later I started cooking, I put dinner in the oven and sat in front of the television to watch the news. I suddenly sat up in my chair. Now I knew where we'd seen each other! I ran to my office and rummaged through our box of old photos.

She was the woman who'd been sitting at the table in that Venetian café, right next to ours, anxiously waiting for someone, fixing her makeup, attentive to the slightest flaw she could find in her compact mirror.

She also appeared in a photo Ricardo had taken of me with the little one asleep on my lap. The Argentine writer, whose face had been a mystery up to now, was there in the background of the snapshot. She gazed out at the sea mist pooling over the darkening waters of the Grand Canal. She looked very attractive that evening, decked out in a blue dress with tiny yellow flowers.

Life is full of coincidences, and literature makes the most of them and turns them into random accidents and amusing incidents. In the end, it tosses them into the fertile pool of memory. It is only by fishing them out and polishing them until they shine that they can be turned into something of unique significance, spun from words.

Santa Maria dei Miracoli. Falling into Zugzwang. Venice, 2008

I discovered, on my own one day, this little church clad in pearl-escent marble, a jewel box blown up to astonishing proportions. I was taking a stroll, and the half-opened church door, together with the simplicity of the portico, powerfully caught my eye.

Entranced by the charm of the place, I crossed the threshold and found no one inside there but me. Not a single visitor.

Neglect was everywhere, the vault was under restoration; filtering through a stained glass window, the sun described a cone of light on a bench in the center of the nave and bounced playfully across the lintel. A thick layer of ash-white dust covered the benches, statues, and altars. I walked around the nave. Might Dora have visited this little church? I pulled out the binder of notes Bernard had photocopied for me, searched for any mention of the church in them. Yes, indeed, they'd all been here together.

I imagined how the three of them had walked in and how, after casing it, stopping in front of every niche, they'd decided to sit down, separately or all together on the same bench, to enjoy a moment of spiritual contemplation as they gazed on every detail in the architecture and the religious objects that adorned the place.

In all likelihood Dora had prayed here. She'd become mawkishly Catholic, though she hadn't yet reached the extreme religious befuddlement that later made her objectionable. Nevertheless, even back then, she like Max Jacob had set off on the path toward holiness by way of astrology, mainly because she was living such a lonely life after leaving the man she most yearned for, the very one who had brought about the deep, disturbing split between her soul and her body.

She had found it almost impossible to admit that she couldn't even give children to the man she loved, because of her sterility. It was even worse to know for certain that she'd never have what Marie-Thérèse Walter did: a son or daughter as proof of her love with the artist—though not even this fact consoled the bosomy blonde for the loss of her absent husband's love, not when he'd always promised to marry her but never did. Marie-Thérèse killed herself four years after Picasso's death. Dora comprehended her desperation, understood the terrible deep chasm that was left after giving up life with Picasso, after his total disappearance. Because she had also edged dangerously close to that cliff.

Jacqueline Roque, his last wife, also couldn't resist and refused to keep on living after the Great Genius's death. She was a strange accident in Picasso's life. And such an accident could only end one way: causing a bigger accident.

Dora had loved life so much—and he had killed that love.

Picasso never asked Dora if she wanted to have children, but she also didn't try to, or push him to live a domesticated life as if she expected to. And then, in the end, she learned she'd never be able. Even so, she harbored the hope he might ask her, might beg her, "I want you to give me babies." If she'd been able to conceive, maybe she would have given him some, though it would only have been to hold onto him a bit longer, since Dora, so cerebral, wasn't the sort of woman to bear or raise children. To top it all, she doubted that if she'd had them Picasso would have given them the time they needed. What would her children with Picasso have been like? She often wondered. "Children to destroy" was the conclusion Dora had always come to in the past.

On various occasions she smiled sarcastically to herself and silently made sardonic fun of the clearly loveless situations she'd had to put up with. Such as the time, for example, when the Great

Genius was telling his friends that his lover Dora obeyed him quicker than his dog Kazbek, an Afghan hound so lazy it barely stirred when Picasso gave it a command. While the dog ignored him doggedly, Dora, to the contrary, ran to his side at the slightest hint of being needed, obeyed him better than his pet, and this filled Picasso with immeasurable joy. "She's just a little girl, like a puppy, a little pet. Throw her a bone, and she'll go running to find it and bring it back to you," he boasted without batting an eye, perversely amazed.

When they made love and he was on top of her, he'd make fun of her expressions, angrily pinch the skin of her neck, of her breasts, leaving excruciating bruises on her. The more he satisfied his libido, and the closer he came to the glory of orgasm, the more bitter he became, and then, rather than giving free rein to his lust—which wouldn't have meant involving himself lovingly, either—he violated her. He was more in love with violence as an artistic convention than with love itself, as art.

It irritated him when she made all those idiotic faces—according to the sarcastic remarks he threw at her in the middle of the sexual act—though he also deplored the way her body was always so rigid, staring straight at him, cold as ice.

Was he capable of ejaculating and emptying himself into her like that, studying her in that way, denigrating her with such cruelty at that most crucial moment in the act of love? It was hard to imagine it possible. He delayed, and delayed, and the longer he delayed, the crueler his thrusting on top of her became. She would dry up and bleed, her heart would turn to a ball of iron.

For Dora, those few days in Venice helped her to understand precisely when she ceased to be an artist, instinctively open to exploring art and passion; she realized that from the moment her special, secret affair with that man began, when she herself had tried to become an idol, her life had been reduced to a series of reeling states of drunkenness. She felt drunk on him, on her passion for him, on his work, and distanced from her own work, fed up with everything having to do with herself. Drunk and cornered. So it was only through him, through his pathetic games, that she learned the meaning of lovelessness, experienced the risk that her willing subjugation could perpetuate the horror, the fear, of letting go of herself, of her life. Her absolute, continual, cruel dependence on that man, with no say of her own about anything.

She knew she couldn't fall ill, couldn't let herself fall ill — not for her own sake, but for his. She anticipated and observed any sign of weakening health in him so that she could care for him with all the devotion he deserved, or all that she thought at first he deserved. But whenever he got sick, he wanted to have nothing to do with her, turning most of all to his secretary, the irreplaceable and grouchy Sabartés. At these moments of weakness, no woman must be at his side, no lover should ever witness his feverish decline. Least of all her, as uneven as she was. He never explained to her what he had meant when he called her "uneven."

James had once pointed out that Picasso would often talk with Kazbek, the Afghan hound, then continue the conversation with his secretary, and finally, when he noticed James was also present, have him join in. But when Dora arrived and tried to give her opinion, Picasso would listen intently, only to declare the subject closed, despotically, abruptly, and without taking into account what his lover had said. For Picasso, Kazbek's attention mattered much more than Dora's. He couldn't care less about her opinion, or at least that's the impression he tried to give his audience at what the artist thought of as his "manly" and "virile" displays of self-assertion.

Perhaps on these benches in the church of Santa Maria dei Miracoli, she and James, with Bernard as witness, could sadly or joyfully recall a few fragments of a past full of unbearable twists and turns, or to the contrary, full of pleasant moments, such as when they joined forces to confront the fury of the Great Genius, of *Cher et Beau*, whose word almost always resonated like sacred oratory.

I took another turn around the church and after a bit hurried back to the hotel. It was raining buckets. My leather sneakers were soaked, and a strange melancholy had taken hold of my spirit. My greatest fear was that I wouldn't be able to interpret the enigma of the passion Dora felt for Picasso, or divine the revelation she had sensed or accepted on this last trip in her life, giving her an iron will to withdraw from the world and to leave her house only to go to the Notre Dame cathedral. After attending Mass, she would return home and shut herself away again, surrounded by the Picasso paintings hanging haphazardly, somewhat carelessly, in no particular order, and with no desire to emphasize their extraordinary value, just as he had left them, on the dreary walls of her dusty apartment, like living personalities that sometimes drew close to cheer her up and, other times, repulsed her fiercely and inscrutably.

In chess there's a position called zugzwang, like being forced to hurt yourself. Being put in zugzwang means a player is obliged to move even though moving means losing a piece. If the player didn't have to move, the situation wouldn't be so dire. It always takes place at the endgame; it's a position that seals the truth, which is that losing is inevitable. I didn't exactly learn all this from playing chess, I got it from reading Guillermo Cabrera Infante. His writing revealed for me the true meaning of obeying when you don't willingly accept your submission and long for it. If you obey, you're forced to lose after one move. When you accept submission as a tactic in the game, you force the other player to be obedient, to play without options, and to lose. Dora traded her liberal state of submission for blind obedience.

Mild and gentle. 1958

James asked if there was anywhere else they wanted to go, since they only had a little time left. They'd have to leave Venice soon and, due to the short stay they'd planned, they hadn't been able to see everything. He would have liked to go back to Peggy Guggenheim's palazzo, but Dora and Bernard objected. With so many other museums and works of art to see, the smart thing would be to go roaming through the byways, discovering new places, entering them randomly, Bernard rather impatiently noted.

They left the hotel and set off together at first, but before long Dora straggled behind, glued to the window of an eye-catching though cramped shop, studying the masks on display. The shopkeeper came out and talked them up, got her inside the shop, and she agreed to try on some of those gems. Excited, she also threw a red velvet cape over her shoulders. Amused and all smiles, she talked with him for several minutes, telling him about her passion for theatrical trappings.

"Ah, the *signora* loves the costumes!" crooned the Venetian.

"No, sir, theatrical trappings; quite different," she now insisted, very serious.

She took one last look around the crowded shop, filled with gilded, brocaded, embossed masks and costumes, laces, cloth so soft you wanted to touch it, caress it, lamps of fine Murano glass, Murano glass jewels as well. "This is all so different from the things I'm surrounded by every day," she thought.

"At last we got her mind off things. I think this trip has really changed her, I find her sweeter now." Bernard was trying to get James's hopes up regarding his friend's personality problems. They had gotten quite a bit ahead of her and she couldn't hear them talk about the worries that turned all their conversations to the complexities of her character.

"It's temporary, it's a passing change," James murmured.

She left the shopkeeper and quickened her pace to catch up with the young men.

"I'd like to go off by myself, wander around out there, without you two." Dora stared at them, expecting a reproach.

"Of course, Dora, but be careful, don't get lost. In any case, here, take this map of the city." James handed her the folded map.

"Are you sure you want to go it alone, Dora?" Bernard asked, more cautiously.

She nodded. With a childish wave goodbye, she took off resolutely down the street, then turned into a lane that led right. Her friends lost sight of her.

She gently ran the tips of her fingers over the damp wall. Suddenly, a strange sensation ran through her, very pleasant, something she'd never experienced before, as if the raw skin of her fingertips was dripping blood and she was slowly sinking into a luminous, mild, and gentle state that warmed her spine. "Blood purifies everything, everything," Picasso was telling her.

"Give me your hot blood, girl." And she was laughing out loud, cutting herself with the knife and letting the red liquid drip over the paper. The brush did the rest.

The steamy, bumpy cobblestone street was eerily vacant. She picked up her pace; in the distance she saw the elongated figure of a man. Was it a man or his shadow? When she was very close, she noticed the strong resemblance between this tall, thin mulatto stranger and the painter Wifredo Lam.

The whispers growing more intense. Venice, 1958

She decided to go back to Piazza San Marco, walking so fast she could barely keep track of where she was, and, dizzy, she almost lost her balance. She had to lean against a chipped wall, tilt her head back, breathe deeply, regain her body's bearings.

She opened the map, clumsily spreading it with both her hands, and stared at the layout of the streets, then lifted her eyes and looked for the street sign on the wall. She'd gotten lost, just as she had yearned to do, to get lost in the city, on her own. Alone and enigmatic. But she'd lost her head at the same time; suddenly she'd forgotten who she was. She'd lost track of her thoughts and her memories when she brushed past the figure of the man who reminded her of Wifredo Lam. She was afraid of going back to the point of no return in her unhinged mind. She was afraid of relapsing, losing her memory, going crazy.

Sitting on the doorstep of some house, she drew her knees up toward her belly, and put her head down, resting it on her knees.

The first time Lam went to the studio of Rue des Grands Augustins, he was coming from Spain to deliver a letter to Picasso from his old friend Manuel Hugué, the fellow who'd shared youth and poverty with Picasso and Mañach at Le Bateau-Lavoir. Picasso liked this young mulatto with thick hair and Asian looks, smiling, shapely, a body like a rustic dancer with no training in dance, wild and brimming with questions.

"Some of my ancestors emigrated to Cuba and set down roots there," Picasso said after getting the letter and the firsthand news from his friend Hugué.

"To Cuba? Your ancestors?" Lam spoke familiarly with Picasso no sooner than they met, with a friendliness that conveyed brotherhood.

Lam's gangling figure took over the room, and he started describing the island landscape, the trees, the *monte*, as he called the Cuban countryside, the birds, the color of the sky, the resplendent blue of the sea. His host studied those long, thin arms, the elegant lines of his legs, the bony face and bulging lips, the eyes with their perfect Asian line, the hair like jungle undergrowth, the countryside furrows in his smooth, chocolate-colored face. Everything about this man evoked tenderness, familiarity, and greatness.

"He is a prince," he told himself, "an indomitable prince."

From the moment he saw Lam's paintings, Picasso knew that, while Lam humbly recognized that he was Picasso's disciple, he could learn a lot himself from the Cuban and African forms created by this young artist, who was only thirty-seven but already a master, a tremendous artist. Picasso did not hesitate to sponsor Lam's exhibition at the Pierre Loeb gallery in Paris.

"We have the same blood; you're like a cousin. Why not sponsor you and your work?" Picasso insisted.

Lam smiled with satisfaction and gave the Spaniard an effusive hug. Just then, Dora walked in and, surprised by the hug and their enthusiasm, asked what they were celebrating.

"We're celebrating Wifredo Lam's exhibition in Paris!" Picasso sounded more effusive than usual.

"My brother, my brother!" Lam sang as he danced around the room smelling of resin, oil paint, ink, and turpentine.

The three spoke their language, Spanish, with different accents. The Cuban's speech, of course, flowed most smoothly. Dora tried to harden her *z*'s and soften her *y*'s so her Argentine accent wouldn't stick out too much for the Spaniard and the Cuban. Picasso opened a bottle of Anís del Mono, the only drink he had to offer, and they toasted with small, thrifty sips.

"Why don't we go to the restaurant on Rue Bonaparte?" Picasso invited, the other two accepted in high spirits.

They flew more than ran to the restaurant; they were starving, especially Lam. Halfway there, Picasso straggled a bit behind, enraptured with observing the two of them: the talented young man, and the woman who so perilously loved him and whom he was already beginning to push away noxiously. Then he felt the fear that always seized his spirit when forebodings crowded his mind and hampered his ability to think and analyze. He wondered fearfully what would happen if over time the two of them became his rivals, his worst enemies. . . . Dora looked back at him; she was shocked to see his blurry, flabby, suddenly aged face. She guessed that something deep had shattered him, old nagging worries. Lam, noticing nothing different, took him by the hand and made him prance about, cheek to cheek, tromping in the glassy puddles on the fogbound street. Just at that moment Picasso reacted, letting loose one of his great horse laughs.

At the restaurant, Lam wolfed down his dinner, seemingly eating with an ancient appetite; he couldn't help it. Dora barely tried her food, while Picasso guffawed, "Look at that, this kid might start eating the table leg next! There's nothing crueler than hunger; I've felt it, I know what I'm talking about. That being said, nobody will contradict me: you can paint better hungry than with a belly full of grub." And the Great Genius went back to laughing thunderously.

Lam wiped the corners of his mouth with the white napkin and drank copious amounts of red wine. Dora asked him, in an oddly prim way, what Cuba was like.

"Surrealist, Cuba is Surrealist!" Lam exclaimed.

"That can't be, no country can be. . . ." she sighed.

"Yes, it is, any absurd situation contains a hefty dose of Surrealism," he asserted.

Picasso asked where they should go after dinner. Dora shrugged; Lam lit a cigarette.

"I know, we can go dancing. That's it, let's go dancing!"

They ended the night in a small cabaret on Rue Vavin, where they met two young women who had each, on her own, been invited to that Spanish *soirée*: the painter Remedios Varo, accompanied at the time by the very drunk Óscar Domínguez, and once again the ethnologist Lydia Cabrera, there with an extremely reserved and elegant young woman, dressed in a sheer toga dyed bone- or ivory-white.

Lam and Lydia hugged, recognizing each other in their shared love for the faraway island. Picasso watched them, jealous of not having an island, the island he had heard so much talk about.

As she walked through the winding streets of Venice, her eyes climbed up the façades.

The façades dissolved, behind them a *monte* thick with trees appeared, and she could hear the beating of drums and melodious Yoruba chants. Then the dense trees closed in around her, tightening, the underbrush grew in every direction. Brash, she ran barefooted, trying out the novel sensation of entering the scrubland on her own. She felt it was like being baptized. The vegetation ended up running into a colorful jungle where reeds wrapped around the broad trunks of ceiba trees. She heard warm murmurings, soporific as the buzzing of bees, and in the end, the lyrical song of a bird she'd never seen before.

Dora had walked nonstop along the vast, labyrinthine cobblestone lane until she reached a dead-end street, or rather, a street whose only outlet was the sea, and she faced a steamy curtain of mist rising off the water of the Grand Canal.

The sun was setting. Never before—except during her illness—had she managed to get so unfathomably far from reality, only to live consciously in the foggy, unreal space of worlds she had invented in a state of lethargy she was unable to control.

The man who looked like Wifredo Lam, the one she'd crossed paths with in the lane, was now right behind her, was going to touch her on the shoulder. She turned around. "I don't think either of us knows where to go. I suggest we keep each other company," she pronounced.

"Señora, I have no choice but follow you, you've chosen me as your shadow," the painter's double stammered.

Dora smiled timidly. This was why only isolation, or what others thought of as solitude, awaited her when she returned to Paris. A solitude overpopulated by phantoms. With them around, Dora would have enough to maintain her balance on the edge between anxious endlessness and indifference to eternity, that hackneyed concept.

She'd held out on that edge, though just barely, hanging on by an imaginary cable, kept aloft by the wind, during her internment at the Sainte-Anne Hospital, not knowing exactly for how long, under a different name, abandoned and forgotten.

The only thing she could recall, could view through a sort of nebula, was the rope high up above, herself hanging, and the wind gently rocking her, helping her to stand. She also saw broad corridors that narrowed into the interminable distance, doors opening and closing, and the faces of dead people, of the living dead, who recognized another dying person in her, just one more among them all.

Her bruised face glimmered with large drops of sweat. She could tell from the sharp pains in her cheeks. Her teeth had gotten loose and her knees trembled all the time. Her body was like a map, marked by bruises and pricked by the needles that tore her skin, for she would impetuously wriggle from the arms of the attendant and run off, intending to pass straight through the walls, and then would crash her body into them.

However, every single night she was there she dreamed of sunny gardens, a field awash in golden oranges, a horse that answered to the name of Jade, a man dressed in white, an Andalusian woman singing at a flamenco show. But the next morning, she would be awakened by the smell of urine mixed with bleach.

An episode of disorder. Venice, 1958

I don't like to daydream; I find it fairly disagreeable, unpleasant, and absurd, quite harmful to my mental health. It isn't just that it fills me with dread, it's that I lose control of myself. That precisely is what happened to me a short while ago. I was walking, and I started recalling the day I met Wifredo Lam, one of the greatest artists I've known and admired. For me there is only Pablo Picasso, Max Jacob, and Wifredo Lam. If I could recognize myself in any of the artists of my time, I swear I'd love to have created the powerful works of Lam. He possesses the lordly gravitas of his ancestors, he's poetic in his forms and exquisite and powerful in his content; he's historical with his content, moreover, deeply anthropological and prophetic. And he's unlike anyone else, because he's telling the story of a world that still hasn't been thoroughly explored and doing it through the desires of a seer. He was able to shake off the influences of Picasso and a Surrealism that was past its prime. Lam had no parallels; he was a natural expert. Only two people equaled his greatness in the world of letters: Lydia Cabrera and Henri Michaux. I would have gladly traded places with either of them. Picasso would have admired and loved me much more if I had turned out like one of them. If Picasso was considered the genius of the twentieth century, then Lydia, Lam, and Michaux should be described as "the sprites of the twenty-first century." Though my male double—as I believe I've already made clear—is Max Jacob. Max Jacob, in my judgment, was the greatest of them all. Neither an angel nor a sprite. A man, a poet.

Unsettled by these thoughts, I head for Piazza San Marco; the city looks deserted, this oppressive drizzle keeps falling. From time to time I cross paths with strangers passing by with umbrellas of every color, all rushing as if they were late to some appointment, anxiously bustling, noticing no one else, for all the time we have available is this tiny crumb dangling over our heads like the edge of a sword. I should hurry along, too, since James and Bernard are waiting for me and have no idea where I am.

At last, my ramble leads me into this enormous space, I've forgotten the name of this famous piazza. The cobblestones gleam like a crocodile's skin. My feet are soaked, I could wring out my sneakers.

I enter Caffè Florian to look for them, I check every room inside, my friends aren't here. Yes, I remember now, this is Piazza San Marco. My favorite waiter has the same name: Marcos. My memory scatters among ragged crags and peaks, I partially recover it, as when we stop to pick a flower and its petals and its fragrance take us back to places where we've never really been. I leave Caffè Florian and nose around in various places: cafés, boutiques, inns, but my friends are nowhere to be found. I return, then, to the hotel. Their room key is not at the front desk. The young man at the front desk doesn't know what's going on with them, or else he doesn't want to tell me.

"They're still not back," the manager calls out from his little office. I get my key and go up to my room.

I undress and take a warm bath.

Sitting on the edge of my bed, I realize just how alone I am. I have no one. This trip is not mine. It's their trip. They've brought me, and I'm superfluous, I'm in the way. From now on I'll always be superfluous everywhere. Because I'm old and I'm alone, and I have more and more gaps all the time in my memory. I'm a woman abandoned by Picasso to a bitter and uncertain fate, that's why I still have some value. Though James and Bernard might tell me it's not true and try to convince me that I mean much more to them, it's only because I'm still his lover in the Great Genius's best paintings, immortalized as *pauvre Dora*, "poor Dora!" as he loved to call me, to humiliate me, just so, in front of friends and enemies alike. I know it's all over. Period. No, now I'm nobody, I'm alone, I'm not his woman anymore, I no longer play any part of Picasso's life. And I am no longer of any interest to those whose one great value is named "Pablo Picasso."

My eyes itch and burn, I try to weep but can't. My tear ducts are dry and gaunt, dusty, cracked. I'm starting to become indecipherable even to myself. Nobody loves me, I love nobody. So much the better. Complete freedom. I can die without hurting them. I bet I could die and everyone would go on their merry way without me, utterly impassive. Isn't that what I've aimed for all my life, for neutrality, for indifference, without the idiotic drama of having to make a confession of it to myself? To disappear without a splash, that's what I've aimed for with my restless, youthful, old-fashioned body.

These last few days have helped me better understand what I've suffered through. My double exile with my parents, my unbearably austere origins, and my calling to a creative life, apprehended on the way toward a cultural blending, a forced and unfinished blending. The oddity of my Surrealist and erotic art world has in the end battered and abused my true, sincere desires because of the inconsolable grief into which I was sinking. My meeting Pablo Picasso, the man I was waiting for to make me what I am today: disorder. And not so far away, I find myself now on a path at last to the unknown, to God, who is unknowability: nothingness, pure and opaline. Is God knowledge? That's what some people think, convinced they'll be able to appropriate divinity for themselves and spoil it. In the same vulgar, inappropriate way they've taken over humanity.

A dream. I see myself in a navy blue dress and matching shoes. A pair of hands is unbuttoning my shirtdress, but I can hardly make out his masculine face, bathed in light. He throws me on the mattress, I'm naked, his hands run over my body. His fingers enter my vulva, I enjoy being masturbated, slow, deep, delicious. The man kisses my lips, his mouth tastes of plums, and I guess that his eyes are green. . . . Then, just at that moment, I'm awakened by a comical melody. But the man was real, and I let him escape, though his fake-phantom shadow still weighs upon my body, once more throbbing.

I lie on the bed for a bit, then go to the chair where I've left my purse, stick my hand in and search the inner pocket where I keep a sort of amulet: my first gift from James, an Egyptian ring, found at Deir el-Bahari according to the man who sold it to him, a fellow named Molattam, quite curiously shaped, ceramic inlaid with a wonderful turquoise gem. The ring shouldn't be worn, the antiquarian warned him, it's extremely delicate. It is simply a sort of spiritual talisman, a gem meant to nurture the spirit of whoever conserves it and observes it in the midst of her dreamworld. I always keep this piece with me. Even after someone shook my hand so roughly they practically reduced it to dust, I'm afraid of losing it. I keep its broken fragments in this bag. This ring may be the cause of our whole misunderstanding. Perhaps I was giving it more significance than it really had. Most likely I accepted the ring with false hopes, and all this was all just a pitiful muddle I brought upon myself, and it was really given to me as a vain and fleeting fancy. Maybe everything in my life, including my relationship with Picasso, has been nothing but a series of misapprehensions, of terrible misinterpretations by my dreamy, mercurial mind.

I was his intelligent, brilliant freak whom he was pleased to cite doggedly: "Dora said this, Dora said that." It was only at such moments that I was of use to him, only then that I ceased to be the beast and turned into as his adorable Dora. Before long he was back to painting me with those gigantic, monstrous feet, representing me in drawings and paintings as a shapeless beast, absurd, dreadful, and so saccharine I even looked stupid. Tediously melancholy eyes

that fall like two gashes to either side of my face. Lips painted in
red that spills over the corners of my mouth, twisted into a pleading
grimace. A smile that inspires pity because there are worms in the
gap between my lips and ants mangling my tongue.

"Get out, go off to the countryside, by yourself!" he'd tell me in
the middle of the war, and I'd have to leave with my problematic
name, a name so dangerous that if I'd fallen into Nazis' hands I
could have disappeared, been deported, been killed. Even so, I had
to leave, alone, by train. "Go by yourself," he'd insist, bored.

But I loved him, and I still do, yes, perhaps I still love him, I'll
always love him. And there was nothing I could do but leave in a
daze, desolated, rush to the station, catch the train with my heart
in my throat, and lightly accept the chance that an ID check could
ruin my life, that I was putting myself at the risk of winding up in
a concentration camp. But he didn't see it, didn't want to see it.
Nor did he hesitate an instant before sending Marie-Thérèse and
his daughter to an apartment quite far from his on Rue des Grands
Augustins and setting them up there, on Boulevard Henri IV. What
difference was it supposed to make to him, the Great Genius, if
the mother of his child had to take the metro or come on foot to
see him in the middle of the occupation, to beg him for the bare
minimum they needed to survive, implore him for the little he'd
allotted them, the little time, the scant resources! He didn't care
if I had to wait anxiously for him to visit me during the rest of the
week, which he'd reduced to two days, and then he'd drop on me
without warning! The other days were for her, the Vestal Mother,
who had received his permission to visit the studio of the man she
still considered her husband, the little girl's father.

I can still hear my paltry reply, dwarfed by the devastating presence of the mother of his daughter Maya: "But I'm the one you
love!" And that unexpected response—or was it really so unexpected
for him to silence me the way he did? "Dora Maar, you know that
Marie-Thérèse Walter is the only woman I love." And the answer

from the only woman he loved: "You heard him. Get out of here!" Repeated like a litany, hammering my temples: "Get out of here!"

Venice is a city where writing paper, blown glass pens, and fine crystal are sold everywhere. These luxurious products—elegant, tinted, embossed paper, and blown glass in all the colors of the rainbow—lift me up and cheer my soul. Standing in front of another shop window, I can be enchanted, captivated for minutes at a time, by all these fascinating kinds of paper and Murano glass ornaments.

On the morning of February 14, 1938, I got the most wonderful letter in my life; my name was written out twenty-one times on it, in Picasso's handwriting and blue ink. How could he not love me? Next, he dedicated a Surrealist story to me in which my name also appeared in a calligraphic form made to resemble a house: ADORA, all capital letters. He also covered one corner of a wall in my room with insects drawn in pencil, spiders. He entertained himself there, drawing little bugs, for hours, days, months. Did that mean that he didn't love me?

Picasso left me just as he washed his hands of Max Jacob; or perhaps he never belonged to either Max or me, and we never belonged to him, the way a beloved trophy would.

"He loved you, Dora, he loved you," James once assured me, "but he didn't know how to show it. He loved you so much, the only way he admitted it was by hurting you."

James liked to recall the famous retort Picasso made to a German who'd asked him if he was the one who made *Guernica*. His response was lashing, no beating around the bush: "No, you were the ones who made it." Nor could Picasso detach himself from the horrors he had committed. Max and I are two examples of the victims no one cares about. What does it matter? What difference do our lives make compared to the life of the Great Genius? None.

"All that time, I had the following image of my life on earth, one that often recurred to me: I'm alone on the edge of the earth. Above my head, a night sky. Below, also the sky. And eternity cascading before me like a black waterfall."

I have the vague recollection of having written this reflection somewhere, but it must surely be about Max Jacob. Not about me.

Or about me, from when I was one of the living dead, in that filthy hospital where they shattered half my brain.

Discussion between overthrown idols. Venice, 1958

"Who did she leave her cat Moumoune with, in the end?" Bernard asked James.

James shrugged, then urged Bernard to ask her about Moumoune himself if he cared so much about the cat mess. James could be too brusque. Ask her what it was like the day she went off the deep end, too, he said, and caused such a ruckus that Picasso, together with Lacan, had her committed to the psychiatric hospital, above all with the approval of their friend Paul Éluard. Bernard shot back that he was in a better position to ask her about that heartbreaking passage in the bleakest part of her personal life.

Madness is something people don't want to deal with, not even from afar. She was mad or she wasn't mad, but something happened, something strange, or they made it look like she was mad, or they drove her mad. And they took her there, like it or not. At the Sainte-Anne Hospital they subjected her to countless electroshock sessions followed by a fairly extreme treatment.

"Was it Picasso who drove her mad? That's what we could make of it at the time, but no one dares to confirm it," Bernard insisted.

"No, he took her out of her own artistic world and inserted her into the exclusive world of Pablo Picasso, he made her a slave to his work and his love. It was Lacan who broke her with the electroshocks. I'm not the one saying it. Others said it first. It's clear that the lovelessness of their breakup weakened her and that the extreme treatments they gave Dora for a disease she didn't have shattered her psyche." James lit a cigarette.

"Is she still mad or was she cured?" Bernard slipped a light cotton sweater over his shoulders.

"I think that Dora the artist was never mad. On the other hand, Dora, Picasso's lover, was mad, very much so, even lingering at death's doorstep because of all her repressed delirium at first, then vomiting out everything her guts conjured up in her. She only had moments of lucidity when she went back to being the artist. That's why they admitted her under the name Lucienne Tecta and turned her into a phantom, erasing any hint of their culpability. Lacan made her one of his case studies. She brought together everything that interested him: her bisexuality, homosexuality, guilt, punishment, paranoia, self-flagellation, arrogance, meanness, awkwardness as a lover; but above all, the mystery of her being a great artist with an astounding mind, a mind of stifled thoughts.

"Poor Dora! Lucienne Tecta . . ." Bernard's voice sent a trail of echoes across the balcony facing the canal. Leaning out, he could see two cats romping with each other on the roof across the street. "Such innocence!"

Yes, such innocence. And such indecency. James lay back in bed to write in his diary. His friend was enjoying the view Venice offered him from the balcony, the narrow street and the people walking down it who had nothing to do with the history they were experiencing, perhaps without realizing its true importance, possibly taking it all too lightly. A beautiful story of their friendship with Dora Maar, the former lover of Pablo Picasso. The sublime photographer, the misunderstood, unfinished painter.

"Do you like her paintings?"

James kept writing in his notebook and chose not to answer.

"I do, a lot. Though, of course, I prefer Leonor Fini," Bernard said, trying to provoke.

"As a painter," James immediately replied, still visibly annoyed, "and as a photographer, Dora is one of the great Surrealist artists.

Don't call her 'poor Dora,' that's what he calls her when he's trying to make fun of her."

"James, have I said or done something to upset you?"

Another doleful silence.

Bernard closed the shutters. He settled in next to his friend in bed. They held hands. Bernard loved this friendship, though their amorous relationship had long since ended. Like this, fingers intertwined, he knew his friendship with James would last throughout his life and that he'd always like him, despite his bad temper.

"You are such a grouch!"

"And you never stop asking questions that don't concern me. The thing is, you seem to have fallen in love with Dora."

"Are you jealous?"

"Bah." James turned over and pretended to fall asleep.

From the street rose the buzz of diners at a nearby restaurant, the clattering of dinnerware and the typical commotion of Venetian waiters.

"Do you think she expects something extraordinary from me?" James suddenly asked.

"She expects everything from you. However, she's resigned to waiting and living in this muddled uncertainty."

"Did you know, for a while, in the past, she and Balthus saw a lot of each other? They are still close friends, of course. We'll really make her happy if we do take her to visit him on the way back to Paris, as we promised."

"Now you're jealous of Balthus."

"No, really, not any more, though I used to be, of course I used to be. . . . Another great artist in her life, imagine, Balthus, Picasso. . . . Picasso actually was jealous, still is jealous, of Balthus, even though he knows Balthus is only attracted to teenage girls."

The blue twilight grew dimmer until the room was left in darkness. Bernard lit another cigarette. The glowing tip moved through the shade toward his mouth. The small burning circle then traced the other male form, silhouetted against the cloud of smoke.

"James, what is Dora to you?"

"A goddess!" he exclaimed without stopping to think, but he immediately reflected, falteringly: "A child."

The Queen of Tibet. Paris, 2010

Secluded at a table in Café Sully on Rue Saint-Antoine, I write in my small notebook and then transcribe it to the laptop. I enjoy transferring my notes to the keyboard, because I'm one of those who still feel that writing by hand in a notebook links us to the great writers of past times. Writing in pencil now belongs to an ancient language, and translating it by keystrokes still represents, for me, a more complex and modern language, less suggestive, and not at all mysterious. I see the text better when it is written on paper. I am still not used to reading on screens, or to correcting my writing directly on the computer.

While I write, I'm thinking about Dora—for years I've been thinking about her, dreaming of her, talking with her—and while I think about her, I'm watching people go in and out of the café from the corner of my eye. At this exact moment I see a haughty, elegant woman with black hair and pearly white skin. She sits at the table next to mine, smiles at the waiter and then at me, then turns back to the waiter and orders a vodka with orange juice, no ice. She isn't very tall, but she looks it. She is wearing lots of Tibetan bracelets on her forearm; she's covered in jewels, as if she were the Queen of Tibet. That's the first image that comes to my mind.

"The Queen of Tibet," I repeat to myself in a litany. That is what Dora Maar started to call herself when she realized, without wanting to admit it, that she was going to lose Picasso. Besides, to make matters worse, she lost her mind. This woman looks like Dora Maar, and she also has something in common with Alicia Dujovne

Ortiz, but she's neither of them, though she manages to be a combination of them both. Now the woman I'm calling "the Stranger" opens a book of Surrealist photography, quite a coincidence. It is a beautiful picture book, and it sold very well when it was published. She thumbs through it, gently, and carefully studies each photograph under a small illuminated magnifying glass that she pulls from a side pocket of her full skirt.

The Queen of Tibet had been found one afternoon naked in the hallway, another time she stripped in front of some neighbors in the entrance hall to the apartment on Rue de Savoie where she lived with her cat Moumoune, a present Picasso had given her after her little dog was stolen.

Later, she walked barefoot down the street and even told the police that her bicycle had also been stolen when, in fact, she had abandoned it by the Seine. The Queen of Tibet began speaking in verse, in what seemed to be incoherent moralizing maxims, tossing out unintelligible messages, tinkling and absurd phrases: "Trees are like balloons about to fly away," she muttered. "Everything is simple, and I admire the utter doom of objects," she stressed in one grim declaration.

Her glassy eyes closed sorrowfully, her lids falling slowly in a strange, deathlike movement that hinted at a psychological rather than physical weariness. Her mouth drooped, her lips had lost their color and even the vibrant pout they used to sport.

She was only thirty-eight years old. Electroshock could only be given to those forty and over, Lacan stipulated.

"It doesn't matter," the Great Genius told the psychoanalyst on the way to the psychiatric hospital. "It is absolutely essential for her to forget. To forget me!"

The Queen of Tibet forgot so much, she even forgot her real name. Now she was going by "the Queen of Tibet" and could recollect, in bits and pieces, that she had once loved someone very important. She could tell this from the precious protuberance she had on her forehead, invisible to other people's eyes, except for the bald, pot-bellied man with the square head and the bulging eyes with large, dark pupils that looked like a pair of dried blood clots, whom she couldn't get out of her most caustic nightmares. He was the only one who noticed the huge horn on her forehead, and he had painted it just so, like a unicorn's horn.

Like an erect penis, to James's eyes.

The Queen of Tibet sensed that James loved her because, thanks to her, he could satisfy his suppressed homosexual passion for Picasso. James also felt attracted to her deified presence because of Picasso's art. No matter where she went, she wasn't going there as herself but as the living art of the Great Genius of the Century, with a tag dangling from her marked with a price still considered cheap. At that moment, she was drastically undervalued in comparison with what she'd be worth later on.

"I am the Queen of Tibet, and you owe me respect and deference. All your belongings and your money shall be mine," she decreed, obliging the young man of thirty-one to kneel in obeisance before the woman of forty-six.

The young man watched her through eyes filled with tears.

The old, ugly dwarf with the crazed eyes had once dominated her. Now it was her turn to subjugate the tall, trim young man with fleshy lips and fine skin, with abundant locks of hair falling over his eyebrows and a prophet's or alchemist's dreamy smile. She also started telling unpleasant stories about herself, describing herself as an avaricious queen whose greatest treasure was the drop of blood belonging to Picasso that she had dripped onto a piece of paper.

She stopped eating, at most nibbling at something when she was by herself. She rarely went out, meeting with a few friends at a restaurant. If they asked if she'd eaten, if she were getting enough to eat, she would assure them she was, but then her friends would discover it wasn't true, because as soon as they weren't looking she would borrow a fork from the person next to her and start grazing off the others' plates. This earned her the nickname *Picassette*, a play on *pique-assiette* (sponger, plate-picker) and a comically feminized form of "Picasso."

Her friend Leonor Fini tried to cheer her up, taking her in her arms, lulling her like a baby against her bosom. Dora's head, resting on the artist's shoulder, would sink into her breast, just as a bone two dogs are playing with will sink into a fluffy cushion. She seemed like a bewildered child, detached from everything, and Leonor was pretending she could take her dead mother's place. Perhaps she was the only one who noticed that Dora was not really cured when she left the sanatorium.

On the other hand, she never wept. Ever. She reasserted herself to her friends with impeccable, admirably incisive body language, with diabolically clever gestures that offered proof of her superb intellect.

The Queen of Tibet had been diagnosed with delirium tremens, persecution mania, schizophrenia, and extreme paranoia. A nice cocktail of pills, electroshock, and isolation would do the rest. She couldn't remember the exact moment when they freed her, that is, when they discharged her and put her back in the original setting where she had consummated and been consumed by her illness. But there she was, once more, for a very long time, longer than expected.

Sitting on the stoop by the entrance, under the lintel of the door to her room in Venice, in the year 1958, Dora could take a deep breath and recall the entrancing aroma of ether. They were using bits of cotton to dry her temples so they could apply the electric shocks to either side of her head. She was angrily biting down on a piece of rubber, her body was contracting into a knot, from her trunk to every muscle in her face. The bright and deadly ray was coursing through her limbs, her waist was twisting, arching, her bones rattling, as if they had split a porcelain doll in half with a single stroke. It was horrible to watch. Dreadful and debilitating to experience.

The roll of cotton kept her from biting her tongue or breaking her jaw. But sometimes it didn't do any good and blood flowed copiously from her mouth. This treatment could supposedly be applied only to patients over forty, she heard the nurses around her emphasize. No one saw fit to check her age. Except Lacan, who again recalled, "She's only thirty-eight."

And the Great Genius of the twentieth century uttered the sentence that finished off Dora's sexual and spiritual life, finished off her emotional life, finished off life itself: "*Je m'en fous*, I don't care! I'm telling you again, she has to forget. Besides, no one else is going to care about her. She's no use to me, she's no good for me. She won't be any use to anyone else, or be any good for anything."

However, the Queen of Tibet would reappear much later, apparently cured. I say "apparently" because she wasn't completely well, but she didn't know that yet. In her nightmares a fist would pound on her throat, the back of her neck, or between her eyes, or would suddenly knock her down and smash all the tiny bones in her tailbone.

In the past, at Chez Francis, she'd had to accept that things were really over with the love of her life when he introduced her to the young woman who was replacing her, Françoise Gilot.

It happened in a seemingly simple way: she recited like an automaton to her young rival that everything between her and Picasso was over, just as her trainer's tactics forced her to do. She feigned savvy by ordering the most expensive dishes and gulped down her pain with fine champagne, caviar, and foie gras. She was no longer the captive wild beast. And she was following a brilliant script.

When the comedy was over, she went off on her own, but first she had to put up with the contemptuous mockery from her *Maître*, her master, her tiger trainer: "At your age you won't need anyone to walk you," he hurled at her with a snideness she recognized from a not very distant past.

She responded no less sarcastically, "At your age, you need to lean on youth, like a cane, to get yourself anywhere."

She pocketed the ashtray Picasso had slipped to her after pilfering it from Chez Francis. She squeezed it angrily, her hand thrust between the silk and wool of her overcoat.

The Queen of Tibet walked awkwardly, as if she would collapse at any moment, while recalling the words of Paul Éluard, one of her few friends: "He's sold too many paintings to the Germans to be trusted as a member of the Communist party." And what the hell good did being a Communist do? she wondered, furiously chewing her lips. It didn't even help you be a man.

I wrote all this and more in the Café Sully, so engrossed in and focused on my writing that I hadn't noticed the woman at the table next to mine had quietly left.

"When did that lady leave?" I asked the waiter. "I hadn't even noticed she was gone."

"About an hour ago, my dear *petite dame*, about an hour ago."

How long had I been writing in the café? Several hours, many hours, I didn't want to calculate it. I was starting to feel bad and didn't know why. I paid the check and decided to go home. It was already dark.

The Café Sully never closes.

Reciprocal offerings between deities. Venice, 1958

God had surely given her this trip as a gift. Now they were nearing its end and she didn't want to spoil it; she had to behave nicely and be good, promise herself to be well-mannered and kind toward James and Bernard. But to be honest, she preferred to be just as she always tried to seem: tough, strict, demanding. Though she was falling apart inside. She'd had a few drinks in her room and felt happy and tipsy. God had also given her three horrific gifts: Picasso, a chair on which he used to paint her, and a church kneeling bench. God sent her those two last gifts through the painter. She got them after they were already living apart, and she was sure that he had sent her both the heavy torture chair and the church kneeler to remind her that she was and would continue to be his lifelong victim, and he her tormentor, and that all she had left to her now was devotion to God. God had formed her exactly as she was now, at fifty years of age: honey on the inside, superior hard rock on the outside.

In exchange for these hideous presents, Dora sent Picasso a rusty, broken, worm-eaten shovel, which James was kind enough to convey to him. Picasso died of laughter when he got it and assured James that no one but that woman, that madwoman, could understand his messages and respond in kind.

God never stopped putting her to the test, but during her youth she couldn't hear him, because what fascinated her was the wonderful sonata of art, its fervent melody, its transcendent meaning, and like all young people she'd been egotistical, greedy for everything earthly that the age demands.

First, God made her Georges Bataille's lover, turned her into his perverted, cultish sadomasochistic muse; after Bataille came others, almost all of them important Surrealist artists; finally, her greatest and hardest test: Pablo Picasso. The Great Genius of twentieth-century Cubism. And, not satisfied with her work, God cast her from the heights, forcing her to fall headlong and smash herself to bits in the harshest, most remote chasm. Would James be her savior, the one to catch her at the last second, just like in the movies?

She had to recover her strength, lift herself up, climb the unmentionable paths of shame and bitterness, reach the summit once more, if there was still time for her, curl up in a bend of the road, wait and get used to it, accept the idea, realize that the only alternative she had left was to surrender completely to Him, to the one, true, authentic Lord of her solitude. God, then, is nothing but abandonment, estrangement, isolation.

In a short time they'd be leaving Venice, they'd take the car and make the trip back to Paris by highway. James promised her they'd visit Balthus. After a few hours, or days, it would all be over, the trip would come to an end. The trip of her life and the journey of life.

In the secret of myself
living you make me live my own secret.
This room where I lived in madness, fear, discomfort
is the simple birth of a summer's day.
Exile is endless but it is summer,
silence under full sun.
An enclave of peace where the soul dreams only happy things.
A child on the highway home.

The verses sprang to mind suddenly, strangely, vaguely. Yet even though she visualized them clearly and sharply, she couldn't remember when she wrote them, or in what context. Nor did that matter to her any more; all that mattered was the essence of the verses: chaste, humble, free from the strident malice that arises from the ridiculous, aggressive egotism of mediocre poets.

Nothing worthwhile happened on this trip, but at least she had restored peaceful relations with James. It had been one more jaunt with him, though longer and farther than their earlier ventures; another stroll by his side through the vast society of solitude that the world had become. Both of the men accompanying her had tried to be nice, and she was deeply and sincerely grateful. Nevertheless, she was expecting much more from her young friend, a more delicate devotion. Though she suspected there wouldn't be any more to him than an interest in having her friendship, just as he aspired to own the artworks Picasso had painted for her. Perhaps she was being unfair, she supposed without getting too upset, but she had to find an excuse for getting away, and she'd already given so much that she now only wanted them to give her the courtesy of letting her be unfair at the last moment, the moment of bidding farewell.

Her friendship with James Lord was slowly being reduced to this, strictly to trading information about Picasso's work, and she knew that the others, his friends, never stopped gossiping about it. She didn't deny James loved her—of course he loved her, in his own way, a way that involved few social obligations. She couldn't even fall back on the powerful treasure of having shared intimate moments of physical love. She hadn't permitted it, and he didn't have the right disposition. It could have succeeded, that night when he lay down by her side, in her bed, at Ménerbes, under the stifling and sustaining light of a candle. She took his hand and placed it on her breast, his hand clutched hers, but she withdrew it, and when he asked her if there was something she desired that he should do, she told him no. Told him everything was better this way.

They packed their bags that same afternoon. They left the Hotel Europa, seemingly having fun, between the fake acid barbs Dora hurled at the couple and their over-the-top retorts, which also papered over their real frame of mind, which was quite low.

They got into the vehicle. The rain was coming down hard. In the car, James and Dora argued over nothing, over nonsense that she preferred to forget or that she had simply erased from her memory. Bernard mediated unsuccessfully, trying each time to tilt the situation in Dora's favor, and incidentally in his own, with the same skill he used when he had to get out and repair the car on several occasions, under the heavy downpour but fortunately with greater success. James also tried to fix the car several times but was unable; he didn't know the first thing about mechanics or any of that nonsense.

In the end, they decided to go to Milan, they visited several museums, and from there they crossed the mountains and reached Zurich. They took in the beautiful scenery and admired the lakes, but above all the hills brimming with pines that so delighted Dora. Basel saddened her; lately it wounded her spirit to see so many paintings at once. There they marveled at a few Holbeins and, as might have been expected, a few magnificent Picassos.

She was unsure whether painting was still an art that was evolving toward new forms of painting. Of painting, not of successive swindles.

They resumed the journey.

Around midnight they arrived at the chateau in Nièvre where Balthus lived. The painter wasn't expecting them, of course.

Bernard and Dora stayed in the Renault; it was James who, after determining that the doors of the chateau were open, went inside in total darkness, turned on the lights, and called out to the artist.

Balthus emerged from Frédérique's room half-dressed and somewhat tipsy; in a rather bad mood, he insinuated that it was not the best time to receive visitors. Leaning against the table, his wandering eyes could only focus on one spot: Dora's face, and his eyes lit up only to dim immediately. As soon as he saw his friend, he started whispering wheezy, incoherent words about her while ruthlessly ignoring her companions. He missed her so much, so much, he endlessly repeated.

"I should have called you, should have called! I missed you so much, my little friend, so much, my Dora!" And with his long, thin hand he caressed her face.

Dora remained stiff, showing no sign of relaxing sentimentally. Stoical and seemingly indifferent, she listened to the artist's laments and even wiped away his tears with the corner of a rumpled handkerchief she pulled from her purse.

"Don't be a baby!" she whispered into the ear of the most babyish of painters.

They decided to turn in, and the following morning Balthus's behavior toward Bernard and James was less gruff, but elegant, as if sleep had afforded him calm and good counsel.

They agreed to have lunch with him. Fortunately, the atmosphere lightened over the course of the meal. Bernard kept trying to force the situation by trying to show himself more sensitive and devoted to Dora than the others. Balthus then leaned away, settling into the back of the chair, half-closed his eyes, and peered slyly through the half-open slits at Bernard, who in turn seemed pleased to see that his grandmother's rug, which he had once given to Balthus as a present, lay in the center of the room. Though Balthus was fond of Bernard, he had gotten to where he didn't trust a soul.

It seemed like Dora didn't want to let go of Balthus, as if the last truly valuable part of her memories of youth were stored up in his company.

But they had to move on, it was getting late; "It's getting beyond late," one of them pointedly noted. And they left.

On the remainder of the trip nothing important happened. During the rest of their journey silence reigned.

On May 8, James and Bernard brought Dora to the front door of her home, where they hurriedly took their leave of her. Though they had agreed to meet during the next few days, they didn't. Thirteen years passed before she and the young American soldier, who had some time before turned into a middle-aged man, dazzling and worldly, saw each other again face to face.

Bernard Minoret, for his part, confessed to me that he didn't know how he had let time slip, just like that, and today he wonders how it could have happened that he never longed to visit her again, that he never again thought about her.

On the other hand, on returning from New York James tried to meet her. After several phone calls, he was bent on going to visit her, but Dora refused to set a day. She didn't do it directly or rudely, no. Quite the contrary, she always brought up a banal or meaningful pretext: her health. James gave up. She was different now, one more woman about to enter the litany leading to old age. She'd been ambushed by the whole string of tumultuous memories piled one on top of another. And to all appearances, she preferred to withdraw into her solitude.

Nevertheless, despite her constant subterfuges, after a long while they unexpectedly agreed, at last, to meet on several occasions. The occasions were few and fleeting, the fleeting imaginary kiss of expectancy.

6–18 Rue de Savoie. January, 1995. December, 1997

I had just gone into exile in Paris. My daughter was not yet a year and a half old, my husband was a year shy of thirty. I would be turning thirty-five on the second of May that year, 1995. Numbers sometimes hold more mystery than words; I mean, there's a quantum enigma to the coincidences in our fates. Born in 1959, I thought of my exile in 1995 (note the last two inverted digits) as a second birth.

I woke up very early that morning, didn't write anything. I was having trouble regaining my drive to write at daybreak.

I thought about our luck in being able to move here and live in Le Marais, though we weren't exactly renting. At first we house-sat in a painter friend's flat while he was off traveling. Though we had the small apartment all to ourselves, we kept to the front room to avoid making ourselves too at home in a place we couldn't think of as ours, despite our host's insistence that we should spread out. We slept on a black IKEA sofa-bed, old and secondhand, my husband and I on either side, the baby in the middle; we had to be careful about how we got out of bed, because if we both stood up at the same time the little one could get trapped, since the sofa-bed was missing a spring and had a dangerous habit of folding shut all at once.

I stood up gingerly and, trying to make no noise, took the few steps to the small, cramped bathroom. I finished washing and dressing, bundling up perhaps more than was called for. In the cluttered, greasy kitchen I had coffee, no sugar, and after a bit wrapped a scarf around my neck and went out swaddled in a thick overcoat.

It was bitterly cold out, but the sun painted the winter day a pearly hue, lending it a sudden exotic joy. I took a deep breath and my lungs froze, I felt like I had a Russian razor, one of those Astra brand shavers the Soviets used to send us in Cuba, coming in through my nose and slicing its way down to my lungs, slitting them mercilessly with its rusty edge. Nevertheless, I breathed deep and instantly felt optimistic and happy because I was free, not thinking with fear and hand-wringing about the future. If I allowed myself to think, I'd be letting in fear. . . . A fear that could settle in like an old friend and become destructive, a writer's block.

I didn't have a penny, not even enough for a metro ticket, so I walked along the Seine toward the Pont Neuf, then turned down Rue de Savoie to number 18, where I was to meet my editor as well as a photographer, since they were going to take an author photo of me for my novel.

When I got to his office I greeted everyone timidly. The press secretary offered me some tea from Mariage Frères, the teahouse a few doors down from the office; she promised to bring it good and hot, for she'd noticed my hands shivering and teeth chattering from the intense cold. Natalie was always so nice to me, she soon had a piping-hot cup in my hands and some cookies on a separate plate.

The photographer was all set, and he decided to go outside to scout for a good location. A few minutes later he came back in to get me so he could take the photos outdoors, since space was so limited inside the office he could barely turn around. We set up right on the corner of Grands Augustins and Savoie, the sun bathing my cheeks, the frozen wind off the Seine tousling and mussing my hair.

Down the opposite sidewalk walked the only pedestrian who shared the deserted street with us at that moment: an old, stooped woman with a pronounced hunch. She halted for a moment to see what we were doing, but not for long. Shaking her hunch as if disgusted by what her eyes were taking in, she shrugged and hurriedly directed her slow steps along Rue de Savoie; she disappeared into number 6. I learned it was number 6 not only because I'd been calculating how far down the street the building was, but because a young editor from Arles who was passing through the city took it upon herself to inform us. "The lady who stopped to watch us is none other than Dora Maar. She lives in number 6 on this street," she whispered fearfully, as if the woman could still hear her.

I jumped up, stunned, it couldn't be true—Dora Maar, living in that house, practically next door? Oh, wow, I couldn't believe it, I'd been that close to Dora Maar—one of my idols! And my mind went back to the afternoon in Havana when I'd tried to act brave, along with Lena, Apple Pie, Lefty Sotera, the time we took part in an impromptu demonstration against the regime; that was the day I showed them Dora Maar's photos.

"And here, around the corner, is the atelier where Picasso painted *Guernica* and where she photographed that extraordinary work of art," added Aline, the editor.

"Do you think I could maybe, I mean, just see . . . ?" I asked, feeling foolish, then added as an excuse and a pretext, "I'm a huge fan, such wonderful artistry."

"See *Guernica*, you mean? No? Sorry. Oh, of course, I see, you meant you wanted to see Dora Maar. Well, of course, you might cross paths with her again. She normally goes to Mass very early, to Notre Dame, but I warn you she tends to be quite rude, though she always returns greetings, she has impeccable manners, as the grande dame she is. . . . But I once tried to start a conversation with her and she brushed me off, saying she was too busy to let me become part of her life, that I shouldn't expect her to bear the luxury of wasting her time on banalities, given that she had her paintings waiting for her. That was our entire conversation. I didn't have time to get a single word in, so it was really more of a monologue."

We finished the photo shoot and I went back home as soon as I could, rushing, my mind absorbed with Dora Maar and the tasks that awaited me: I had to cook, since it would soon be lunchtime, and finish a translation that I was getting paid 500 francs to do, of a preface several pages long for an art catalogue. I'd make something light to eat—anyway, without money I had no other choice—and then devote the rest of the day to working.

Yet I could barely concentrate. All day long I kept thinking about that hunchbacked old woman with the face wizened by age and the clear eyes, dressed in black and carrying a purse slung from her shoulder that was almost bigger than she was. That's how the great Dora Maar first appeared to me, who could have guessed?

The next morning I returned at the same time with the sole objective of bumping into her again. As I left the run-down old hotel where I was temporarily residing, I ran right into another painter friend of mine, also Cuban; we exchanged impressions of our plunge into exile, and he gave me some pointers. I asked after Yendi, who had been his girlfriend in Havana in the eighties. "Oh, her, yeah, a real exaggerator, she made me miss a trip and ruin my life for no reason!" I told him I was sorry, and we agreed to meet for dinner some night.

I hurried on to my imaginary appointment, afraid of getting there late.

Positioning myself near the main door, I got a clean view inside her building when the concierge came out to collect the empty garbage cans. She asked me, as she looked me over uneasily from head to toe, if I was waiting there to meet one of the tenants. From her accent, I realized she was Spanish or Portuguese. I was just about to ask after Dora, but I stopped myself because I suspected she would shoo me off with the broom in her hand, which she held at the ready.

"I'm waiting for someone from the publisher's."

"The publisher's office is at number 18; this is number 6," she growled.

I apologized, pretending I'd made a mistake, and made as if to leave.

After a while, no more than ten minutes later, I caught sight of the little old woman, who was almost back to the building, which had to be her apartment building. Coming from the other direction I almost ran toward her, while she barely noticed me, being so completely wrapped in thought, perhaps more worried about falling and hurting herself than about crossing paths with someone like me.

When I was almost on top of her she looked up, and those beautiful eyes that changed color like the weather rested on mine. The look in them was private, sad, yet not at all dull, but rather sparkling and full of zest.

I wanted to say a few words and introduce myself, but she drew back, opened the door, and entered the building, faster than I reckoned. As the door swung slowly shut behind her fleeing figure, I managed to watch, not without deep sorrow, this scrawny bundle of a woman fearfully crossing the courtyard and disappearing up a stairway that led to an apartment with colossal picture windows. She firmly shut the door facing the street.

I told myself I'd have really loved living in a building like this and being Dora Maar's envied neighbor so I could interview her about her life and work and make friends with her; yes, I even began to feel the peculiar and unexpected need to become her friend. Then nostalgia once again seized me, something that shouldn't be happening, given my still brief separation from the island and my nonexistent desire to go back. But I was gripped by a nostalgia that had nothing to do with my own past; instead, it was about hers, a longing to have been a part of this great woman's era and the days of her youth.

After this took place, for the next two years I kept on crossing paths with Dora Maar—because I had set my mind to do so. Finally, toward the end of our furtive encounters, she began to greet me with a smile and a gracious nod of her head, and I would be overcome by a wild, barely controllable desire to hug her, to confess to her how much I admired her, and to tell her I had even begun to love her with an indescribable, constant, and despairing tenderness.

One spring morning I bought some carnations that I hoped to give her. I offered her the bouquet when we greeted each other, and she accepted them ceremoniously, simply wishing me, in her embarrassed little voice, slightly cracked, still hinting at the verve she had in years past, a happy summer. We never strayed, however, from our strict routine of maintaining a respectful distance.

On another morning in 1997—a morning when I arrived fatefully late—Dora set out for the cathedral but never made it. She fell stricken in the middle of the solemn esplanade in front of Notre Dame. I suppose the hands of strangers picked up her dead body there.

That day I'd been waiting for her as usual, but due to my unforgiveable lateness and seeing that she wasn't coming back, and of course never imagining the worst, I decided to go home and resume my translation and editing work, which I was behind on.

I learned of her death the following day. Early that morning I got a call from a journalist friend who knew how much I admired the artist. It was a hard blow, not easy to recover from. My first hard shock in exile. My first loss.

All these years, not a day has gone by that that I haven't thought about her, read about her life and her work, though so little has been written about her in comparison with the grandeur that defines her; I've done this quietly and sadly, not daring to share with anyone.

When I walk past a bookstore and catch sight of books by Man Ray, the covers of which are most often adorned with his beautiful photo of Dora Maar, all I can do is regret not having the courage to approach her and talk with her, beyond what little I did, about whatever might interest her. About herself, perhaps, about her paintings, about her photography, about the era she lived in. About Picasso. She would have picked the topic, after all.

Yes, it was a shame I never dared; it would have helped me so much at the time, during my first months of definitive separation from my country, to have been able to count on her help, as a friend, as the foreigner she had been, if she had accepted my friendship. Because, though it might seem that a vast historical abyss separated us, in truth that chasm, which the remains of the century were beginning to brim over, instead brought us together.

Notes from the last litany about the beyond. Paris, 2011

I will never truly understand why a woman like Dora Maar loved Picasso, beyond his art, but I'm not interested in delving into it too deeply. The time she spent with the painter isn't what attracts me—unlike James Lord—to the story of her life. Frankly, I'd rather investigate why she kept up her friendship with Lord himself, which was also complicated and damaging to her later artistic career; and on the more irrational side, I'm interested in why Lord put so much effort into that trip to Italy, which ultimately led to her total withdrawal from social life.

Perhaps surrounded by the tumult of memories invading her solitude, she hoped and dreamed that the "decaying scenery of Venice," in the words of Terenci Moix, would allow her to "exorcise the ghosts" of her life with Picasso, and later with Lord, and that the trip would distance her from her youthful indiscretions in Paris.

Yet such a prudent desire to blot out an entire life with one trip, to seek refuge in solitude through an ordinary friendship with a gay man instead of remaining shackled to love for a genius, is hard to believe. I'd find it more plausible if she'd stuck with the nasty ogre, given the way Picasso treated her, since he did his best to destroy her as a woman and disparage her as an artist. And, naturally, in most cases we women opt for the ogre.

Even if I can begin to understand Dora's fascination with the Master, with the Genius, and how she transferred her admiration into a demonic and possessive love, what I'll never get is her slavish dependence on him to the end of her days. I guess having the platonic, yet equally complicated love—rather than a simple friendship—that she had with James Lord afforded her a breath of freedom, a taste of excitement, and a gutsy decisiveness, that lasted longer than she could have imagined.

Besides, it's not that she was enthralled by James Lord himself; her genuine feeling of love for him arose from an aesthetic visual image: the image of him in the enormous, sculpture-crammed room where the Great Genius worked, surrounded by all sorts of stuff, true masterpieces along with vulgar bric-a-brac, in the midst of which the soldier looked like an ephebe from ancient Greece, yet another object to be preserved and adored.

Dust reigned in that room, so eclectic it tired your eyes to look at it all, where you could hardly make out the stained and threadbare old red crepe sofa, or Kazbek, the dopey dog, lolling in the spot where the sofa sagged most deeply.

That afternoon when she first discovered the lad, he was half-naked in the suffocating heat, and the smell of the cushions mingled with the smell of James's sweat (and the sweat of previous guests), while he slept, or pretended to sleep, stretched out on the garish couch, making him scandalously seductive. His face shined as if bathed in a patina of marble, looking keen and serene, as if time's glacial passing had turned him into a Taino stone artifact polished by calm and silence. Picasso was painting nearby. He approached the sleeper when he saw Dora enter. With an aristocratic gesture of his hand he indicated she should take care not to disturb him. He chuckled. "Be careful, Dora, don't wake him. This little American soldier is my war trophy, you know."

The Master skipped off playfully, pleased with himself. After a while he came back, still smiling, muttering flirtatious remarks at his guest. Dora still stared in amazement at that pile of fresh, tasty, delectable flesh, assembled as neatly as a jigsaw puzzle. Picasso began showing off to the other visitors who were now arriving what he called the "Sleeping Liberation Warrior," as if he were one more object in his personal collection.

"Look, look! Isn't he stunning? Isn't he absolutely glowing with health?" he whispered.

Picasso's admirers had no choice but to utter compliments to each other, faking an admiration for the living work of art outstretched before them, whom the Cubist genius would have titled *Sleeping Soldier.* To all appearances, the sleeping lad's utter surrender had transformed the artist into a passive spectator, chosen by the object of his observation, flattered and satisfied in the deepest part of his ego, since everything indicated that the lad had made an exclusive and everlasting gift of his sleep to Picasso alone.

This image, these memories, these events, had captivated Dora more than the actual person behind them. From that day forth, Dora appreciated James Lord for his boldness and his brilliant ability to turn his own self into a Picasso.

Years later, when the painter had abandoned her and Lord had begun to woo her, she realized that Picasso had unknowingly led her to a man who would go to any lengths to help her heal from her irreparable loss. Actually healing was another story.

As she wandered over the rusty, cobblestoned streets of Venice, a putrid odor arose from the lagoon, shattering her rose-colored image of palazzos with their prominently displayed coats-of-arms of old families of the Novecento, some waning, some prospering. Most had already disappeared by then, with their burning desire to amass more riches and titles, or else had grown perfectly accustomed to sneering bitterly at the end of their frippery and frills and the triumph of the bourgeoisocracy.

On one of her walks she realized—as if receiving a memo from the past—that the first time her body had been aroused about James was when Picasso told her he had kissed the good-looking soldier. She had not witnessed it herself, but she had indeed been there at the moment when the lad awoke from his long sham sleep and rose from the sofa to go to the living room, constantly trailed by the frightening shadow of the sickly, skeletal, skeevy Afghan hound that responded lethargically to the stupid name of Kazbek.

The guests paid no attention to the dog, much less to James. The lad announced in a drowsy voice that he was about to leave. Dora returned to the other room, followed by the entourage of visitors. It was then that Picasso, taking advantage of his being alone with James, took him in his arms, brought his lips close, and planted them on young man's blushing cheeks. The American was overwhelmed by the kisses of his idol, and he let Picasso do it, ecstatic, immobilized by excitement and desire.

He was unable to respond, however, because he didn't know whether he should return the kiss, and at the same time he was overcome by an inner thrill that, although enjoyable, was too unsettling and too exquisite for his taste. He had desired this kiss and he accepted it happily, but innocently, rather like a child. James later told Dora that this show of exaggerated affection had been totally unexpected and unprecedented for him, and it had stopped him in his tracks, given that nothing of the sort ever happened in his own country between two men, and even though it had, of course, aroused him from head to toe, like a teenaged boy fingered and caressed for the first time, the worst shock had been discovering that it gave him an erection.

Much later, once again recalling the event with Dora, she had told him, "In France, a kiss like that doesn't mean anything sexual; it's usually the same as shaking hands. Of course, who knows what Picasso intended by embracing you and kissing you so passionately. You never can tell with him. Can I share something with you? He used to love pulling my hair just to hear me scream—that's what he'd say—and he did it so savagely I almost passed out, and when I screamed he couldn't hide the endless delight and pleasure my pain gave him."

She could now smile as she listened to James relate how Picasso talked about her when she wasn't around, though she could imagine the sarcastic sorts of comments he threw at her, meaning to take her down a peg, making fun of her to his heart's content. Sure, he'd say, she was a first-rate photographer, but then he'd add that she had never picked up a brush before she met him. Of course, he'd say, she was a brilliant photographer and yes, certainly, as soon as they met Dora began taking hundreds of photos of him, and she wouldn't have been happy if someone like James took the place she'd always held as his portrait photographer.

While she stood apart from the pair, aiming her camera to take her famous photograph of them, the vain Picasso shared these bits of gossip with his newly-arrived guest, whom he would later consider an upstart.

"Take your time, Dora. This will be a one-of-a-kind portrait. I will never pose with such an attractive American soldier again," he jabbered, laughing his head off.

Click. Dora captured a superb shot of the two. Two such different men, who would nevertheless play such complementary roles in her future.

She dragged her feet along the dense evening streets of Venice, feeling the decadent humidity of the cobblestones, wondering if she would ever return to this city with James and Bernard, or perhaps just James. And if Picasso ever asked her to make this trip again, would she accept? No. Never. They'd never do it. It was too late to bring Picasso back into her life, and she couldn't allow herself to be seduced again by someone she now knew she should handle very carefully. A woman's life is a perfect litany, like a Bach fugue, basically unvarying, then building in a crescendo to nowhere, until at some point it all collapses and nothing is ever the same again. Nothing in this infinite song of life, not a single melody, ever repeats, not even one faltering note.

She was spontaneously overcome by a fit of nervous laughter. James had once told her how he sometimes passed himself off as Picasso's son, and how he used this trick to mess with more than one stuffy, old-fashioned gallery owner, the sort who loathed the Spaniard for his "incompetent" paintings, his unbearable moodiness, and his uncontainable verbal diarrhea.

"It got worse when he decided to join the Communist Party. Louis Aragon and Paul Éluard were the ones who got him all fired up and talked him into agreeing to become a Bolshevik."

"He's just a Commie, yes, sirree! That father of yours is really something!" blurted out one of those old schoolmarm dealers who found Picasso's work horrendous and who never completely believed *l'américain* Monsieur Lord when he claimed to be the Great Genius's son. "Aragon can be very persuasive, because he not only dresses the part, so elegant, but he's also attractive; he has a free hand with gifts and an ingratiating tongue for flattery. At least, that's what the women who hang around him say," said the "schlock handicraft saleswoman," as Picasso called her type of dealer.

James never could stand Aragon, who was too devious and twisted, a real reptile, truly a snake, doing whatever it took to charm and humor those beguiled by his sibylline circumlocutions. Paul Éluard was a different story. James liked him from the start, since he always treated James with tactful kindness. James was a nobody, but Éluard talked to him one-on-one and gave him his full attention. He seemed so nice, and besides, James never knew how he managed it but he could always entrap him in an intricate conversation, full of the big-boned words that Éluard loved to employ: "pistil," "limbo," "nonchalance," "demon," "rhinoceros," "pitch-black."

Dora felt a viscous liquid sloshing against her feet; a reddish trickle started to fill the cracks of the pavement and cover the soles of her shoes. The overcast sky offered a crushing view of the city, as if it were about to fall with all its leaden weight flat upon her. She felt as if the walls were closing in on her, as if the streets were narrowing until she would be squashed between the buildings. She felt trapped, scarcely able to breathe.

James had once told her that "every adventure is about going to a particular place, arriving at a destination, whether physical or spiritual, normally at some distance from where you started, which in any case is irretrievably lost in time. There's also the possibility of a quest, if only a quest to find yourself." Why could she always remember what James Lord had told her and hardly ever what Picasso said? Was it just that whatever words Picasso said to her weren't particularly memorable or eternal? She could vividly remember every sensation from every moment she'd spent with Picasso, but the things he had expressed in words had been few and scarcely interesting. So far from wise that she hadn't added any to the album of famous quotes she jealously treasured in the most hidden recesses of her mind.

The walls that had closed in on her now withdrew again, until she suddenly found herself in the middle of a vast space, with that same black cloud still looming overhead, and she did nothing but prance about stomping in puddles as viscous as coagulated blood.

Two phantasmagoric figures appeared before her, like silhouettes drawn in pencil, embossed in graffiti dust, specters subordinated by their long-limbed movements. One of them was the painter, the other the young soldier. Picasso lay on a pile of big cushions, motioning for the lad (also drawn as if in an animated cartoon) to cross the threshold. James lay down next to Picasso, who pulled him close and kissed him on the lips, then backed off in surprise, staring into James's eyes, and let out a sonorous guffaw.

"You are a miracle, a miracle!" he exclaimed, excited.

The vision was gone in a flash, and Dora found herself once more squeezed between the old palazzos and the foul stench of the lagoon. After that fever dream, another Picasso appeared, fuming in repressed fury.

The war with Picasso had long since ended, but as he himself had once told Lord, hostilities would persist forever. Any time they met, even if only in phantom form, it would trigger uncontrollable rage in them both, but especially in her, choking her, smothering her, making her sick. She didn't want that, didn't want to get sick, and didn't want to spend the rest of her life remembering him with hatred.

Down below, mist spread in the opaque light of dusk, and a fine drizzle fell; up above, on the bridge, she gazed through her tiny opera glasses as if watching Assia, her former model, diving into water streaked with too much concentrated sunlight. Everything seemed framed like one of her early photos of Paris in the rain, or in the sun, a low-angle shot, the sort she took with Kefer in the early thirties. The water of the lagoon churned bottle-green, turbulent, stinking. She could photograph water like no one else, and no one could create liquid images better than she, finding the choppy waves in a model's hair or in a body whose pores could be made to look, through the magic of the lens, like cresting foam or like the craters of some newly discovered hydraulic planet under study.

She knew she would spend her final years alienated and entrapped by a heap of memories, foremost among them those from her trip to Venice, where she made one of her last attempts to revive the water woman, the enthusiastic woman who stirred within her, always struggling to outsmart the clay woman who wept heartbroken, striving to reclaim her artistic self and eager to forget her lover. Maybe her memory was playing tricks on her, mixing up her success as a Surrealist photographer with that trip to Venice; maybe, too, Picasso's phantom apparition came to her with the intention of dashing to bits the last hopeful dreams that were bringing her past back to life. So in order to make up for the turbulent invasions of her inner peace by these smooth, placid memories, she ran from home, from her solitude, with a stifling desire to seek the banal, furtive, iconically unnatural refuge of a church.

Sitting on a pew beneath the vault of Notre Dame, she was able to calm her spirit and redirect it toward a single figure: God. But when she resurfaced, out on the street again, the past seized her throbbing inner mind and then, as if hypnotized, she retraced the steps her old spirit had traveled.

In the middle of the crowded street, she imagined she saw James coming toward her with a bunch of russet orchids specked with emerald green, and she guided him to the staircase landing, after first happily accepting his embrace.

Thanks to the calling card that the florist had carefully pinned to the bouquet, she noticed that it had been bought on Rue Royale, at the Lachaume flower shop, a pricey location; she held onto that information, and then she appreciated the gift more for its cost than for its beauty. Her idea of beauty, especially when it came to art, tended to be less practical than the idea of beauty found in everyday life; if it was expensive it was good, better than beautiful, an idea that had caused not a few misunderstandings: people took her to be more selfish and egotistic than sensitive to expressions of generosity or poetic brilliance. She loved poetry, but she was a practical woman and hated people who used poetry as a means to other ends. She detested the tiresome use of lyrical wordplay for passing as the intellectual of the moment or the pearl found in the pigsty.

Picasso was very prone to this very type of false lyricism. She had learned it from him and also rejected it on account of him. Though it's true that *Cher et Beau* — the nickname she and James had given him, "Beloved and Beautiful" — could be counted on to pull one of them out of thin air at the drop of a hat, as a clever reply to something more about politics than art. No one was ever able to trip him up in a conversation that dropped art in favor of politics; Picasso always came out ahead. Asked a million times why he had joined the Communist Party, he always answered it was because everyone had to demonstrate their commitment to a cause back then, and not just any cause, so he too felt obliged to belong to something and had gladly joined, and so had put himself in the role of a loyal individual, since he valued loyal commitment, a thing that many people had undoubtedly found beneficial. Why wouldn't he find it profitable, too?

"Since one party is as good as another," he said, amused, "I joined the party of my friends, who are Communists. In the end, I only did it out of friendship."

Well, of course, doing it out of friendship gave him the apolitical status he needed in order to claim he was far above ideology. Dora also understood that this evasive behavior was what best suited a genius, that it was the equivalent of responding with a truthful performance in art. Frankly, it was better to be evasive than to surrender eagerly and fanatically to politics, because for artists, politics led to nothing but hate, bitterness, and slavery.

All the hours that she and James spent together in Ménerbes, they devoted most of their time to puzzling out the painter's social and political persona.

Nevertheless, she now drove off the fervent visions and stances that cast doubt on Picasso, always deferring to the attractive opinions that James brilliantly inserted in his languid and intelligent conversations as well as to the fabulous, fascinating stories he told on returning from America, from Egypt, or from some other captivating journey.

In New York, James had met Thomas Mann, and their meeting spurred a series of beautiful, joyous, lucid letters. "The gift of feeling astonishment is one I have spent my whole life endeavoring to cultivate," Mann wrote in one letter. And indeed, that was the only thing Dora still had in her after she lost her capacity for love: astonishment at all the great artists who had, in one way or another, destroyed her life. She detested them as lovers, but as artists she admired and venerated them to the end of her days. The greatest of them was Pablo Picasso.

This ability to separate her feelings from artistic judgments hadn't come to her overnight. Living with James had helped her view things clearly and analytically without getting defensive.

James was a cultured, refined man who never proved to be the great writer he claimed to be, and because of this, his inability to demonstrate greatness, he never became a full-fledged poet or painter either, much as he was set on it and dreamed of succeeding. That was why, no matter what he did, even when he annoyed her, she indulged him as a loyal friend, her most devoted and most loyal. If she had maintained her friendship with him for this long, without sex or any other sort of commitment in the middle, it was because James hadn't been egotistical enough to reach the artistic heights to which he aspired and was dying to attain.

His egotism revolved around needs and ambitions that were all too earthly; for example, when he first set foot in Dora's home he stopped to count how many Picasso paintings he saw in the living room; eight all told. And just knowing that he was in Dora Maar's living room, surrounded by eight Picassos, more than satisfied him: it was bliss. He was on top of the world. His artistic egotism could be sated through osmosis, through the adventures of someone else who had taken over his dreams. And when the illusion of someone else's adventures monopolizes your own dreams, you've lost a major part of your struggle for talent.

It was still possible to travel without being overwhelmed by so many trifles; journeys were relaxed, and a trip to a faraway place (back then, everything was far away) had not yet become the horror it is today: a sort of hustling to and fro with no meaning beyond sticking your nose into other people's business.

Nowadays you can't appreciate what you see out of the corner of your eye fully or deeply enough, because you're watching everything idly, through the lens of the superfluous. To top it off, you've got Japanese tourists behind you, with their flashing cameras, their feet getting in your way, all hunched over; American tourists to one side, in their Bermuda shorts, showing off the scraggly hair on their legs; over there, Spaniards shouting themselves hoarse, wrapped up in their disparate ways of expressing their self-imposed, commercialized nationalisms; and farther back, Saudi fat cats handing out bribes left and right—actually, it's never right—using the oil-bought gold that they cart about in sequined moneybags or in safes in the form of designer handbags. Don't put it past them to tip the hotel receptionist a couple of gold ingots as if they were loose change to get the best seats in the restaurant and the most attractive Russian whores, even in the middle of Ramadan, or precisely because it's the middle of Ramadan. Everything has devolved into a genuine, absolute human error turned scientific horror. When people still dropped Latin phrases as a stroke of distinction and culture, it was called, as in antiquity, the *horror vacui*.

Traveling to Venice in the era when Dora, Bernard, and James made their trip was still a matter of confronting the unexplored and mysterious world with an imperiously adventurous spirit, and you might even brandish a romantic notion of getting far away, a fervor for consuming miles. Why even travel to Egypt today, if we get calluses just from visiting the pyramids by Internet, not on our feet, but on our eyes and on the finger pressing the mouse button?

James Lord was right when he admitted he was terrified by the idea that the coming years, with their obsession over a future of marked egalitarianism and ideological comfort, of greed and Puritanism hiding behind a false show of pleasure and lewdness, and of the deranged and pretentious possession of vain and pointless wealth, would destroy their present day, when people still valued the desire to listen to those who could express themselves well and when the presence of others mattered; the need to know other people, and theirs to be known in turn, was surrounded by a halo of deep wisdom that always went along with a pleasant bit of eccentricity.

Culture was still far from being mere spectacle. And music was really music, melody, not deafening noise.

True enough, money still served to manipulate people's destinies, and many of them were flush with cash before, during, and after the war, and it has always been the solution for every sort of scarcity, especially the scarcity of morals. Why wouldn't they claim that clinging to a belief that money mucks up everything is stunningly immoral and cretinous? With the disappearance of cash and the appearance of banks, the mediocre provincial illusion spread that everybody could be rich, brilliant, and, the height of stupidity, powerful. How cynical!

All-embracing stupidity. Totalitarianism became a sentiment, an overwhelmingly idiotic sentiment. You can fight against an idea, the Cuban novelist Guillermo Cabrera Infante used to say, but not against a sentiment that is deep-seated, inbred, and immature, and therefore the perfect glue for holding an ideology together.

She wanted to push all these distressing thoughts aside. She made a scornful flick of her hand, and in so doing noticed the ease of that gesture. Her hand was no longer heavy, wrinkled, arthritic, and covered with the thick, swollen dark spots that old age had provided her. Her hand had become unexpectedly bright, smooth, and youthful, sporting nails painted red; it seemed to be jutting out in the most unusual way from a sea snail emerging from a gleaming shell, against a backdrop of perfectly spaced clouds, as in that Surrealist photo she had manipulated through photomontage, way back in the thirties.

Peals of thunder shook her and broke her daydream, and she had to run over to the big windows at the entrance to the hotel, which crashed thunderously every time the wind shoved them violently open and slammed them closed. The storm had risen up without warning, one of those unforeseeable events orchestrated by the master instrument, nature. Everyone was asleep; everyone but her and a tabby cat prowling around a roof across the street.

PART IV

THE FINAL WORD
AND FINAL PRAYER

Time as handle

She wrote, possessed by her text, eagerly to rid herself of all she knew, to erase it from her mind by writing it down, returning to the point of departure, once and again, as in a leaden litany; thoughts compiled in her diaries led her through shrinking, labyrinthine tunnels, down narrow byways elegantly edged by the bitterness of memory. She revised it yet again, went over it and over it, to be certain there were no mistakes, that she hadn't left out any detail, conceiving each repetition as a string of bewitching and melodious events in which figures from her photos mingled with landscapes she had photographed or painted and anecdotes she relived. She corrected, rewrote, crossed out, interwove and meticulously stitched together what she had written, as if it were a medieval tapestry. As if an invisible stranger's hand had taken hold of hers and set it moving with unwonted verve, forcing her to spill everything she had hitherto tried to keep hidden. She obeyed, and this act of obedience, of renunciation, flooded her with feelings of desire and pleasure more satisfying than any she had ever felt.

She went back over the passage about the meeting at the restaurant: years earlier, that night in La Méditerranée, she was smiling and her voice lilted like a singer's. James watched her, intrigued: no, this wasn't the impenetrable, morbidly melancholy Dora he was used to dealing with. At that moment she appeared a stranger, a mysterious and unrecognizable companion, perfectly dreamy, reinvented. Her eyes had a new sheen to them, and she sucked on her cigarette holder, slowly inhaling the smoke, moving with such expressive and sensual body language that he blushed in embarrassment. Cigarette ash rolled down her silk blouse, collecting in a small pile that rose and fell with the movement of her breasts. Dora looked delicious, delectable. James would never forget how she looked at that moment, and pressing his lips to her shoulder dabbed with an exotic Oriental perfume, he even told her that if he wanted to describe the universe, he could find no better definition tonight than her.

Douglas Cooper was the first to break the enchantment when he asked how much some Picasso canvases cost. Dora answered him, a slight shift in her features denoting nervous tension. "Oh, I'd rather be talking about movies or the weather, but here we go, I have to get back to talking about Picasso and the prices of paintings. I get it, that's what people expect of me, nobody knows it better than I do, but—prices! How boring can we get? You give me so much grief. Please, have pity on me!"

"This is the century of Picasso, the evidence is inescapable, and you're part of it, part of its fabulous fatalism, a key character in the drama. It isn't just that Picasso is the most important personality of the century, bigger than Einstein or Freud; it's also that his works are getting more expensive every week." Douglas Cooper paused as if to underline his conviction regarding this point, his hand fluttering in the air, an arrogant frown on his face. "That's right, I wouldn't doubt it for a second. This is the century of Picasso."

"Poor century!" she exclaimed, and a corrosive, bitter taste burned her throat.

Her distraught face wrinkled into a grimace of confusion, and she was no longer the charming woman who had been flirting with a man much younger than herself only minutes before.

"Still, Douglas, you've had your doubts, I mean, you had to think about it before you came out with such a big statement," James said, trying to save the situation and recover the woman who had made him compare the gleam in her eyes to the twinkling of the stars, just as unbearably twee as that, sincere as the comparison was on his part.

"Dora, let's set the inessentials aside. Can you tell me the prices?" Douglas Cooper insisted, pretending to ignore Lord's opinion.

"No, leave me alone, I beg of you, for pity's sake, I have nothing to do with those prices, I'm sorry, I'm not up to talking about Picasso sales."

"But, you've sold . . . you've sold . . ." he persevered, pouring salt into the wound.

"I've sold a piece or two that were less important to me, as you well know, because I sold them to you, dear Douglas, but I'll never sell another one, much less speculate on my 'memories of lost love.'"

That was what Dora called the paintings that represented the passion and the deep, ill-fated love, which—according to what she declared when she showed off in front of her friends—had been mutual, until the interest and enthusiasm waned.

The paintings rattled against the walls, or at least that's what she seemed to see through the darkness. She was an old woman now, and she took all these revelations as warnings or proofs that she was already passing into some sort of antechamber before the journey to the beyond. As in her 1935 photograph, *Forbidden Games*, where the smallest detail pointed to a beyond, to a never-never land, both possessed and possessing. She couldn't even remember why she had titled the photograph like that, given that it only showed a young boy sitting under a table and watching a couple in full erotic play: the man in the dark business suit, to all appearances a real gentleman, bent over double to play horsey, and the half-naked dancer riding him. The woman's breasts were exposed, and her attitude was not very lascivious or even provocative; rather, she looked businesslike and contagiously, sinfully bored.

She could see the subjects of the photograph now, as if she had plunged into the frame and could move around to look at it from different angles; the paintings on the walls had been replaced by Picassos, and the mirror wasn't completely black anymore but reflected James's face. A viscous, honey-tinted liquid flowed from worn striped silk wallpaper, the same sticky glop that had soaked her shoes and ankles a little while ago, and the red of it looked the color of slippery purplish clots jammed into a laboratory test tube.

She studied this space, framed in a hexagonal format that she had invented in a photomontage, yet inspired by a standard bourgeois Parisian apartment from the turn of the century, and she felt satisfied when she observed her own anachronism, her figure an unneeded addition to the overflowing, eclectic jumble.

Trying to climb into the spaces that her imagination had created allowed her to recycle her apathy. This new game made her feel less alone and less useless, she had managed to make her artworks accompany her, to enter into them, melt into their phantasmagoria, though to do so she paradoxically had to distance herself even more from the real world and listen more closely to the burbling litany of time that played inside her head. The uneasy rhythmic cadence that accompanies and imprisons an old woman.

Yes, she should resist, remain immaculate, reject the tainted human tide swarming sullenly around those weak and execrable spirits out there. She would keep her resistance intact, would look more and more like the portraits where Picasso painted her as confined, as shamed by her tears, bitter, covered with stigmata. Her solitude itself would merely be a product of the Great Genius's creativity. Yes, because Picasso had only been able to be generous toward her when he kept her isolated and offered her a mélange of solitudes. Majestic solitudes, crushed into a shapeless lump of imperishable traces, turning her from a woman into a sort of savage goddess, as James described her, covered all over in scars and tattoos. Nobody would come anymore to seek out the real Dora but rather the goddess created by Picasso, the image established in museums around the world, framed in precious woods. All her beauty, as seen and revisited by the eyes of the Great Genius, all her magnificence, as translated by Picasso and offered up to the onlookers who flocked from every corner of the planet to worship her, entranced by the moist, absent gleam in her eyes: sheer hieroglyphics. They are more interested in how much it costs than in the sheer artistic value emerging from the creation and the painting.

The woman who would become most visible was now, however, the most deeply hidden. The one who in the future would be surrounded by the largest crowds of viewers stopping to gaze at her various portraits, was for now the loneliest one, sitting and fanning herself in the large armchair of the drawing room, or pushing herself forward and back in the rocking chair, a repetitive motion of mundane inertia.

Picasso painted nothing but his fury and, though she didn't want his wrath to pass on to posterity, she had been unable to stop it. Their show was all sacrifices and lies, because his fury never actually lasted long, the sting of a bumblebee. He did get those fits, indeed, but they quickly passed, because he wasn't spiteful and he readily forgot—perhaps too quickly and too readily. Yet he had labored to immortalize those dreadful attacks of anger. And from then on, for everybody else only what Picasso had seen and painted would count, not what she had been or done, really, much less what she had felt.

But it would be different for James. Perhaps he knew much more about her, since he had probed her deepest secrets in his eagerness to become a writer. He was searching her inner life for the words he lacked, and she knew that with the passage of time she had become an inexhaustible wellspring of waiting words, of unwritten phrases, and that she could have written down everything she had wished to weep. James would do it, she had no doubt. And others would do it, too. Even if she steadfastly opposed it in her last testament. Posterity would pass her by, and she wouldn't be able to decide on it or add anything, she wouldn't be in any condition to do so, because she'd be dead, like the poor, mediocre human she was; though on the other hand, she knew, she'd be immortal, eternalized, in the portraits of Dora Maar signed by Pablo Picasso. Likewise, and no matter what other people wrote, even if James Lord did his best to do her justice, nothing would change the vision Picasso had of her through his works.

Her hands would be tied, like when they stole her dog; he came in and, without saying a word, reached down the neck of his shirt and pulled out that cat, that skittish little devil. He brought it home precisely because he knew she loathed cats. And right then, to torture her, he gave her Moumoune, and she could never get rid of the annoying animal, for which she came over time to feel a sort of morbid affection, or compassionate disgust.

Nor could she ever get rid of the view that others had of her, through Picasso, through James, and through those to whom her past, her life, had something more or less relevant to say.

Despite all these fears and hesitations, she was convinced that James would not betray her. She knew. She was sure of it. He couldn't. Picasso, on the other hand, already had, first by painting her, then by abandoning her. By erasing her from his most important work, or trying to: *Guernica*. Not completely, though. The evidence of her presence had gone over the Master's brilliant head. The work would still exist, with her impassive face and her voice caught in her throat.

James wouldn't betray her in the future. James would write exactly what had happened between them, and intuitively sensing this gave her comfort.

They began seeing each other, one on one, when she was already forty-six and he was thirty-one. Another litany of numbers she wouldn't dare give up: the day she met Picasso, her age, his age, the day she met James, his age, her age, and so on; figures she jotted down here and there, amassing them in address books and in her beleaguered brain. Despite it all, she recited once more, James was the genuine article, even when his elegance sometimes failed him and his American coarseness betrayed him.

"How much do you figure the Picassos are worth, the ones in my house?" Dora asked with satisfaction, once when she felt like boasting about her Picasso possessions.

"Half a million dollars, maybe more," he reckoned.

"Quite a bit more." Her arms waved in agitation and the haughty frown on her face deepened. She shook her cigarette holder, scattering ashes everywhere. "You know why they're worth so much? I'll tell you, confidentially: they're worth a fortune because they're mine, they belong to me, and the longer I hold onto them, the more value they accrue. Most likely if they were hanging on the walls of some gallery they'd go for the laughable sum of half a million, but being on the walls of Picasso's lover adds a hefty surcharge. On Dora Maar's walls, they have another sum tacked on by a story of love lived and love betrayed. As if they'd been saved from a fire. . . . Picasso showed me all sorts of tricks, I learned things from him nobody had been able to teach me, and he always said that money isn't important, not at all, but you should consider it absolutely vital or it will destroy you."

"I wish I owned one of those paintings," James muttered. She pretended not to hear him.

Her parents hadn't taught her anything relating to money, so in the first years of her adult life as an artist, though she was still practically a teenager, she was completely unable to manage her money, spending, misspending, overspending the little she made. She had to admit, she told herself, the person who got her started saving and administering her money carefully, who even turned her into a penny-pincher, was Picasso. On top of that, and this wasn't positive at all, he had passed on the vice of gossip to her. It's a known fact that when two people get to understand each other deeply and begin to identify as a couple, the virtues and defects of one will reproduce and multiply in the other. For the best and for the worst.

However, Picasso loved his parents and respected them. She loved her father more than her mother. Her relationship with her mother had always been tense; there were moments when she wished her mother would die, and she even dreamed about killing her. Her mother meddled too much in her affairs, and with her constant squabbling over nothing she made a mess of everything. Picasso didn't pick up this defect from Dora and start hating his mother, nor did she pick up his mother-worship or soften toward her own.

This kept up until her mother died in the most ridiculous way imaginable: in the middle of an argument with Dora, and she couldn't even remember what it was about. That night they were having a real row over the phone. Dora was gesticulating, pacing back and forth as far as the cord would reach. After a moment, she heard a rattling breath, followed by a heavy, devastating silence on the other line. She thought her mother had hung up, but she was surprised to hear the absolute vacuum of the sound of silence in the infinite depths of the phone line.

The Nazi occupation was then in full swing, and the curfew made it impossible to go check up right away. She wasn't able to leave her house until the following day, when she ran desperately to her mother's house and found her there, dead, sprawled across the phone, the receiver still in her hand. She knelt beside her body and looked at her for the longest time. She didn't want to forget any detail from that instant. "Photographer's habit," she told herself.

After a while Picasso joined her and, without skipping a beat, he set about displaying the corpse to everybody who came, as if it were a circus, evidently proud to be the son-in-law of the woman who had "sung 'The Peanut Vendor'" (a Cuban expression that Wifredo Lam had taught him, referring to someone who had passed away). She had died getting worked up in an argument over the phone with her daughter, who was his lover!

That defining incident could never have happened the other way around, because he would never have allowed anyone to show off his dead mother like a worm-eaten doll broken by helplessness and separation.

Dora sometimes dreamed of her mother, who appeared to her sleeping, or dead, with her hair lying in an untidy mess on a pillow placed on top of a brick, her arms at her sides, her mouth gaping open, her body covered with a grayish-white bedsheet. She was lying on the ground under a vault of arches and columns, much like the arcades in the Place des Vosges, a wave of white foam surging into what seemed to be her home. It was simply an evocation of another photograph of Dora's from 1935, when she was in her full Surrealist glory.

Her dreams often transformed into a jumble of random nightmares.

In one of them, repeated endlessly, her mother, standing erect, was showing her the gilded Dunhill cigarette lighter, embossed with a small face that looked like Dora's, that Picasso had made for her. She threatened to throw it into the sea or into a stony chasm, then she carried out the threat after letting out a dreadful cackle. Dora would wake up feverish from this nightmare, soaked in sweat, her head burning. She would take a cold bath and gulp down a glass of chilled white wine. Surrounded by Picasso's paintings, she'd spend the early hours of the morning staring at one spot on a canvas. After a while, she would get up, wander around the apartment, searching fruitlessly in every nook and cranny for the lost lighter with trembling hands: in the bottoms of drawers, in the pockets of dresses, in the wardrobe—without finding it.

She'd go back to bed. In the bit of sleep she could still grab, nightmares would befuddle her again: her hand fluttering about while holding her porcelain doll, as in the photo where you can see the shimmering ocean and, in the distance, the Statue of Liberty. In the foreground, her fingers, nails painted, clutching the bisque plaything, holding it perpendicular to the woman who symbolizes the triumph of life and the free world.

In her dream, however, what she clutches is a Roman glass bottle with a fairly common shape but a rare color: a purple patina with shades of peacock blue and Pompeiian green. The bottle was a present from James; it had slipped from her fingers and broken the same day he gave it to her. In the nightmare, it shatters over and over again, in slow motion. Then, to get back at her, James steals the bird he had wanted so badly, a bird Picasso had fashioned from wire, wood, and plaster especially for her. Dora had felt so sorry for breaking James's gift that she had offered it to him, but she later took it back, in one of her unbearable fits. James kept drooling over that beloved treasure, but she knew how to torture him and prevented him from having it to the end.

Now she is the one being tortured, because she can't stop dreaming about that bird, dreaming that James is pinching it from her and she can't run after him because she keeps falling, always falling. Tormented, she then looks for a phone number, the number for the police, but only manages to recite her own phone number in a deafening litany: ODE 18–55, ODE 18–55, ODE 18–55. . . .

She roams all over the house, grabs her overcoat and runs out, distressed, to Chez Georges, the restaurant on Rue Mazarin where she has arranged to meet Marie-Laure de Noailles and her lover, Óscar Domínguez, the painter. The lover, drunk as always, sets about making unpleasantly nasty jokes, making fun of Dora and her relationship with Picasso, then attacking Lord. Isn't Lord a faggot? Why does she hang out with that fag American? The spectacle gets louder and louder and more and more dismal. She can't stand it. She flees the restaurant without saying goodbye to her friend. Furious, powerless, doubly annoyed because her patroness didn't even bother to stop her lover from talking such nonsense.

Then she runs into James Lord in the middle of a street very much like the one she had photographed years ago: to the left, a glimpse of a set of stairs; by it, a passageway with windows in rounded arches, lots of light, carved stone columns; a boy in shorts, shirtless, carrying another naked-chested boy on his shoulders. The lad is bent over double, like a stevedore carting a heavy sack on the docks. In the background, a plump, half-naked woman in a Roman helmet and carrying a spear, comically trying to stand guard. And Lord reemerges in the middle of all this. What is Lord doing here?

"Dora, I need to talk to you. I can't bear this ridiculous situation. It's killing me. Look, I'm giving you back Picasso's bird." He hands her the tiny sculpture, she clumsily catches it. "I don't know if I'd be willing to be your lover. Don't you see that I can't compete with him? He holds all the winning cards; for all the bad things he's done to you and the way he's tortured you, he'll always win. And I'll lose, I'll lose."

"You can do it, James, you can," she whispers, smoothing his cheek with the palm of her hand, holding it there for a moment, taking his temperature. "You're very important for me."

"I can also satisfy a woman sexually, I know, and I'd really love to do it with you, but . . ."

"But? Are you afraid of the marks Picasso has left on me? You'll never be able to erase those marks, as I warned you then and I'm telling you again now. This isn't about you leaving your own mark on top of his; you just have to accept that you'll leave a very small mark compared with Picasso, but it will be there, and it will endure."

James steps back from her, crushed, hurt by her words. Then Bernard appears in the background and jealously calls out to his friend. "Don't do it, James, don't you dare, don't be ambiguous. Don't make a fool of her. She'll never forgive you. Don't join up with a fallen goddess, because when it's your turn she'll destroy you."

She woke up from the dream exhausted, her body burning with fever. It was barely dawn. Sitting up in bed, pale, sad, she smiled bitterly. Though her friend was younger than she was, he had never paid much attention to the difference in their age; that wasn't the issue. But she sensed that there was more standing between them than the "existential, intellectual, and moral inequality" that he referred to, because she had so much more experience and wisdom; and besides, he had never been frank with her, not the way she had been with him. He had other love toys; he had Bernard, and he could let off steam by going to bed with any of his lovers, until it reached the point where Dora had nothing but his ambiguous presence on the increasingly rare and more formal occasions when he showed up. So, she couldn't stand being dependent for one more minute on the crumbs men left her, the scraps from this man. Picasso had brought them together; Picasso drove them apart.

Turning to the mirror, she inspected her wrinkled face. She had stopped wearing makeup as she once did. When she was young, she used to put it on first thing in the morning, but no more; it wasn't worth the trouble, her face was no longer the guiding light, the radiant glow that illuminated and inspired Picasso, James, her other friends. Now she could go out and calmly watch people, study the youth, whereas nobody saw her, few even noticed she existed. She was one more old woman among all the grumpy, angry, abandoned old people wandering lonely around the city.

That was why she was surprised to find that young woman—a foreigner, yes, as far as she could tell, by her accent, her appearances, the way she walked, she was a foreigner—waiting for her every morning on Rue de Savoie, a few steps from her house, then following her to Notre Dame, and for nearly two hours walking a certain distance behind her, though she never dared to say anything to her. Yes, she found the girl's timidity amusing, because it indicated a kind of monastic withdrawal. She told herself she really ought to say hello to the girl, without being too friendly or giving her too much access, because she had struck her as a nice person from the first. The girl was posing for a photographer, shivering with cold but still standing there, smiling, shy and stoic, barely resisting the photographer's lens, silenced by duty. That persistent girl reminded her of Nusch, and of Leonor Fini, and of herself.

She realized that the girl was actually more attractive when she handed her a bouquet of carnations, reminding her of the time she gathered those white flowers in Ménerbes, with James.

She and James had filled the car with dozens of bouquets of those white flowers, spending that whole morning and afternoon in the middle of the field, surrounded everywhere by pure white petals, carried away, overwhelmed, by the scent still floating in the air after a passing drizzle.

Picasso was a Scorpio, she a Capricorn. Her astrological chart resembled a diamond crushed and viewed edge-on, cut wafer-thin. She was a fiery Capricorn, a goat enveloped in flames.

She kept this drawing from her astral chart under her pillow, and it often appeared to her in dreams like the atlas of her destiny, floating in three dimensions above her head, alternating with Picasso's portraits of her.

So it was with her now: tossing and turning in bed, she was looking at the picture. Suddenly, she heard knuckles rapping at the door. She half-opened her eyes, and the knocking stopped. No sooner had she returned to a brief, shallow sleep than the knocking on the front door started up again. "Who's out there?" she sleepily asked.

"*Maman, c'est moi,*" but she had no children. It was, to all evidence, the voice of a young women whispering behind the door: "*Maman, c'est moi,*" the voice drooped hoarsely.

She got up with difficulty—her kidneys were giving her trouble, she found it hard to raise her swollen legs. She made an effort, put on her slippers, and went to the front door. Nobody there. She went back to bed. She stood facing the bed for a while, looking at a portrait that Picasso had made of her in which she appeared nude, young, and plump, her legs spread and her sex entangled with what looked to be some species of perfidious two-headed insect.

At length she lay down and, squeezing her eyes shut, she clung once more to sleep. It was easier, more comfortable, to live in her fantasy and dream world. When she was awake, she was plunged into that whole ordinary real and repetitive world which, like a worn, blunt needle, was tattooing on her temples the little time she had left and, on top of that, stressing that she would die very soon. She could put up with it better asleep because in that other dimension, her life grew; sleeping, she encompassed the vast, limitless eternity provided by the impalpable dream unreality.

She saw herself sitting, years ago, on that square chunk of cement, shaped like a column, in the middle of the beach, forest and shimmering shoreline in the background. She had crossed her legs and was holding the toe of one foot with one of her hands, as if to comfort it after some imperceptible sting. She was gazing out into infinity, which at that moment might seem to be, from her perspective, Picasso's profile. He, on the contrary, sat comfortably by her side, one leg tucked under him, eyes staring straight ahead. Both seemed carefree, she more loving and attentive than he. He was still acting like a free man, she was already becoming his slave, guided by a pact of obedience. But there was no fear, no pity, no forgetfulness, no rage between them yet. Though, she remembered, the Spanish Civil War had already broken out and he seemed a bit saddened, without being terribly distressed, but he still tried to avoid looking slightly lost and to hide his worries.

"Roland Penrose, Roland Penrose," Dora mumbled in the middle of her semi-insomnia. Penrose had taken that photograph of them, and she struggled not to lose that frozen image of the first symptoms of cruel everyday apathy; in any case, bad memories are the last to vanish; they are the ones that endure.

In the hours before dawn, she felt thirsty, her throat was dry, she stretched out her hand to grab the water glass; as she drank it, she noticed that the furniture had grown hooves and a kind of mold, and that huge masses of long, thick hair were emerging from the drawers, like horse tails and manes. Dear God, dear Virgin Mary! She pressed her hands together to pray, but she couldn't recite any prayer correctly, none came to her lips.

The bedroom filled with galloping horses.

In a murmur she heard the word *jade*.

The warm water from some beach flooded across the old parquet floor and, a posteriori, the landscape of Porquerolles poured into the living room. "Posterior," "a posteriori," words that Picasso used.

In the distance, James was killing time by catching tiny fish in the hollow of his hands and throwing them back. Catherine Dudley prattled next to her, "They tell me you're badmouthing Picasso. You shouldn't do that, it won't do you any good, people are already making fun of you behind your back. After all, you owe everything to him, you owe him everything."

"Come on, Catherine, could you try being a little less idiotic? That is so stupid! Please, don't get me mad. I don't owe him anything at all. Actually, it's the other way around. He used me, savagely. He used me for his art, I was his raw material. He used me ruthlessly and tossed me aside when I wasn't any more use to him. Don't forget the motley and misshapen portraits he did of me. The ones he says are me."

"The ones you hold onto like they're all the gold from Peru," Catherine said sarcastically.

"And what would you have me do? They're mine, I'm me, it's my business. Of course I hold onto them like gold dust. He abused me, sapped my intelligence. I don't hold a grudge against him — don't you think that's enough? Besides, I don't have them all; he kept most of them for himself."

"They're going to exhibit more of his things, have you heard? They've put together an incredible selection in Russia. Nobody in Paris has seen these paintings. It's going to be wild, people are going to go crazy about them. The only problem is that they're putting the exhibit up at the Maison de la Pensée Française, that Communist dive."

Catherine fiddled with a dry branch, making rings of sea foam on the sandy beach.

"As far as I'm concerned—well! I don't care about any of that, couldn't care less, to tell you the truth. I've seen my fill of Picassos, they sicken me. I've seen enough Picassos for this life and a hundred thousand more."

"I don't believe for one second that you don't care."

Dora left a long pause before replying.

"You see that young man there? Lord? Maybe I like him, and perhaps he loves me. Isn't that good enough for a woman my age? Well, of course I care about Picasso, and his paintings, but I have to pretend I don't, make a show of not giving a damn. It's so unbearably boring when everybody's in love with Picasso, even James. Especially James." She pointed him out with an elegant movement of her chin. "He loves Picasso more than me. That's the problem that keeps us apart, but on the other hand, it's the advantage that brings us together. Tomorrow he'll take off as cool as can be to brownnose him and leave me here alone."

James had walked over and heard the last phrase, at which he defended himself. "Of course I'll go visit him, but I'll be bringing him a present from you."

"Yes, that humiliating thing, the perverted piece of junk." Dora let out a guffaw that ended in a deep sigh. "A rusty shovel, in response to a torture chair he sent me. It's a sinister code only we understand."

Dora got out of bed. She didn't want the dream to keep going, like a sorrowful encumbrance of dangerous old obsessions, not very advisable for one's mental health.

Sitting in the rocking chair, she thought she should find someone who would force her out of this rut.

Could it be the woman who persisted in following her? Could she be the answer that would get her to break momentarily from her solitude? Maybe paying attention to her now and then, sitting down to talk with her in a café, making friends with this young woman would do her more good than not. But what could she tell this woman? What did they have in common? She wasn't sure if the woman even knew who she really was.

But there couldn't be any doubt. The woman wasn't following her because she was any woman; she intentionally wanted to get close to her. She must know who Dora Maar was, the great Surrealist photographer, the painter and lover of . . . Or could she only be interested in her because she'd been Pablo Picasso's lover, like all the rest? In that case, what could she do to attract her more to herself and keep her from growing bored with her stories about her past adventures, while she erased Picasso from her life?

Yes, absolutely, she'd do it, and she wouldn't leave out the Great Genius. She'd start with that phrase he once blurted out to her contemptuously, the sort of verbal jab he readily shared with everybody: "The uglier my paintings get, the crazier people get about buying them." Because the worse he painted, the more accessible they became to common people, the bourgeois crowd. He was right about that: the worse artists paint, the greater and more incomprehensible the blind fury in which they paint, the more people snatch up their paintings.

She could also tell her about the conversation between Lord and Picasso, when the two of them were alone, in which Lord finally made the best, the most beautiful statement any man had ever made about her: "I've never known anyone like her."

"Neither have I." At last there was something they agreed about, James sighed, but Picasso couldn't restrain himself: "I've never known anyone so—how can I describe her?—so handy. Dora was whatever you insisted she be, a dog, a mouse, a bird, an idea, a storm, a formula. That's a huge advantage when you've fallen in love, don't you think?"

And that was undoubtedly the ugliest thing anyone had ever said about her. Inevitably, Picasso had no scruples about putting her down. No, she wouldn't repeat this anecdote that Lord had hesitatingly, downheartedly shared with her. It might be interpreted some other way, she might again become an object of humiliation to so many ignorant people.

She must, yes, she had to meet this young woman as soon as possible. Tomorrow, she'd agree to talk with her tomorrow, and if the young woman wouldn't approach her—because from what Dora could see, she was still very shy—she'd find a pretext to start a conversation. "She'll probably find Picasso's comic side interesting," she sneered. "Like the time he painted the bathroom of the house in Ménerbes, and then joked about it, saying he'd only wanted to give it a touch of Pompeii, and this way the great Dora Maar, meaning me, could enjoy the chance to sit down and defecate on his work, take a shit on him once and for all, on his goddamned genius, on his shocking solemnity, on his putrid art." Ugh! The damned Spaniard's broad, blustering sense of humor was enough to make her sick. How had she put up with him for so long? How could she have deviated so far from her fundamental impulses and made her heart beat only for him?

Much later that night, she pulled out an ordinary school notebook and began writing down some of the stories she'd tell the stranger after they finally met and became friends. She didn't want to forget a single one of the unbelievable adventures that formed her life. Nothing should be left out, not the smallest detail, she told herself, repenting of her desire to sideline Picasso. However, she didn't have the slightest idea how to put order into the tidal wave of thoughts and their unexpected evocations that surged rebelliously, crashing chaotically in her mind.

She'd tell the young woman how she once explained the one true meaning of Picasso's art to James, and she'd do it in the same way, referring to the meaning of a simple tree, its obvious interpretation: a tree isn't much until it has been observed by a genius and his vision. No tree is important if Picasso hasn't seen it, hasn't painted it. "Take a good look at it, James, observe it," she had told him. "For you, it's a plain, ordinary plant, with that meek trunk and those shrubby branches hanging from it, just something growing on the side of the road, completely commonplace, spectacularly trite. If *Cher et Beau* painted the tree, the story would be totally different, James. He'd turn that tree into a matchless object, a treasure, a jewel, an unquestionable object of worship. To a person of faith, it's already a miracle in itself, since it's a tree. It's pedestrian, rustic, but it represents all that is beautiful on earth and in the world, because it comes from the earth, it's alive, visible, tangible, an explicit message from every living being on this planet. It represents you and me and all the universe, the whole conceivable and inconceivable world. Picasso will always go deeper, because he can catch more than the obvious message; he'll reveal the majestic mystery of the tree's roots to us, beginning deep down with the soul of the tree, because he'll give the tree a soul, invent one for it if it doesn't have one already."

James readily understood, because even though he wasn't exactly a genius, far from it, he was a very sensitive person, open to mysteries, and he wrote down everything she told him in his diary. That was how James got ahead of her and wrote everything she wished to weep before she wrote it herself, before she even finished weeping over it.

She wasn't sure whether the woman who would soon become her listener, and a very special one, would be able to understand how hurt she was when James moved far away and fell out of contact for some time. Kept his distance, relatively speaking, from her distressing self (she knew that was how he talked about her with others), first in a comfortable flat on the Avenue Georges Mandel, later on Rue de Lille. At the time, he was feeling more Parisian than the Parisians. After a while they met again. No, it isn't easy to understand how you can love someone so much that you prefer to keep them out of reach, even if the grief of being apart ties our feelings and our bodies in knots, in a physical and heartrending sense.

During one conversation, James grew so sad that his eyes teared up and he almost started to cry. This happened when Dora said of Lacan, rather admiringly, "He's the high arbiter of lost causes. I'm one of them."

Sending her into one of those desperate, irreversible downward spirals until she was saved at the very end, almost miraculously, in extremis.

"Dora, can I say something to you? I want you to know that nobody has meant as much to me as you have."

She smiled and ran her hand over his head with deliberate and painstaking sweetness.

James loved her, no doubt of it; he gave her so many presents — and she gave him so few in return. Rather, none at all, until she decided to offer him the tiny original etching used to print her face on the Dunhill matchboxes, made by Picasso.

When he got home, he was so happy that he ran to greet Bernard. He admitted to his friend that he thought the right thing to do was to ask Dora to marry him.

"Are you crazy? Think about it. Dora isn't just Dora, she is Picasso, too. Do you want to marry Picasso?"

Why did James insist on being honest with her, as if she were his mother? And why did Bernard slight her so cruelly? Yes, it was true, she and James would never be free of Picasso. James and Bernard were right. No, they could never go anywhere without the phantom presence of *Cher et Beau*.

"You know something, James? Being Picasso wasn't enough for him, he also wanted people to love him for being himself," she whispered once.

Now it was James asking her if she was crazy for denying some bit of nonsense that she couldn't even recall. She could only visualize the moment this happened and hear the cruel question on his lips, "Are you crazy?"

She abruptly turned to face him, gritted her teeth, dropped the lilting nightingale pitch of her voice to snarl an uncharacteristic, unexpected growl, like that of a wounded wolf. How dare he? How, how dare he?

"Don't you ever, ever, even think of telling me I'm crazy, hear me? Never!"

No, this fragment of her at her wit's end, of the delirium into which her life descended, would not be to the point; her interlocutor would doubtless overwhelm her with too many questions, most of them awkward, and then she really would have to go back over the chapter of her illness and figure out how to cover it and in what order: the madness, the psychiatric hospital, the electroshocks, the unbearable string of events she went through, up to the irredeemable ending.

No, better not distress or confuse the young woman, because if she did, she might run off, whereas her mission was to keep the woman here as much time as she could. The little time she had left.

The light at sunrise gilded the furniture and lent a coppery glow to the worn leather and polished wood of the old sofa. She crossed the drawing room to the bathroom, relieved herself of a long stream, and got the impression that her urine smelled of antibiotics gone bad, which wasn't normal at all, not a bit. She couldn't allow herself the luxury of falling ill, especially not in the kidneys.

By then Picasso had died, most of the major characters from her era had passed away, from a natural death or from suicide. She, however, was still there, resisting, growing older, slowly wasting away. Just like James, he must also be getting old, and even though they were growing old apart, Dora always received a bouquet of orchids, roses, lilies, and gladioli. A courtesy she no longer returned, not even with a scribbled postcard as a show of thanks; she had even lost the spirit one gets from having good manners.

She thought intensely about the young woman, whom she was quite sure she would see again that morning, and felt very nervous, more nervous than ever, because she hadn't concocted a speech, hadn't even thought up some solid, interesting phrase to open a conversation with her. Of course it would be easier if the other woman approached her first, but what if she never made up her mind?

In fact, this is how it happened. After getting dressed, always in black from head to toe, she went outside and there was the young woman, leaning against the house across the street, smoking. Dora was glad to see she smoked. She was wearing leather shorts, a black velvet jacket, red socks, and black leather boots to the middle of her calves. Dora walked slowly and observed that, as usual, the woman didn't fall behind or lose track. Then Dora turned around sharply and began to walk in the young woman's direction, but when they crossed paths, neither one dared say anything but good morning, accompanying the greeting with a slight smile.

Dora took time to walk all the way around the block and then along the Seine so she could enter Notre Dame by the main door.

Tomorrow, without fail, she told herself, she would surprise the stranger with some phrase, the most powerful she could come up with. She wouldn't expect more than that, she couldn't expect more. She mused nervously.

She heard Mass, entertained herself strolling along the waterfront, and went home to eat something and to paint. Though she was quite elderly and her whole body ached as she neared her final rest, she could still sit before an easel and imagine and create, in short, slow brush strokes, the landscapes that she could no longer stretch, as she had in the distant past, to cover the endless expanse of gigantic canvases. She consoled herself with the thought that at least she had enough strength and spirit to paint. Taking shelter in color and getting caught up in the enigma of the unusual journey of the line toward nothingness were the best imaginary ointments for her rheumatic bones. She worked for two hours. She had a light lunch, washed the dishes, and sat down to write in her lined Clairfontaine notebook.

For her there was nothing like the sea. She came to identify so deeply with the bluey vastness that when she swam underwater, deep beneath the azure surface and far from shore, she felt she could stay there for the rest of her life, dying slowly, little by little, without putting up any resistance to death. Her body undulated like a dolphin, like a manatee, like some ancient sea deity. The ocean revived her, projected her into another dimension, and gave her a sense of security such as she had never experienced with her feet on dry land. The sea swell enwrapped her in a supernatural halo that made her feel herself, in the foaming crest of a surge, a fluid woman, composed and assembled piece by piece from drops of water. She had the sense that Picasso would be watching, bewitched by this image of the dolphin woman, the salty goddess with the body of a bird. Picasso ran to find something to sketch her with, returning in exultation, and from this image of her, liquid and intensely blue, he dreamed up and elaborated the drawing of the beautiful bird woman, radiantly indigo, an owl with firm breasts, a winged face, like a sphinx, standing an elegant vigil on a rocky promontory. She knew that when Picasso said she could be anything, "whatever you insisted she be," as he told Lord, he had said it in the name of creativity, of painting, scorning the effect of human insensitivity his words might have on someone who heard them out of context without paying attention to the artistic obsession that overcame him, nor to everything he appropriated for himself with the brilliance of his gaze.

That vision of Dora rising from the waves had a different meaning for James, however. The only time he saw her emerge from the ocean, he was petrified by the sexual desire her image aroused in him. A sudden and imperious urge to possess her carnally overcame him, as she could tell from a slight physical excitation visible in his swimming trunks, which sadly lasted only a short while.

There was a period when she preferred to inspire men with physical desire rather than aesthetic ardor. That period lasted an immoderately long time and disturbed her deeply.

She paused. At length she continued writing for the stranger, her hand held straight above the paper, but she had to stop once more when, suddenly, another strange and very specific image came between her memories and the young woman who was to receive this rosary of written anecdotes.

It was set in a not too distant future: she saw the woman with a man and another girl, apparently even younger, rather short in stature and with the most maleficent guinea-pig eyes she had ever seen. Sitting in a café, they were talking about Anaïs Nin; then they moved to what looked like a plaza, after which she found them without much difficulty as they walked through a museum. They rushed out of there and jumped into a car. The second woman intentionally forgot her gloves on the back seat, feigning absentmindedness; they were nightmarish black lambskin gloves with red backstitching.

"Don't touch them, don't touch them!" Dora felt an impulse to warn the stranger not to pick up the gloves dropped by the ungrateful, malicious woman whose company, she deeply intuited, would bring her no good luck.

Exhausted by this vision, she decided to lie back in the rocking chair, holding a cup of rosehip tea in one hand. What secrets did she still have that at this date might interest a woman of today? What could she reveal that the woman might care about? She racked her brains. "That's it, I know! The trip to Venice!"

The eight days with James and Bernard. Those days were almost too much, so definitive that they had made her long to move "far from the madding crowd." But the trip to Venice had also been unquestionably wonderful.

Though afterwards there was dead quiet, a wall of silence. She hoped, she waited for a phone call. . . . No special, tactful attention came her way, and yet she always imagined that James would always be *à portée de main* for anything she might need. Despite the way her friends brushed her off afterwards, the Venice trip would be a good topic of conversation and wouldn't be too great a commitment on her part, since the young woman wouldn't have to wait for the next chapter or to keep up a friendship based on an intimidating and submissive relationship with Picasso's work, or with her own.

Waiting, waiting inordinately, for what? She'd waited so long already! Picasso and James had both left her on the doorstep one fine day, no explanations, no dedication, no special manners. What happened with James after the Venice trip had occurred in the same way, long before, with Picasso. He had also left her at the door of the house on Rue de Savoie as if he were setting out a worn old piece of furniture for the trash collectors to pick up, and bid her a warm farewell, perhaps too warm. She knew right then it was all over. And she didn't discover the real reason until some time later: a younger woman. It must have taken her more than two weeks to verify it. The disillusionment of having the rumor confirmed added to the sense of estrangement. She missed him tremendously, because they had been seeing each other almost daily for ten years, and it was hard for her to get used to how it had ended so suddenly, without a word, without so much as a relevant gesture, other than his telling her he was going to leave there, not walk up with her, since she could walk on her own.

What she would never forgive Picasso for was the fact that he hadn't had the courage to tell her, as a gentleman would, that everything was over between them. Even worse, she supposed that to keep from having to talk it through with her, he had hoped that his silence would push her to suicide, that she'd have died for him, without a complaint, that she'd have ceased to exist, tormented and silenced, so he would be able to live more comfortably with the other woman who by then had definitely taken her place.

His indifference was extremely stinging. Criminal. And so she became ill. So ill that one day when Paul Éluard came to visit, he came in and found her on the stairs, in her nightgown, weeping desperately. The poet picked her up and called the doctors. He let

Picasso know right away. That incoherent, unbearable scene would run through her head like a litany for the rest of her life.

From that day forth, she swore, she would never again make a spectacle of herself; but it was too late, the illness had attacked her, with no solution. The contagious and irreversible madness of women who wail streams of baleful invocations, occupying the minds of men who expect from women only moans that reaffirm their tragic manliness, had taken root in her battered body.

Still hopeless, she managed to more or less heal, and once she was completely over the breakup she swore again that she'd never run the risk of depending on somebody else, that she'd depend exclusively on herself. No, she would never live with a man again. To this oath she added a promise that she would sweep aside any amorous intentions that might plunge her life into another anesthetic state of desolation, no matter how healthy and attractive it might look at the beginning. As Marlene Dietrich might say, life is a circus. "Believe me, everything's just a circus," and every one of her misadventures in love represented one of its terrible performances.

But then James reappeared, with his aroused youthfulness, and sat on that bench under the fig tree in Ménerbes, and, sitting there, she had no choice but to paint him. She had no other option but to dream again. She couldn't help it; he seemed eternal, brimming with vigor. Besides, he knew to treat her tenderly, pampering her and never tiring of telling her that he wanted nothing but to be with her always, by her side. *Trop mignon, n'est-ce pas?*

After that they became great friends, almost lovers; the only thing missing was the sex, because even though he made serious and truthful declarations to her in bed, they never touched, just a few light pats, more tender than puritanical. Dora had grown resentful, distrustful, and more headstrong than before her illness, and she brandished her new character as her only weapon of resistance against idleness; but for all that, she accepted having a man's friendly and concrete presence again.

"James Lord." She whispered his name thoughtfully. Now, that's a topic. Quite an interesting topic for anyone who might try in the future to puzzle out much of what she called her "anodyne existence."

He also wrote down everything that occurred to him, everything he experienced with her, in his interminable diary, a notebook that he purposely left on the night table, where his hostess could see it, in Ménerbes, though Dora never dared to read it, not even to open it. That diary undoubtedly shaped the writer he would become, but she was the one who provided and prepared the ingredients from which he produced the work.

Yes, he was a real writer now, Dora thought, in large measure because she had turned him into a mature man capable of being one.

"Never trust men," she repeated, "much less writers." They dramatize what they know, and she didn't want anyone to write about her part from a single point of view, an idea she found execrable.

And then, inevitably, all her friends had begun to grow old, just like her, some of them even prematurely; but unlike them, she never showed herself, keeping out of sight and away from the implacable judgment of others.

Likewise, Picasso almost frivolously remade his life; falling in love with Françoise Gilot, he had children with her. More children! And then came Geneviève Laporte for a short time, and finally Jacqueline Roque. And at last, with time, the terrible news came: Pablo Picasso had died. Picasso dead! The end of all possible ends!

Dora, who like everyone else had toyed with the idea that Pablo Picasso would live forever, collapsed when she found out, but before much time had passed she came to accept it, much more readily than she would have believed possible. The apparent reason it did not tear her apart to accept his death was simply that he was always around, at her side, in her living room, lurking in the shadows, keeping her company through his paintings, his sculptures, down to the most trivial objects or nuisances she had kept of his.

This was the only time she called him by his Christian name: Pablo. But he wasn't around to hear her pronounce, for the first and last time, the only word that might have softened his heart coming from her lips: Pablo.

Sometimes she even managed to laugh uproariously in his shadow's presence, in the presence of Picasso's ghost, when he merrily repeated in the stubborn litany typical of the dead, "I'm a lesbian, Dora, I'm a lesbian."

James had long since stopped coming by; phone calls became ever more distant. The last time she had seen him was in 1980. They met after Picasso's death, in 1974, but it was in exactly 1980 that she saw him for the last time.

She still found him very good-looking, even more so than when she had known him, though he was far too tanned for her taste and had become ceremonious and clumsily patronizing. She was already the pious and stooping little old woman she had been transformed into by resentment and God. She observed enormous bitterness in James's eyes, quickly receding in view of the old age of the person he had once considered the most beautiful and youthful woman in the world, an eternal child and a Surrealist goddess.

On that last occasion, Dora of course asked about his friend Bernard, who she had heard was on his way to becoming a successful playwright and screenwriter. Aside from Bernard, she was interested in the few old friends who were still living. The living friends were doing well, the dead ones better, she told herself a while later, after James Lord had vanished through the front door of the house and the small pile of dry leaves that the caretaker had swept up was blowing away in a gust of wind.

She went over everything she'd written and was satisfied. The next day she would invite the stranger for tea at Ladurée on Saint-Germain-des-Prés and give her these fragments, handwritten in a scattered way, though entirely correct and faithful to her memories of an entire era that, much like herself, refused to disappear.

She read an old book for a while longer and went to bed early. Then, for the first time in quite a while, she dreamed of a simple, pleasant landscape: the sea in the background, foamy, just as it appears in her paintings, and Picasso there in front of the waves, bare chest, hairy legs, sitting on the rocks, hiding his face behind a minotaur skull. Meanwhile she focused on him, pressed the shutter, and snapped his picture.

The aged woman stepped into the courtyard, carrying her old, worn, half-empty shopping basket with difficulty. In the basket were the notebook, an umbrella, and a coin purse. She wasn't startled when the caretaker ran after her with her thinly veined coarseness.

"Off to Mass again, ma'am?" she asked. The caretaker had the bad habit of getting between her and the door every time she wanted to go out and asking her the same question every morning, but Dora was fond of her after so many years together and looked at her more with affection than with respect.

"Yes, I am going to Mass again, as I have done every morning since you've known me. And on my way back I will pass by the market, but I will not be long, don't you worry. Au revoir! Goodbye!"

Reaching the sidewalk, she scanned in every direction and got a terrible feeling of apprehension when she didn't see the stranger. She told herself that perhaps the young woman hadn't shown up on time because of the storm overnight. She decided to hurry so as not to miss the beginning of Mass. Then she'd come back through the market; surely her future friend would bet here by then, as always, waiting for her.

As she walked to Notre Dame, she felt a slight dizziness, then a second spell, followed by a sort of strange throbbing up around her groin, and another more intense throbbing in her brain. She stopped briefly and after a while went back to walking.

She was so happy. For the first time in so long she smiled to passersby, greeted the *bouquinistes*, and even came close to buying an old edition of *The Graveyard by the Sea* by Paul Valéry and a woolen hat offered by a woman selling on the street. But stopping to shop would slow her down, she thought, and she needed to be back early.

She was walking faster than usual, and the morning, though cold, sparkled in the bright sun; the wind had abated. She begged God to give her a little more time; over the past few years she had always asked for the same thing, as if it were her last prayer, the final line in a stern litany: "God, please grant me a little more time, a little more."

"Jade, Jade!" A mother called out to her little girl, who was playing with the Dalmatian that a very elegant gentleman was pulling by a leash along the esplanade of Notre Dame.

"Jade." The last word she heard.

I had been running very late, and even though I sprinted onto the metro and dashed headlong across the Pont Neuf, I didn't arrive on time to meet Dora Maar and, at last, in a few perhaps stammering words, declare how much I admired her. I might have even heard her voice in an unforgettable and instructive conversation that would endure, like her friendship, in which she would tell me, "Art, after all, can only embellish the truth. It is not the truth in itself."

Afterwards we would say goodbye, I would watch her walk away, and she would enter her house, promising me we would meet again.

From that same building, a short time later a beautiful and mysterious woman wrapped in a dark leather overcoat would emerge. Her profile would slowly grow smaller as she walked away along Rue de Savoie, and vanish entirely when she turned the corner onto Rue des Grands Augustins.

She would then walk, head held high, her firm steps clacking rhythmically against the sidewalk, and would carelessly drop a glove embroidered with tiny flowers. I would pick it up, intending to return it to her right then, or the next day. The glove would be dripping with blood.

Perhaps I would not have time to catch up to the elegant imaginary lady, her silhouette stretching into a lethargy of shadow, as in the photograph of Assia nude. I would be left waiting for her in vain. Because she would never return from that last appointment.

Yet I am still waiting for her today, on the vague and tremulous edge of a page.

Epilogue

On a freezing February day in 2006, I made arrangements with the photographer Marcela Rossiter to go see the exhibit "Picasso–Dora Maar, 1935–1945" at the Musée Picasso. From late winter through spring of that year, hundreds of thousands of people from all over the world packed the galleries of the museum in Le Marais. I returned to see it again and again.

I had never been so close to Dora and Picasso before, as they loved each other through time, their love immortalized in art. I have reconciled with Picasso, but it was not easy. How are we supposed to understand how, "when German officers came to his door, Picasso was unable to turn them away," as we read in Alan Riding's book *And the Show Went On: Cultural Life in Nazi-Occupied Paris?*

Standing there once more, looking at his work, I was completely taken by the vastness of the Great Genius. Then, after a long process, I again came to admire his skill, to love it.

I had the sense that at that moment, and for the first time, Dora Maar was also being recognized and valued rightly for her greatness as an artist and as a lover.

Paris, August 2011

Pour Zoe,

avec ma pensée

Picasso et Dora

cordiale, en attendant
de voir moi-même vu
par vous!

James Lord.

Paris, le 5 janvier 2007.

Author's Note on Sources

Part of the story told in this novel is based on facts that can be found the books cited below, and can verified in others unmentioned here that I consulted only in passing. I was also inspired by the personal testimony of several people whom I interviewed at the beginning of this project, including James Lord and Bernard Minoret. The rest is pure imagination, artifice, and invention, as should be expected in a work of fiction. This is a novel.

Avril, Nicole. Moi, Dora Maar: *La passion selon Picasso*. Paris: Plon, 2002.

Baldassari, Anne. *Picasso: Life with Dora Maar: Love and War, 1935–1945*. Paris: Flammarion, 2006.

Caws, Mary Ann. *Dora Maar with and without Picasso*. London: Thames & Hudson, 2000.

———. *Les Vies de Dora Maar: Bataille, Picasso, et les surréalistes*. Paris: Thames & Hudson, 2000.

Dujovne Ortiz, Alicia. *Dora Maar: Prisonnière du regard*. Paris: Grasset, 2003.

Lachgar, Lina. *Arrestation et mort de Max Jacob*. Paris: Différence, 2004.

Lake, Carlton and Françoise Gilot. *Life with Picasso*. New York: McGraw-Hill, 1964.

Lord, James. *Picasso and Dora: A Personal Memoir*. New York: Farrar, Straus and Giroux, 1993.

O'Brian, Patrick. *Pablo Ruiz Picasso: A Biography*. New York: Putnam, 1976.

Ray, Man. *Man Ray: Portraits: Paris-Hollywood-Paris: From the Man Ray Archives of the Centre Pompidou*. Munich: Schirmer Mosel, 2011.

Richardson, John. *A Life of Picasso*. New York: Random House, 1991.

Riding, Alan. *And the Show Went On: Cultural Life in Nazi-Occupied Paris*. New York: Alfred A. Knopf, 2010.